SAVAGE VISITORS

The hallway was dark and silent. Perhaps it was my overwrought imagination, but the silence had a chill feel to it. It was not the blessed silence of a house asleep. It was the silence of a house that is empty. A tinge of smoke hung in the air. We came to my room. The door was partially open and I distinctly remembered having shut it when I left.

I stepped to the door, looked inside, and stood, transfixed.

The bed had been ripped open by what appeared to be giant claws. Long slashes cut through the mattress. Gouts of feathers lay in heaps on the floor. My knapsack had been torn apart, my clothes strewn about the room. My other possessions—shaving kit, comb, brush—were scattered everywhere.

"You see," said Scylla. "They were searching for the Darksword."

Despair robbed me of breath. I ran to Saryon's room. Eliza stood dazed in the hall, staring with disbelief at the destruction. . . .

Other Bantam Spectra Books
by Margaret Weis and Tracy Hickman

THE DARKSWORD TRILOGY
Forging the Darksword
Doom of the Darksword
Triumph of the Darksword

DARKSWORD ADVENTURES

ROSE OF THE PROPHET
The Will of the Wanderer
The Paladin of the Night
The Prophet of Ákhran

THE DEATH GATE CYCLE
Dragon Wing
Elven Star
Fire Sea
Serpent Mage
The Hand of Chaos
Into the Labyrinth
The Seventh Gate

by Margaret Weis

STAR OF THE GUARDIANS
The Lost King
King's Test
King's Sacrifice
Ghost Legion

by Tracy Hickman

Requiem of Stars

LEGACY
OF THE
DARKSWORD

MARGARET WEIS
&
TRACY HICKMAN

BANTAM BOOKS
NEW YORK   TORONTO   LONDON   SYDNEY   AUCKLAND

LEGACY OF THE DARKSWORD
A Bantam Spectra Book

PUBLISHING HISTORY
Bantam hardcover edition published July 1997
Bantam paperback edition / June 1998

SPECTRA and the portrayal of a boxed "s" are trademarks
of Bantam Books, a division of Bantam Doubleday Dell
Publishing Group, Inc.

ISBN 0-553-57812-X

Published simultaneously in the United States and Canada

Bantam Books are published by Bantam Books, a division of
Bantam Doubleday Dell Publishing Group, Inc. Its trademark,
consisting of the words "Bantam Books" and the portrayal of
a rooster, is Registered in U.S. Patent and Trademark Office
and in other countries. Marca Registrada. Bantam Books,
1540 Broadway, New York, New York 10036.

PRINTED IN THE UNITED STATES OF AMERICA
OPM 10 9 8 7 6 5 4 3 2 1

Dedicated to all our readers
who keep asking us,
"And then what happens?"

~

CHAPTER ONE

Finally, a child may be born to the rarest of all the Mysteries, the Mystery of Life. The thaumaturgist, or catalyst, is the dealer in magic, though he does not possess it in great measure himself. It is the catalyst, as his name implies, who takes the Life from the earth and the air; from fire and water, and, by assimilating it within his own body, is able to enhance it and transfer it to the magi who can use it.

~ *FORGING THE DARKSWORD*

Saryon, now somewhere in his sixties or seventies, as reckoned by Earth time, lived very quietly in a small flat in Oxford, England. He was uncertain of the year of his birth in Thimhallan, and thus I, who write this story out for him, cannot provide his exact age. Saryon never did adapt well to the concept of Earth time relative to Thimhallan time. History has meaning only to those who are its products and time is but a means of measuring history, whether it be the history of the past moment or the history of the past billion moments. For Saryon, as for so many of those who came to Earth

from the once-magical land of Thimhallan, time began
in another realm—a beautiful, wondrous, fragile bubble of a realm. Time ended when that bubble burst,
when Joram pricked it with the Darksword.

Saryon had no need for measuring time anyway. The
catalyst (though no longer required in this world, that
is how he always termed himself) had no appoint-
ments, kept no calendar, rarely watched the evening
news, met no one for lunch. I was his amanuensis, or so
he was pleased to call me. I preferred the less formal
term of secretary. I was sent to Saryon by command of
Prince Garald.

I had been a servant in the Prince's household and
was supposed to have been Saryon's servant, too, but
this he would not allow. The only small tasks I was
able to perform for him were those I could sneak in
before he was aware of it or those which I wrested
from him by main force.

I would have been a catalyst myself, had our people
not been banished from Thimhallan. I had very little
magic in me when I left that world as a child, and none
at all now after living for twenty years in the world of
the mundane. But I do have a gift for words and this
was one reason my prince sent me to Saryon. Prince
Garald deemed it essential that the story of the Darksword be told. In particular, he hoped that by reading
these tales, the people of Earth would come to understand the exiled people of Thimhallan.

I wrote three books, which were immensely well received by the populace of Earth, less well received
among my own kind. Who among us likes to look
upon himself and see that his life was one of cruel
waste and overindulgence, greed, selfishness, and ra-
pacity? I held a mirror to the people of Thimhallan.
They looked into it and did not like the ugly visage that

glared back at them. Instead of blaming themselves, they blamed the mirror.

My master and I had few visitors. He had decided to pursue his study of mathematics, which was one reason that he had moved from the relocation camps to Oxford, in order to be near the libraries connected with that ancient and venerable university. He did not attend classes, but had a tutor, who came to the flat to instruct him. When it became apparent that the teacher had nothing more to teach and that, indeed, the teacher was learning from the pupil, the tutor ceased to make regular visits, although she still dropped by occasionally for tea.

This was a calm and blessed time in Saryon's tumultuous life, for—although he does not say so—I can see his face light when he speaks of it and I hear a sadness in his voice, as if regretting that such a peaceful existence could not have lasted until middle age faded, like comfortable jeans, into old age, from thence to peaceful eternal sleep.

That was not to be, of course, and that brings me to the evening that seems to me, looking back on it, to be the first pearl to slide off the broken string, the pearls that were days of Earth time and that would start falling faster and faster from that night on until there would be no more pearls left, only the empty string and the clasp that once held it together. And those would be tossed away, as useless.

Saryon and I were pottering about his flat late that night, putting on the teakettle, an act which always reminded him—so he was telling me—of another time when he'd picked up a teakettle and it wasn't a teakettle. It was Simkin.

We had just finished listening to the news on the radio. As I said, Saryon had not up until now been particularly interested in the news of what was happening on Earth, news which he always felt had little to do with him. But this news appeared, unfortunately, to have more to do with him than he or anyone else wanted and so he paid attention to it.

The war with Hch'nyv was not going well. The mysterious aliens, who had appeared so suddenly, with such deadly intent, had conquered yet another one of our colonies. Refugees, arriving back on Earth, told terrible tales of the destruction of their colony, reported innumerable casualties, and stated that the Hch'nyv had no desire to negotiate. They had, in fact, slain those sent to offer the colony's surrender. The objective of the Hch'nyv appeared to be the annihilation and eradication of every human in the galaxy.

This was somber news. We were discussing it when I saw Saryon jump, as if he had been startled by some sudden noise, though I myself heard nothing.

"I must go to the front door," he said. "Someone's there."

Saryon, who is reading the manuscript, stops me at this point to tell me, somewhat testily, that I should break here and elaborate on the story of Joram and Simkin and the Darksword or no one will understand what is to come.

I reply that if we backtrack and drag our readers along that old trail with us (a trail most have walked themselves already!) we would likely lose more than a few along the way. I assure him that the past will unfold as we go along. I hint gently that I am a skilled journalist, with some experience in this field. I remind him that he was fairly well satisfied with the work I'd done on the first three books, and I beg him to allow me to return to this story.

Being essentially a very humble man, who finds it overwhelming that his memoirs should be considered so impor-

tant that Prince Garald had hired me to record them,
Saryon readily acknowledges my skill in this field and per-
mits me to continue.

"How odd," Saryon remarked. "I wonder who is
here at this time of night?"

I wondered why they did not ring the doorbell, as
any normal visitor would do. I indicated as much.

"They have rung it," Saryon said softly. "In my
mind, if not my ears. Can't you hear it?"

I could not, but this was not surprising. Having lived
most of his life in Thimhallan, he was far more attuned
to the mysteries of its magicks than I, who had been
only five when Saryon rescued me, an orphan, from the
abandoned Font.

Saryon had just lit the flame beneath the teakettle,
preparatory to heating water for a bedtime tisane
which we both enjoyed and which he insisted on making for me. He turned from the kettle to stare at the
door and, like so many of us, instead of going immediately to answer it or to look through the window to see
who was there, he stood in the kitchen in his nightshirt
and slippers and wondered again aloud.

"Who could be wanting to see me at this time of
night?"

Hope's wings caused his heart to flutter. His face
flushed with anticipation. I, who had served him so
long, knew exactly what he was thinking.

Many years ago (twenty years ago, to be precise,
although I doubt if he himself had any concept of the
passage of so much time), Saryon had said good-bye to
two people he loved. He had neither seen nor heard
from those two in all this time. He had no reason to
think that he should ever hear from them again, except

that Joram had promised, when they parted, that when his son was of age, he should send that son to Saryon.

Now, whenever the doorbell rang or the knocker knocked, Saryon envisioned Joram's son standing on the doorstoop. Saryon pictured that child with his father's long, curling black hair, but lacking, hopefully, his father's red-black inner fire.

The psychic demand for Saryon to go to the front door came again, this time with such a forceful intensity and impatience that I myself was aware of it—a startling sensation for me. Had the doorbell in fact been sounding, I could envision the person leaning on the button. There were lights on in the kitchen, which could be seen from the street, and whoever was out there, mentally issuing us commands, knew that Saryon and I were home.

Jolted out of his reverie by the second command, Saryon shouted, "I'm coming," which statement had no hope of being heard through the thick door that led from the kitchen.

Retiring to his bedroom, he grabbed his flannel robe, put it over his nightshirt. I was still dressed, having never developed a liking for nightshirts. He walked hastily back through the kitchen, where I joined him. We went from there through the living room and out of the living room into the small entryway. He turned on the outside light, only to discover that it didn't work.

"The bulb must have burned out," he said, irritated. "Turn on the hall light."

I flipped the switch. It did not work either.

Strange, that both bulbs should have chosen this time to burn out.

"I don't like this, Master," I signed, even as Saryon was unlocking the door, preparing to open it.

I had tried many times to convince Saryon that, in this dangerous world, there might be those who would do him harm, who would break into his house, rob and beat him, perhaps even murder him. Thimhallan may have had its faults, but such sordid crimes were unknown to its inhabitants, who feared centaurs and giants, dragons and faeries and peasant revolts, not hoodlums and thugs and serial killers.

"Look through the peephole," I admonished.

"Nonsense," Saryon returned. "It must be Joram's child. And how could I see him through the peephole in the dark?"

Picturing a baby in a basket on our doorstoop (he had, as I said, only the vaguest notion of time), Saryon flung open the door.

We did not find a baby. What we saw was a shadow darker than night standing on the doorstoop, blotting out the lights of our neighbors, blotting out the light of the stars.

The shadow coalesced into a person dressed in black robes, who wore a black cowl pulled up over the head. All I could see of the person by the feeble light reflected from the kitchen far behind me were two white hands, folded correctly in front of the black robes, and two eyes, glittering.

Saryon recoiled. He pressed his hand over his heart, which had stopped fluttering, very nearly stopped altogether. Fearful memories leapt out of the darkness brought on us by the black-clothed figure. The fearful memories jumped on the catalyst.

"*Duuk-tsarith!*" he cried through trembling lips.

Duuk-tsarith, the dreaded Enforcers of the world of Thimhallan. On our first coming—under duress—to this new world, where magic was diluted, the *Duuk-tsarith* had lost almost all of their magical power. We had heard vague rumors to the effect that, over the past twenty years, they had found the means to regain what had been lost. Whether or not this was true, the *Duuk-tsarith* had lost none of their ability to terrify.

Saryon fell back into the entryway. He stumbled into me and, so I vaguely recollect, put his arm out as though he would protect me. Me! Who was supposed to protect him!

He pressed me back against the wall of the small entryway, leaving the door standing wide open, with no thought of slamming it in the visitor's face, with no thought of denying this dread visitor entry. This was one who would not be denied. I knew that as well as Saryon, and though I did make an attempt to put my own body in front of that of the middle-aged catalyst, I had no thought of doing battle.

The *Duuk-tsarith* glided over the threshold. With a brief gesture of his hand, he caused the door to swing silently shut behind him. He put back the cowl, revealed his face, and stared intently at Saryon for several seconds, almost as if expecting some response. Saryon was too flustered, too upset to do anything except stand on the braided rug and shiver and tremble.

The Enforcer's gaze shifted to me, entered my soul, caught and held fast to my heart, so that I feared if I disobeyed, my beating heart would stop.

The *Duuk-tsarith* spoke. "First, I caution you both to remain silent. It is for your own protection. Do you understand?"

The words were not spoken aloud. They were fiery letters, traced across the back of my eyes.

Saryon nodded. He didn't understand what was going on, any more than I did, but neither of us was going to argue.

"Good," said the Enforcer. "Now I am going to

perform a magic spell. Do not be alarmed. It will not harm you."

The *Duuk-tsarith* spoke inaudible words, that came to me only in whispers. Fearfully, not terribly reassured by the *Duuk-tsarith*'s promise, we stared around, waiting for the Almin knew what to happen.

Nothing happened, at least that I could see. The *Duuk-tsarith,* his finger on his lips, again to enjoin silence, led the way into the living room. We shuffled along behind him, keeping close to each other. Once we were in the living room, the Enforcer pointed one long, white finger.

A painting hung on the wall, a painting which had been acquired along with the flat and which depicted a pastoral scene of cows in a field. From behind that painting now glowed an eerie green light.

The *Duuk-tsarith* pointed again, this time to the phone. The same green light surrounded the phone.

The *Duuk-tsarith* nodded to himself, as if he'd expected to find this phenomenon, whatever it was. He didn't bother to explain. Once again, and this time emphatically, he silently cautioned us not to speak.

And then the *Duuk-tsarith* did a most peculiar thing. He turned with the calm repose of a guest who has been invited to remove his hat and coat and stay to tea. Moving with quiet grace among the furniture, the Enforcer walked to the window, parted the curtain a minuscule crack, and looked outside.

I was overwhelmed by a series of fleeting impressions as my brain tried frantically to grapple with the strange occurrence. At first, I thought that the *Duuk-tsarith* was signaling reinforcements. Logic arrived to remark dryly that the apprehension of one elderly catalyst and his scribe would hardly call for a SWAT team. That first impression was replaced by another.

The *Duuk-tsarith* was looking outside to see if he had been followed.

Not knowing what else to do and, by now, more curious than fearful, both Saryon and I stayed with the *Duuk-tsarith* in the living room. Through force of habit, I fumbled for the light switch.

"You needn't bother. It will not work."

The voice of the *Duuk-tsarith* inside my head was vibrant and sent a mild shock through me, reminding me of the first time I had encountered electricity on this strange world.

"Don't move," the inner voice commanded.

We remained standing in the darkened living room. I could sense Saryon shivering in his nightshirt, for he'd turned the heat down in the flat and his thin robe was woefully inadequate. I was wondering if I might be allowed to bring my master a sweater, when the *Duuk-tsarith* spoke silently again. And though the words were not addressed to me, I understood them.

"You don't remember me, do you, Saryon?"

Having had many encounters with the *Duuk-tsarith*—all of them extremely unpleasant—Saryon later told me that he feared this must be one of the Enforcers who had caught him in the forbidden library of the Font, or maybe even one who had performed the Turning to Stone, that excruciatingly painful punishment inflicted on those catalysts who rebelled against the Church's authority. Why one of these people should drop by Saryon's house for a chat in the small hours of the night was beyond him. He could only stare and stammer and whisper to me something to the effect that, if the person would permit us to turn on the lights and let us see a face, such an act would aid recognition considerably.

"All will be made clear soon enough," said the Enforcer, and it seemed to me that there was a sad quality to his words, as if the man—it was a man, I had at last ascertained that much—was disappointed that Saryon had not recognized him. "Now, follow my instructions. Return to the kitchen and prepare your tea, as you normally do. Take the cup to your bedroom, as you normally do, and lie down to read to this young man, as you normally do. Don't deviate from your nightly habits in even one instance, either of you. You can be seen from the bedroom window. I do not think that I was followed, but I can't be certain."

This last sentence was not conducive to relieving our apprehension. We did as we were commanded, however. As a catalyst, Saryon was accustomed to obedience, as was I, having been raised a servant in the royal household. In this case, it made no sense for my master to stand around in his nightshirt, arguing. We went to the kitchen.

The *Duuk-tsarith* remained in the darkened living room, but I could feel the man's eyes on me. It was extremely unnerving. Until now, neither Saryon nor I had realized that we had developed "nightly habits." Consequently, when this fact was brought to our attention, and we were forced to think about what we did every night, we couldn't remember doing any of it.

"Don't think," came the voice of the *Duuk-tsarith*. "Let your body take over. When you are settled in your bed, Father, then we will talk."

This was not exactly the way we would have chosen to spend our evening, but we didn't have much choice. Saryon took the Enforcer's advice and tried not to think about what he was doing. He turned off the kettle, which had been whistling loudly, though we'd been too distraught to notice. He poured the water, stirred the tea. I added to it a plate of digestible biscuits. We tottered—tea and biscuits in hand—off to his bedroom.

The *Duuk-tsarith* glided along silently behind.

Saryon, remembering the duties of a host, paused, turned, and held up the teacup, asking in dumb show if his visitor would like to share our repast.

"Keep moving!" The voice in my head was urgent. Then it added, in softer tones, "No, thank you."

Saryon went to his small bedroom, where he placed the tea and the biscuits on the nightstand beside his bed. I pulled up the chair. Picking up the book, I found the place where we had left off reading last night.

Saryon climbed into bed and it was only when he was safely tucked beneath the sheets that he remembered he usually brushed his teeth at this point. He looked at me, made a motion of using a toothbrush. I shrugged my shoulders, helpless to advise or assist.

Flustered, he was about to mention it to the Enforcer, then changed his mind. Giving me another glance, he settled himself. He opened the book, and drank a sip of tea. I usually ate a biscuit, but at that moment, due to the dryness in my mouth, I couldn't have swallowed one and I feared I would choke.

The *Duuk-tsarith,* watching us from the shadowed hallway, appeared satisfied. He left momentarily, returned with a chair from the kitchen, and sat down in the hall. Again came the whispered words of magic, and both Saryon and I looked about expectantly, wondering which of the pictures on the wall was going to turn green.

None did.

"I believe," said the silent voice, "that you usually listen to music, do you not?"

Of course! Saryon had forgotten. He switched on the CD player, which was, as far as he was concerned,

LEGACY OF THE DARKSWORD

one of the most miraculous and wondrous devices of this technological world. Beautiful music—I recall that it was Mozart—filled the room. Saryon began to read aloud from the book *Right Ho, Jeeves* by P. G. Wodehouse, one of our favorite authors. We would have been quite content had not the shadowy figure been perched, like Poe's raven, in the hall.

"It is now safe to talk," said the *Duuk-tsarith,* and this time he spoke the words aloud, albeit in a low voice. He drew the cowl back from his face. "But keep your voice down. I have deactivated the devices of the *D'karn-kair,* but there may be others present of which I am not aware."

Now that we could talk, all the questions which had been crowding my mind fled. Not that I could have spoken them myself, but I could have let my master speak for me. I could see that Saryon was in much the same state.

He could only munch his biscuit, sip his tea, and stare. The face of the *Duuk-tsarith* was in the direct light and Saryon seemed to find something vaguely familiar about the man. Saryon would later tell me that he did not experience the sensation of overwhelming dread one usually feels in the presence of the Enforcers. Indeed, he felt a small thrill of pleasure at the sight of the man and, if he could only have remembered who he was, knew that he would be glad to see him.

"I'm sorry, sir." Saryon faltered. "I know that I know you, but between age and failing eyesight . . ."

The man smiled.

"I am Mosiah," he said.

CHAPTER TWO

One by one, after each had been coldly rebuffed by the strange, dark-haired child, the other children let Joram severely alone. But there was one among them who persisted in his attempts to be friendly. This was Mosiah.

⁓FORGING THE DARKSWORD

I believe that Saryon would have exclaimed aloud in astonishment and pleasure, but he remembered in time the injunction to keep our voices down. He started to rise from his bed to go enfold his old friend in a fond embrace, but the *Duuk-tsarith* shook his head and motioned with his hand that Saryon was to remain where he was. Although the bedroom shades were drawn, the light was visible from outside and so was the catalyst's silhouette.

Saryon could only stammer, "Mosiah . . . I can't . . . I'm so sorry, my dear boy . . . twenty years

. . . I'm getting old, you see, and my memory . . . not to mention my eyesight . . ."

"Don't apologize, Father," Mosiah said, falling back on the old form of address, though it was hardly applicable now. "I have changed a lot, over the years. It is small wonder you did not recognize me."

"Indeed you *have* changed," said Saryon gravely, with a sorrowful glance at the black clothing of the Enforcer which Mosiah wore.

Mosiah seemed surprised. "I thought perhaps you might have heard that I had become one of the *Duuktsarith*. Prince Garald knew."

"We rarely speak, the Prince and I," said Saryon apologetically. "He felt it was best, for my own safety, or so he was kind enough to say. Remaining in contact with me would have damaged him politically. I could see that clearly. It was the main reason I left the relocation camp."

And now it was Mosiah who looked sadly upon Saryon, and the catalyst who was stricken with confusion and guilt.

"I . . . deemed it was best," Saryon said, flushing. "There were those who looked at me . . . if they didn't blame me, I brought back memories. . . ." His voice died away to silence.

"There are those who say you abandoned them in return for favors," Mosiah said.

I could no longer contain myself. I made a quick and violent gesture with my hand, to negate these cruel words, for I could tell that they wounded my master.

Mosiah looked wonderingly at me, not so much in astonishment that I did not speak—for he, as an Enforcer, must already know everything there was to know about me, including the fact that I was a mute—but that I was so quick to defend Saryon.

"This is Reuven," said Saryon, introducing me.

Mosiah nodded. As I said, he must have known all about me.

"He is your secretary," Mosiah said.

"That is what he has me call him," Saryon said, glancing in my direction with a fond smile. "Though it has always seemed to me that 'son' would be the more appropriate term."

I felt my skin burn with pleasure, but I only shook my head. He was dear as a father to me, the Almin knows, but I would never take such a liberty.

"He is mute," Saryon continued, explaining my affliction without embarrassment.

Nor did I feel any embarrassment myself. The handicap which one has had a lifetime seems more normal than not. As I had foreseen, Mosiah had advance knowledge of this, as his next words proved.

"Reuven was only a small child when the Shattering"—the term the people of Thimhallan now use for the destruction of their way of life—"occurred. He was left an orphan. Whatever happened to him was so traumatizing that it bereft him of speech. You found him, critically ill and alone in the abandoned Font. He was brought up in the household of Prince Garald, educated in the relocation camp, and sent to you by the Prince to record the story of the Darksword. I read it," Mosiah added, with a polite smile for me. "It was accurate, as far as it went."

I am used to receiving mixed compliments for my work, and therefore I made no reply. It is never dignified to defend one's creative endeavors. And I made allowances for the fact that Mosiah had been one of the central participants.

"As for my leaving the relocation camp," Saryon

said, continuing the earlier conversation, "I did what I thought was best for everyone."

His hand holding the teacup began to shake. I rose, went to him, and removed the cup, placing it on the nightstand.

"This house is quite nice," said Mosiah, glancing around, somewhat coldly. "Your work in the field of mathematics and Reuven's work in literature have made you a comfortable living. Our people in the relocation camps don't live as well as this—"

"They could if they wanted to," Saryon said, with a flash of the old spirit.

Knowing him as I do, and knowing his history, I guessed that this must be the same driving spirit which led him to seek out the forbidden books in the Font library. The same spirit that helped Joram forge the Darksword. The same spirit that faced the Turning with such courage and kept his soul alive, though his flesh had been changed to rock.

"No barbed wire surrounds those camps," Saryon said, speaking with increasing passion. "The guards at the gates were placed there when we first came to keep out the curious, not to prevent our people from leaving. Those guards should have been gone long ago, but our people begged for them to stay. Every person in the camp could have entered into this new world and found his or her place.

"But do they? No! They cling to some hopeless dream of returning to Thimhallan, of going back there to find—what? A land that is dead and blasted. Thimhallan has not changed since we left. It will not change, no matter how much we wish for it. The magic is gone!" Saryon's voice was soft and aching and thrilling. "It is gone and we should accept that and go on."

"The people of Earth do not like us," said Mosiah.

"They like me!" Saryon said crisply. "Of course, they don't like you. You refuse to mingle with the 'mundane,' as you call them, although many of them have as much magic in their bodies as you do in yours. Still, you shun them and isolate yourselves from them and it is no wonder they look upon you with distrust and suspicion. It was this same pride and arrogance which brought about the collapse of our world and put us into those relocation camps, and it is our pride and arrogance which keep us there!"

Mosiah would have spoken, I think, but he could not do so without raising his voice to interrupt my master, who, now conversing on his pet topic, was on his soapbox—a quaint term used by the natives of this world.

Indeed, Mosiah appeared moved by this speech. He did not reply, at first, but remained seated in thought a short space of time.

"What you say is true, Father," he said. "Or, rather, it was true at the beginning. We should have left the camp, gone forth into the world. But it was not pride which kept us behind those barricades. It was fear. Such a strange and terrifying world! Oh, admittedly, the Earthers brought in their sociologists and their psychologists, their counselors and teachers to try to help us 'fit in.' But I am afraid that they did more harm than good. The more they showed us of the wonders of this world, the more our people shrank away from them.

"Pride, yes, we had our share," he continued. "And not misplaced. Our world *was* beautiful. There *was* good in it." Mosiah leaned forward, his elbows resting on his knees, gazing earnestly at Saryon. "The Earthers could not believe in it, Father. Even the soldiers who had been there had difficulty believing what they had seen with their own eyes! On their return, they were ridiculed, and so they began to doubt their own senses, saying that we drugged them, made them see things that weren't there."

Mosiah shrugged. "The 'ologists' were kind and they tried to understand, but it was beyond their capacity to do so. Such an alien existence to them! When they looked at a young woman of twenty, to all appearances healthy and normal—by their standards—who did nothing all day but lie in bed, they could not understand what was wrong with her. When they were told that she was lying in bed because she was accustomed to floating through the air on wings of magic, that she had never walked a step in her life and had no idea how to walk, nor any inclination to do so, now that her magic was gone, they could not believe it.

"Oh, yes, I know that they appeared to accept it on the surface. All their medical tests confirmed the fact that the girl had never walked. But deep inside, in the inner core of their being, they did not believe. It is like asking them to believe in the faeries of which you wrote in your book, Reuven.

"Do you talk to your neighbors of your visit to the faeries, Father? Have you told the woman who lives next door, who is a secretary for a real-estate broker, that you were nearly seduced by the faerie queen?"

Saryon's face was exceedingly red. He stared down at the sheets, absently brushed away a few biscuit crumbs. "Of course not. It wouldn't be fair of me to expect her to understand. Her world is so . . . dissimilar. . . ."

"Your books." Mosiah's penetrating gaze shifted to me. "People read them and enjoy them. But they don't believe the stories, do they? They don't believe that such a world ever existed or that such a person as Joram ever lived. I have even heard it suggested that you pretend to have this affliction of yours to avoid interviews, because you are afraid that you would be revealed as a fraud and a fake."

Saryon glanced anxiously at me, for he was not aware that I had heard these accusations. He had gone to great lengths to spare me. I therefore took care to indicate that they caused me no concern, which, in truth, they did not, for so long as my work pleased one man, and that my master, I cared nothing for what others thought.

"And herein was created a strange dichotomy," said Mosiah. "They do not believe us, they do not understand us, and yet they are afraid of us. They are afraid that we will regain powers they do not believe we possessed in the first place. They try to prove to themselves and to us that such power never existed. What they fear, they destroy. Or try to."

An uncomfortable silence fell between us. Saryon blinked and attempted to stifle a yawn.

"It is your normal time to retire," Mosiah said, suddenly coming back to the present. "Do so. Keep to your routine."

It was my custom to bid my master good night and go to my room, to spend some time writing before I, too, went to bed. I did so, going upstairs and turning on the light. Then I crept back down the stairs in the darkness. Mosiah did not look particularly pleased to see me, but I think he knew that nothing short of my death would keep me from my master's side.

Saryon's room was now dark. We sat in the darkness, which was not, after all, very dark, due to a street lamp right outside the window. Mosiah drew his chair closer to Saryon's bed. The CD player remained on, for it was Saryon's habit to fall asleep to music. It was much past his usual hour for retiring, but he stubbornly refused to admit he was tired. Curiosity kept him awake and fighting his body's need for rest. I know because I felt the same.

"Forgive me, Father," said Mosiah at last. "I did not mean to be drawn down that old road, which, in truth, has long been overgrown with weeds and now leads nowhere. Twenty years have passed. That young girl of twenty is now a matron of forty. She learned to walk, learned to do for herself what had previously been done for her by magic. She learned to live in this world. Perhaps she has even come to believe something of what the mundanes tell her. Thimhallan is nothing but a charming memory to her, a world more real in her dreams than in her waking life. And if, at first, she chose to cling to the hope that she would return to that enchanted world of such miraculous beauty, who can blame her?"

"A world of beauty, yes," said Saryon, "but there was ugliness there, too. Ugliness made more hideous by being denied."

"The ugliness was in the hearts of men and women, was it not, Father?" Mosiah asked. "Not in the world itself."

"True, very true," Saryon said, and he sighed.

"And the ugliness lives still," Mosiah continued, and there came a change in his tone, a tension, which caused both my master and me to glance at each other and brace ourselves, for we each felt that a blow was coming.

"You have not been back to the camps for many years," Mosiah said abruptly.

Saryon shook his head.

"You have not been in contact with Prince Garald or anyone else? You truly know nothing of what has been going on with our people?"

Saryon looked ashamed, but he was forced to shake his head. At that moment I would have given all I own to be able to talk, for it seemed to me that there was accusation in Mosiah's tone, and I would have spoken most vehemently in my master's defense. As it was, Saryon heard me stir in restless anger. He set his hand on mine and patted it gently, counseling patience.

Mosiah was silent, wondering, perhaps, how to begin. At length he said, "You maintain that our people could leave the camps of their own free will, as you did. In the beginning, that might have been true. It is not true now.

"The guards of the mundane left us years ago. To give them credit, they fought to protect us, as they were ordered, but they were not equal to the task. After several had died and more had deserted, the army pulled out. The guards of the mundane were replaced—by our own."

"Fought against whom? Who attacked you? I've heard nothing of this!" Saryon protested. "Forgive me for doubting you, Mosiah, but surely, if such dreadful things were happening, journalists from all over the world would have descended on the camp."

"They did, Father. The Khandic Sages spoke to them. The journalists believed the lie—they could not help themselves, for the Khandic Sages coat all their bitter lies with the sweet honey of their magic."

"Khandic Sages! Who are they?" Saryon was bewildered, shocked beyond coherent speech. "And Prince Garald . . . How could he . . . He would have never allowed . . ."

"Prince Garald is a prisoner, held hostage by his love for his people."

"A prisoner!" Saryon gaped. "Of . . . of the mundanes?"

"No, not of the mundanes. And not of us Enforcers, either," Mosiah added, with another slight smile, "for I see that question in your mind."

"Then of whom? Or what?" Saryon asked.

"They call themselves *T'kon-Duuk*. In the language of the mundanes—Technomancers. They give Life to that which is Dead. Most horribly"—Mosiah's voice lowered—"they draw Life *from* that which is dead. The power of their magic does not come from living things, as was true in Thimhallan, but from the death of the living. Do you remember the man who called himself Menju the Sorcerer? The man who sought to murder Joram?"

Saryon shuddered. "Yes," he said in a low voice.

"He was one of them. I know them well," Mosiah added. "I used to be one of them myself."

Saryon stared aghast, unable to speak. It was left to me—the mute—to communicate. I made a gesture, pointing from Mosiah to Saryon and myself, asking in dumb show why Mosiah had come to us with this information now, at this time, and what this all had to do with us. And either he understood my gesture or he read the question in my mind.

"I have come," he said, "because *they* are coming. Their leader, a Khandic Sage known as Kevon Smythe, is coming tomorrow to talk to you, Father. The *Duuk-tsarith* chose me to warn you, knowing that I am the only one of that order you would trust."

"The *Duuk-tsarith*," Saryon murmured, perplexed. "I am to trust the *Duuk-tsarith* and so they send Mosiah, who is now one of them and who used to be a Technomancer. Technomancy. Life from death."

Then Saryon looked up. "Why me?" he asked. But he knew the answer, as well as I did.

"Joram," Mosiah replied. "They want Joram. Or perhaps I should say, they want the Darksword."

Saryon's mouth twitched. I realized then the subtlety of my master, one might almost say cunning, if a man as gentle and honest could be accused of such a thing. Though he had not known the news Mosiah had imparted, Saryon had known from the outset that this was why Mosiah had come, and yet my master had not mentioned it. He had been stalling, gaining information. I regarded him in admiration.

"I am sorry, Mosiah," said Saryon, "but you and King Garald and this Kevon Smythe and apparently a great many other people have wasted your time. I cannot take you to Joram and Joram cannot give you the Darksword. The circumstances are all detailed in Reuven's book."

Saryon shrugged. "The Darksword no longer exists. When Joram thrust the sword into the altar in the Temple, the sword was destroyed. Joram could not give you the sword if he wanted to."

Mosiah did not appear astonished or chagrined; nor did he rise to his feet and apologize for having disturbed us over nothing.

"A Darksword exists, Father. Not the original. That, as you say, was destroyed. Joram has forged a new one. We know the truth of this, because an attempt was made to steal it."

CHAPTER THREE

This is what the Duuk-tsarith *are trained for—to be aware of everything going on around them, to be in control of everything, yet manage to keep themselves above and apart from it.*

~*FORGING THE DARKSWORD*

Saryon was angry. His hand clenched, his anger flickered in his eyes. "You had no right! If Joram did forge a new sword, it must have been because he felt threatened. Was King Garald behind this? His own law clearly forbids—"

"What care do they have for the law?" Mosiah interrupted impatiently. "They know no laws but their own."

"They?"

"The Technomancers. Don't you understand yet, Father?"

Slowly, Saryon's hand unclenched. Fear replaced his anger. "Is Joram safe? He was supposed to send the boy to me to be educated. I've heard nothing and I feared—"

"Joram is alive, Father," Mosiah said, smiling slightly. "And he is well and so is Gwendolyn. As for Joram not sending his son to you, he did not do so because he and Gwen did not have a son. They have a daughter. His only child, she is precious in his sight. He is loath to send such a jewel to this world—and I can't say that I blame him." Mosiah sighed.

"How do you know this?" Saryon demanded, his voice sharp. "You are spying on him!"

"Protecting him, Father," said Mosiah softly. "Protecting him. He doesn't know of our watchfulness. He doesn't suspect. How could he know, who has no magic Life within him? We are careful not to disturb him or his family. Unlike others.

"Just recently, an arm of the Technomancers known as the *D'karn-darah* defied the law which prohibits any person from traveling to Thimhallan. They had read Reuven's book"—he gave me a wry smile—"and they went to the altar at the Temple of the Necromancers to try to recover the Darksword. They found what one might have expected. As you know, Father, the altar itself was made of darkstone. The sword had fused with the stone.

"The Technomancers used every device known to man to try to free the sword, from the most sophisticated laser cutting tools to old-fashioned blowtorches. They attempted to cut the altar itself into pieces, to haul it back to their laboratories. They did not even scratch its surface."

Saryon appeared relieved. "Good." He nodded. "Excellent. Thank the Almin."

"Don't be so quick to thank Him, yet, Father," Mosiah said. "Failing to make a dent in the altar, the Technomancers went to Joram."

"They were wasting their time. He would have been furious," Saryon predicted.

Mosiah's smile twisted. "He *was* furious. The Khandic Sages had never seen such fury. His anger astonished them, and they are not easily astonished. Kevon Smythe himself talked to Joram, though now Smythe denies that he did so. He thought to win Joram with his charm, but, as you know, Father, our friend is not easily charmed. Smythe offered Joram vast wealth, power, whatever he wanted in exchange for the location of raw darkstone and the secret of the forging of Darkswords.

"Smythe barely escaped with his life. Joram threw Smythe—literally picked him up and threw him—out the door and warned him that the next time he returned he could count his life as nothing. By this time, the Border Patrol had arrived. You ask what took them so long? How the Technomancers evaded their defenses? Easily. Several of their own had managed to get themselves assigned to the duty. They shut down the alarm signals, permitted their brethren to cross the Border without notice.

"When the Border Patrol arrived, they escorted Smythe and his followers off-planet. To our relief, the Technomancers lost interest in the Darksword after that. Their scientists studied the reports brought back from Thimhallan and made the determination that the original sword could never be removed from the altar and it was therefore useless to them. Without Joram's assistance, and without permission to take teams of workers to Thimhallan—permission that would never be granted—the search for raw darkstone would be too difficult and too costly to undertake.

"King Garald hoped that this incident would be an end of the Technomancers' desire for the Darksword and it might have been, Father, except that Joram did a very foolish thing."

Saryon looked as pained and unhappy as if he himself had been responsible for Joram's behavior. "He forged a new sword."

"Precisely. We are not certain how. Smythe's visit had made Joram suspicious and paranoid—"

"Made him feel as if he were being watched," Saryon interrupted.

Mosiah paused a moment, then slightly smiled. "I have never known you to be sarcastic, Father. Very well. I grant that Joram had some basis for his feelings. But if he had only gone to King Garald or General Boris instead of trying to fight the whole world all by himself!"

"Battling life alone was always Joram's way," Saryon said, and his voice was filled with affectionate sorrow and understanding. "His blood is that of Emperors. He comes from a long line of rulers who held the fate of nations in their hands. To ask for help would be a sign of weakness. You recall the effort it took him to ask me to help him create the Darksword. He was—"

Saryon paused. I had been wondering when this would occur to him.

"Joram could *not* have forged a Darksword," he said excitedly. "Not without a catalyst. I drew Life from the world, gave Life to the Darksword, which in turn used that Life to drain Life from those who possessed it."

"He didn't need you to forge the sword itself, Father. He only needed you to enhance its abilities."

"But without a catalyst to do that, the sword is no more dangerous than any other sword. Why would the Technomancers still want it?"

"Consider the number of catalysts among our people, Father. Catalysts living in poverty in the relocation camps, who would be more than willing to exchange their gifts for the promise of wealth and power from the Technomancers. Though the corrupt Bishop Vanya is now dead, his legacy lives on among some of his followers."

"Yes, I can see how that could be true," said Saryon sadly. "How did Joram manage to escape the watchful eye of the *Duuk-tsarith* long enough to forge the sword?"

Mosiah shrugged and spread his hands. "Who knows? Such a feat would be relatively simple, especially if he had an amulet made of darkstone. Or, for all we know, he forged this sword years ago, before we began to keep watch. None of that matters now, however. We attempted to keep word of this new Darksword secret, but the Technomancers found out. Their interest has been rekindled."

"Are Joram and his family in danger?" Saryon asked anxiously.

"Not for the moment, mainly because of the efforts of the *Duuk-tsarith*. Ironic, isn't it, Father. Those who once sought Joram's death now risk death themselves to guard his life."

"You?" Saryon asked. "You're risking death?"

"Yes," Mosiah replied, very calmly. He gestured around the darkened room. "Thus the reason for these precautions. The *T'kon-Duuk* are eager to get their hands on me. I know too many of their secrets, you see,

Father. I am a great danger to them. I have come to warn you of them, of the techniques they will try to use to persuade you to take them with you to Joram—"

Saryon raised a hand to halt the flow of words. Mosiah ceased speaking instantly, with a quiet respect for the elderly catalyst which did much to increase his favor with me. I could never trust him completely, not while he wore the black robes of the Enforcers. The *Duuk-tsarith* never worked for just one end. They worked for several and sought to gain the middle into the bargain.

"I will not go," Saryon said firmly. "Have no fear of that. I would be of no use. I don't know what you or they or anyone else thinks I could do."

"Joram respects and trusts you, Father. Your influence with him is—" Mosiah broke off.

He was staring at me. They were both staring at me. I had made a noise. It must, I realize, have sounded very strange—a guttural sort of croak in my throat. I made a signal to my master.

"Reuven says that there is something out there," Saryon said.

The words had not yet left Saryon's lips before Mosiah was standing next to me. This sudden movement of his was at least as startling as the apparition I thought I had seen outside the window. One moment he was across the room from me, sitting in the darkened hallway, and the next instant he was by my side, peering out the window. In his fluid, silent motion, he was one with the shadows. Imagine my astonishment when, glancing back at my master to be certain he was all right, I caught a glimpse of Mosiah, seated in his chair!

I realized, then, that the Enforcer next to me was

insubstantial. Mosiah's shadow, so to speak, had been sent on an errand by its master.

"What did you see? Tell me! Immediately!" he demanded. The words blazed in my mind.

I signaled with my hands. Saryon translated.

"Reuven says he thinks he saw a person dressed all in silver—"

Mosiah—the Mosiah seated in the chair—was on his feet. His shadow had returned to its body.

"They are here," he said. "The *D'karn-darah*. Blood-doom knights. Either they followed me or they have come for their own reasons. I fear it is the latter. You are not safe here, either of you. You must come with me. Now!"

"We're not dressed!" Saryon protested.

It must be a very real and present danger which sends an elderly man dashing out into the cold winter night clad only in his nightshirt and bedslippers.

"You don't need to be," Mosiah replied. "Your bodies aren't going anywhere, except to bed. Follow my instructions exactly. Father, remain where you are. Reuven, go upstairs to your room and climb into your bed."

I was not happy at the thought of leaving my master, though what I could have done against the power of the *Duuk-tsarith* was open to question. Saryon indicated with a nod that we were to obey Mosiah and that is what I did. I urged Mosiah to care for my master and left to go upstairs to my small room.

Saryon always waited until he heard me in the bedroom, which was on the level above his, before turning out the downstairs light. Tonight was the exception since his light was already off. As I have said, it was usually my practice to spend some time writing, but—acting on Mosiah's orders—I abandoned this custom and retired immediately to my bed. I turned out my light and the house was dark.

Lying alone in the darkness, I began to be afraid. It is easy to frighten oneself at this time of night. I recalled childhood terrors of monsters lurking in the closet. The fear I experienced could not be banished by a flashlight, however. I wondered why I was experiencing this feeling of dread and I realized it was because I felt Mosiah's fear.

Whatever is out there in the night must be terrible, I thought, to have frightened someone as powerful as the *Duuk-tsarith*.

I lay in my bed, ears stretched to catch every sound. The night had its usual noises, I suppose, but they were all alarming to me, who had never before paid them much heed. The bark of a dog, the whine and snarl of fighting cats, a lone automobile traveling up the street. I invested these with such sinister meanings that when Mosiah's words again lit up my mind, I was so startled that my shudder shook the bed frame.

"Come to me," said Mosiah. "Not your body. Leave that behind. Let your soul rise from its shell and walk with me."

I had no idea what the man was talking about.

I think I would have laughed—in fact, I am afraid that I did giggle, perhaps from nervous tension—except that I felt his dire urgency. Bewildered, I lay in my bed, wondering what I was supposed to do, wondering if my master knew what to do. Mosiah—or perhaps I should say the "shadow" of Mosiah—took form in the darkness, standing at the foot of the bed.

He held out his hand to me. "It is quite simple," he said. "*You* are coming with me. Your body is staying behind. My body is downstairs right now. Yet here I stand before you. Picture yourself rising up out of bed and walking with me. You are a writer. You must have traveled like this in your imagination many times. When I read your description of Merilon, I could see it again in my mind, it was so vivid. You are a professional daydreamer, one might say. Simply concentrate a little bit more."

And when I did not immediately move, Mosiah's tone sharpened. "Saryon will not leave without you. You are putting him in danger."

He knew that would rouse me. It would have roused me from my grave. I closed my eyes and imagined myself rising up from my bed and joining Mosiah. At first, nothing happened. I was in such a flutter of excitement and fear that it was difficult to concentrate.

"Relax," Mosiah said softly, hypnotically. "Relax and slough off the heaviness of the body that weighs you down."

His words no longer burned in my mind, but seemed to flow through it like running water. I found myself relaxing, letting the water run over me. My body did, in fact, feel very heavy, so heavy that I knew I could not lift it. And yet, there was the imperative *that I had to leave*!

I stood up and I walked over to join Mosiah. When I looked back, I was not surprised to see the heavy body still lying in the bed, slumbering soundly, to all appearances.

My fears were forgotten in my wonder and awe.

I started to move toward the door, thinking to go through it and down the stairs to my master's bedroom, as I was accustomed, but Mosiah stopped me.

"You are no longer constrained by physical barriers, Reuven. A thought will take you to Saryon."

And he spoke truly. The moment I thought about being with my master, I was there beside him. At the

sight of me, Saryon smiled and nodded and then, hesitantly, as if having to relearn skills long forgotten, his
soul left his body.

I was not surprised to see his spirit suffused with a
soft radiant white glow; a distinct contrast to Mosiah,
whose spirit seemed cloaked with the same black robes
his body wore.

My master was pained by this, as I could tell. And so
could Mosiah.

"Once—you remember, Father—my soul was bright
and crystal clear as Reuven's. The dark and terrible
things I have seen since have left their mark upon me.
But we must hurry. They will wait only until they think
you are asleep. Don't be afraid, I will not let them harm
either of you."

Mosiah's soul slid back into its body. He spoke a
word, reached out with his hand as if to some invisible
door, pushed on nothing, and walked inside.

"Hurry!" he commanded. "Follow me."

The mind thinks of the strangest things at the most
inappropriate times. I remembered, suddenly, a televi-
sion cartoon I had seen as a child, in which the character—perhaps a rabbit, I'm not certain—is being chased
through the forest by a hunter with a gun. The rabbit is
cornered, apparently, until he opens a hole in the cartoon, crawls inside, and pulls the hole in after him,
leaving the hunter extremely befuddled.

Mosiah had done the very same thing. He had
opened a hole in our bedroom and was urging us to
crawl inside!

Saryon, having lived for many, many years in the
magical world of Thimhallan, was much more accustomed to such arcane manifestations than I was. He
immediately entered the hole, then beckoned to me to
follow. I started to cross the room, remembered that I

didn't have to rely on my feet, and wished myself at my master's side.

I was in the hole. The hole closed behind me and formed a bubble around us, holding us suspended in the air, floating somewhere near the ceiling of Saryon's bedroom.

"A Corridor?" Saryon asked, amazed. "Here on Earth?"

I must mention, by the way, that we did not speak, but communicated mind to mind. And it occurred to me that, in this spirit realm, I was no longer mute. I could talk and be heard. The knowledge filled me with such trembling joy and terrible confusion that I was immediately rendered more silent than I had ever been in the physical realm.

"Not as you mean it, Father. Not a Corridor in time and space such as we had on Thimhallan," Mosiah replied. "That skill has been lost to us, and we have not regained it. But we do have the ability to slip inside one of time's folds."

I must try to explain the sensation of being hidden in a "fold" of time, as Mosiah called it. The only way I can put this is to say that it was very much like hiding behind the folds of a heavy curtain. And, in fact, I began to feel an almost smothering constraint upon me, which is caused by, so I learned later, the knowledge that time was passing for my body and I—the spirit—was standing still.

The sensation is not as bad, I understand, for those who enter the fold with both mind and body, for one has only to step out again to be caught up in time's flow. But, despite the fact that my body was slumbering, I began to feel a panic inside me akin to that felt by someone fearing he may miss the last train home. The train—i.e., my body—was moving on ahead, and I was running frantically to catch up. I think I would have attempted to escape, then and there, but I would not leave Saryon.

I found out later that he felt the same, but that he would not leave because of me. We laughed over that, but our laughter was hollow.

"Shh, hush! Look!" Mosiah cautioned.

He did not silence us so that we would not be heard—for that was not possible, not even for the *D'karn-darah*. He silenced us that we might hear them. What we heard and what we saw chilled us.

Though we could move through physical barriers, we could not see through them. Trapped inside time's fold, we could not move to another part of the house or see what was transpiring in any other part of the house except Saryon's bedroom. My hearing is acute, however, and the nervous tension I was under accentuated it. I heard a slight clicking sound, which was our front-door lock giving way. The creak of the door's hinges (which Saryon had been asking me to oil) meant that the front door was being stealthily opened. At the same time I heard the snick of the lock of the back door, heard the door itself scrape across the mud rug which we had placed at the entrance.

Whoever had been out there had entered the house by the front and by the back. But try as I might, I could not hear them moving at all through the front part of the house. One of them was in the bedroom before I was fully aware of his coming.

He was clad all in paper-thin silver robes that clung to his body and crackled faintly as he moved, occasionally emitting tiny blue sparks, like the fur of a cat in the darkness. His face was plastered with the same paper-thin silver, so that only the outline of features—a nose and mouth—were visible. Silver fabric covered his hands and feet like a second skin.

He stood in the bedroom and Mosiah, with a whispered thought, called our attention to a strange phenomenon. The machines in the bedroom knew the *D'karn-darah* was there. The machines responded to his coming.

The machines' response was not overt or dramatic. I would not have noticed it, except for Mosiah's mention. The bedroom's overhead light, which had, of course, been turned off, flickered on. A faint hum of music came from the compact-disc player. The reading lamp gave a feeble gleam.

The *D'karn-darah* ignored all this and went immediately to Saryon's body, which continued to sleep soundly. He put out a silver-covered hand and shook the catalyst by the shoulder.

"Saryon!" he said loudly.

Beside me, I could feel Saryon's spirit shiver. I was thankful, then, for Mosiah's arrival and his timely warning. If my master had been wakened in the night and seen such a horrific sight bending over him, he might never have recovered from the shock.

At that moment I heard a female voice say "Reuven!" loudly. I felt a slight brushing sensation across my shoulder. Then I knew that the second person, the one who had entered by the back door, had gone to my room. She was standing over my body.

The *D'karn-darah* shook Saryon again, more forcibly, turning the sleeping body over in the bed. "Saryon!" the man repeated, and his voice was harsh.

I trembled, for I was afraid he would do Saryon some harm. Mosiah again reassured both of us.

"They will not hurt you," he repeated. "They do not dare. They know you may be of use to them."

The one who had been in my room now appeared in Saryon's bedchamber.

"Same thing?" she asked.

"Yes," answered the *D'karn-darah* who stood beside my master. "Their souls have fled. They were alerted to our coming."

"*Duuk-tsarith.*"

"Of course. Undoubtedly the one named Mosiah, that Enforcer who was once the catalyst's friend."

"You were right, then. You said we would find him here."

"He has been here. He is probably still here, hiding in one of their cursed time folds, no doubt. And the other two are probably with him right now. Very possibly"—the man's silver faceless face turned and gazed around the bedroom—"they are listening to us at this moment."

"Then it is simple. Torture the body. Pain will cause their spirits to return. They will be only too glad, after a while, to tell us where to find the Enforcer."

The female *D'karn-darah* raised her hand, and where before had been five fingers were now five long steel needles. Electricity began to arc from one to another. She reached the hand with the horribly crackling needles toward Saryon's defenseless form.

Her partner halted her, his own hand closing around her wrist.

"The Khandic Sages will be here tomorrow, working their own methods of persuasion. They would know that we had been here and they would not be pleased."

"They know that we are hunting this Enforcer. They want him as much as we do."

"Yes, but they want this catalyst more." The

D'karn-darah sounded irritated. "Very well, we will leave him to them. A pity we could not have arrived a few moments sooner. We would have been able to capture the *Duuk-tsarith*. As it is, our meeting is only delayed, Enforcer!" He spoke to the air. "And, you, Catalyst." The silver face turned toward the figure in the bed. "I leave this, my . . . business card."

He opened the palm of his gloved hand, reached into his other palm, gave a twist, freeing some object—I could not see what. He tossed that object onto the bed, at the feet of Saryon's slumbering figure. Then the two of them left the bedroom, left the house by the back door.

At their departure, the machines in the house returned to normal. The lights went off, the CD player ceased to play.

We waited, hidden, for some time, to make certain the *D'karn-darah* were gone and that this was no trick to lure us out of hiding. When Mosiah permitted us to return, my spirit drifted back to find my body. I looked down upon myself.

This was much different than looking into a mirror, for the mirror shows us what we see every day, what we have grown accustomed to seeing. Before now, I had never seen myself with such clarity. And though I was eager to return to Saryon and had questions to ask of Mosiah, I was so entranced by this ability to see myself as a casual observer might see me that I took a few moments to do just that.

Physical attributes I knew well. The mirror shows us these. Fair hair, worn long, that someone in my childhood once called "corn silk." Brown eyes beneath eyebrows that I did not like. They were thick and dark brown, in stark contrast to my fair hair, and gave me a

grave and overly serious aspect. The features of my face
tended to be sharp, with prominent cheekbones and a
nose that was called aquiline. It would grow beaky as I
aged.

Being young, my body was lithe, although certainly
not strong. Exercise of the mind suited me far better
than running very fast on a machine that took me nowhere. Yet now I looked at those thin hands and spin-
dly arms with disfavor. If Saryon was in danger, how
could I defend him?

I found that I did not have the leisure to spend long
on this inspection. The nearer my spirit drew to my
body, the more it longed to return, and I had the impression that I dove down to my body from a great
height. I awoke, shaking, stomach clenching, as one
does from a falling dream. And I have wondered, ever
since, if perhaps those dreams aren't really the first
tentative journeys our spirits make.

I sat up in my bed, shaking off the feelings of sleep
that clung to my body. Hurriedly grabbing my robe, I
wrapped it around myself, and switching on the hall
light, hastened down the stairs. Light came from
Saryon's bedroom. I found my master, looking as
groggy as I felt, staring at the object which the *D'karn-
darah* had left upon the blanket.

"It will not harm you," Mosiah was saying as I entered. "You may pick it up, if you like."

"I will do so, sir," I signed, and swooped down
upon the object, gathering it into my hand before
Saryon could touch it.

Mosiah watched me with a slight smile, which was, I
think, approving. Saryon just shook his head with fond
exasperation.

When I was certain that the object was benign, not

likely to explode or burst into flame or—I don't know what I'd expected exactly—I opened my hand and held it out. Saryon and I peered down on it wonderingly.

"What is it?" he asked, puzzled.

"Death," said Mosiah.

CHAPTER FOUR

*Like a Living being, the sword sucked the magic
from him, drained him dry, then used him to
continue to absorb magic from all around it.*

∼FORGING THE DARKSWORD

"Death!" Saryon tried to snatch the object from me,
but I was too quick for him. I clasped my hand over it
tightly.

"I do not mean for any of us, here and now," Mosiah said. His voice held a note of gentle rebuke. "I
would not have allowed this to remain in this room if it
had been dangerous."

Saryon and I exchanged glances, both considerably
ashamed.

"Of course, Mosiah," Saryon said. "Forgive me—
forgive *us*—for not trusting you. . . . It's just . . . it

has all been so strange. . . . Those dreadful people. . . ." He shivered and drew his robe closer around his tall, spare form.

"Who were they?" I gestured. "And what is this?"

I opened my palm. In it lay a round medallion about two inches in diameter made of very hard, heavy plastic. The medallion had what appeared to be a sort of magnet on the back. One side was clear. I could see inside and what I saw was very strange. Encased in the medallion was some sort of bluish-green, thick, and viscous sludge. As I held the medallion in my hand the sludge began undulating, surging against the sides of the medallion, as if it were trying to escape. It was not a pleasant sight and made me feel queasy to watch it.

I was loath to hold on to the medallion longer and I fidgeted with it in my hand.

"It . . . it looks as if it's alive!" Saryon said, frowning in disgust.

"They are," Mosiah answered. "Or rather they were. Most are already dead, which is why the *D'karn-darah* gave this up. The rest will be dead shortly."

"The rest of what! What's trapped in there?" Saryon was horrified and looked about vaguely, as if for something he could use to crack the medallion open.

"I will explain in a moment. I am first going to remove the listening devices which the *D'karn-darah* placed in your living room and in the phone. They made their presence known. There is no longer any reason to keep up the pretense."

He left the room, returned a moment later. "There. Now we may speak freely."

I handed over the medallion, thankful to be rid of it.

"A very elemental organism," Mosiah said, holding it to the light. "A sort of organic soup, if you will.

Single-celled creatures, who are born and bred by the Technomancers for one purpose—to die."

"How terrible!" said Saryon, shocked.

"But not much different from calves," I pointed out, "who are born only to become veal."

"Perhaps," Saryon said with a smile and a shake of his head.

The only disagreements—I can't even call them arguments—he and I have ever had have been over the fact that I am a vegetarian, while he enjoys a bit of chicken or beef on occasion. Early in my arrival, I made the attempt—in my zeal—to convert him to my way of thinking. I made life very unhappy for us both, I am sorry to say, until we reached an agreement to respect each other's opinions. He now views my bean curd with equanimity and I no longer stage a protest over a hamburger.

"The living always feed off the dead," said Mosiah. "The hawk kills the mouse. Big fish eat their smaller cousins. The rabbit kills the dandelion it devours, if it comes to that. The dandelion feeds off the nutrients in the soil, nutrients which come from the decomposing bodies of other plants and animals. Life thrives on death. Such is the cycle."

Saryon was quite struck by this. "I never looked at it that way."

"Nor have I," I signed, thoughtful.

"The Dark Cultists have, for generations," Mosiah continued. "They carried their beliefs one step further. If death was the basis for life—"

"Then Death would be the basis for Life!" Saryon said, suddenly understanding.

It took me a moment longer to understand, mainly because I did not, at the time, hear the capital letters in his words.

Of course, when he spoke of Life, he was referring to magic, for the people of Thimhallan believe that magic is Life and that those born without the ability to use magic are Dead. And that, one might say, was the beginning of the story of Joram and the Darksword.

The magic—or Life—is present in all things living. The dandelion possesses its tiny share, as do the rabbit and the hawk, the fish, and we humans ourselves. In very ancient times certain people discovered how to take the Life from things around them and used it to perform what others considered miracles. They termed such miracles "magic" and those who could not use the magic feared and distrusted it immensely. Wizards and witches were persecuted and slain.

"But who are the Dark Cultists?" Saryon asked.

"Recall your history lessons, Father," Mosiah said. "Recall how the magi of ancient times came together and determined to leave Earth and find another world—a world where magic could flourish and grow, not wither and die as it was bound to do on this one.

"Recall how Merlyn, the greatest of us all, led his people into the stars and how he founded the new world, Thimhallan, where magic was concentrated, trapped, so that it seemed to have disappeared from Earth completely."

" 'Seemed to have'?" Saryon repeated.

"Excuse me," I signed, "but if we are going to stay up for the rest of the night, may I suggest that we move to the kitchen? I'll turn up the heat and make tea for everyone."

We had been standing, shivering—at least Saryon and I were shivering—in Saryon's bedroom. He looked haggard and weary, but neither he nor I could sleep now, after so many astounding and puzzling events.

"That is," I added, "unless you think those terrible beings will return."

Saryon translated my gestures, but I had the feeling that wasn't necessary. Mosiah understood me—either my thoughts or the sign language.

"The *D'karn-darah* will not come back this night," Mosiah said with confidence. "They thought to ambush me, to take me by surprise. They know now that I am aware of them. They will not face me in direct battle. They would be forced to kill me and they do not want my death. They want to capture me—they *must* capture me—alive."

"Why?" Saryon asked.

"Because I infiltrated their organization. I am the only disciple of the blood-doom knights to have ever escaped their clutches alive. I know their secrets. The *D'karn-darah* want to find out how much I know and, most importantly, who else knows. They hope, by capturing me, that I will tell them. They are wrong," he said simply, but with firm conviction. "I would die first."

"Let us have some tea," Saryon said quietly.

He put his hand on Mosiah's arm, and I knew now that my master trusted this man implicitly. I wanted to, but it was all so strange. It was hard for me to trust my own senses, let alone trust another person. Had what happened really happened? Had I truly left my body? Had I hidden away in a fold of time?

I filled the teakettle with water, put it on the burner, brought out the teapot and cups. Mosiah sat at the table. He declined to have tea. He held, in his hand, the medallion. None of us spoke, the entire time we waited for the water to boil, the tea to steep. When, at last, I poured my master's tea, I had begun to believe.

"Start at the beginning," said Saryon.

"Do you mind," I indicated, "if I take notes?"

Saryon frowned and shook his head, but Mosiah said he did not mind and that our experiences might, someday, make an interesting book. He only hoped people would still be left alive on Earth to read it.

I retrieved my small computer from my bedroom, and seated with the computer in my lap, I wrote down his words.

"The Dark Cultists have existed down through time, although we, in Thimhallan, had no record of them. What we knew as the Council of Nine on Thimhallan, representing the nine magical arts, was once the Council of Thirteen here on Earth. At that time the Council believed that all magi should be represented, even those who held diverse ethical views, and so those who practiced the dark side of magic were included. Perhaps some of the more naive members hoped to turn their brothers and sisters who walked in the shadows back to the light. If so, they did not succeed and, in fact, they incorporated their own eventual downfall.

"It was the Dark Cultists who poisoned the mundane of Earth against magi. Life did not come from life, for them. Life—or magic—came from death. They engaged in human and animal sacrifice, believing that the deaths of others enhanced their power. Cruel and selfish, they used their arcane arts only to indulge themselves, to further their own ambition, to enslave and seduce, to destroy.

"The mundane fought back. They held witch trials, inquisitions. Magi were rounded up, tortured until they confessed, and were burned or hanged or drowned. Among these were many members of the Council who had used their magic for good, not evil. Shocked and saddened by their losses, the Council of Thirteen met to consider what to do.

"The Four Dark Cults—the Cult of the White Steed, the Black Steed, the Red Steed, and the Pale Steed—all advocated war and conquest. They would rise up and destroy those who opposed them, enslaving all who survived. The Nine Cults of Light refused even to consider this option. Furious, the Four members stormed out of the meeting. In their absence, the other members made their decision. They would leave Earth forever. Realizing now the danger the Dark Cultists represented to their order, the Council took care that the Dark Cultists were excluded from all their plans.

"In A.D. 1600, when Merlyn and the Council of Nine left this world, the Dark Cultists found out about the exodus, but—so well kept was the secret—they were too late either to impede the exodus or to force their way along. They were left behind on Earth.

"At first, they welcomed the change, for the Council of Nine had long curtailed the activities of the Dark Cultists. They saw themselves as rulers of the people of Earth and so they set out to advance their goals. But during this time on Thimhallan, Merlyn established the Well of the World, which drew magic from Earth and concentrated it within the boundaries of Thimhallan. The Dark Cultists found themselves bereft of their magical power.

"They were enraged, but helpless. They knew well what had happened, that magic was being kept within Thimhallan. Their powers dwindled, except for times of famine or plague or war, when Death stalked the world and increased their power. Even then, they could perform only small magicks, mostly for their own personal benefit. They never lost their ambition, nor their memory of how powerful they had once been. They believed that there would come a time when they would rise again.

"And so, down through the ages, the Four kept their loose-knit organization. Parents would pass on this dark inheritance to their children. Worthy recruits were brought into the circle. Fearful of discovery, the Four worked their Dark Arts in isolation, keeping apart from others. Yet they always knew each other, one mage recognizing a fellow mage by certain secret signs and countersigns.

"A central organization existed, run by the Khandic Sages. So secret was this that few of the members ever knew who was in control. Once a year the *Sol-huena*, the Collectors, appeared at the door of every Dark Cultist, demanding a tithe, which was used to keep the Council operational. The only time members ever came together was if one of their own had been lax in payment of funds or had broken one of their strict rules. The wizards of the Black Steed, the *Sol-t'kan* or Judges, sat in judgment and passed sentence. The *Sol-huena* carried out that sentence.

"Eventually, as time passed, the modern world no longer believed in witches and warlocks. The Dark Cultists were able to leave their cellars and their caves, where they had once practiced their arts, move into apartments and town houses. They entered politics, became government ministers and rulers of nations, and when it suited their purposes, fomented war and rebellion. They delight in suffering and death, for by such is their power enhanced.

"And then came the day when the Darksword was created."

Mosiah glanced at Saryon, who smiled gently and sighed softly and shook his head. For though he did not regret his part in the creation of the Darksword and the eventual downfall of Thimhallan and often said that he would do it again, he as often added that he wished change could have been accomplished with much less pain and suffering.

"The Four knew of the sword's creation," said Mosiah. "Some of them said that they were aware of it from the very hour it came into being."

Saryon was perplexed. "But how is that possible? They were so far away. . . ."

"Not far enough. Like it or not, threads of magic bind us together, like the gossamer strands of a spiderweb. If one strand is broken, the shock is felt throughout the web. The Four had no idea what had happened, but they felt the sword's dark energy. They had strange dreams and portents. Some saw the shadow of a black sword, shaped like a man, rise out of flames. Others saw the same image of a black sword shattering a fragile glass globe. They took it for a symbol of hope. They believed that its creation would bring magic back to them. They were right.

"Twenty years ago, by Earth time, Joram used the Darksword to shatter the Well of the World. Magic spewed out into the universe. The magic was diluted when it reached Earth, but to the parched members of the Dark Cults, the magic fell upon them like a renewing shower."

"But I don't understand why they should want the sword," Saryon protested. "The Darksword nullifies magic. It was invaluable to Joram in Thimhallan, because he was the only person alive who did not possess any magical powers. It was his only means of defense against a world of magi. But what would these Technomancers do with the Darksword here on Earth? Its power is nothing compared to that of . . . of . . . a nuclear bomb."

"On the contrary, Father. The Technomancers believe that the Darksword would give them immense power. Power similar to that of a nuclear weapon, in that they could control entire populations. And the Darksword would provide such power on an individual basis in a handy, compact, and inexpensive form. Far more convenient to use than a nuclear bomb and not nearly so messy."

"I am afraid I still don't understand—"

"The Darksword absorbs Life, Father. You have said yourself—and your young friend has written—how the sword drew from you the magic that you were drawing from the world. 'The magic surged through him like a blast of wind,' is, I believe, how Reuven phrased it."

Saryon paled. He had lifted his teacup, to drink, set it down again with haste. His hand shook. He gazed at Mosiah with sorrowful anguish.

"I am afraid so, Father," Mosiah answered the look, the unspoken protest. "The Technomancers know that the Darksword has the power to absorb Life. Once the sword is in their possession, they plan to study it, determine how to mass-produce it, and distribute Darkswords to their followers. The swords will absorb magic, then give up that Life, much as a living being gives up life when the being dies. And because the Technomancers are accustomed to taking magic from the dead, they believe they can use Darkswords to fuel their power—a far cheaper and more efficient means than that which they are now using."

A kind of magic battery, I typed.

"What are they using to fuel their power?" Saryon asked, his voice low. His gaze was on the medallion, which had now gone almost completely dark—a brownish, blackish green.

Mosiah picked up the medallion, held it to the light. "Imagine these organisms grown in immense vats—

vats seven times the size of this house, whose circumference would encompass this block. Various gases are pumped into the vats. An electrical current is passed through the gases. The result is this simple form of life. Great quantities are manufactured. The living mass seethes and bubbles in the vats as it grows and reproduces. Now imagine many more vats, dedicated to the death of these organisms. Again, the electric current. But this time it destroys, it does not create.

"As the catalysts give us Life . . ." Mosiah paused, looked at Saryon. "As you used to give me Life, Father. Do you remember? We were fighting Blachloch's henchmen and I transformed into a gigantic tiger. . . . I was very young," he added, with a slight smile, "and prone to flaunt my power."

Saryon smiled. "I remember. And I remember being quite happy to see that tiger at the time."

"At any rate"—Mosiah shook off memory—"as the catalysts give us Life, drawing the magic from all living beings and pouring it into those of us who use it, so the Technomancers receive their power from the deaths— not only of these manufactured organisms, but from the deaths of all things in this universe. The war with the Hch'nyv has been a blessing to them," he added, his tone bitter.

"I will never take the Technomancers to Joram," Saryon said with absolute conviction. "Never. Like you"—he looked at Mosiah—"I would die first. You need have no worry."

"On the contrary, Father," said Mosiah. "We *want* you to take them to Joram."

Saryon stared at Mosiah, stared a long time in silence. His pain was so great that it grieved me to look at him.

"*You* want the Darksword," he said. His brows drew together. "Who sent you?"

Mosiah leaned forward, his hands clasped together. "The Technomancers are extremely powerful, Father. They have seduced a great number of our people, who are now finding it easier and faster to gain what they want in this world by exchanging magic for technomancy. King Garald—"

"Ah!" Saryon exclaimed, and he nodded.

"King Garald dares not openly defy them," Mosiah continued resolutely. "Not now, not yet. But secretly, we are building our strength, readying our resources. When the day comes, we will take action and—"

"And what?" Saryon cried. "Kill them? More killing?"

"If you do not acquire the Darksword from Joram, what do you think they will do to him and to his family, Father?" Mosiah asked coldly. "The only reason they have left him in peace thus far is due to the laws of the mundane, which prohibit anyone from setting foot on Thimhallan. The Technomancers have not yet been ready to reveal themselves to the mundane.

"All that is about to change, however. Their leader—this man Kevon Smythe—has gained great political power among the mundane, who do not know he is a Technomancer and wouldn't believe it if they were told. Smythe has convinced the heads of Earth Force that, using the power of the Darksword, the Technomancers can defeat the Hch'nyv. At this juncture in the war Earth Force is desperate enough to try anything. Tomorrow, Kevon Smythe, King Garald, and General Boris will call on you, Father Saryon. They will urge you to go to Joram and, speaking in the name of all the people of Earth, beg him to hand over the Darksword."

"He will not." Saryon shook his head, firm with conviction. "You know that, Mosiah. You know him."

Mosiah hesitated a moment, then said, "Yes, I know him. And so does King Garald. We are counting on the fact that he won't give up the Darksword. We don't want the Technomancers to obtain it."

Saryon blinked in confusion. "You want me to ask him to give up the sword that you don't want him to give up?"

"In a way, yes, Father. Simply ask Joram to show you where the sword is hidden. Once we know where it is, we will take over. We will retrieve it and keep it in our possession. We will keep it secret and safe, guard it with our very lives, as we will guard Joram and his family. Of that, you can rest assured."

Saryon's long hair was quite gray and very thin and lay on his shoulders, soft as a child's. He had acquired a stoop, and sometimes a slight palsy made his hands tremble. These physical attributes, combined with a generally benign expression, caused people to take him for a weak, gentle old man. There was nothing gentle about him now as he sat bolt upright, his body rigid, the warmth in his eyes igniting to fire.

"You've tried before to find the Darksword, haven't you? Tried and failed!"

Mosiah regarded Saryon steadily. "It would have been better for Joram if we *had* been able to discover the sword's location and safely remove it. The Technomancers would then have no interest in him. Rest assured, Father, if you do not acquire the Darksword by peaceful means, they will take it by whatever means they can."

"And what about the *Duuk-tsarith*?" Saryon demanded, the fire within him burning bright. "What means will *you* use to take the sword?"

Mosiah rose to his feet. His black robes fell in folds about him. He clasped his hands together. "Know this, Father. We will not let the Darksword fall into the hands of the Technomancers."

"Why not?" I signed. "What if they can use it to defeat the Hch'nyv? Wouldn't it be worth it?"

"The Hch'nyv plan to exterminate humankind, the Technomancers to enslave us. An unhappy choice, wouldn't you say, Reuven? And, of course, for me and those like me, there would be no choice at all. And, there are those among the *Duuk-tsarith* who think that *we* may be able to use the sword in the battle against the Hch'nyv.

"Well, Father?" Mosiah waited for an answer. "Through King Garald's intercession, we give you this chance to acquire the Darksword by peaceful means. If you do not, the Technomancers will take it from Joram by force. Surely your choice is clear."

"And what *of* Joram?" Saryon rose to face him. "What of his wife and child? He is the most hated man in the universe. The *Duuk-tsarith* once pledged his death. Perhaps the only reason you haven't killed him before now is because you don't know where he's hidden the sword!"

Mosiah's face was stern, pale. "We will protect Joram—"

Saryon gazed steadily at the Enforcer. "Will you? And what about the rest of our people? How many countless thousands have vowed to kill Joram and his wife and child on sight?"

"How many people will the Hch'nyv kill?" Mosiah countered. "You speak of *Joram*'s child, Father. What of the millions of innocent children who will die if we lose the battle against the Hch'nyv? And we *are* losing,

Father! Every day they draw nearer Earth. We must have the sword! We must!"

Saryon sighed. The fire died within him. He seemed suddenly very old, very frail and feeble. He sank back down into his chair, rested his head in his hands. "I don't know. I can't promise."

Mosiah frowned, appeared prepared to add to his arguments.

I rose from my chair, confronted the Enforcer.

"My master is very tired, sir," I signed. "It is time you left."

Mosiah glanced from one of us to the other.

"This has been an unnerving experience for you both," he said. "You're not thinking clearly. Go to bed, Father. Sleep on your decision. The Almin grant that it be the right one."

To our intense astonishment, two *Duuk-tsarith* materialized. Black-hooded, black-robed, faces hidden, they appeared, one on either side of Mosiah.

Bodyguards, reinforcements, witnesses . . . Perhaps all of these. Certainly they had been here this entire time, watching, guarding, protecting, spying. The three formed a triangle. They raised their hands, each placed the palm of one hand on the palm of the hand of the person beside him. Thus linked, their power merged, they vanished.

Saryon and I stared at the place where they had been standing, both of us shaken and disturbed.

"They planned this!" I signed, when I was over my shock enough to be able to give expression to my thoughts. "They had advance knowledge that the Technomancers were coming here this night. King Garald could have sent us warning, told us to leave."

"But he didn't. Yes, Reuven," Saryon agreed. "It was all staged for our benefit, to make us fear the

Technomancers and force us to join sides with the *Duuk-tsarith*.

"Do you know, Reuven?" my master added, glancing at the chair in which Mosiah had been sitting. "I grieve for him. He was Joram's friend, when it was not easy to be Joram's friend. He was loyal to Joram, even to death. Now he has become like all the rest. Joram is alone now. Very much alone."

"He has you," I said, touching my master very gently on his breast.

Saryon looked at me. The sorrow and anguish on his pale and haggard face brought tears to my eyes.

"Does he, Reuven? How can I say no to them? How can I turn them down?" He stood up, leaning heavily upon the chair. "I am going to bed."

I bid him have a good night, though I knew that was impossible. Taking my computer, I went up to my room and entered all that had happened while the incidents were still fresh in my mind. Then I lay down, but I could not sleep.

Every time I drifted off, I saw, once again, my spirit rise from my body. And I was afraid that next time, it would not know how to return.

CHAPTER FIVE

"*What you did was right, my son. Always believe that! And always know that I love you and honor you.*"

~SARYON'S FAREWELL TO JORAM;
TRIUMPH OF THE DARKSWORD

The next morning, quite early, an army of police entered our neighborhood and took over our quiet row of flats. Arriving shortly after the police was a cadre of reporters in huge vans with various gadgets all pointing skyward.

I can only imagine what the neighbors thought. Again it struck me as odd, how the human mind dwells on the most inconsequential issues at times of crisis. While I was busily engaged in preparing our dwelling to receive three such notable dignitaries—the three most powerful men in the world—my biggest worry was how we were going to explain this to Mrs. Mumford, who lived in the flat across the street.

She was (or thought she was) the conductor of the orchestra of our lives here on our street and nothing was supposed to happen—be it divorce or a case of breaking and entering—without the wave of her baton.

So far she had left Saryon and me in peace, our lives being, up until this juncture, extremely uninteresting. Now I could see her pinched, inquisitive face pressed close against the glass of her living-room window, avid with frustration and curiosity. She even made a tentative foray out into the street, to accost a policeman. I don't know what he told her, but she dashed like a rabbit to the home of her assistant conductor, Mrs. Billingsgate, and now two faces pressed against the latter's living-room window. They'd be pressed against our front door tomorrow.

I was arranging some last-of-the-season roses in a vase, and trying to think what we would say to our neighbors in the way of explanation, when Saryon entered the room. The idle curiosity of two snoopy old ladies vanished from my mind.

My master had not risen for breakfast, nor had I disturbed him. Knowing he had been up late, I left him to sleep as long as he could. He didn't look to have slept a moment. He had aged twenty years during the night; his face was bleak and drawn, his stoop more pronounced. He peered about the room vacantly and smiled and thanked me for tidying up, but I knew well that he wasn't seeing any of it.

He went to the kitchen. I brewed tea and brought him buttered toast. He stared hopelessly at the toast, but he drank his tea.

"Sit down, Reuven," he said in his quiet, gentle manner. "I have made a decision."

I sat down, hoping to persuade him to eat. At that moment the doorbell rang, and at the same time there was a knock on the back door. I gave my master a helpless glance, and with a wry smile and a shrug, he went to answer the front door while I took care of the back.

The army of policemen, having secured the street, now moved into our house. A woman in a business suit, who said she was head of Earth Force security, took charge of Saryon and me, telling us that her people would be searching and securing the premises. She marched us back into the kitchen, sat us down, and laid out The Plan. A team of cool-eyed, professional, and thorough people moved in behind her, bringing with them cool-eyed, professional dogs.

I could soon hear them upstairs, down in the cellar, and in every room in the house. Whether or not they found any more green-glowing devices I do not know. I assume they did, they found everything else, including a half-eaten biscuit from beneath a couch cushion, which one of the men politely handed over to me. I offered it to his dog, who was, however, far too professional to accept such treats while on the job.

Seeing that Saryon's thoughts were turned inward and that he was not paying the slightest bit of attention to The Plan, I devoted myself to listening and understanding what it was we were to do. All the while I wondered what decision he had made.

"His Majesty King Garald and General Boris and their aides and entourage will arrive in the same vehicle at precisely thirteen hundred hours. The Right Honorable Kevon Smythe and his aides and entourage will travel in a second vehicle and will arrive at precisely thirteen-thirty. They will all depart at fourteen hundred."

Pardon me, ma'am. I started to write my words on a tablet, which I usually kept with me, but she indicated that she understood sign language, for which I was grateful. "How many aides and entourage will there be?"

I was thinking of our small living room and wondering where on earth we would put them all. Also if we would be expected to serve tea. If so, I was going to have to make a run to the store!

She reassured me. We were not to worry about a thing. She and her staff would handle all the arrangements. I could tell, by the sounds of furniture scraping over the floor, that the living room was being adjusted.

At this point Saryon, with a blink and a sigh, rose from the table, and with a slight bow and a vague smile for the woman—I'm convinced he had no idea who she was or why she was there—he left, saying something to the effect that he would be in his study and to call him when it was time.

The woman frowned, displeased. "He appears completely insensible to the fact that he is being paid a great honor. For such eminent and important figures to completely rearrange their schedules, and travel—some of them—halfway around the world, all to honor this gentleman on his birthday! . . . Well! It seems to me that he should be exhibiting far more gratitude."

His birthday! I had forgotten, in all the turmoil, that this date corresponded approximately to the date he had been born in Thimhallan. I was the one who had figured it all out (Saryon would have never bothered) and I had, in fact, planned a small celebration for us that evening. His gift, a new chessboard, with figures formed of dragons and griffins and other supposedly mythic animals, was neatly wrapped upstairs in my room. I wondered how anyone else knew it was his birthday, for we had shared this with no one. Then I remembered the green-glowing eavesdropping devices.

So this was to be the excuse—visiting the old catalyst on his birthday. How fortunate for them that it fell on this date. I wondered what other excuse they would have cooked up, had this one not been conveniently provided. I was extremely angry, more angered at this than at the invasion of our house by the silver-robed Technomancers.

It is, sometimes, a blessing to be mute. Had I the gift of speech, I would have used it to lash out at this woman and probably would have spoiled everything. As it was, being forced to sign my words, I had time to consider them. I could see, on reflection, that it was wisdom on the part of the King and the General to keep the true nature of this meeting secret.

"You must forgive Saryon," I signed to the woman. "My master is a very humble man, and completely overwhelmed by such a great honor, to the point where he is dazed by all the attention. He feels himself very unworthy and he deplores all the fuss and bother."

She was somewhat mollified by this, and we went over the rest of the details. The guests would be staying one hour, no more, and fortunately, there would be no need to serve them tea. She hinted that Saryon might want to change out of the brown robes he was wearing—the robes of a catalyst, such as he had worn all his life—and into a suit, and that it would be well if I also changed out of my blue jeans into something more appropriate to the occasion. I replied that neither of us owned a suit, at which point she gave up on us both and left to go check on how things were proceeding.

I went to my master's study, to inform him that it was his birthday, which I was sure he had forgotten. I made more hot toast and took a plate of it and the tea with me.

I explained everything—rather heatedly, I'm afraid. Saryon regarded my flashing hands with a weary, indulgent smile and shook his head.

"Intrigue. Politics. All of them were born into the game. They live in the game. They have no idea how to leave the game and so they will play the game until they die." He sighed again and absentmindedly ate the toast. "Even Prince Garald. King Garald, I should say. He held himself above it, when he was young. But I suppose it's like quicksand. It sucks even good men down."

"Father," I asked him, "what decision have you made?"

He did not speak aloud, but signed back to me, "The men were just in this room, Reuven. For all we know, they may have planted their electronic ears and eyes in this room. And there may be others watching, listening, as well."

I remembered the two *Duuk-tsarith* who had appeared out of the air of our kitchen, and I understood. It seemed strange to me to think that there might be a dozen people crowded into that small study and my master and I the only two visible. I felt nervous when I walked out, returning the plate to the kitchen. I kept fearing I would bump into one of them.

The dignitaries arrived precisely on time. First came the black limousine with flags of Thimhallan flying and the royal coat of arms upon the door. Mrs. Mumford and Mrs. Billingsgate had, by this time, abandoned all pretense. They were standing on their front doorstoops, openmouthed and jabbering. I couldn't help but feel a swelling of pride as His Majesty, dressed quite conservatively in a dark suit, but wearing his medallions and ceremonial sash, accompanied by the General in his uniform with all his medals and ribbons, stepped out of the limo. Aides trailed after them. Soldiers came to stiff attention and saluted. Mrs. Mumford and Mrs. Billingsgate stared until I thought it likely they might strain something.

My pride advanced a step further as I imagined having tea with the two women tomorrow, explaining, with suitable modesty, how the King was an old friend of my master's; the General once a worthy adversary. It was a harmless, if vain, fantasy—one that unfortunately never came about. I was never to see either of our neighbors again.

King and General entered our house, where Saryon and I both waited with extreme trepidation. My master knew these men were going to put enormous pressure on him and he feared this meeting. I was nervous, for Saryon's sake, but I must admit that I was looking forward to seeing once again two people whom I had written about, especially the King, who had once had such a notable effect on Joram's life.

King Garald had been Prince Garald then. Of him I had written:

> The beauty of the voice matched the features of the face, delicately crafted without being weak. The eyes were large and intelligent. The mouth was firm, the lines about it indicative of smiling and laughter. The chin was strong without arrogance, the cheekbones high and pronounced.

My description, taken from my early memories and Saryon's account, was accurate, even now, when the

King was in his middle years. The lines around the firm mouth had darkened, graven by sorrow and suffering and wearisome toil. But when the mouth smiled, the lines softened. The smile was warm and genuine, the source of its warmth coming from deep within. I saw at once how this man had won the respect and perhaps even the affection of the sullen, obdurate boy Joram.

Saryon started to bow, but Garald took my master's hand and clasped it in both his own.

"Father Saryon," he said, "let me be the one who does you reverence."

And the King bowed to my master.

Between pleasure and confusion, Saryon was completely taken aback. His fears and trepidation melted in the warmth of the King's smile. He stammered and blushed and could only protest incoherently that His Majesty did him far too much honor. Garald, seeing my master's embarrassment, said something light and inconsequential, to put them both at ease.

Saryon gazed at the King, now without restraint, and clasped his hand and said over and over with true pleasure, "How do you do, Your Highness? How do you do?"

"I could be better, Father," the King replied, and the lines on his face deepened and darkened. "Times are very difficult, right now. You remember James Boris?"

But the spell was broken. Garald had lifted, for one moment, the burden from my master's shoulders, only to cast it back on the next. James Boris—short, square-shouldered, solid as one of his own tanks—was a good man, a good soldier. He had been merciful, in Thimhallan, when, by rights, he could have been vengeful. He was genuinely pleased to see Saryon and shook hands with my master quite cordially. So cordially that Saryon winced as he smiled. But James Boris and his army represented Thimhallan's doom. He could not help but be a bleak omen.

"General Boris, welcome to my home," Saryon said gravely.

He led the way into the living room, the move being an absolute necessity, for four of us were a tight fit in the small entryway and the aides and entourage were forced to camp out on the front lawn. In the living room, Saryon presented me. The King and the General both made polite comments on my work in writing the history of the Darksword. The King, with his innate charm, relaxed into another of those warm and disarming smiles and told me he thought my portrayal of him far too flattering.

"Not half so flattering, Your Majesty," I signed and Saryon translated, "as *some* would have had me make it." I cast a fond glance at my master. "I had to dig very hard to discover some human flaws in you, to make you an interesting and believable character."

"I have flaws enough, the Almin knows," Garald said with a slight smile, adding, "Several of my staff members have taken a great interest in your work, Reuven. Perhaps you would be so kind as to do them the favor of answering their questions while your master and the General and I talk over old times."

I admired and appreciated the smooth way he was getting rid of me. Rising to my feet, I was about to leave when Saryon reached out a hand and clasped me by the wrist.

"Reuven is in my confidence."

Garald and General Boris exchanged looks. The General gave a slight nod, and the King responded with a nod in his turn.

"Very well. General, if you please?"

The General went to the entrance to the living room,

spoke a few words to a member of his staff. The soldier gestured to several of his men and they departed, leaving the four of us in the room. I heard booted footsteps resound throughout the house, making one last check, then the booted footsteps departed and the front door closed. I saw, through the window, the soldiers deploying, securing the area.

Though four of us remained in the house, it seemed empty and alone, the house of a stranger who has moved away. A chill raised my flesh. It was as if we had already left this house, never to return.

Of the four of us, Saryon was the most at ease. His decision made, he was calm, gracious, and—oddly enough, with a King and General in attendance—it was my master who was in command of the situation.

In fact, when Garald was about to speak, Saryon interrupted him.

"Your Majesty, your emissary Mosiah explained matters quite clearly to me last night. The visit from the Technomancers was also quite instructive."

At this, King Garald shifted uncomfortably on the couch and would have again spoken, but Saryon continued on, placid and imperturbable.

"I have reached a tentative decision," Saryon said. "I need more information before I can make my decision final. I hope you two gentlemen, as well as the gentleman who is expected to arrive later, will be able to provide it."

"About the one expected later," General Boris said. "There are a few things you should know, Father, in regard to Kevon Smythe."

"I know quite a bit about him, already," Saryon said, with a half smile. "I spent the night researching him on the World Wide Weave."

"Web," I signed, correcting him.

"Web," Saryon replied. "I always get that confused."

The two gentlemen seemed amazed. If they knew Saryon at all, they should not have been. Though the technology of the combustible engine left him baffled, he had adapted to the computer world like a duck to water.

"I tapped into various sources," he continued, and I suppressed a smile, for I knew now he was innocently showing off. "I read articles on Smythe written by political analysts. I read newspaper reports, and even scanned a biography, which is in the works. Not one of these mentioned that Kevon Smythe is a Technomancer."

"Of course not, Father," said Garald. "He has taken care to keep that part of his life secret. And, after all, who would believe it? Only those of us who were born and raised on Thimhallan. And," he added, including General Boris, "those who once visited there. Surely, you don't doubt it! After last night . . ."

"Indeed, Your Majesty." Saryon was calm. "As I said, last night was most instructive. All the accounts of Kevon Smythe speak of his ambition, his meteoric rise to fortune and fame, his charismatic ability to sway people to his cause. They all marveled at his luck— what they term 'lucky breaks'—that gained him wealth, or put him in the right place at the right time, or caused him to make exactly the right decision."

"What they call luck, some of us call magic," said King Garald.

"How is it possible that no one knows?" Saryon asked mildly.

"Are you doubting His Majesty?" General Boris's face flushed.

Garald waved him to silence. "I can understand Father Saryon's concern. It was difficult for me to believe, at first. But this is how the Technomancers have long worked in this world.

"You've heard, undoubtedly, stories of those who practice so-called Black Magic; cults of Satan worshipers, who don black robes and mutilate animals and dance around graveyards at midnight. This is what most of the people on Earth equate with the dark arts. This is *not* the Technomancer. They laugh at such nonsense and even use it for their own purposes—it deflects attention away from them.

"Who would believe that the businessman in the three-piece suit who is said to be a genius at playing the stock market uses his magical ability to make himself invisible, sits in on board meetings of various companies, and thus gains inside information? Who would believe that the embezzler who left her firm in financial ruin was able to mislead everyone because of the magical hold she had on their minds?"

It sounded ludicrous, even to me, and I had seen with my own eyes the silver-robed Technomancers invade our house.

King Garald grew bitter. "When I first discovered that the Four Cults of Dark Magic still existed, I tried to warn people in Earth government. Even my best friend did not believe me." He looked at James Boris, who smiled ruefully and shook his head. "I will not waste time by relating what occurred that finally convinced him. It nearly cost us both our lives, but—in the end—he believed. The General suggested that I was wasting my time and energy attempting to fight the Technomancers in the open. I must adopt their own strategy."

"Mosiah told you he had been one of them," said General Boris. "Did he tell you that he volunteered to become one of them? To go undercover? To risk his life ferreting out their dark secrets?"

"No," said Saryon, and he looked relieved. "No, he did not."

"Through him we found out much about their organization; we discovered the true nature of this 'chemical factory' which they operate and for which"—King Garald smiled wryly—"they even receive lucrative government grants!"

"You work with Smythe," Saryon said. "You do not denounce him."

"We have no choice," said King Garald, and his voice was grim and harsh. "He holds our people and the people of Earth hostage."

"The Technomancers have infiltrated every part of the military," said General Boris. "They do not commit sabotage. Oh, no. They are far too clever for that. They have made themselves indispensable to us. Because of their power and their skill, we are holding our own against the Hch'nyv. Should they withdraw their magical assistance—worse yet, should they turn their magic against us—we would be lost."

"How do they do this?" Saryon was perplexed.

"I'll give a very simple example. We have a torpedo that has an electronic brain. We can program that brain to aim the torpedo to hit its target. The enemy detects the torpedo, sends out an electronic signal which scrambles its brain. But they can't send out a signal to scramble magic. A Technomancer, magically guiding that torpedo, will send it unerringly to its target.

"And if"—General Boris's voice dropped—"they were to magically alter that torpedo's programming, cause it to turn and strike a different target. *Not* an enemy target . . ." He shrugged his massive shoulders.

"From what they have told us, they control nuclear armaments in the same way," said King Garald. "From our investigations, we have reason to believe that they are telling the truth."

"To put it another way, we dare not call their bluff," said the General bluntly.

"I don't see how the Darksword could possibly aid you in any way against these people," said Saryon, and I was convinced then that I knew his decision.

"Frankly, we don't either," said King Garald.

"Then why—"

"Because they fear it," said the King. "We don't know why. We don't know what they've found out or how they found out, but they have received a warning from their researchers, those called the *D'karn-kair*, that the Darksword could be both an asset to them and a danger."

Saryon shook his head.

Garald regarded him silently, then said, "There is another reason."

"I thought as much," said Saryon, adding dryly, "You would not have gone to this much trouble to recruit me otherwise."

"No one knows about this except the *Duuk-tsarith*, and they, as always, are sworn by their oaths of loyalty to secrecy. Otherwise, Mosiah would have told you last night. Do you remember Bishop Radisovik, whom you used to know as Cardinal Radisovik?"

"Yes, yes. I remember. A good, sensible man. So he is Bishop now. Excellent!" said Saryon.

"The Bishop was working alone in his study one day when he sensed someone in the room with him. He lifted his head and was astonished to find a woman seated in a chair in front of his desk. Now this was a very unusual occurrence, for the Bishop's secretary has strict orders never to introduce anyone into the Bishop's office without an appointment.

"Fearing that perhaps the woman was there to do him some type of harm, the Bishop talked to her pleasantly, all the while using a secret button, hidden beneath his desk, to alert the guards.

"The button apparently did not work. No guards appeared. The woman, however, assured the Bishop that he had no reason to be afraid.

" 'I have come to give you information,' she said. 'First, I suggest that you discontinue your war against the Hch'nyv. You have no chance—absolutely none— of defeating the aliens. They are far too strong and too powerful. You have seen only a smattering of their entire force, which numbers in the billions of billions. They will not negotiate with you. They have no need. They intend to destroy you and they will succeed.'

"The Bishop was astonished. The woman, he said, was very calm and imparted this terrible information in a tone which left no doubt in his mind but that she spoke the truth.

" 'Excuse me, madam,' the Bishop said, 'but who are you? Whom do you represent?'

"She smiled at him and said, 'Someone very close to you, who takes a personal interest in you.' Then she continued, telling him, 'You and the people of Earth and Thimhallan have one chance for survival. The Darksword destroyed the world. It may now be used to save it.'

" 'But the Darksword no longer exists,' Bishop Radisovik protested. 'It was itself destroyed.'

" 'It has been forged anew. Offer it to Thimhallan's maker and find salvation.'

"At that moment the Bishop's intercom buzzed. He turned to answer it, and when he looked back, the woman was gone. He had not heard her leave, any more than he had heard her enter. He questioned his secretary and the building's security people, who said that no one had either gone into or come out of the Bishop's office. The button on the desk was discovered to be operational. No one could say why they hadn't heard the alarm.

"What was truly remarkable," Garald added, "is that the security cameras in the building show no evidence of this woman, not even the camera which is placed in the Bishop's office. Even stranger—at that point in time we knew nothing of the fact that Smythe had been to visit Joram or that Joram had, as the woman said, forged a new Darksword."

"To what does the Bishop attribute this visit, then?" Saryon asked.

Garald hesitated, then replied, "Judging from what the woman said, about representing someone very close to the Bishop, someone who takes a personal interest in him, the Bishop is convinced that he was visited by an agent of the Almin. An angel, if you will."

I noted that General Boris shifted in his chair and looked extremely embarrassed and uncomfortable.

"An agent, maybe," said the General. "CIA, Interpol, Her Majesty's Secret Service, FBI. But not of God."

"How very interesting," said Saryon, and I could see him mulling over this in his mind.

"Whoever brought us this information, our own researchers now want that sword," said General Boris. "To determine if there really is some way we can use it to stop the Hch'nyv."

"But that wasn't what the an—the woman said," Saryon interposed. "She said that the sword must be returned to Thimhallan's maker."

General Boris had the look on his face of a man indulging a child's whim to hear a fairy tale. "Who is that supposed to be—Merlyn? You find him, Father, and I'll give him the Darksword."

Saryon appeared very stern, considering this sacrilegious.

"At the very least," said King Garald in mollifying tones, "we must keep the Darksword out of the hands of the Technomancers."

Saryon now appeared troubled, as if he were rethinking an already-thought-out determination. The other two would have pressed him further, had not an enormous black limousine rolled up at that moment.

General Boris put his hand to his ear.

"I see it," he said, speaking to an aide through a communicator. The General looked around grimly at us, adding, "Smythe is here."

CHAPTER SIX

"This is my magic," said Joram, his gaze going to
the sword lying on the floor.

~ *FORGING THE DARKSWORD*

Saryon and I had watched a performance of Gou-
nod's *Faust* on the BBC recently and Mephistopheles
was much in my mind as I waited to meet the head of
the Technomancers. Smythe certainly did not look the
part of Mephistopheles, being of medium height with
flaming red hair and a smattering of freckles across his
nose. But in the light blue eyes, that were glittering and
changeable and cold as diamond, was the reputed
charm which the devil purportedly possesses and which
he uses to tempt mankind to its downfall.

Smythe was witty and effervescent and brought light

and air into our house, which seemed gloomy and suffocating by contrast. He undoubtedly knew what terrible things the King and the General had been saying
about him and he didn't care. Smythe spoke no word in
his own defense, he said nothing against either of them.
In fact, he greeted them both with deference and pleasure. In their cold and stilted greeting of him, they
seemed, by contrast, ungracious, bitter, twisted.

"Father Saryon." Kevon Smythe took my master's
hand and a radiance shone from him that engulfed
Saryon, who actually blinked, as if looking into a
blinding light. "I am honored to meet you at long last. I
have heard much of you, all good, and of Joram. It is a
subject that fascinates me. Tell me, Father," he said as
he accepted a proffered seat in a chair, not on the
couch where sat the other two, stiff and upright. "Tell
me the story of Joram and of the Darksword. I know
bits of it, but I would like to hear it from your own lips.

"I am sorry to say, Reuven," he added, looking at
me, "that I have not read your account, of which I've
had the most favorable reports. My time is such that it
does not give me leisure to read as much as I would
like. Your books are in a prominent place in my library,
and someday, when the pressures of leadership are removed, I look forward to reading them."

It was very odd, but I felt a glow of pleasure suffuse
me, as if he had paid my books the best of compliments, when—in bald truth—part of me knew perfectly well that he had undoubtedly received distilled
accounts of what was in the books from his subordi-
nates and that, though he might indeed own them, he
had no intention of ever looking at them.

What was even stranger was that he was aware of
the dichotomy of feelings he produced in others and
that he did so on purpose. I was fascinated and re-

pulsed at the same time. In his presence, all other men, including the King and the General, appeared petty and ordinary. And although I liked and trusted them and I did not like and did not trust him, I had the uneasy impression that if he called me, I would follow.

Saryon felt the same. I knew because he was talking about Joram, something he was always very reluctant to do with any stranger.

". . . Thimhallan was founded by the wizard Merlyn as a land where those blessed with the art of magic could live in peace, using that art to create beautiful things. There were Nine Mysteries of Life present in the world, then. Each person born into that world was gifted with one of these mysteries."

Kevon Smythe's lips parted, he whispered beneath his breath the number "thirteen" and a chill went over me. The Four Dark Cults, who had remained behind, would have made the number thirteen.

Saryon, unconscious of the interruption, continued on.

"There are Nine Mysteries, eight of them deal with Life or Magic, for, in the world of Thimhallan, Life *is* Magic. Everything that exists in this land exists either by the will of the Almin, who placed it here before even the ancients arrived, or has since been either 'shaped, formed, summoned, or conjured,' these being the four Laws of Nature. These Laws are controlled through at least one of the eight of the Mysteries: Time, Spirit, Air, Fire, Earth, Water, Shadow, and Life. Of these Mysteries, only the first five currently survived at the time of the Darksword's creation. The Mysteries of Time and Spirit were lost during the Iron Wars. With them vanished the knowledge possessed by the ancients—the ability to divine the future and the ability to communicate with those who had passed from this life into Beyond.

"As for the last Mystery, it is practiced, but only by those who walk in darkness. Known as Death, its other name is Technology."

"Quaint." Kevon Smythe was amused. "I was told you people believed something along those lines. And the other two . . . um . . . Mysteries, you called them. Time and—what was it—Spirit? They are lost? Perhaps just as well. As Macbeth discovered, looking into the future is dangerous. Are we doing what was truly destined or is it a self-fulfilling prophecy? I think it is safer—and more honest—to be guided by one's *vision* of the future. Don't you agree, Father Saryon?"

My master was thoughtful, introspective. "I don't know," he said at last. "The tragedy that befell Joram and all of Thimhallan was, in a way, brought about by a vision of the future—a vision which terrified. Would we have caused our own destruction if we'd never heard the Prophecy concerning the Dead child?"

"Yes, we would have. So I believe," said King Garald. "Our downfall began long before Joram was born, as early as the Iron Wars. Intolerance, prejudice, fear, blind faith, greed, ambition—these would have destroyed us eventually, with or without Joram and the Darksword."

He looked pointedly at Kevon Smythe as he spoke, but if His Majesty meant those words for the edification of Smythe, His Majesty wasted his breath. Smythe's attention—and perhaps his magic, if that was what he used to charm—was focused on Saryon, to the exclusion of all else.

"To me, Thimhallan was symbolized by Joram's mother, the Empress," said Saryon softly, sadly. "Her husband refused to admit that she was dead, though all in court knew it. He kept her corpse animated by magicks. The courtiers bowed, paid homage, gossiped with her . . . reveled with a lifeless and corrupt shell of something that had once been alive, vibrant, beautiful. Such a dreadful charade could not have gone on forever.

"Joram's story is really very simple. A Prophecy was given immediately following the Iron Wars, which stated: 'There will be born to the royal house one who is dead but will live, who will die again and live again. And when he returns, he will hold in his hand the destruction of the world.' Joram was a child of the royal house, born to the Empress and Emperor of Merilon. He was born Dead—that is, he had no magic in him at all. I know," said Saryon, with a sigh. "I was present when they performed the tests on him.

"Bishop Vanya, knowing of and fearing the Prophecy, ordered that the baby be refused all sustenance. Vanya took the baby away to die. But the Almin is not so easily thwarted. A madwoman named Anja found the baby and stole him, took him to the farms near the Outlands, raised him as her own child.

"Anja knew Joram was deficient in magic. She knew that if this deficiency were discovered, the *Duuk-tsarith* would seize him and that would be the end of him. She taught him sleight-of-hand tricks so that he could keep up a pretense of possessing magic.

"Joram was raised as a field magus, a peasant. It was here he met Mosiah, who became Joram's one true friend. It was also here that, when he was a teenager, Joram killed a man, a harsh overseer, who had discovered Joram's secret. In an effort to protect her son, Anja attacked the overseer, who killed her in self-defense. Furious, Joram killed the overseer.

"Joram fled to the Outlands, where he was found by

the Order of the Ninth Mystery, who were also living out there—the Technologists. They had broken the laws of Thimhallan, used Technology to supplement their magic. It was here, among them, that Joram learned the art of forging metal. It was here he discovered darkstone and its ability to nullify magic. Joram developed the idea of forging a weapon made of darkstone, a weapon that would compensate for his lack of magic, a weapon that would give him the power he craved.

"For reasons of my own, I assisted him in making the Darksword," Saryon said, adding pointedly, for Smythe's benefit, "Darkstone must be given magical Life through the intercession of a catalyst. Otherwise, its properties are those of any other metal."

Smythe was gracious. "How interesting. Please continue, Father."

Saryon shrugged. "There is not much more to tell. Rather, there is, but the story is a long one. Suffice to say, through a series of circumstances, Joram came to learn who he was. He came to learn of the Prophecy. He was sentenced to death. He could have destroyed his attackers, but he chose instead to leave the world. He crossed the Border into what we all thought was the realm of Death. Instead, he traveled to another part of the planet we know as Thimhallan. Here, he and the woman who loved him were found by a member of Earth's Border Patrol. He was taken to Earth and dwelled there for ten years with his wife, Gwendolyn.

"Discovering that there were some on Earth who were plotting to travel to Thimhallan and conquer it, Joram returned, bringing the Darksword, to fight those who sought to destroy our people, our way of life. He was betrayed and would have been assassinated, but for another strange twist of fate. Realizing that Earth

Forces"—Saryon glanced at General Boris, who was red-faced and extremely uncomfortable—"were winning and that our people were going to be either enslaved or slaughtered, Joram chose to end the war. He plunged the Darksword into the sacred altar, released the magic that was pent up in the Well. The magic flowed back into the universe. The war ended.

"The magical shell that had been cast protectively over Thimhallan was broken. The terrible storms that had once swept the land returned. The people had to be transported to a place of safety, and so they were brought here, to Earth, and placed in relocation camps. Only two remained behind: Joram and his wife, Gwendolyn. Now the most hated man in the universe, Joram knew that his life would be in danger if he ever returned to Earth. He chose to stay alone on Thimhallan, the world he had destroyed, as the Prophecy predicted."

Saryon's tale had gone on rather longer than the half hour Kevon Smythe had allowed for this business. He made no motion to interrupt, however, nor even glanced at his timepiece, but sat immovable, completely immersed in the catalyst's story. King Garald and General Boris, who had lived parts of the story, glanced at their own watches and fidgeted, yet they would not leave Smythe alone with us and so they were forced to sit and wait. Looking outside, I saw their aides speaking into handheld phones, undoubtedly rearranging schedules.

I was just thinking that if they stayed much longer, we would be expected to offer them something to eat and drink, and wondering if there were enough biscuits to go around, when Saryon ended his tale.

"Truly," said Kevon Smythe, and he appeared to be much affected by the story, "the Darksword is an inter-

esting object. Its properties should be analyzed, to see
of what benefit it may be to mankind. I know that
several theories have been advanced concerning it. It
seems to me important that these theories be tested.

"In one of my corporations, I have a team of scientists—top professionals in their fields—who are even
now making preparations to study the weapon. They
understand"—Smythe glanced smilingly at the irate
King, who was on his feet—"that this artifact is extremely valuable. These scientists would treat it with
the utmost respect, removing only small portions as
necessary for study. Once the testing was completed,
the weapon would be returned to the people formerly
of Thimhallan—"

"Like hell you would!" General Boris stood up as
well.

King Garald was livid. "Of course, we all know that
the testing would never *be* completed, would it,
Smythe? There would always be one more test to perform, one more theory to either support or deny.
Meanwhile you would be using the Darksword's
power—"

"For good," said Kevon Smythe quietly, "as opposed to those, such as your black-robed Enforcers,
who would use it for evil."

King Garald's face muscles contracted and stiffened,
so that when he tried to speak, no words would come
through his fury. Smythe was able to continue.

"Father, it is your duty as one of the brotherhood of
men to persuade Joram of his duty in these troubled
and dangerous times. He used the Darksword to destroy. Let him now redeem himself and use it to create.
Create a better life for us all."

At this, I saw King Garald pause in his attempt to
speak. He was keeping close watch on Saryon. The

King knew, as well as I, that Smythe had made a mistake. His vaunted charm—be it of magical origin or born in his blood—would not cover his error. He would have done much better to have read my books, not left his research to underlings. He would have then known the nature of the man with whom he dealt.

Saryon's face grew shadowed.

But if King Garald thought that he had gained a victory by his enemy's mistake, he, too, was mistaken. I knew my master's decision, even before he spoke it. I, alone in that room, was not surprised.

Saryon rose to his feet. His gaze encompassed all three men. His voice was rebuking.

"Joram and his wife and child live alone on Thimhallan now. They are under the protection of Earth Forces. They are not to be hounded, or bothered, or mistreated in any way. That is the law." He turned to Kevon Smythe. "You speak very glibly of redemption, sir. Redemption is the Almin's province. He alone will judge Joram, not you, not me, not the King, nor any other mortal!"

Saryon took a step backward, raised his head, regarded them all with a gaze that was steady and unwavering. "I have made my decision. I made it last night. I will *not* go to Joram. I will *not* be part of any attempt to trick him into revealing the whereabouts of the Darksword. He has suffered enough. Let him live out the remainder of his days in peace."

The three men were bitter enemies, yet they had the same desire. They glanced at each other.

Kevon Smythe spoke. "The Hch'nyv will not permit Joram to live in peace."

"They will slay him," General Boris said, "as they have already slain tens of thousands of our people. All the outposts that remain in our system are being evacuated, their people brought back to Earth for protection. Our fleet is too decimated to be divided. Here, on Earth, we will make our final stand against the invaders."

Saryon regarded them gravely, troubled. "I had not heard the situation was that critical."

Garald sighed. "We have made a mistake with you, Father. We have put our worst argument first and we have done it badly. Now you don't trust us, and I can't say that I blame you. But very few people on Earth know just how desperate the situation is. We want to keep it that way, for as long as possible."

"The panic that would follow, the damage it would do our cause, is incalculable," said the General. "We need troops prepared to fight the enemy, not used to quell riots in the streets."

"What you have heard here, Father," said Kevon Smythe, "you must not repeat, except to one person, and that is Joram. You may tell him the truth, if only to make him understand the danger. Then it is my hope and my prayer, Father, that he will relinquish the Darksword willingly—to whomever he chooses. We are fighting for the same cause, after all."

He looked like a saint, in his self-sacrificing humility, and the King and General came off shabbily by contrast. Yet the charm, once dispelled, could not be recast.

Saryon sank down in his chair. He looked ill from worry and anxiety. It wasn't proper etiquette or protocol, but I was past caring. Ignoring the three, I went to Saryon and, leaning over his chair, asked him with a sign if I should bring him some tea.

He smiled at me and thanked me, shook his head no. He kept his hand on mine, however, indicating that I was to remain at his side. He sat and thought a long time, in distraught, unhappy silence.

The King and General returned to their seats. Smythe had not left his. All three tried to look sympathetic, but they could none of them hide an air of smugness. They were certain they had won.

At length, Saryon raised his head. "I will go to Joram," he said quietly. "I will tell him what you have told me. I will warn him that he and his family are in danger and that they should evacuate to Earth. I will say *nothing* to him of the Darksword. If he brings it with him, you may each go to him and present your own need. If he does not, then you may each go to Thimhallan—once Joram and his family have departed—and search for it."

It was a victory for them—of sorts. They were wise enough not to continue to argue or cajole.

"And now, gentlemen," said Saryon, "you have been kept here past your time. I don't mean to seem rude, but I have travel arrangements to make—"

"All that has been taken care of for you, Father," said General Boris, adding lamely, "on the . . . er . . . off chance that you would decide to make this trip."

"How convenient," said Saryon, and one corner of his mouth twitched.

We were to leave that night. One of the General's aides would remain with us and assist us with packing, drive us to the spaceport, escort us on board ship.

Kevon Smythe left with gracious words and seemed to take the sunlight with him. General Boris hurried out, relieved to have it all over with, and was immediately surrounded by his staff, who had been impatiently awaiting his release. King Garald remained a moment behind.

Saryon and I had gone to the door to see our guests out. King Garald looked almost as ill as my master, and he, at least, had the grace to apologize.

"I am sorry to put this burden on you, Father," he said. "But what could I do? You've met the man." We knew who he meant. There was no need to name him. "What could I do?" he repeated.

"You could have faith, Your Majesty," said Saryon gently.

King Garald smiled, then. Turning to Saryon, there on the doorstoop, the King reached out his hand and clasped my master's. "I do, Father. I have faith in you."

Saryon was so extremely startled by this response that it was difficult for me to hide my smile. Garald left, walking tall, with his shoulders back; a kingly air. General Boris was waiting in the limousine. Kevon Smythe had already departed.

Saryon and I ducked hastily back inside, narrowly avoiding a mob of reporters, who clamored for interviews. The General's aide was skilled in handling the press, and all in all, they did not give us too much trouble. After breaking only one window and trampling the flower beds, they eventually left us in peace. I saw several interviewing Mrs. Mumford.

I suppose that a birthday celebration for one elderly cleric was not considered worth the expenditure of time and money. Had they known the true story, they would have stormed the house.

Another of the General's aides was in the study, on the phone, confirming and updating arrangements for our transport to Thimhallan.

Saryon paused a moment in the hallway. Noting the expression on his face, I touched his arm, drew his attention.

"You did the right thing," I signed, and added, a

little teasingly, I'm afraid, hoping to cheer his mood. "You must have faith."

He smiled, but it was a wan, pale smile. "Yes, Reuven. So I must."

Sighing, his head bowed, he went to his room to prepare for our journey.

CHAPTER SEVEN

*The Watchers had guarded the Border of
Thimhallan for centuries. It was their enforced
task, through sleepless night and dreary day, to
keep watch along the boundary that separated the
magical realm from whatever lay Beyond.*
    What did lie Beyond?

~ *TRIUMPH OF THE DARKSWORD*

I will spare you the details of our journey, which was,
I suppose, the same as any other interplanetary flight,
with the exception that we were in a military ship with
a military escort. For me, the trip into space was awe-
inspiring and exciting. This was only my second flight
and the first I remembered clearly. I had only the vaguest recollection of leaving Thimhallan, traveling on the
evacuation ships.

Saryon kept to his quarters, on the pretext that he
had work to do. He was, as I believe I have neglected to
mention, developing a mathematical theorem having to

do with light-wave particles or something of the sort. Not being mathematically inclined, I knew little about it. The moment he and his tutor began to discuss it, I began to feel a throbbing in my temples and was glad to leave. He claimed to be working on this, but every time I entered his room, to see if he needed anything, I found him staring out the porthole at the stars gliding past us.

He was reliving his life in Merilon, I guessed. Maybe he was once more in the court of the faerie queen or standing, a stone statue, on the border of Beyond. The past was for him both painful and blessed. At the expression on his face, I silently withdrew, my heart aching.

We landed on the world he and I had known as Thimhallan, the first ship from Earth in twenty years, not counting those that arrived only to off-load supplies to the station then left again, and not counting those that arrived secretly, carrying the *Duuk-tsarith* and the Technomancers.

Saryon remained alone in his quarters for so long after the ship settled to the ground that I began to think he had reconsidered his decision, that he was not going to talk to Joram after all. The General's aide was exceedingly worried and panicked calls were made to both General Boris and King Garald. Their images were on-screen, prepared to badger and plead, when Saryon appeared.

Motioning me to follow him, he walked past the aide without a word, did not even glance at the screens. He moved so swiftly through the ship that I barely had time to grab the knapsack in which I had packed a few necessaries for us both and hurry after him.

By the beatific expression on his face, Saryon was lifted far above the remembrance of such things as clean socks, bottled water, and shaving kits. Blessing the forethought which had prompted me to pack for both of us, I slung the knapsack over my shoulders and was following at his heels when he reached the hatch.

Whatever doubts he may have entertained were gone. The weight of his responsibility and even the weight of the intervening years had fallen from him. This was more than a dream come true, for my master. He had never dared dream the dream. He had never thought this reunion would take place. He had believed that Joram—in his self-imposed exile—was lost to him forever.

When the hatch opened, Saryon shot out the doorway and dashed down the ramp, his robes flapping wildly about his ankles. I clattered down behind, struggling with the heavy knapsack, which was throwing me off balance. We were met at the foot of the ramp by a contingent of people from the research station. Saryon halted only because it was either stop or run them over.

He paid them very little attention, however; his hungry gaze going above their heads to the land beyond, a land that, as he had known it, would have been shrouded in magical, protective mist. The mist was gone. The land was now laid bare for all to see.

Saryon tried to see it, tried to see everything he could of his homeland. Craning his neck and peering above the heads of the group, he made only brief and generally incomprehensible statements and, at length, gave up all attempts at politeness. He walked off, leaving the commander and the urgent message he was trying to impart in mid-sentence.

Saryon walked across the rock-strewn ground, walked toward the land of his birth.

The base commander would have gone after him, but I had seen the tears on my master's face. I intervened, indicating to the commander by emphatic signs that Saryon wanted to be left alone. The General's aide had arrived by now. She and the commander and I made the plans necessary for our stay.

"You *must* make him understand," said the base commander, frustrated. "As I was attempting to tell the priest, we received our orders to pull out yesterday, evacuate the station. So don't linger. Remind the priest he's not on holiday. The last ship leaves seventy-two hours from now."

I was shocked. I stared at the man, who understood my wordless question.

"Yes. The Hch'nyv are that close," he said grimly. "We'll be taking you and the prisoner and his family out of here. I guess you and the priest there are responsible for making him see reason, eh?

"Well, I don't envy you." The commander turned his gaze toward the distant hills. "That Joram—he's gone insane, if you ask me. He was like a wild man when we went up there to rescue Senator Smythe. Not but what he had cause, I grant you. Still, no harm was done and there was Joram standing over the poor Senator, fists clenched, seeming ready to bash the life out of him. And such a look Joram gave me, when I asked him if his wife and daughter were well? He fair roasted me with those black eyes of his and told me that the health of his family was none of my concern. No, sir. I don't envy you and the priest. I recommend an armed escort."

I knew that would be out of the question, as far as Saryon was concerned, and so did the General's aide.

"They do not have far to travel and the catalyst is familiar with this land," she told the base commander. "The priest is an old friend of Joram's. They will not be in any danger. And they will have communicators in the air car, which they can use should they run into any unforeseen circumstances."

She gave me a sideways glance as she said this, to see my reaction. I guessed then that we would have escorts—of an unseen kind. The *Duuk-tsarith*, perhaps hidden in their folds of time, would be guarding us.

"What about a driver?" asked the commander.

"I will drive—" the aide began.

I shook my head emphatically and tapped myself on the chest. On my handheld computer, I typed out, *I will drive*.

"Can you?" the aide asked me, clearly dubious.

Yes, I replied stoutly, which was almost the truth.

I had driven an air car once before, at an amusement park, and had just about got the hang of it. It was the other cars, coming every which way at me, which had confused me and caused my driving to be slightly erratic. If mine was the only air car in this part of the solar system, I figured I would be fairly safe.

Besides—I held up the computer for the aide to see what I had written—*you know that he will not let anyone else come with us.*

She did know, but she didn't like it. My guess was that this had all been arranged—the air car, I mean—with the understanding that she would drive us, keep an eye on us, make her reports.

Haven't you got spies enough? I thought bitterly, but did not put into words. I had won this round and could afford to be magnanimous.

"Keep in contact," the base commander warned. "Circumstances with the enemy could change. And probably not for the better."

The aide returned to the ship, to complain to the General. The base commander accompanied me to the air car, gave me quick refresher lessons in operating the thing—lessons which served to confuse me thoroughly. I tossed the knapsack in the backseat and left the air car to fetch Saryon, who, in his eagerness, had started walking in the direction of the distant mountains.

I hadn't taken six steps when the commander called after me. I turned to see him picking something up off the ground.

"Here." The commander handed it to me. "The priest dropped this."

He held out Saryon's leather scrip, one of the few objects he had brought with him from Thimhallan. I recalled it well, for it was given an honored place in his study, carefully arranged upon a small table near his desk. I always knew when Saryon was thinking about Joram or about the past, for he would rest his hand upon the scrip, his fingers stroking the worn leather.

I thought it touching that he had brought the scrip with him, perhaps as a holy relic, to be rededicated. I couldn't imagine, though—cherishing the scrip as he did—how he had come to carelessly drop it. Thanking the commander, I placed the scrip in the backseat along with the knapsack. Then I went to retrieve my master.

"Air car," he said, and gave me a sharp look. "And who's to be the driver?"

"I am, sir," I signed. "It's either that or the General's aide will drive us, and I knew you wouldn't like to have a stranger along."

"I would much prefer that alternative to being splattered against a tree," said Saryon irritably.

"I have driven an air car before, sir," I returned.

"In an amusement park!" Saryon snorted.

I was hoping that in his excitement, he would have forgotten the circumstances. Apparently not.

"I will go find the General's aide, sir," I signed, and started to head back toward the ship.

"Wait, Reuven."

I turned around.

"Can you . . . really drive one of those contraptions?" He cast a nervous glance at the air car.

"Well, sir." I relaxed, smiled, and shrugged. "I can try."

"All right, then," he said.

"Do you know the way?" I asked. "Where are we going?"

He looked out again across the landscape, toward the mountains that rose, snowcapped, on the horizon.

"There," he said. "The Font. The only building left standing, after the terrible storms broke over the world with the destruction of the Well of Life. Joram and Gwendolyn took refuge there, and there, according to King Garald, is where they live still."

We started walking back to the air car. "We have seventy-two hours," I told him, "before the last ship leaves."

He gave me the same shocked look I had given the commander. "So short a time?"

"Yes, sir. But surely it won't take nearly that long. Once you explain the danger to Joram . . ."

Saryon was shaking his head. I wondered if I should tell him what the base commander had said about Joram's being insane, decided that I would keep that to myself. I did not want to add to my master's worries. My research on the book had seemed to indicate that Joram was a manic-depressive and I thought it quite possible that the isolation of his life, plus the tension created by the arrival of the Technomancers, might well have driven him to the breaking point.

Reaching the car, I opened the door for Saryon and

saw the leather scrip draped over the backseat. I pointed at it.

"You dropped it," I signed. "The base commander found it for you."

Saryon stared at the scrip in perplexity. "I couldn't have dropped it. I didn't bring it. Why would I?"

"Is it yours?" I asked, thinking that perhaps it might belong to someone on the base.

Saryon peered closely at it. "It looks very much like mine. Somewhat newer, perhaps, not quite as worn. Odd. Such a thing could not come into the possession of anyone on base, because such a thing has not been made for twenty years! It *must* be mine, only . . . Mmmm. How strange."

I reminded him that he had been distracted and upset, that perhaps he had brought it and not remembered. I also hinted that his memory had failed him before—he was constantly forgetting where he put his reading spectacles.

He cheerfully acknowledged that I was right and admitted that it had crossed his mind to take the scrip, but that he had been fearful of losing it. He thought that he had put it back in its accustomed place.

The scrip remained lying on the backseat. We entered the car and my thoughts centered on trying to remember all that the commander had told me about the operation of the vehicle. The odd discovery of the leather scrip passed clean out of my mind.

Saryon settled into the passenger's seat. I assisted him with his seat belt and then fastened my own. He asked worriedly if there weren't more safety restraints and I said, with more confidence than I felt, that these would be adequate.

I pushed the ON button. The air car began to hum. I pushed the button marked JETS. The humming grew louder, followed by a whoosh of the jets. The air car rose off the ground. Saryon had fast hold of the door handle.

All was going very smoothly. The car was drifting upward when Saryon spoke. "Aren't we going too high?" he asked in a cracked voice.

I shook my head, and taking the wheel, I pressed on it, intending to level us off.

The wheel was far more sensitive than I had anticipated, certainly more sensitive than the wheel of the air car in the amusement park. The car lurched downward and headed at a high rate of speed straight for the ground.

I jerked back on the wheel, pulled up the nose. At the same time I inadvertently increased the power and we soared up and jumped forward, the sudden thrust nearly snapping our necks in the process.

"Almin save us!" Saryon gasped.

"Amen to that, Father," came a sepulchral voice.

Saryon stared at me and I think it was in his mind that perhaps the whiplash had miraculously restored my speech. I shook my head emphatically and motioned with my chin—my hands were gripping the wheel so tightly that I dared not let go—that the voice had come from the backseat.

Twisting around, Saryon stared.

"I know that voice," he muttered. "But it can't be!"

I don't know what I expected—the *Duuk-tsarith,* I suppose. Not completely certain how to stop the air car, I kept driving and at last managed to stabilize it. I cast a quick look in the rearview mirror.

There was no one in the backseat.

"Ouch! I say!" The voice had a peevish quality to it now. "This great smelly green bag has fallen on top of me. I'm being frightfully dented."

LEGACY OF THE DARKSWORD

Saryon was searching wildly around the backseat and was now groping about with his hands. "Where? What?"

I managed at last to halt the air car. I kept the jets on, and we remained floating in the air. Reaching back, I shoved aside the knapsack.

"Thanks awfully," said the leather scrip.

CHAPTER EIGHT

"Let me be your fool, sire. You need one, I assure you."

"Why, idiot?" asked Joram, the half smile in his dark eyes.

"Because only a fool dares tell you the truth," said Simkin.

~ *FORGING THE DARKSWORD*

"**S**imkin!" Saryon gulped, swallowed. "Is that you?"

"In the flesh. Leather, actually," replied the scrip.

"You can't be," Saryon said and he sounded shaken. "You're . . . you're dead. I saw your corpse."

"Never buried," the scrip returned. "Grave mistake. Speaking of stakes, one through the heart. That or silver bullet or sprig of holly in the heel. But everyone was so busy those last few days, destroying the world and so forth, I can see how I came to be overlooked."

"Stop the nonsense." Saryon was stern. "If it *is* you, change into yourself. Your human self, that is. I find this very disconcerting. Talking to a . . . a leather scrip!"

"Ah, bit of a problem." The scrip wriggled, its leather ties curled in upon themselves in what might have been embarrassment. "I don't seem to be able to do that anymore. Become human. Rather lost the knack. Death takes a lot out of a fellow, you know, as I was saying just the other day to my dear friend Merlyn. You remember Merlyn? Founder of Merilon? Adequate wizard, though not as good as some would have you believe. His fame due entirely to his press agent, of course. And spelling his name with a *y*! I mean—how pretentious! But then anyone who goes around dressed in a blue-and-white star-spangled bathrobe—"

"I insist." Saryon was firm, ignoring the desperate attempt to change the subject. He reached out his hand for the leather scrip. "Now. Or I shall toss you out the window."

"You won't get rid of me that easily!" said the scrip coolly. "I'm coming with you, no matter what. You can't imagine how boring it has been! No amusement, absolutely none. Toss me out," the scrip warned as Saryon's hand drew nearer, "and I'll change into an engine part on this simply fascinating vehicle. And I know very little about engine parts," he added, as an afterthought.

Recovering from the initial shock of hearing what I considered to be an inanimate object speaking, I was regarding Simkin with a great deal of interest. Of all those whose stories I had written, those concerning Simkin intrigued me the most. Saryon and I had argued in friendly fashion over just exactly what Simkin was.

I maintained that he was a wizard of Thimhallan with extraordinary powers—a prodigy, a genius of magic, like Mozart was a genius of music. Add to this a chaotic nature, an addictive lust for adventure and excitement and a self-centered, shallow personality, and you have a man who would betray his friends at the drop of an orange silk scarf.

Saryon admitted that all this was true and that I was probably right; still, he had reservations.

"There are things about Simkin that your theory doesn't resolve," Saryon had once said. "I think he is old, very old, perhaps as old as Thimhallan itself. No, I can't prove it. Just a feeling I have, from things he's mentioned. And I know for a fact, Reuven, that the magic he performed is not possible. It is simply, mathematically, not possible. It would take far more Life than a hundred catalysts could give for him to transform himself into a teapot or a bucket. And Simkin could perform this magic, as you say, at the drop of his orange silk scarf! He died when Technology invaded the realm."

"What do you think he is, then?" I had asked.

Saryon had smiled and shrugged. "I have absolutely no idea."

My master was about to pick up the scrip.

"I'm warning you!" Simkin told us. "Carburetor! I have no notion what one is or what it does, but the name attracts me. I will become Carburetor if you so much as lay a finger—"

"Don't worry, I'm not going to throw you out," Saryon said mildly. "On the contrary, I'm going to carry you safely—where I would normally carry my scrip. Around my waist. Beneath my robes. Next to my skin."

The scrip vanished so suddenly that I found myself doubting my senses, wondering if I had actually seen (and heard) it. In its place, in the backseat of the air car, was the pale and ephemeral-looking image of a young man.

He was not ghostlike. Ghosts, from what I've read about them, are more substantial. It is difficult to describe, but imagine someone taking watercolors, painting the figure of Simkin, then pouring water over it. Ethereal, transparent, he faded into the background and would not have been noticed if you weren't already looking for him. The only bright spot of color anywhere about him was a wisp of defiant orange.

"You see what I've become!" Simkin was doleful. "A mere shadow of my former self. And who is your silent friend here, Father? Cat got his tongue? I recall the Earl of Marchbank. Cat got his tongue, once. Earl ate tuna for lunch. Fell asleep, mouth open. Cat enters room, smells tuna. Ghastly sight."

"Reuven is mu—" Saryon began.

"Let him speak for himself, Father," Simkin interrupted.

"Mute," Saryon resumed. "He is mute. He can't speak."

"Saves his breath to cool his porridge, eh? Must eat a considerable amount of cold porridge. This finger-wiggling. Means something, I presume?"

"It is sign language. That is how he communicates. One way," Saryon amended.

"How jolly," said Simkin, with a yawn. "I say! Could we get a move on? Nice to see you again and all that, Father, but you were always a bit of a bore. I'm quite looking forward to talking to Joram again. Been ages. Simply ages."

"You haven't seen Joram? All this time?" Saryon was skeptical.

"Well, there's 'seen' and then there's 'seen,' " Simkin said evasively. " 'Seen' from a distance, 'seen' to one's best advantage, 'seen' to the task at hand, 'seen' off on a long ocean voyage. I suppose you might say that I have, in fact, 'seen' Joram. On the other hand, I haven't 'seen' him, if you take my meaning.

"To put it another way," he added, having seen that we were both lost, "Joram doesn't know I'm alive. Quite literally."

"You propose to go with us, to have us take you to Joram," said Saryon.

"Jolly reunion!" Simkin was enthusiastic. "In your ecclesiastical company, Padre, our dark and temperamental friend might be willing to overlook that harmless little joke I played on him there toward the end."

"When you betrayed him? Plotted to murder him?" Saryon said grimly.

"It all turned out right in the end!" Simkin protested. "And it wouldn't have, you know, if it hadn't been for me."

Saryon and I looked at each other. We really had no choice in the matter, as Simkin well knew. It was either take him with us or throw him out, and although his magic might be weakened, he was, as he had so cleverly proved, still adept at altering his form.

"Very well," Saryon said testily. "You may come with us. But you are on your own. What Joram chooses to do *with* you or *to* you is up to him."

"What Joram chooses . . ." Simkin repeated softly. "It seems to me, from what I've heard—Merlyn is such a gossipy old busybody—Joram is running out of choices. I say, you don't mind if I change back to the scrip, do you? Very fatiguing in this form—breathing and all that. You must promise, though, Father, that you won't put me next to your skin!" Simkin shivered. "No offense, Father, but you've gone all wrinkly and prunelike."

"What do you mean about Joram running out of choices?" Saryon demanded, alarmed. "Simkin! What—the Almin take him!"

The watercolor image was gone. The leather scrip was back, resting on the seat of the air car. And it had gone mute, apparently. As mute as myself.

Nothing Saryon did or said could induce it to talk.

I wondered if the scrip had ever talked at all. And if it hadn't, what did that make me? Delusional? That would be a kind word. I glanced at my master to see if he was prey to the same uncomfortable feelings.

He was certainly regarding the scrip very grimly.

"We better drive on, Reuven," Saryon said, adding with a frown for the scrip. "We've wasted precious time as it is."

We crossed the Borderland which had, for endless ages, separated Thimhallan from the rest of the universe and separated magic from the rest of the universe as well. A field of magical energy, created by the founders of Thimhallan, the Border permitted people to leave, but prevented them and all others from entering or reentering. It was Joram, the Dead child of a dying world, who not only crossed that Border, but was able to return. He had brought the two realms—one magical, one technological—together. They had met with the violence of a thunderclap.

Keeping the speed of the air car slow, I was able to handle the vehicle with some proficiency, although our ride was still rough and we were jounced about considerably. Not having had much experience with air cars—or cars of any type, for that matter—Saryon attributed the roughness to the buffeting winds. I am ashamed to say that I did not disabuse him.

As for Simkin, we had barely started off again when the leather scrip slid to the floor. The knapsack tumbled down on top of it. We heard a muffled shriek, but Saryon couldn't reach the scrip.

"Should I stop?" I mouthed. With the wind tossing around the air car, I was reluctant to do so.

"No. Serves him right," Saryon said.

I had not thought my master could be so vindictive.

We drove past a red beacon light that was now no longer operational. Saryon stared at it, twisting around to gaze at it when it was behind us.

"That must be the alarm beacon," he said, turning back around. He was holding fast to a hand strap above the door on his side. "The one that used to alert those in the outpost to anyone crossing the Border. Next, we should see the Stone Watchers. Or what is left of them."

Along the Borderland had once stood enormous statues known as the Watchers, the guardians of the Border. They had been living men, before their flesh was changed to rock, frozen forever, while their minds remained active.

Such a dreadful fate had once been Saryon's.

I recognized the site, when we reached it, though I had never seen it. During the last days of Thimhallan, when violent quakes and fierce storms swept the land, the Watchers fell; the spirits in them freed at last. Now the shattered remains littered the ground, some of them completely covered over by windblown sand. The mounds looked very much like graves.

Noticing the pain of memory contort Saryon's face, I was about to increase our speed by giving more power to the rear thrusters, taking us quickly away from this tragic site. Saryon understood my attempt and forestalled it. I hoped he was not going to ask me to stop, for the wind, though lessened somewhat, was still strong. If I tried to halt the air car, we might be blown out of control. Stinging sand blasted our windshield, rattled against the doors.

"Slow down a moment, Reuven," he said. He stared long at the mounds as we drove slowly past. "They cried their warning, but no one paid heed. The people were too intent on their own ambitions, their own plots and schemes to listen to the voices of the past. What voices call to us now, I wonder?" Saryon mused. "And are we listening to them?"

He fell silent, thoughtful. The only voice I heard was a faint one coming from the floor of the backseat of the air car. The language it was using was shocking. Fortunately Saryon could not hear Simkin over the rush of the jets and his sad reverie remained undisturbed.

We left the Border behind, crossing over the vast stretch of sand dunes, and entered the grasslands. Saryon gazed around blankly and I realized that he recognized nothing, no landmarks looked familiar to him. Not only had the land changed during the cataclysmic upheavals that followed the emptying of the Well of Life, but, I reasoned, my master had been accustomed to traveling the magical Corridors, built by the long-lost Diviners, which whisked the people of Thimhallan through time and space from one place to another.

I continued flying toward the mountains on the horizon, that being our general destination, but I was growing worried. Heavy blue-gray clouds were massing; lightning flickered on their fringes, which dragged the desolate ground. The wind was increasing. One of the fierce storms for which Thimhallan is noted was fast approaching. The mountains were my only guide and I would lose sight of them in the driving rain. The air car was equipped with all manner of devices to assist one in navigation, but I did not know how they worked.

Bitterly I regretted the impulse which had prompted me to turn down the offer of a driver. We would have to stop the air car when the storm hit, not only because we might easily lose our way, but because we ran the risk of slamming into a tree or the side of a cliff. Heavily forested lands lay ahead and, beyond that, the foothills.

A gust of wind hit the car, blew it sideways about three feet. The rain began, large drops splatting into the windshield. I thought of the small, lightweight tent we had brought and shook my head. I couldn't share my fears and doubts with Saryon, for my hands were my voice and I was forced to keep both hands on the steering mechanism.

There was only one thing to do and that was to turn back before the storm grew any worse. I cut the power, lowered the car to the ground. Saryon turned to look questioningly at me. Once the air car had settled, I was about to explain to him our predicament, when his eyes—looking at me—suddenly widened and shifted their gaze to a point behind me. I turned swiftly and shrank back, startled, at the sight of the apparition which loomed in the window.

I don't know why I was surprised. I should have known they would be around.

The black-robed and -hooded Enforcer made a motion. I touched the button, the window slid into the side of the car. Rain struck me in my face. The wind blew my hair into my eyes and howled so that I could barely hear. Yet the black robe of the *Duuk-tsarith* remained dry, its folds still and unruffled. He might have been standing in the eye of the cyclone, while we—only inches from him—were in the teeth of the storm.

He pushed back his hood and I recognized Mosiah.

"What do *you* want?" Saryon shouted. He didn't look pleased.

"You are wasting time," Mosiah said. "Abandon this technological monstrosity. You can be with Joram in an instant if you use the magic."

Saryon looked questioningly at me.

"We don't know the way, sir," I signed to him. "The storms will only grow worse. We dare not travel blind. And we have only seventy-two hours."

"It seems we have no choice," Saryon admitted. "How will you take us there?"

"The Corridors," said Mosiah. "You must leave the vehicle. Bring your things with you."

I opened the door. The wind nearly pulled it out of my hand. I was instantly soaked. Reaching into the backseat for my knapsack, I lifted it from the floor and looked beneath it for the leather scrip. At least this would be an opportunity to rid ourselves of Simkin.

The leather scrip was gone.

With deep misgivings, I pulled the knapsack out of the backseat. I wondered what strange object I was now carrying inside the knapsack—a teapot, perhaps.

Saryon, his robes whipping about his lean body, stood next to Mosiah. With some difficulty caused by the wind, I hoisted the knapsack onto my shoulders.

"Did you bring my leather scrip?" Saryon shouted.

"No, sir!" I signed back. "I couldn't find it."

"Oh, dear," said Saryon, and looked extremely worried. "It is always better to know where Simkin is than where he isn't," he said to me in a low voice.

"Have you lost something?" Mosiah asked.

"Probably not," Saryon said gloomily. He peered at Mosiah through the rain. "How do we travel the Corridors? I thought they were destroyed!"

"We thought so, too," Mosiah said. "We searched

for the Corridors, after the destruction of Thimhallan, and couldn't find them. We assumed that they were lost to us, because the magic that had supported them was gone. But it seems that they had only moved, shifted with the upheaval of the land."

Saryon frowned. "I don't see how that's possible! Mathematically speaking, it isn't! Admittedly we never knew exactly how the Corridors functioned, but the calculations necessary to open them precluded any—"

"Father!" Mosiah interrupted, with a smile, as if reliving old memories. "I would be interested to hear about these calculations, but at a later date. Now shouldn't we be going?"

"Yes, of course, I'm sorry. Here's poor Reuven soaked to the skin. I told you to wear something heavier than that jacket," he added in concern. "Didn't you bring a warmer coat?"

I indicated that I was warm enough, only very wet. I was wearing a white cable-knit sweater and blue jeans, with a jacket over that. I knew my master, however. Had I been wearing fur, wrapped up from head to toe, Saryon would have still been worried about me.

"We should hurry, sir," I signed.

Not only was I looking forward to getting out of the rain, I was eager to see the magic.

"Am I supposed to open the Corridor?" Saryon asked. "I'm not sure I remember . . ."

"No, Father," Mosiah replied. "The days are gone when you catalysts controlled the Corridors. Now anyone who knows the magic may use them."

He spoke a word and an oval void appeared in the midst of the rain and the wind. The void elongated, until it was tall enough for us to enter. Saryon looked back uncertainly at Mosiah.

"Are you coming with us? Joram would be glad to see you."

Mosiah shook his head. "I do not think so. Step into the Corridor, before you catch your death." He turned to me. "The sensation you will feel is very frightening at first, but it will soon pass. Remain calm."

Saryon started to enter the void, then he halted. "Where will it take us?"

"To the Font, where Joram lives."

"Are you sure? I don't want to end up in some shattered castle in Merilon—"

"I am certain, Father. I said the Corridors had shifted. Like spokes in a wheel, they now all lead either to the Font or away from it."

"How strange," said Saryon. "How very strange."

He entered the void. Urged by Mosiah, I followed quickly after my master, almost tripping on his heels. I lost sight of him immediately, however. The Corridor closed around me, as if it would compress me into nothingness. I felt squeezed and smothered, unable to breathe.

Remain calm. . . .

All very well for Mosiah to say! He wasn't suffocating! I struggled for air, struggled to free myself. I was drowning, dying, losing consciousness. . . .

Then suddenly the Corridor opened, like a window shade in a dark room springing up to let in bright sunlight. I could breathe. I was on a mountaintop. The air was crisp and cool. No rain fell. The storm clouds were in the valleys beneath us.

I looked into blue sky, saw white, scudding clouds that were so close I felt as if I might snag one.

Saryon stood next to me, gazing around with the eager, wistful, hungry look of one who has returned at long last to a site where memories, painful and pleasant, were forged. We stood on the ramparts of what had once been an immense city-fortress.

He shook his head, looking a little dazed. "So much has changed," he murmured. He drew near, took me by the arm, and pointed. "Up there, on the mountain's peak—made *from* the mountain's peak—was the cathedral. It is gone. Entirely gone. It must have collapsed later on, after we left. I never knew."

He stared at the ruins, which lay scattered over the mountainside, then he turned and looked in a different direction. His sadness brightened somewhat. "The University is still here. Look, Reuven. The building on the side of the mountain. Magi from all over Thimhallan came to study there, to perfect their art. I studied mathematics there. What happy hours!"

Tunnels and corridors burrowed into the mountain. The work of the Church had been done here, its catalysts living, working inside the mountain, worshiping at its peak. Deep within the mountain was the Well of Life, the source of the magic on Thimhallan, now empty and broken.

It occurred to me, suddenly, that—but for Joram and the Darksword—I might now be a catalyst, walking these very corridors, bustling about importantly on the business of the Church. I could picture myself here very clearly, as if that same shade that snapped open to reveal the sunshine had also afforded me a glimpse of another life. I looked out that window and saw myself looking back in.

Saryon saw his past. I saw my present. It was exhilarating and unnerving, yet eminently satisfying. This was the land of my birth. I was a part of this mountain, the sand, the trees, the sky. I took a deep breath of the crisp air, and felt uplifted. And though I had no idea how to go about it, I think—at that moment—I could have drawn Life from the world around me, focused it within my body, and given it away.

A sound touched my reverie. Concern for my master drew me back to reality.

Saryon stood with bowed head. He brushed his hand swiftly across his eyes.

"Never mind," he said, when I would have offered comfort. "Never mind. It was for the best, I know. I weep for the beauty that was ruined, that is all. It could not have lasted long. The ugliness would have overwhelmed it, and like Camelot, it might have been destroyed and irretrievably lost. At least our people still live and their memories live and the magic lives, for those who seek it."

I had not sought it, yet it had come to me anyway. I was not a stranger to this land. It remembered me, though I had no memory of it.

Like Saryon, I had come home.

CHAPTER NINE

*"I will run to Joram and he will take me in his
arms and we will be together forever and
ever. . . ."*

~GWENDOLYN; *DOOM OF THE DARKSWORD*

"I say!" came a peeved voice from the vicinity of the
knapsack. "Are you two going to stand around and
slobber over each other all day? I'm dying of ennui—
the same sad fate that befell the Duke of Uberville, who
was such a boring old fart that he bored himself and
died for lack of interest."

I considered overturning the knapsack and searching
for Simkin, but to do so would have wasted precious
time. I had spent hours trying to see to it that everything fit inside and I dreaded the thought of having to
do all that over again.

I signed to Saryon, "If we ignore him, perhaps he'll go away."

"I heard that," Simkin said. "And I can assure you, it won't work!"

I was astonished, for I had not spoken, and I don't think that even Simkin could have learned sign language in the space of the few hours we had known each other.

Saryon shrugged and wryly smiled. "The magic lives," he whispered, and there was a warmth in his eyes that was rapidly drying up the tears.

"Where are we?" I asked.

"I was just trying to figure that out myself," said Saryon, peering down from our perch on the ramparts.

"*I* know," said a muffled voice from inside the knapsack, adding huffily, "but *I'm* not telling."

Below us was a courtyard, its paving stones cracked and overgrown with a wide variety of plant life, including several varieties of wildflower. Across the courtyard was a long, low building with a great many windows, to let in the sunlight. Some of the windows had been broken, but the holes had been neatly covered over with pieces of wood. Here and there, in the courtyard, some attempt had been made to cut back the weeds, sweep away the dead leaves, and make the area more attractive.

"Ah, yes! In that building"—Saryon pointed to the building past the courtyard—"the Theldara, the healers, had their infirmary. Now I know where I am."

"Did I ever tell you about the time the Theldara came to treat my little sister for ringworm? Or was it tapeworm? I'm sure there's a difference. One eats you and you eat one. Not that it mattered to poor little Nan, for she was eaten by bears. Where was I? Ah, yes, the Theldara. He—"

Simkin prattled on. Saryon turned and began to walk along the ramparts, making his way toward a flight of stairs which led down into the courtyard. "There was a garden here, on the other side, where they grew herbs and other plants which they used in healing. A quiet, restful, soothing place. I came here once. A very fine man, that Theldara. He tried to help me, but that proved impossible. I was quite unable to help myself, which is always the first step."

"It looks as though someone lives here," I signed, pointing to the boarded-up windows.

"Yes," Saryon agreed eagerly. "Yes, this would be an excellent place for Joram and his family to reside, with access to the interior portions of the Font."

"Oh, jolly," was the opinion of the knapsack.

Rounding a corner of the retaining wall, we found further evidence of habitation. One part of the courtyard, where the great Bishop Vanya had once walked in ceremony and state, was now apparently a laundry. Several large washtubs occupied the paving stones and lengths of rope had been strung between two ornamental trees. Fluttering from the ropes were shirts and petticoats, sheets and undergarments, drying in the sun.

"They *are* here!" Saryon said to himself, and he had to pause a moment, to gather his strength.

Up to this point he had refused to let himself believe that at last, after all these years, he would see the man he loved as well or better than he could have ever loved a son.

Courage regained, Saryon hurried ahead, not thinking consciously of where he was going, but allowing his memory to show the way. We circled around the laundry tubs, ducked beneath the clothes.

"Joram's flag—a nightshirt. Well, it figures," said Simkin.

A door led into the dwelling. Looking through a window, we could see a sunlit room, with comfortable couches and chairs, and tables decorated with bowls of blooming flowers. Saryon hesitated a moment, his hand trembling, then he knocked at the door. We waited.

No answer.

He knocked again, staring intently, hopefully, through the glass windowpane.

I took the opportunity to search the area. Walking the length of the building, I looked around the corner and into a large garden. Hastening back to my master, I tugged on his sleeve and motioned him to follow me.

"You've found them?" he said.

I nodded and held up two fingers. I had found two of them.

I stayed behind as he entered that garden. The women would be startled, frightened, perhaps. It was best that they saw him, at first and alone.

The two were working in the garden, their long, cream-colored skirts kilted up around their waists, their heads protected from the sun by wide, broad-brimmed straw hats. Their sleeves were rolled up past the elbow, their arms were tanned brown from the sun. Both were hoeing, their arms and the tools they held rising and falling with swift, strong chopping strokes.

Wind chimes, hanging on a porch behind them, made music for them, to lighten their work. The air was filled with the rich smell of freshly turned loam.

Saryon walked forward on unsteady legs. He opened the gate that led into the garden, and that was as far as his strength and courage would bear him. He put out a hand to support himself on the garden wall. He tried, I think several times, to call a name, but his voice was mute as my own.

"Gwendolyn!" he said at last, and spoke that name with so much love and longing that no one who heard it could have been the least bit frightened.

She wasn't fearful. Startled, perhaps, to hear a strange voice where no strange voice had spoken in twenty years. But she wasn't afraid. She stopped her hoeing, lifted her head, and turned toward the sound.

She recognized my master in an instant. Dropping her hoe, she ran to him straight across the garden, heedless of the plants she crushed, the flowers she trampled. Her hat flew off, in her haste, and a mass of hair, long and golden, tumbled down behind.

"Father Saryon!" she cried, and flung her arms about him.

He clasped her tightly, and they both held on to each other, weeping and laughing simultaneously.

Their reunion was sacred, a private special moment for only the two of them. It seemed to me that even watching must intrude, and so, deferentially and with some considerable curiosity, I turned my gaze on the daughter.

She had ceased her work. Standing straight, she regarded us from beneath the broad brim of her hat. In figure and stature, she was the twin of her mother, of medium build, graceful in her movements. That she was accustomed to physical labor showed in the well-defined muscles of her bare arms and legs, her upright stance and posture. I could not see her face, which was hidden by the shadow of the hat. She came no closer, but stood where she was.

She *is* afraid, I thought, and who can blame her? Having grown up apart, isolated, alone.

Gwendolyn had taken a step back, out of Saryon's arms, though not out of his hold, to gaze fondly at him and he at her.

"Father, it is good to see you again! How well you look!"

"For an old man," said Saryon, smiling down on her. "And you are lovely as ever, Gwen. Or lovelier, if that is possible. For now you are happy."

"Yes," she said, glancing behind her at her daughter, "yes, I am happy, Father. *We* are happy." She laid emphasis on the word.

A shadow crossed her face. Her grip on Saryon tightened. She looked back up at him, with earnest pleading. "And that is why you must leave, Father. Go quickly. I thank you for coming. Joram and I have often wondered what became of you. He was worried. You had suffered much for his sake and he feared it might have damaged your health. Now I can give him ease, tell him you are well and prospering. Thank you for coming, but go quickly, now."

"Pulled the welcome mat right out from under him, didn't she?" said Simkin.

I gave the knapsack a whack.

"Where is Joram?" Saryon asked.

"Out tending the sheep."

A muffled, derisive snort came from the knapsack. Gwen heard it. Glancing at me, she frowned and said defiantly, "Yes, he is a shepherd now. And he is happy, Father. Happy and content. For the first time in his life! And though he loves and honors you, Father Saryon, you are from the past, you are from the dark and unhappy times. Like that dreadful man who came here before, you will bring those terrible times back to us!"

She meant that we would bring the memory to them. I saw, by the pain in Saryon's face, that he gave her words another meaning, a truer meaning. It was not the memory we were bringing to them, but the reality.

He swallowed. His hands on her arms trembled. His

eyes grew moist. He tried several times to speak, before
the words finally came out. "Gwen, I stayed away from
Joram all these years for this very reason. Much as I
longed to see him, much as *I* longed to know he was
well and happy, I feared I would only disturb his tranquillity. I would not have come now, Gwen, but that I
have no choice. I must see Joram," Saryon said gently,
and now his voice was firm. "I must talk to him and to
you together. There is no help for it. I am sorry."

Gwen gazed long into his face. She saw the pain, the
sadness, the understanding. She saw the resolution.

"Do you . . . have you come for the Darksword?
He won't give it up, not even to you, Father."

Saryon was shaking his head. "I have *not* come for
the Darksword. I have come for Joram, for you and
your daughter."

Gwen kept fast hold of him, for support. When she
let go, it was only to lift her hand, to wipe her eyes.

I had been so intent on their conversation that I had
forgotten the daughter. At the sight of her mother's
distress, she dropped the hoe and ran toward us, moving with long, free strides. She pushed back the hat, to
see better, and I realized that I had misjudged her. She
hadn't been afraid of us. She had been pausing to consider us, to study us and to study herself, to determine
how she felt about us.

I paused to consider her. My life paused, at that
moment, to consider her. When life resumed, a second
later, it would never be the same. If I never saw her
again, from that moment on I would see her forever.

Thick, black, and unruly hair fell in disordered curls
from a central part, glistened in luxuriant clusters
about her shoulders. Her brows were also thick and
black and straight, giving her a stern and introspective
aspect that was dispelled by the sudden, dazzling light

of large, crystalline blue eyes. That was her father's legacy. Her mother bequeathed the oval face and pointed chin, the ease and grace of movement.

I did not love her. Love was impossible, at that first moment of our meeting, for love is between humans and she was something extraordinary, not truly human. It would have been like falling in love with the image in a painting or with a statue in a gallery. I was awed, admiring.

Prospero's daughter, I said inwardly, recalling my Shakespeare. And then I smiled derisively at myself, remembering her words on seeing the strangers washed ashore by her father's art: "How many goodly creatures are there here! How beauteous mankind is!"

I could tell from her glance that raked across me with curiosity and little more that I was *not* providing images of brave new worlds. And yet I interested her. Though she had her parents for company, youth yearns for its own, to share the newfound dreams and budding hopes that belong to youth alone.

But for now, her first care was for her mother. She put her arms protectively around her mother's shoulders and faced us boldly, accusingly, her black brows a straight, heavy line.

"Who are you? What have you said to upset her? Why do you people keep intruding upon us?"

Gwen lifted her head, dashed away her tears, and managed a smile. "No, Eliza, don't talk in that tone. This man is not like the others. He is one of us. This is Father Saryon. You've heard us speak of him. He is an old friend and very dear to both your father and to me."

"Father Saryon!" Eliza repeated, and the heavy line lifted, the blue eyes were light and radiant, like the sun shining down after a thunderstorm. "Of course, I have

heard of Father Saryon. You have come to teach me!
Father said I was to go to you, but he kept putting it off
and now I know why—*you* have come to *me*!"

Saryon reddened, swallowed again, and, embarrassed, looked to Gwen for guidance, to know what to
say.

She was unable to assist him, but her assistance
wasn't necessary because Eliza's quick gaze went from
one to the other and she realized her mistake. The light
dimmed. "That is not why you've come. Of course not.
My mother would not be crying if that were the case.
Why are you here, then? You and your"—she turned
her brilliant gaze on me, made a guess—"your son?"

"Reuven!" said Saryon. He turned around and
stretched out his hand, urging me forward. "My boy,
forgive me! You're so quiet . . . I forgot you were
here. He is my son by affection, though not by birth.
He was born in Thimhallan, born here in the Font, as a
matter of fact, for his mother was a catalyst."

Eliza regarded me with cool intensity and suddenly I
had another of those strange flashes, such as I had experienced earlier, where I seemed to be looking through
a window into another lifetime.

I saw myself a catalyst, standing in a crowd of catalysts. We were dressed in our best ceremonial robes, all
blending together, our tonsured heads bowed in respect. And she walked past us, regal, gracious, clad in
silks and jewels, our queen. I lifted my head, greatly
daring, to look at her and she, at that moment, turned
her head and looked at me. She had been searching for
me in the crowd and she smiled to see me.

I smiled at her, we shared a secret moment, and
then, fearing my superiors would notice, I lowered my
gaze. When I next dared look again—hoping that perhaps she was still looking at me—I saw only her back,

LEGACY OF THE DARKSWORD

and even that vanished, for she was followed by all her courtiers, every one of them walking. Walking. Why did that seem strange to me?

The image faded from before my eyes, but did not fade in my mind. Indeed, it was so clear and well defined that the words *Your Majesty* were on my lips and I think I would have spoken them aloud, had I been able to speak. As it was, I felt bewildered and disoriented, much as when Mosiah released us to return to our own bodies.

Recovering, I signed that I was honored and pleased to meet those who held a special place in my master's heart.

Eliza's eyes widened at the sight of my flashing hands. "What is he doing?" she demanded, with the frank and open honesty of a child.

"Reuven is mute," Saryon explained. "He talks with his hands." And he repeated to them aloud what I had said.

Gwendolyn gave me a preoccupied smile and said I was welcome. Eliza appraised me, those blue eyes studying everything about me with unabashed curiosity. What she saw was a young man of medium height, medium build, long blond hair pulled back from a face that always seemed to inspire women with sisterly affection. Honest, sweet, gentle were words women used to describe me. "At last, a man we can trust," they would say. And then they would proceed to tell me all about the men they loved.

As for what I saw in Eliza, the statue was gaining life and warmth, becoming human.

Gwendolyn cast a glance at me and it seemed that she suddenly had a new worry. A glance at Eliza reassured her somewhat. Turning back to Saryon, Gwen drew him away, to speak to him in a low, pleading tone. Eliza remained, staring at me.

My situation was extremely embarrassing and uncomfortable. Never before had I cursed my handicap as I cursed it now. Had I been a man like any other, I could have made polite conversation.

I considered bringing out my electronic notepad, writing on it. Writing what? Some inanity? *What a lovely day. Do you suppose we shall have rain?*

No, I thought. Better to keep my notepad shut.

And yet I wanted to do something to hold her interest on me. Already, she was starting to turn her head, to look back to her mother and Saryon. I had some notion of plucking a flower and handing it to her, when I heard a *plop* at my feet.

Eliza gave a glad cry. "Teddy!"

At my feet sat a stuffed teddy bear; well worn, most of its fur rubbed off, one ear missing.

Eliza swooped down, picked up the bear, and held it up, calling in delight, "Look, Mother, Reuven's found Teddy!"

Gwen and Saryon turned from their conversation. Gwen smiled, a strained smile. "How nice, dear."

Saryon flashed me an alarmed glance. All I could do was helplessly shrug.

Around his neck, Teddy wore an orange ribbon.

CHAPTER TEN

"*Nevertheless, there I sat, a perfect teapot upon his desk.*"

~SIMKIN; *TRIUMPH OF THE DARKSWORD*

"I've had Teddy ever since I was a little girl," Eliza said, cuddling Teddy in her arms.

I have never seen a more self-satisfied and smug-looking stuffed bear. I wanted very much to throttle it.

"I found him in one of the old parts of the Font," she continued, "where I used to play. It must have been a nursery, because there were other toys there. But I liked Teddy best. I used to tell him all my secrets. He was my companion, my playmate," she said, and a wistful tone crept into her voice. "He kept me from being alone."

I wondered if Eliza's mother knew the truth, that Teddy was, in reality, Simkin—although one might contend that Simkin and reality had little to do with one another.

Gwendolyn bit her lip and cast a warning glance at Saryon, asking him to keep silent.

"I lost Teddy years ago," Eliza was saying. "I don't remember quite how. One day he was there and the next day, when I went to look for him, he was gone. We searched and searched, didn't we, Mama?"

Eliza looked to me, then to Saryon. "Where did you find him?"

My master was, for the moment, struck mute as myself. He was hopeless at lying. I made a sign, indicating that we'd found the bear somewhere near the Borderlands. It was not quite a lie. Saryon, in a faint voice, repeated what I had said.

"I wonder how he came to be there!" Eliza exclaimed, marveling.

"Who knows, child?" Gwendolyn said briskly. She smoothed her skirt with her hands. "And now you should go find your father. Tell him—no, wait! Please, Father? Is there no other way?"

"Gwendolyn," said Saryon patiently, "the matter on which I come is very urgent. And very serious."

She sighed, bowed her head. Then, with a forced smile, she said, "Tell Joram that Father Saryon is here."

Eliza was doubtful. Her delight in recovering the bear faded at the sight of her mother's troubled face. For a moment she had been a child again. The moment passed, gone forever.

"Yes, Mama," she said in a subdued voice. "It may take me a while. He is in the far pasture." And then she looked at me and brightened. "Could I—could Reuven come with me? You say he was born in the Font. We

must go through it on our way. He might like to see it
again."

Gwen was doubtful. "I don't know how your father
would react, child. To have a stranger come suddenly
on him, without any warning. It would be better if you
went by yourself."

Eliza's brightness began to dim. You could see it
fade, as if a cloud had passed over the sun.

Her mother relented. "Very well. Reuven may go if
he wishes. Make yourself presentable first, Eliza. I can
refuse her nothing," she added to Saryon in an under-
tone, half-proud, half-ashamed.

And that was why they had not taken "Teddy"
away, when both Gwen and Joram knew quite well
that the bear was not a real bear. I could imagine the
guilt both felt, forced to raise their child in isolation.
Joram's own childhood had been one of bitter loneliness and deprivation. He must have believed it a sad
legacy to pass on to a daughter, a legacy that pained
him deeply.

Eliza set Teddy in a flower basket and gave him a
laughing admonition not to go and get himself lost
again.

"This way, Reuven," she said to me, smiling.

I had gained great favor with her by the "discovery"
of the bear, which hadn't been my doing at all. I
glanced back at the bear as I followed after Eliza.
Teddy's black button eyes rolled. He winked.

I deposited the knapsack next to the bear, though I
took my electronic notepad with me. Saryon and
Gwendolyn sat together on a stone bench in the shade.
Eliza and I walked together through the garden. Eliza
shook her skirts down, covering her legs. She pulled the
broad-brimmed hat over her head, hiding the shining
black hair and leaving her face in shadow. She walked

swiftly, with long strides, so that I had to adjust my normally slower pace to match hers.

She said nothing the entire way across the garden. I, of course, maintained my accustomed silence. But the moment was a comfortable one. The silence was not empty. We filled it with our thoughts, making it companionable. That her thoughts were serious I could tell by the somber expression on her shadowed face.

A wall surrounded the garden. She opened a gate and led me through it, down a flight of stone steps, which crisscrossed the cliff face. The view from the mountain, overlooking the other buildings of the Font—some whole, many crumbling—was breathtaking. The gray stone against the green hillsides. The mountain peaks against the blue sky. The trees dark green clumps against the light green of the grass. As of one accord, unspoken, we both stopped on the narrow steps to gaze and admire.

She had gone down before me, to lead the way. Now she looked back up at me, tilting her head to see me from beneath the brim of her straw hat.

"You find it beautiful?" she asked.

I nodded. I could not have spoken had I wanted to.

"So do I," she said with satisfaction. "I often stop here on my way back. We live down there," she added, pointing to a long, low building attached to another, much larger building. "My father says it is the part of the Font where the catalysts used to live. There is a kitchen there and a well for water.

"Father made looms for Mother and me. We use the rooms up here for our work. We spin our own thread, weave our own woolen cloth. That comes from the sheep, of course. And the library is here, too. When our work is finished, we read. Sometimes together, sometimes separately."

We were walking down the stairs as we talked. Or I should say, as *she* talked. But with her I did not feel as if I were in a one-sided conversation. Sometimes people, embarrassed by my handicap, talk around me instead of talking to me.

Eliza continued to discuss books. "Papa reads the books on carpentry and gardening and anything he can find on sheep. Mama reads cookery books, though she likes best the books about Merilon and the treatises on magic. She never reads those when Father is around, though. It makes him sad."

"And what books do you like?" I asked with sign language, moving my hands slowly.

I could have used the notepad, but it seemed out of place in this world, an intrusion.

"What books do I like? That's what you said, wasn't it?" Eliza was delighted to understand me. "The Earth books. I know a great deal about Earth's geography and history, science and art. But my favorites are fiction."

I looked my astonishment. If there had ever been Earth books on Thimhallan, they must have been ancient, brought here at the time of Merlyn and the founders. If she has learned science from those, I thought, she must think the Earth is flat and that the sun revolves around it.

I remembered then that, according to Saryon, Simkin had once gotten hold of a copy of Shakespeare's plays. How he managed to do this, Saryon was not certain. He speculated that back before the Iron Wars, before Simkin's magical power began to wane as the magic Life in Thimhallan began to wane, Simkin had once traveled freely between Earth and Thimhallan. It's possible that he either knew Shakespeare or—as

Saryon used to say ironically—perhaps Simkin *was* Shakespeare! Had "Teddy" given Eliza books?

Eliza answered my questioning look. "After Thimhallan was destroyed, the evacuation ships came to take the people to Earth. My father knew he would be staying here and he requested that the ships bring supplies, tools, food until we could raise our own. And he asked them to bring books."

Of course. It all made sense. Joram had spent ten years of his life on Earth, before returning to Thimhallan. He would know exactly what he needed to survive with his family in exile, what was needed for both body and mind.

We had, by this time, reached the portion of the Font where Joram had taken up residence. We did not enter, however, but skirted around the Gothic-style buildings (I was reminded of Oxford). We followed various meandering paths and walkways past the enormous edifice and I soon became quite lost. Leaving the buildings behind, we continued down the mountainside, but only for a short distance. Ahead of me was lush green hillside. Running against the green grass of the hill, I saw a white blotch—a flock of sheep, and one dark spot—the man tending them.

At the sight of Joram, I halted. My coming did not now seem like such a good idea. I pointed to Eliza, then out to her father. Touching my breast, I patted the top of the stone fence, which was, by the smell and the sight of one or two sheep resting in sheds, the sheep pen. I indicated I would wait here for their return.

Eliza looked at me and frowned. She knew quite well what I had said; indeed, the two of us were communicating with an ease which, had I thought about it, was quite remarkable. I was too dazzled and overwhelmed to think coherently about anything then.

"But I *want* you to come with me," she said petulantly, as if that would make all the difference.

I shook my head, indicated that I was tired, which was true enough. I am not much accustomed to physical exertion and we must have walked two kilometers already. Taking out my notepad, I typed, *Your mother is right. You should see him alone.*

She looked at the notepad and read the words. "Father has something like this," she said, touching it hesitantly with one finger. "Only much larger. He keeps records on it."

She was silent. Her frowning gaze turned from me to the sheep and the distant, dark, roving figure that kept watch over them. Her frown eased; her gaze was troubled. She turned back to me.

"Mother lied to Father Saryon, Reuven," Eliza said calmly. "She lied to herself at the same time, so perhaps it doesn't really count as a lie. Papa is *not* happy. He was content, before that man Smythe came, but ever since then Papa has been brooding and silent, except for when he talks to himself. He won't tell us what's wrong. He doesn't want to worry us. I think it will be good for him to have Father Saryon to talk to. What is it," she asked, in a pretty, wheedling tone, "that he plans to say?"

I shook my head. It was not my place to tell her. I indicated again that I would wait for them here and motioned that she should go to her father. She pouted some, but I think that was mostly reflexive, for she was really very sensible and finally agreed—though reluctantly—that perhaps this way was best.

She ran off down the hill, her skirts flying, her hat blown back, her dark curls rampant.

I thought about her, when she was gone. I remembered every word she said, every expression on her face, the lilt and tone of her voice. I was not falling in love. Not yet. Oh, maybe just a little bit. I had dated several women before now—some of them seriously, or so I thought—but I had never been this at ease, this relaxed with a woman. I tried to figure out why. The unusual circumstances of our meeting, the fact that she was so open and unabashed and free to speak her mind. Perhaps the simple fact that we had been born on the same world. And then the oddest thought came to me.

You did not meet as strangers. Somewhere, somehow, your souls know each other.

I grinned at this impossibly romantic notion, though the grin was a little shaky, considering the vivid image I'd experienced of Eliza as Queen and myself as one more dull, plodding catalyst.

Banishing such foolish notions from my mind, I reveled in the beauty of my surroundings. Though I could see wounds upon the land, wounds caused by the war and later the storms and quakes and firestorms which had raged over Thimhallan, the wounds were healing. Young trees grew amid the ashes of the old. Grass covered the ragged scars and gouges on the landscape. The constant wind was softening the tooth-sharp cliffs.

The solitude was peaceful, quiet. No jets roared overhead, no televisions yammered, no sirens wailed. The air was crisp and clean and smelled of flowers and grass and far-off rain, not petrol and the neighbor's dinner. I was immensely content and happy as I sat there on the low stone wall. I could picture Joram and Eliza and Gwen living here, reading, working in the garden, tending sheep, weaving fabric. I could picture myself here and my heart suddenly yearned for a life so simple and serene.

Of course, I was oversimplifying, romanticizing. I

was deliberately leaving out the hard work, the drudgery, the loneliness. Earth was not the horrid place I was picturing by contrast. There was beauty to be found there, as well as here.

But what beauty would be left to any of us if the Hch'nyv destroyed our defenses, reached our world, and ravaged it as they had ravaged all others? If the power of the Darksword could truly be used to defeat the aliens, then why shouldn't Joram relinquish it? Was this the conclusion Saryon had reached?

I worried and wondered and dreamed as I sat upon the wall, watching Eliza on the hillside, a bright speck against the green. I saw her meeting with her father. I could not see, from this distance, but I could imagine him staring over to where I sat. They both stood still, talking, for long moments. Then they both began to round up the sheep, driving them down the hill and back toward their pen.

The stone wall on which I sat grew suddenly very cold, very hard.

CHAPTER ELEVEN

The sword was made of a solid mass of metal—hilt and blade together, possessing neither grace nor form. The blade was straight and almost indistinguishable from the hilt. A short, blunt-edged crosspiece separated the two. The hilt was slightly rounded, to fit the hand. . . . There was something horrifying about the sword, something devilish.

⤳ FORGING THE DARKSWORD

Eliza and her father came back, driving the sheep before them. I watched them the entire way, the sheep flowing like a huge woolly caterpillar across the grassy hillside. Joram walked steadfastly behind, reaching out now and then with his shepherd's crook to guide an errant ewe back into the flock. Eliza dashed about them like a sheepdog, waving her hat and flapping her long skirts. I have no idea, knowing nothing of the tending of sheep, if she did harm or good, but her grace and exuberance brought joy to her father's dark eyes and so of course she was permitted to have her own way.

That joy dimmed considerably and vanished altogether when those dark eyes turned their intense and unsettling gaze upon me.

The sheep flowed past me in a woolly wave, smelling strongly of damp wool—for it had rained upon the hillside—bleating and baaing so that it was impossible to hear. I stood to one side, keeping out of the way, trying not to hinder Joram's work. I was very uncomfortable and wished devotedly I had not come.

Joram's gaze raked me from head to toe as he came up the hillside. When he was level with me and I started to bow my greeting, he abruptly withdrew his gaze and did not once glance in my direction again. His face was so cold and set that it might have substituted for the granite cliff face opposite me and no one would have noticed the difference.

He paid me not the slightest attention. Since he was involved with his work, I was able to study him, curious to see the man whose life story I had written.

Joram was in his late forties at this time. Of a serious, somber mien, he looked older than he was. The rugged life, spent mostly out-of-doors, in the wayward and harsh Thimhallan weather, had tanned his skin a deep brown, left his face weathered and seamed. His black hair was as thick and luxuriant as his daughter's, though his was touched with gray at the temples and gray strands mingled with the black throughout.

He had always been strong and muscular and his well-knit, well-muscled body might have belonged to an Olympic athlete. The face had too many years etched on it, however; years of sorrow and tragedy which those happier years following could never smooth away.

No wonder he paid me scant attention and probably wished with all his heart that I would evaporate on the spot. And he did not even know the portent of our coming, though I am sure he must have suspected. I was Joram's doom.

The sheep being safely penned and watered and bedded down for the night, Eliza took her father by his calloused, work-hard hand and would have brought him over to where I stood. He removed his hand from hers, however; not roughly, he could never be rough or harsh with his heart's treasure. But he made it very clear that the two of us—he and I—would not be connected in any way, especially not through her.

I could not fault him or blame him. I felt such guilt within myself—as if this were all my doing—and such grief and compassion for him, whose idyllic life we were destined to destroy, that tears stung my eyelids.

Hurriedly, I blinked them back, for he would despise any weakness on my part.

"Papa," said Eliza, "this is Reuven. He is Father Saryon's almost son. He cannot speak, Papa. At least not with his mouth. He talks whole books with his eyes."

She smiled, teasing me. That smile and her beauty— for she was flushed with her exertion, her hair tousled and windblown—did nothing to add to my composure. Charmed by Eliza, awed by Joram, consumed by guilt and unhappiness, I bowed my respects, glad for the chance to hide my face and try to regain my self-command.

This was not easy. Joram said no word of greeting. When I raised my head, I saw that he had folded his arms across his chest and was regarding me with dark displeasure, his heavy brows drawn into a frown.

His cold forbidding darkness dimmed his daughter's sunshine. Eliza faltered, looked uncertainly from him to me.

"Papa," she said, chiding gently, "where are your manners? Reuven is our guest. He has come all the way from Earth just to see us. You must make him welcome."

She did not understand. She could not understand. I raised my hand, to ward off her words, and shook my head slightly, all the while keeping my gaze fixed on Joram. If, as Eliza had said, I could speak with my eyes, I hoped he would read in them understanding. Perhaps he did. He still did not speak to me. Turning away, he walked up the steps that crisscrossed the hillside. But before he turned, I saw that his frowning aspect had lightened a little, if only to be replaced by sorrow.

I think, all in all, I would have preferred his displeasure.

He strode up the steps very rapidly, taking them two or three at a time. I marveled at his endurance, for the steps went directly up the hill; there must have been seventy-five of them, and I was soon panting for breath. Eliza kept beside me, and she was troubled, for she was silent and her gaze was on her father's back.

"He is eager to see Father Saryon," she said abruptly, in apology for Joram's rudeness.

I nodded yes, that I understood. Pausing to catch my breath and try to ease the cramps in my calves, I signed to her that I was not in the least offended and that she was not to worry about me.

This she didn't understand. I took out the electronic notepad and typed it in, showing the words to her. She read them, looked at me. I nodded, smiled, reassuring. She smiled back, tentative, and then sighed.

"Things are going to change, aren't they, Reuven? Our life is going to change. *His* life is going to change." Her gaze went again to her father. "And it's all my fault. I've longed for this day, prayed for it to come. I didn't realize . . . Oh, Papa, I'm sorry! I'm so sorry!"

Gathering her long skirts, she left me, running up the stairs with the long stride that matched Joram's. I could not have kept up with her if my life had depended on it. As it was, I was not disappointed to be left behind. I needed time to sort out my own thoughts. I trudged slowly and painfully after them.

Eliza caught up with her father. She twined her arm through his, rested her head on his shoulder. He folded her in a loving embrace, stroked and smoothed her black curls.

His arm around her, her arm around him, they continued up the stairs until they reached their living quarters, where they vanished from my sight.

I kept climbing, my strength sapped by the ache in my legs, the burning in my lungs and my heart. Below, I could hear the sheep, snug and safe in their barn, bleating contentedly as they settled down for the night. In the distance, the rumble of thunder; another storm ravaging the land below.

I wondered, then, what would happen to the sheep when we took Joram and his family away from their home. Without their shepherd, they would die.

CHAPTER TWELVE

*The rounded knob on the sword's hilt, combined
with the long neck of the hilt itself, the handle's
short, blunt arms, and the narrow body of the
blade, turned the weapon into a grim parody of a
human being.*

⮑ *FORGING THE DARKSWORD*

It occurred to me that I would miss the reunion, the
first meeting between my master and Joram, and that
fear impelled me up the stairs at a much more rapid
pace than I would have thought myself capable of. I
was gasping for breath when I reached the top. Dusk
was falling and the lights had been lit inside the dwelling place and so I was able to find their rooms, when
most of the rest of the building was dark and deserted.

Entering a door nearest the lights, I made my way
along a shadowy hall into what must have been, in the
days of the Font's grandeur, the dortoir, where lived

the young catalysts in training. I say this, because of the innumerable small rooms opening off the central corridor. In each room was a bed and desk and a washstand. The stone walls were chill, the rooms dusty and darkened by the sadness which comes to a place when the life that once filled it is withdrawn.

In this corridor, I lost sight of the lights of Joram's dwelling, but found them again when I entered a large, open room that had probably been a dining hall. I heard voices through a door to my left. I walked from darkness and chill to light and warmth. A kitchen, which had once fed several hundred, was now not only kitchen but the central living area for Joram and his family.

I could see easily why they chose it. An enormous stone fireplace provided heat and light. Twenty years before, when the Font had teemed with life, magi hired to work with the catalysts would have conjured up fire to cook the food and warm the body. Possessed of no magic whatsoever, Joram cut and hauled wood to the fireplace. The flames crackled and danced, smoke and sparks fled up the chimney. I reveled in the warmth. The air was growing cool outside, with the setting of the sun.

Saryon and Gwen sat near the fire. Gwen was pale and silent, staring into the flames. Occasionally she would shift her gaze to the back part of the room, in part expectation, part dread. Saryon, ill at ease, suddenly stood up and began roaming aimlessly about the room. Just as abruptly, he sat back down. Joram was not present and I feared he might refuse to see Saryon at all, which would have hurt my master terribly. Then Eliza entered at almost the same time I did, although from a door opposite.

"Papa bids you welcome, Father Saryon," she said,

coming to stand before the catalyst, who rose to meet her. "Please sit down and be comfortable. Papa has gone to wash and change his clothes. He will join us shortly."

I was relieved and I think Saryon was, too, for he smiled and gave a deep sigh before resuming his chair. Gwen stirred, at this, and said we must be hungry and she would fix the evening meal. Though Eliza had done a very good job of attempting to wash away the traces, I saw that she had been crying.

She said she was certain I would like to wash up, which was true, and offered to show me the way. I crossed the room to join her. We were both being watched by the teddy bear with the orange ribbon around his neck, who was seated in a small chair that must have been specially made for a child. Just at the moment we were walking past, the bear gave a lurch and tumbled out of the chair, landing on his nose on the floor.

"Poor Teddy," Eliza said playfully. Picking up the bear, she dusted him off, kissed him on the top of his well-worn head, and settled him more comfortably in the chair. "Be a sweet Teddy," she admonished, still in her playful tone, "and you shall have bread and honey for your supper."

Glancing back at the bear, I saw Simkin smirk.

Eliza led me into the sleeping quarters of the family, rooms which she told me had once belonged to the higher-ranking catalysts. These rooms were larger and much more comfortable than the narrow cells I had passed. She took me to one at the end of the hallway.

"Here's where you will spend the night," she said, opening the door.

A fire burned on the small hearth. The bed was covered with clean, sweet-smelling sheets, scented with lavender. The floor was newly swept. My knapsack rested near the bed. On the nightstand was a jug of steaming water and a washbasin. Eliza told me where to find the outbuildings.

"No need to hurry," she said. "Papa is bathing and taking his evening swim. He won't be ready for at least another half hour."

Like her mother, she was pale and preoccupied. The only time I'd seen her smile was when she was playing with Teddy and that smile had faded quickly. She was about to leave when I stopped her.

Since we had time, I typed on the notebook. *Tell me more about Teddy.*

Her smile returned. "I told you how I found him in the old nursery. I took him everywhere with me—he went with Papa to tend the sheep, with Mama to work in the garden or wash the clothes.

"You're going to think this is silly." Her cheeks flushed faintly. "But I seem to remember Teddy telling me stories—all about faeries and giants, dragons and unicorns." She laughed self-consciously. "I suppose I must have made them up myself and told them to Teddy, though I have the oddest impression that it was the other way around. What do you think?"

I don't remember what I responded. Something about lonely children having vivid imaginations. What could I say? It was not up to me to tell her the truth about Simkin!

She said that this must be true and started to leave, but paused, just before she shut the door. "Now that I recall them, some of those stories were quite horrible. Tales about duchesses sneezing their heads off and the heads landing in the soup and earls being buried alive by mistake and faerie queens who took men captive and used them as slaves. What a morbid little imp I must have been!"

Laughing again, she left me, shutting the door behind her.

Chaotic, treacherous, Simkin was quite capable of leading grown people to ruin just for the entertainment value. It shocked me to think that Joram and Gwen—Joram in particular, who knew what Simkin was—had allowed him to be the playmate of their child. Yet Simkin obviously had not harmed her and had provided her with pleasant—albeit strange—childhood memories.

And what would happen when we took Joram and his family back to Earth? Eliza would undoubtedly want to take along her "Teddy." The image of Simkin loosed upon Earth was appalling. I made a mental note to myself to discuss this with Saryon, who, worried and preoccupied himself, had probably not given this matter much thought.

I found the outbuildings—one for men and one for women—which must have dated back to the very early days of life in the Font. They were as clean as was possible, but being open-air, they made me consider that one of mankind's most wonderful achievements had been indoor plumbing.

Back in my room, I washed myself from the basin—envying Joram his swim—combed my hair, and changed my clothes, which smelled strongly of sheep. Dressed in clean blue jeans and a blue cable-knit sweater I'd purchased in Ireland and which was one of my favorites, I returned to the living quarters.

Eliza and her mother were busy in the kitchen. I offered my services and was put in charge of slicing loaves of freshly baked bread, which had been cooling on a rack. Eliza set out bowls of dried fruit and

honeycombs filled with honey that tasted of clover.
Gwen was stirring a pot of beans, cooked with mutton.
I understood then that the sheep meant not only wool
for their clothes, but meat for their table.

Saryon looked at me rather anxiously, when Gwen
talked about the mutton, for I had been known, when
younger, to express my disapproval of meat-eaters at
the dinner tables of our hosts, usually over the prime
rib. I smiled at him and shook my head, and even accepted the responsibility of tasting the beans, when
Eliza offered them, to see if they were seasoned prop-
erly.

I think they were bland. I don't remember. It was
then, when she held the wooden spoon to my lips, that
I realized I was falling in love with her.

At that moment Joram entered the room.

I could not see him, from my angle in the kitchen,
but I knew by the sight of Saryon's face, which had
become as white as polished bone. Gwendolyn and
Eliza exchanged glances—conspiratorial glances. It had
been by their design that we three were in the back part
of the kitchen, leaving Saryon and Joram in the living
area alone.

Joram advanced in my view, and my heart sank, for
he was every bit as grim and stoic and cold as I had
seen him on the hillside. Saryon stood tall and straight,
his hands at his sides. The two gazed at each other long
minutes without moving or speaking. I don't know
what I feared—that Joram would denounce his mentor
and order him out of the house. I could envision this
stern, proud man doing anything.

Eliza and Gwen clasped hands. My own hands grew
chill and I was worried for Saryon, who had begun to
sag and was looking very ill. I was going to go to him. I
had already taken a step in that direction.

Joram reached out, clasped his arms around Saryon, and held him in a fast embrace.

"My boy," Saryon murmured brokenly, stroking the grown man on the back as perhaps the catalyst had once lovingly stroked the baby. "My dear boy! How good it is . . . You and Gwen . . ." Saryon broke down completely.

Gwen was sobbing into her apron. Eliza stood watching, tears rolling unheeded down her cheeks, on her lips a sweet, sad smile. I had tears in my own eyes, and quickly dried them on the sleeve of my sweater.

Joram straightened. He was taller than my master now; Saryon having become stooped with the years. Joram placed his hands—brown and rough—on Saryon's shoulders and smiled briefly, darkly. "Welcome to our home, Father," he said, and his tone belied his affectionate gesture, for his voice was cool and shadowed. "Gwen and I are pleased that you have come to visit us."

He turned to her and his dark countenance lightened somewhat when his eyes fell upon her, as if the sun had broken through the clouds and was shining on his face. His tone to her softened.

"Our guests must be hungry. Is supper ready?"

Gwen hurriedly wiped her eyes on the tail end of her apron and replied, in a faint voice, that the table was laid and invited us to sit down. I was going to help serve, but Eliza said no, I was to sit with the other men.

Joram took his place at the head of the long plank table. He placed Saryon at his right hand. I sat down next to Saryon, on my master's right.

"I believe you have met Reuven," Saryon said mildly. "My assistant and scribe. Reuven wrote your story, Joram. At King Garald's behest, so that the people of Earth could understand our people. The books were very well received. You would like them, I think."

"*I* would like to read them!" said Eliza, placing the bowl of steaming beans on the table. She clasped her hands and stared at me in awe. "You write books! You didn't tell me. How splendid!"

My face was hot enough that we could have toasted the bread by holding it to my cheek. Joram said nothing. Gwen murmured something polite; I'm not sure what, I couldn't hear for the pounding of blood in my head and the confusion of my thoughts. Eliza was so beautiful. She was regarding me with respect and admiration.

Shipboard romance, I expostulated with myself sternly. You are in a strange and exotic location, meeting under unusual circumstances. Not only that, but I am the first man near her own age she has ever met. It would be completely wrong of me to take advantage of this situation. She would need a friend, in that brave new world to which she was going. I would be that friend and if, after she had met the hundreds of thousands of other young men who would be clamoring for her attention, she happened to still think well of me, I would be there for her.

One more catalyst in the throng . . .

Saryon nudged me with his bony knee beneath the stone table. I came back to reality with a jolt, to find that Gwen and Eliza were taking their seats; Eliza sitting directly across from Saryon and Gwen across from her husband. As the women sat down Joram rose to his feet in respect. Saryon and I did the same.

We all returned to our seats.

"Father," said Joram, "would you offer a prayer?"

Saryon looked astonished, as well he might, for in the past Joram had never been at all religious. Indeed, he had once held a grudge against the Almin, blaming Him for the tragic circumstances of his life, when by rights the blame should have fallen on the greed and evil ambition of men.

We bowed our heads. I thought I heard a snigger, coming from the vicinity of Teddy, but no one else seemed to hear anything.

"Almin," Saryon prayed, "bless and keep us in these dark and dangerous times. Help us to work together to defeat this dread enemy, who seeks to destroy and defile the glory of Your creation. Amen."

Eliza and Gwen murmured "Amen" in response. I said it myself, silently. Joram said nothing. Lifting his head, he sent a black look at Saryon that, if he had seen it, must have struck him to the heart. Fortunately, he did not. My master was studying Eliza, who sat across the table from him.

"You are very much like your grandmother, my dear," Saryon said to her. "The Empress of Merilon. She was said to be the most beautiful woman in Thimhallan. And she was, one of them." He turned his mild gaze to Gwen. "The other, of course, was your mother."

Gwendolyn and Eliza both flushed at the compliment and Eliza asked Saryon to tell her about the Empress, her grandmother.

"Papa never talks about the old days," Eliza said. "He says that they are gone and it is useless to think about them. I've read about Merilon and the rest in the books, but that isn't the same. Mother has told me some, but not much. . . ."

"Did she tell you about how she saved us from the *Duuk-tsarith* when we first came to Merilon?" Saryon asked.

"No! Did you, Mama? Will you tell the story?"

Gwen smiled, but she, too, had seen the look her husband cast on Saryon. She said something to the effect that she was a poor storyteller and would leave that to the good father. Saryon launched into his tale. Eliza listened with rapt attention. Gwen stared at her plate, made only the barest pretense of eating. Joram ate his food in silence, looked at nothing and everything.

"Simkin changed himself into a tulip," Saryon was saying, bringing the story to its conclusion. "He planted himself in the bouquet your mother was carrying and urged her to tell the guards at the city gate that my young friends and I were all guests of her father's! And so they admitted us—who were in reality fugitives from the law—safely into Merilon. She told a lie, of course, but I believe that the Almin forgave her, for she acted out of love."

Saryon smiled benignly and gave a gentle nod toward Joram. Gwendolyn lifted her head, looked at her husband. He returned the look and again I saw the darkness, that seemed to hang over him perpetually, lift. The love that had been kindled that day still burned, its warmth surrounded us and blessed us.

"Mama! You were a heroine! How romantic. But tell me more about this Simkin," Eliza said, laughing.

At this, Saryon looked extremely discomfited. My glance went involuntarily to the stuffed bear, which seemed to be quivering with either anticipation or suppressed laughter. Saryon opened his mouth. I'm not sure what he would have replied, but at that moment Joram, his face grim, shoved his plate back and rose to his feet.

"We've had enough stories for the night. You came here for a reason, or so I understand, Father. Come into the warming room and tell us. Leave the dishes,

Gwen," he added. "Father Saryon has important work to do back on Earth. We don't want to prolong his visit unnecessarily. You and Reuven will be our guests tonight, of course."

"Thank you," said Saryon faintly.

"It will only take a moment to clear the table, Joram," Gwendolyn said nervously. "You and Father Saryon go into the warming room. Eliza and Reuven and I will—"

Her chill, trembling hands dropped a plate. It struck the stone floor and shattered.

All of us stood and stared at it in unhappy silence.

Everyone in that room read its dread portent.

CHAPTER THIRTEEN

*The sword lay like a corpse at Saryon's feet, the
personification of the catalyst's sin.*

~*FORGING THE DARKSWORD*

Eliza brought a broom and swept up the remnants of
the plate.

"Reuven and I will do the dishes, Mama," Eliza said
in a low voice. "You stay with Papa."

Gwendolyn did not reply, but she nodded, and going to Joram, she put her arm around him, rested her
head on his chest. He held her fast, bowed his dark
head over her blond hair, and kissed her gently.

I cleared the table, carried the plates into the kitchen.
Eliza tossed the broken plate into a bin, then filled a tub
with hot water from a kettle that had been steaming on

the hearth. She didn't look at me once, but kept her eyes on her work.

I guessed what she must be feeling: guilt, remorse. Prospero's daughter wanted to see this brave new world. She was certain in her own mind that this was why we had come—to take her back with us. She wanted to go, to see the wonders about which she had only read. Yet she realized, perhaps for the first time, how her going would grieve her parents. She would never leave them.

She won't have to. They will come with her. The knowledge cheered me.

Joram made certain that Saryon was settled comfortably near the fire, then sat down in what I must assume was his accustomed chair. Gwendolyn took her place in a chair beside Joram's, near enough that they could reach out and touch hands.

On tables beside each chair were several books and, near Gwen's chair, a basket holding balls of yarn, hand-carved knitting needles, and another basket of mending. She reached, by habit, for one of these. Only when the basket was in her lap did she look at Father Saryon, and with a sigh, she put her work away and folded her hands together tightly.

No one said a word. We might have been a party of mutes, except that then the silence would have been alive, with thoughts flying from one to another, faces animated, eyes bright and speaking. Each person in that room stood behind a wall—a wall of time and distance, fear and mistrust and, in my master's case, deep sorrow.

Finishing the dishes, we joined the others. Eliza lit candles. I added another log to the fire. Eliza went to her own chair, near a table piled with books and another basket of handwork. There not being any more chairs, I retrieved one from the kitchen and placed it near my master.

Joram regarded Saryon with grim expectation, black brows drawn in a straight heavy line above his eyes, his expression stern and impregnable, a solid rock cliff, challenging Saryon to hurl himself against it.

Saryon had known this would not be easy. I don't believe he imagined it would be this hard. He drew in a breath, but before he could speak, Joram forestalled him.

"I want you to take a message to Prince Garald, Father," Joram said abruptly. "Tell him that his commands have been thwarted, the law broken. My family and I were to have been left alone and in peace on this world. That peace has been disturbed by a man named Smythe, who came seeking the Darksword. He dared to threaten my family. I threw him out with orders to never return. If he does come back, I take no responsibility for what might happen. That goes for anyone else seeking the Darksword as well."

This statement obviously included us and made Saryon's task no easier.

"I cannot think why they have come in the first place," Joram continued. "The Darksword was destroyed when the world was shattered. They are wasting their time searching for something that doesn't exist."

He was not lying, not outright. True, the original Darksword had been destroyed. But what about the new one, the one he had most recently made? Or did it truly exist? Perhaps the *Duuk-tsarith* were mistaken. Saryon did not dare ask. To do so would be to admit that Joram was being spied upon and that would send him into a rage.

My master had the look of a man about to go swim-

ming in an icy lake. He knows that entering the water
little by little will only prolong the agony and so he
plunged straight in.

"Joram, Gwendolyn"—Saryon's compassionate
gaze included them both—"my business here does not
concern the Darksword. I am here to take you and
your family back to Earth, where you will be safe."

"We are safe here," said Joram sternly, glowering,
"or we would be if Garald would keep his word and
enforce his law! Or does he want the Darksword, too?
That's it, isn't it?" He bounded out of his chair,
loomed over us threateningly. "*That's* why you've
come, Father!"

I knew then, of course, that the reports were true.
Joram had made another Darksword. He had as good
as admitted it.

Saryon stood to face him. His cheeks were flushed,
his voice shook, not with weakness, but with anger. "I
am not here for the sword, Joram. I have stated as
much. You know—or at least you should know—that I
would not lie to you."

Gwendolyn was on her feet, her hands on Joram's
arm.

"Joram, please!" she said softly. "You don't know
what you're saying. This is Father Saryon!"

Joram's fury subsided. He had the grace to look
ashamed of himself and to apologize. But the apology
was brief and it was cold. He returned to his chair.
Gwen did not go back to hers, but remained standing
behind Joram, her presence strong and supportive, defending him, though he had been in the wrong.

Eliza was troubled, confused, and a little frightened.
This was not what she had expected.

Saryon sat back down, looked gently, grievingly, on
Joram. "My son, do you think this is easy for me? I see

the life you have made for yourself and your family. I see that it is peaceful and blessed. And I am the one telling you it must end. I wish I could add that it would be possible to regain such peace back on Earth, but that I cannot promise. Who knows whether any of us will find peace when we return, or if we will all be plunged into terrible war.

"Smythe spoke to you of the Hch'nyv, the aliens who have one avowed purpose and that is to destroy the human race. They have no interest in negotiating, they refuse all contact with us. They have slaughtered those we sent to them in hopes of obtaining a truce. They are closing in on us. Our military forces have pulled back, in order to make a final stand on Earth. This outpost is the last to be evacuated.

"I cannot even promise that you will be safe on Earth," Saryon admitted. "I can't promise that any of us will. But at least there you will have the protection of the combined Earth Forces. Here, you and Gwen and Eliza would be at the aliens' mercy. And, from what we have seen, they have no concept of mercy."

Joram's mouth twisted. "And if you have the Dark-sword—"

Saryon was shaking his head.

Joram amended his statement, though the twist of his mouth deepened and his tone was bitter and ironic. "If *someone* has the Darksword, then *someone* could use it to stop these fiendish aliens and save the world. Still trying to redeem yourself, Father?"

Saryon gazed at him sadly. "You don't believe me. You think I am lying to you. I am sorry, my son. Very sorry."

"Joram," Gwen whispered in gentle reproof, and placed her hand on his shoulder.

Joram sighed. Reaching up, he took hold of her

hand and rested his cheek against it. He kept fast hold of her as he talked.

"I do not say you are lying, Father." Joram spoke in a softened tone. "I am saying that you have been tricked. You were always gullible," he added, and the bitter smile warmed into one of affection. "You are too good for this world, Father. Much too good. People take advantage of you."

"I do not know that I am particularly good," Saryon said, speaking slowly, earnestly, his words gathering force as he went, "but I have always tried to do what I believed was right. This does not mean that I am weak, Joram, nor that I am foolish, though you always equated goodness with weakness. You imply that these aliens do not exist. I've seen the news reports, Joram! I've seen the pictures of the ships attacking and destroying our colonies! I've read the accounts of the terrible slaughter, the senseless butchery.

"No, I have not seen these aliens with my own eyes. Few men have and lived to tell of it. But I have seen the anxiety, the concern, the fear in the eyes of General Boris and King Garald. They are afraid, Joram. Afraid for you, afraid for all of us. What do you think this is— an elaborate hoax? To what purpose? All to trick you out of the Darksword? How is that possible, when you have said yourself that it was destroyed?"

Joram made no response.

Saryon sighed again. "My son, I will be honest with you. I will leave nothing hidden, though what I have to tell will anger you and rightly so. They know you have forged a new Darksword. The *Duuk-tsarith* have been watching you—only to protect you, Joram! Only to protect you from Smythe and his associates! So the *Duuk-tsarith* claim, and I . . . I believe them."

Joram was indeed furious, so furious that he was

choked by his rage and could not speak. And so my master was able to continue.

"I know why you made the sword, Joram—to protect yourself and those you love from the magic. And that is why you cling to it. And, yes, I admit that they want the Darksword and its secrets, Joram. Bishop Radisovik—you remember him? You know him to be a good, wise man. Bishop Radisovik received a message which he believes came from the Almin concerning the Darksword and how it might be used to save our people. Whether you take the sword to Earth or not is your decision. I will not try to influence you. I care only for the safety of yourself and your family. Do you care about the Darksword so much, my son, that you would sacrifice your family for it?"

Joram rose to his feet. Releasing Gwen's hand, he stepped away from her placating touch. His voice was deep with anger. "How can I trust them? What have I known from these people in the past, Father? Treachery, deceit, murder—"

"Honor, love, compassion," Saryon countered.

Joram's face darkened. He was not accustomed to being contradicted. I don't know what he might have said next, but Gwendolyn intervened.

"Father, tell us what King Garald plans for us," she said.

Saryon did so. He related how a ship was waiting for them at the outpost. The ship would take them back to Earth, where housing had been arranged. He spoke with regret of things left behind, but there was not enough room on the ship to store many personal belongings.

"Just room enough for the Darksword," Joram said, and sneered.

"The hell with the Darksword!" Saryon said angrily,

losing patience. "Consign it to perdition! I do not want to see it! I do not want to hear of it! Leave it! Bury it! Destroy it! I do not care what you do with it. *You,* Joram! You and your wife and your child. These are all that matter to me."

"To you!" Joram countered. "And that is why they sent you! To make exactly this plea in this tone! To scare us into running. And when we are gone, then they will be free to come and search and take what they know I would die for before I give up!"

"You can't mean this, Father!" Eliza spoke for the first time. Rising to her feet, she faced him. "What if they are right? What if the power of the Darksword could save lives? Millions of lives! You have no right to withhold it. You must give it to them!"

"Daughter," said Gwendolyn sharply, "hold your tongue! You can't possibly understand!"

"I understand that my father is being selfish and obstinate," Eliza returned. "And that he doesn't care about us! About any of us! He cares only for himself!"

Joram glared darkly at Saryon. "You have accomplished your task, Father. You have turned my child against me. No doubt that, too, was part of your plan. She can go with you to Earth, if she wants. I will not stop her. You may stay the night, you and your accomplice. But you will be gone in the morning."

He turned and started to leave the room.

"Father!" Eliza pleaded, heartbroken. "I don't want to leave! Father, I didn't mean . . ." She stretched out her hands to him, but he walked past her without a glance and disappeared into the darkness. "Father!"

He did not return.

With a ragged cry, Eliza ran from the room, into another part of the dwelling. I heard her footsteps and then, in the distance, a door slam.

Gwendolyn stood alone, drooping and pale as a cut flower.

Saryon began to stammer out an apology, though the Almin knows he had nothing for which to apologize.

Gwendolyn lifted her gaze to meet his. "They are so alike," she said. "Flint striking flint. The sparks fly. And yet they love each other. . . ." Her hand went to her mouth and then to her eyes. She drew in a shuddering breath. "He will reconsider. He will think about this through the night. His answer will be different by morning. He will do what is right. You know him, Father."

"Yes," said Saryon gently. "I know him."

Perhaps, I thought. But in the meantime it will be a long night.

Gwendolyn gave Saryon a kiss on his cheek. She bid me good night. I bowed silently, and she left us.

The fire had died to embers. The room was dark and growing chill. I was afraid for Saryon, who looked very ill. I knew how exhausted he must be, for the day had been a tiring one. The evening's stressful and unpleasant scene had left him empty and shaken.

"Master," I signed, going to him, "come to bed. There is nothing more we can do this night."

He did not move, nor did he seem to see my speaking hands. He stared into the glowing coals, and from his words, spoken to himself, I shared his vision. He was seeing the forge fire, the making of the sword.

"I gave the first Darksword life," he said. "A thing of evil, it sucked the light from the world and changed it into darkness. He is right. I *am* still searching for redemption."

He was shivering. I looked around the room, spotted a woolen throw tossed on a stool near the fireplace.

As I went to retrieve it, my eye caught a tiny flash of orange light, in the corner between the fireplace and the wall. Thinking it might be a cinder that had caught the wood on fire, I started to brush it off, intending to stamp it out.

The moment my hand touched it, a shiver went through my body. Smooth, plastic, it was not of this world. It did not belong here. I saw again the green glowing listening devices Mosiah had discovered in our house. Except why should this one glow orange . . . ?

"No reason," said a furry voice, near my elbow. "Except that I happen to like orange."

Teddy sat upon the stool. The orange glow of the listening device was reflected in his button eyes.

I might have asked how Simkin knew what such a device was, or even if he *did* know what it was. I might have asked why he waited to show it to us now, now that it was too late. I might have asked, but I did not. I think I feared the answer. Perhaps that was a mistake.

And I did not tell Saryon that all we had said had been overheard by the Technomancers. Perhaps that, too, was a mistake, but I was afraid it would only add to his misery. Whereas, if Gwen was right—and she should surely know Joram—by morning he would have reconsidered. By morning, we would all be gone from this place and the Technomancers could listen to the silence.

Picking up the throw, I placed it over Saryon's shoulders, and rousing him from his bleak reverie, I persuaded him to go to bed. We walked together down the dark hallway, with only the lambent light of the stars to guide us. I offered to make his tea for him, but he said no, he was too tired. He would go straight to bed.

Any doubts I had about concealing my knowledge of

the listening device vanished. It would only worry him to no purpose, when he needed rest.

And if that was a mistake, then it was the first of many to be made that night. Still another mistake, and perhaps the most drastic, was that I neglected to keep an eye on "Teddy."

CHAPTER FOURTEEN

> *"Wrap the sword in these rags. If anyone stops*
> *you, tell them you are carrying a child. A*
> *dead child."*
>
> ~JORAM; *FORGING THE DARKSWORD*

I woke up, thinking I heard a sound, but unable to place what the sound had been. Lying in bed, trying to recollect what it was and not making much headway, I heard the creak of hinges, as of a door being either opened or shut very slowly, so as not to disturb anyone.

Thinking perhaps it was Saryon and that he might need me, I left my bed, pulled on my sweater and jeans, and went out into the hall and down to his room. Listening at the door, I could hear his gentle snoring.

Whoever was up and wandering around in the night, it
was not my master.

"Joram," I thought, and though I had been angered
by his obduracy and his show of disrespect for Saryon,
I felt sorry for the man. He was being forced to leave a
home he loved, a life he had made.

"Almin give him guidance," I prayed, and returned
to my room.

Restless, knowing I would not be able to go back to
sleep, I walked to the window and parted the curtains
to look out upon the night.

My window opened up onto one of the many gar-
dens with which the Font was surrounded. I have no
idea of the name of the flowers which grew out there;
some sort of large, white blooms that hung heavy on
their stems and seemed, to my imagination, to be hanging their heads in sorrow. I was thinking to myself that
this would make a good metaphor to use in a new book
I was then planning. I was about to turn away, to note
it down, when I saw someone enter the garden.

Of course, Joram has taken his worries outside, I
thought. I felt uneasy about disturbing his privacy and
also about the possibility of him seeing me through the
window and thinking I was spying on him. I was about
to draw shut the curtains when the figure stepped out
into an open walkway, almost directly opposite me,
and I saw that it was not Joram.

It was a woman, wearing a cloak and hood and
carrying a bundle in her arms.

"Eliza!" I said to myself. "She's running away from
home!"

I went cold all over. My heart constricted. I stood
bolted to the floor in that terrible indecision which
sometimes comes over one in a crisis. I had to do something, but what?

Run and wake Saryon and have him talk to her? I recalled his weariness and how ill he had looked and decided against that.

Wake her parents?

No. I would not betray Eliza. I would go to her myself, try to persuade her to stay.

Grabbing up my jacket, I threw it on and dashed out into the hall. I had only the vaguest idea where I was going, but on reflection, I seemed to remember passing the garden on my way to the outbuildings. I found the door after only one wrong turn and stepped out into the night. The creak of the hinges, as I passed through, was the same creak I'd heard earlier.

The night was bright and it was easy to see the shadowy figure ahead of me. She had been moving at a fairly rapid pace when I first saw her from my window, and I was afraid she might have already crossed the garden and disappeared over the wall before I could reach her. As it was, she had reached the wall, but the bundle she was carrying had slowed her down. She had placed the bundle on the top of the wall and with it something else, the sight of which gave me another cold chill—Teddy.

Teddy, a.k.a. Simkin, sat on the top of the wall beside the bundle while Eliza vaulted over the wall, in a flurry of cloak and skirt. Turning, she reached for the bundle with one hand and Teddy with the other. She saw me.

Her face, framed by its night-dark cloud of hair, was pale as the heavy flowers; pale but resolute. Her eyes widened when she saw me, and then narrowed in displeasure.

Frantically, I waved my hands, though what I hoped to accomplish by this gesturing was beyond me. Whatever it was, it didn't work. She snatched up the bundle, and it was obviously heavy, for she had a difficult time managing it. She was forced to drop Teddy—on his head, I hoped—and use both hands to grasp the bundle.

There was a muffled clang—steel wrapped in cloth striking stone.

I knew then what she carried and the knowledge knocked the breath from my body. I faltered, came to a halt.

She saw that I knew, which served only to increase her haste. Securing her burden, she turned away from me and I heard her footsteps slipping on the rocks of the hillside.

I came to my senses and hurried after her, for now it was more imperative than ever that I catch up to her.

The Technomancers were listening. But according to Mosiah, the *Duuk-tsarith* were watching!

Expecting to see their dark forms leap out of the shadows any moment, I scaled the wall, scrambling over it clumsily. I have said that I was not very athletic. I could not see the ground beneath me in the dark shadow cast by the wall. I misjudged the drop and fell heavily, bruising my knees against the wall and scraping away the skin on the palms of my hands.

"Oof! Zounds! Oaf! You've knocked the stuffing out of me!" came a voice.

I was too busy trying to regain purchase on the steep slope to pay any attention to the lamenting Teddy. My feet scrabbled on a loose rock, which bounded down the hillside and started a small avalanche. I slipped and slithered and then she hovered over me. The folds of her cloak settled around me. Hands grasped my arms and pinched my flesh.

"Stop it!" she whispered furiously. "You're making enough noise to wake the dead!"

"Happened once," said a doleful voice, somewhere near my elbow. "The Duke of Esterhouse. Dropped dead, sitting in his armchair, reading the paper. Everyone afraid to tell him. Knew he'd take the news frightfully hard. So we left him there. And then one day cook forgot and rang the dinner bell—"

Startled, Eliza let go of me and sat back on her heels.

"You can talk!" she said to me in a tight voice. She was not carrying the bundle.

I shook my head emphatically. Reaching underneath my scraped rump, I pulled out the alleged stuffed bear and gave it a shake.

Eliza looked at the bear and bit her lower lip and the sudden inkling of the truth formed in my mind.

"Are you hurt?" she asked in a grudging tone.

I shook my head.

"Good," she said. "Go back to bed, Reuven. I know what I'm doing."

And without another word, she snatched the bear from my hand and was up and gone in a flutter of skirt and cloak. She stopped some distance on the hill below to pick up her heavy bundle, and then I lost her in the darkness.

She knew where she was going. I did not. She was accustomed to climbing and walking these steep hills. I was not. I could not shout after her, although I wouldn't have, in any case. The last thing I wanted to do was call attention to her and what she carried. I hoped to be able to persuade her to return home before any harm was done. But first I had to catch her.

It would cost more time in the long run, I reasoned, if I stumbled blindly down the hillside. There had to be a trail; she could not be moving so fast otherwise. I took time to search, my knees stiffening and my palms burning. My patience was rewarded. Not far from where I had fallen I found a crude trail, half-natural, half-man-made, carved into the hillside. It was an old trail; the feet of many catalysts had trodden it before me. The trail was formed of deep gouges in the hillside, reinforced here and there with large embedded rocks or exposed tree roots.

The rocks gleamed white in the starlit night; the tree roots, worn by the passage of many feet, were slick and shiny. I made my way down the trail, wondering as I did so where it led.

The way was steep, and despite the help from rocks and other foot and handholds, my going was difficult and slow. I could no longer hear Eliza's footfalls and knew she must be far ahead of me. My taking this route was a foolish idea. If I slipped and fell, I would probably break my leg or my ankle, and be forced to lie out here all night with no hope of rescue.

If only I could move faster! I could see, in my mind, those catalysts who had once made this trail and walked it every day, bounding down it like goats. . . .

I was bounding down it, if not like a goat, at least swiftly and easily. Brown robes hiked up to my waist, sandals flapping, a bag of scrolls flung over my shoulder, I ran down the trail in the bright sunshine of a fine day. All the young catalysts and occasionally some of the old ones took this route when they were late for classes, for this trail led straight to the University.

The vision was eerie and startling, just like the other vision I'd had before—of myself in brown robes, of Eliza my queen. . . . Of course, as an author, I was accustomed to living in my imagination and my fancies and dreams are very real to me. But not as real as this. Again, I lifted a curtain to look out a window and saw myself on the other side, looking back in.

But—could I use this to my benefit? Did I dare?

I was light-headed from exhaustion and the thin air of the high altitude. Plus I was desperate, fearful for Eliza's safety. Otherwise I do not believe that I could have done what I did. I let go of myself in this life and gave myself to the other life, if that's what it truly was. I became that catalyst, late for class, certain to be in trouble with the master, and I plunged down the hillside.

My feet knew where the stones would be, my hands knew where to grasp. I knew where I could safely slide and once I even jumped from one ledge to another. It was madness, it was exhilarating. If I had stopped to think about what I was doing, I would have frozen in place and been unable to move another step.

When I finally reached the bottom, I gasped for breath and stared up the hillside and the catalyst that I was vanished. I realized what I had done and my stomach turned within me. Quickly, I looked away and started to search for Eliza. I had a final image of the catalyst running in the opposite direction from the one I was taking and part of me was sorry to let him go.

I had reached a broad, flat, white-stone-paved road. It must be the main highway, leading down from the Font to the foothills and the long abandoned city below, a city whose sole reason for being had been to support the Font and the University. This road must have been clogged with wheelless carts that floated on the wings of magic and the exotic and fanciful carriages of the nobility coming to pay their respects or to ask for favors or visit sons and daughters attending the University.

I stared down the road's bending, winding length, shining like a white ribbon in the night, and after a moment I saw a dark shadow moving along it, keeping to the side, but not taking any other precautions. She was not far ahead of me and moving slowly. I guessed her burden must have weighed more than she'd imagined when she started. I was thankful to see that she was still alone, not counting Teddy, of course.

I hastened after her, my way comparatively easy now. She heard my footsteps, when I drew near, and made a halfhearted attempt to increase the speed of her pace, but that didn't last long. Realizing the futility of trying to escape, she stopped and turned to face me. Her extreme pallor made her face ghostly in the starlight; her black eyes beneath their thick brows were bright with anger and defiance. But I saw that she was tired, too, and perhaps a little frightened, and that there was something in her which was glad she was no longer alone.

I caught hold of her arm beneath her cloak and started to draw her into the shadows of the trees that lined the road.

"What are you doing?" she demanded, breaking free.

I pointed to the shadows, then to the gleaming white road, and shook my head.

"He's trying to tell you that we stand out like a mole on the Countess D'Arymple's backside. She had a very white, smooth backside," Teddy added helpfully.

"I don't see what difference it makes," Eliza said petulantly. She held the bear tucked under one arm, the heavy bundle awkwardly in the other hand. "No one is around to notice us, anyway."

"From your mouth to the Almin's ear," said Teddy, which was, more or less, exactly what I had been thinking.

I took hold of Eliza's arm again and this time she allowed me to lead her off that gleaming highway and into the shadows of the trees. She carried the bundle. I did not try to take it from her.

Once in the deep shadows, she dropped the burden on the ground, in a pile of leaves. Then she sank down on a low, crumbling wall and stared at the bundle at her feet.

"I didn't know it would be so heavy," she said. "It didn't seem heavy when I first picked it up. But now it weighs more and more. And it's awkward and difficult to carry."

I pulled out my electronic notebook from the pocket of my jacket; thanking the Almin that I'd put it there earlier, for such had been my haste at departure that I had not thought to bring it along. I typed the words.

The Darksword.

"Yes," said Eliza, looking at what I'd written.

What are you doing with it? Where are you taking it? I asked.

"To the army base," she replied.

I was so astonished, I stared at her and forgot to type.

"My father is wrong," she said in a low, determined voice, looking down at the sword at her feet. "It's not his fault." She defended him loyally, glanced at me defiantly, as if I'd accused him. "You don't know him! If he finds it hard to trust people, can you blame him? Time and again he was betrayed by those he trusted."

It was not quite as simple as that, but I honored her for defending him.

"I'm taking the sword to the army base, to give it to the Border Patrol to take back to Earth. Then people will leave us alone and our lives will be peaceful once more. And when the sword is gone, no one will hurt Father, ever again."

I saw the tears shine in her dark eyes that were looking forward to that life, a life that would be empty for her, isolated and alone on this deserted world. I saw her generous, noble spirit in that moment and I loved her. I could not tell her. It would not be fair to take advantage of her. But silently I pledged my heart and my soul to her service, as I knew in that other life the catalyst had pledged his heart and soul to serve his queen.

How do you know about the army base? I typed.

"I've been there," she said with a smile at my surprise. "Simkin showed me. It was his idea to take the sword there tonight."

She fondled the bear, rubbing his head.

"Oh, no one at the base ever saw me," she said. "I made certain of that. Simkin used his magic to keep me invisible. I would sit on crates and watch the people come and go and listen to them talk. I'd do that for hours, when Mama and Papa thought I was in the library studying." She grinned impishly. "I used to watch the skyships take off, blasting fire and roaring like thunder. Simkin said they were traveling to Earth. I would imagine what it would be like to be on one. Yesterday, when you and Father Saryon came, I thought—"

Her smile faded. Resolutely, she buried her dream. "I was wrong," she said, and started to stand up.

I stopped her. I had a great many questions, mostly concerning Simkin. I thought it extremely odd and perhaps even sinister that he was suggesting giving the Darksword away. But those questions could wait.

The army base is a long distance from here, I told her. *Many miles. You could not reach it tonight or even tomorrow by walking. Certainly not carrying the heavy sword.*

"We weren't planning to walk all the way," she said,

avoiding my eyes. "We can't use the magical routes we normally travel, because of the Darksword destroying the magic. But Simkin said that you . . . um . . . had an air car. We were only going to borrow it. I would have brought it back. I know how they operate. I've even ridden in one before, though no one knew I was there."

So much for Prospero's daughter. The brave new world was old hat to her.

Please come back home, I wrote. *This burden is not your burden. That is why it seems so heavy. It is your father's and he alone can cast it off or choose to carry it. Besides, you could be in danger.*

"What?" She stared at me, amazed and disbelieving. "How? There is no one here beyond the Border but Father Saryon, my parents, and ourselves!"

I did not feel that I could offer adequate explanation. *Come back. Talk to Father Saryon. Besides,* I added, *your mother told us that, by morning, Joram will have had a change of heart. He is reacting out of hurt and anger. When he thinks about things, he will do what is necessary. You shouldn't take that decision away from him.*

"You are right," Eliza said, after a moment's thought. "It was only by accident I found the sword. We missed Papa one afternoon—it was the day after that horrible Smythe-man came. Mama was worried and sent me to look for him. I searched all over and no sign of him. When I finally found him, where do you think he was?"

I shook my head.

"In the chapel," she said. "I came in the door and there he was. He wasn't praying, like I thought at first. He was sitting on the stair beneath the altar and this— the Darksword—was across his knees. He was staring at it as if he hated and loathed it, but yet as if he loved it and was proud of it."

Eliza shivered and drew her cloak more closely around her. I pressed my body a little nearer, to warm her and warm myself both. The picture she painted with her words was not a pleasant one.

"The look on his face frightened me. I was afraid to say anything, because I knew he would be furious. I wanted to leave. I knew I *should* leave, but I couldn't. I sneaked into a little alcove near the door and I watched him. He sat for a long, long time, just staring at the sword. And then he gave a great sigh and shook his head. He wrapped the sword up in this cloth and opened up a little hidden door inside the altar itself. He put the sword in there, inside the altar, and he shut the door and left. I waited until he was gone before I dared move. I felt ashamed. I knew I had seen something I shouldn't have seen. Something that was secret and private to my father. And now he'll know." Her head drooped. "He'll find out I was spying on him. He'll be so terribly disappointed."

Maybe not, I typed. *We'll take the sword back to its hiding place and he'll never realize it was gone.*

"Are you sure that would be right?" she asked me, troubled. "Wouldn't that be lying, in a way?"

The truth will serve no purpose, I wrote, *and only hurt him. Later, when all this is passed, then you can confess to him what you did.*

She liked that. She agreed to return to the Font with me, although she refused to let me carry the sword.

"It is my burden now," she said with a half smile. "At least for a little while."

I was given the honor of carrying Teddy. Trying to ignore the fact that the bear winked its button eye at

me as I took hold of it, I was about to ask Eliza how
long she had known Teddy was Simkin or vice versa,
when suddenly the bear said, in quite a different tone, a
serious alarming tone, "We are not alone."

"What?" Eliza asked, pausing and staring around.
"Who's there? Is it Papa?"

"No, it is not Papa! Keep quiet! Don't move! Don't
even breathe! Too late." Teddy groaned. "They've
heard us."

Silver shimmered in the night. Two figures clad in
silver robes, their faces hooded and masked, were
walking along the highway. They were twenty paces
from us and coming up on us rapidly. Eliza opened her
mouth. I put my fingers on her lips, to warn her to keep
silent. We stood in the shadows, hardly daring to
breathe, as Teddy had cautioned. The figures continued
walking and they came to a halt, right opposite us.
Their faceless faces turned slowly in our direction.

"This is where we heard voices, sir," one was saying, speaking into some sort of communication device.
"They came from somewhere around here. Yes, sir,
we'll check it out."

Eliza shrank close to me. Her free hand clutched
mine. She pressed the Darksword to her body. I put my
arm around her, held fast to her, and thought frantically of what to do if they found us, which it seemed
they must do any moment. Should we make a break for
it? Should we—

"Almin's blood," said Simkin irritably. "It seems I
must get you out of this."

The bear vanished from my hand. A translucent
form, much as if smoke had taken the shape of a young
and foppish nobleman from about the time of Louis
XIV, materialized right in front of the Technomancers.

"Oh, I say! Lovely night for a walk, isn't it?" Simkin languidly waved his orange scarf in the air.

I must give the Technomancers credit. They would have been more than human if they had not been startled by the apparition materializing before them, but they kept amazingly calm. One thrust her hand into the molten fabric of the silver robe, held up a gob of it, and a device shaped itself out of the fabric.

"What is this thing?" asked the other Technomancer, a male by his voice. The faceless head was gazing at Simkin.

"I'm analyzing it now," the woman replied.

"Analyzing me? With that?" Simkin cast the device a scathing glance and smiled smugly. He seemed to find the entire idea hilarious. "What does it say I am? Spirit? Specter? Spook? Ghost? Ghoul? Wraith? I know—doppelganger! No, better yet. Poltergeist."

He sidled around, craned his head to try to get a look at the device. "Perhaps I'm not here at all. Perhaps you're hallucinating. Sleep deprivation. A bad acid trip. Or maybe you're going mad." He appeared eager to help.

"Residual magic," the woman reported. Snapping shut the device, she slid it back into the robe, which seemed to swallow it whole. "We postulated that there are likely to be pockets of leftover magic all over Thimhallan."

"Residual magic!" Simkin quivered, his voice cracked with outrage. He could barely speak for his emotion. "Me! Simkin! The darling of Kings, the play toy of Emperors! Me! Magical leftovers! Like some damn moldy sandwich!"

The Technomancer was reporting in again.

"The voices checked out, sir. Nothing to worry

about. Residual magic. A substanceless phantasm, possibly an Echo. We were warned about such. It poses no threat."

He paused a moment, listening, then said, "Yes, sir."

"Our orders?" the woman asked.

"Continue. The other teams are on site and advancing."

"What do we do with this thing?" The woman gestured at Simkin. "It has a voice. It could warn the subject."

"Unlikely," the man responded. "Echoes mindlessly repeat words they've heard others speak. They mimic, like parrots, and like parrots, sometimes give the illusion of appearing intelligent."

I cannot describe the look on Simkin's face. His eyes bulged, his mouth opened and shut. Perhaps for the first time in his life—which, considering that he was probably immortal, had certainly been a long one—he was struck dumb.

The man started to walk on. The woman was more dubious. Her silver face was turned toward Simkin.

He hung in the air, appearing more nebulous than when he had first taken shape; a wisp of smoke and orange silk that looked as if it could be puffed away in a breath.

"I think we should disrupt it," the woman said.

"Against orders," the man returned. "Someone might see the flash and raise the alarm. Remember, those damn *Duuk-tsarith* are around here, too."

"I suppose you are right," the woman agreed charily.

The two walked on, moving at a rapid pace up the highway toward the Font.

Eliza and I kept still, waiting until they were out of earshot and beyond. I hushed Eliza when she would have spoken, for I could see by the Technomancers' swift and easy movement that they had some sort of night vision and I was afraid they might have technologies which enhanced their hearing, as well.

When they had disappeared, going down a dip in the highway, I moved cautiously to where I could get a better view. I guessed from their words what was going forward, but I needed to see it for myself.

Here and there across the hillside, figures, shining silver in the lambent light, formed a cordon around the Font, moving inexorably toward it, closing in.

"Who are they? What are they?" Eliza demanded.

"Evil," I signed, and she needed no translation.

"They've come for the Darksword, haven't they?" she asked fearfully.

I nodded and recalled the glowing listening devices in the living room.

"Would they . . ." She had to pause to find the courage to speak. "Would they *kill* to get it?"

I nodded again, reluctantly.

"They won't believe Papa when he says he doesn't have the sword," Eliza said, thinking through the scenario, as I was myself. "They'll think he's lying, trying to keep it from them. If we give it to them, perhaps they'll leave us alone. We must take it back! We'll use the shortcut."

I agreed. I could see no other way. But it occurred to me that even taking the shortcut, burdened as we were with the heavy sword and forced to keep to the shadows, we would arrive long after the Technomancers had stormed the building.

Simkin! Simkin could warn Joram, could tell him that we had the sword and we were bringing it back.

I turned to see the diaphanous figure floating over

the highway. The words *residual magic* blew hot against my face, like a dry desert wind.

"No threat? Well, we'll see about that!" cried Simkin. "Merlyn? Merlyn, where are you? Never around when you might be of the slightest use, of course. The old fool!" and with that, he was gone.

CHAPTER FIFTEEN

*"Your fool is here to save you from your folly.
Rather a nice ring to that. I must remember it."*

~SIMKIN; *DOOM OF THE DARKSWORD*

I hoped that Simkin had read my thoughts and was gone to alert Joram and the others to their danger. Capricious and erratic as I knew Simkin to be, however, my hope was a forlorn one. And I did not think it likely we could count on Merlyn—with a *y* or an *i*—to save us.

"Hurry!" urged Eliza, taking my hand and drawing me back among the trees. "This way is faster! Through the fields."

We had to cross the wall, not difficult, as it was low to the ground. Eliza was hampered by her long skirt and her cloak, and needed both her hands to climb over. She hesitated only a moment, looking into my eyes, then she handed me the Darksword, wrapped in its cloth blanket.

I knew immediately what she'd meant about the physical burden of the sword. The sword's weight was considerable, for it was made of iron, mixed with dark-stone, and had been designed to be wielded by a grown man with immense physical strength. But as heavy as the sword was to carry, it weighed far more heavily on the heart than it did on the hands. Holding it, I glimpsed the soul that had produced it—a dark maelstrom of fear and anger.

Bitter lessons learned, Joram had struggled up from the darkness of his soul, saved himself from drowning beneath the perilous waters. He had returned the original Darksword to the stone from which it was made. He had released magic into the universe. And though he had destroyed a world, he had saved the lives of many thousands who would otherwise have perished in the great war Earth waged for Thimhallan. If Joram did not walk in the light, at least he could feel the sun upon his upturned face.

The Darksword had passed out of his life.

Through anger and fear, it had been reforged.

Eliza climbed over the wall. Turning, she held out her hands. I gave the Darksword back to her and the biblical quote about the sins of the fathers came to mind.

We trudged up a long, grass-covered slope, moving cautiously, keeping watch in all directions for the silver-shining Technomancers. We didn't see any; probably—I said to myself—because they are already nearing their goal. We did not make very good time. Clouds moved in, hiding the stars, thickening the darkness, and making it difficult to find our way.

We reached the crest of the hill. Not far from us, I could barely make out the scattered white rocks which marked the trail. I was already winded and Eliza, keeping up gamely, was breathing heavily from the exertion of climbing and carrying the sword. I gazed at the trail in despair. It had not seemed so steep or so long, coming down. Tired as we were, I wondered how we would manage, even without the sword.

I turned to Eliza and saw my dismay reflected on her pale face. Her shoulders and arms must have been burning with fatigue. The point of the sword dropped to the rocky ground, hitting it with a metallic thunk.

"We have to keep going," she said, and it was not me she was exhorting to further effort but herself.

I was about to offer to take the sword, to give her rest, when a concussive blast rocked the land. The ground shuddered beneath our feet. The blast echoed among the mountains and then finally died away.

"What was that?" Eliza gasped.

I had no idea. Though storms raged in the valley below us, that sound had not been thunder. It was too sharp and I had seen no lightning. I looked up toward the Font, terrified of seeing fire and smoke erupt from the building.

Logic eased my fear. The Technomancers would never destroy the Font if they could not find the sword.

The blast and the concern it brought lent us strength. Eliza and I resumed our climb when, for a second time, a strange sound caused us to halt. This was nearer and more frightening—the sound of footfalls, coming from very close behind us.

We were caught out in the open, with no cover. We lacked the strength to run and would not have been able to run far, in any case, hampered as we were by the heavy sword.

Eliza heard the steps the same moment I did. We both turned, and such are the incongruities of the mind that my first thought was one of relief. At least, if the Technomancers captured us, I wouldn't have to climb that damn hill!

The person was a dark shadow against the backdrop of the trees, so dark that I couldn't distinguish features. At least, I thought, my heart resuming its beat, the person was *not* clad in silver.

"Wait there a moment, Reuven and Eliza, will you?" called a clear voice, a woman's voice.

The woman materialized out of the night, and as she came to us she flicked on a flashlight and played it swiftly over us.

We blinked painfully in the harsh light, averted our faces, and she switched the flashlight off us and played it down around her feet.

"What do you want?" Eliza asked, her voice strong and unafraid. "Why do you stop us?"

"Because," answered the woman, "you should not return home. There's nothing you can do to help, and much you might do to harm. By great good fortune, the Darksword has been kept out of their hands. It would be folly to cast away this opportunity."

"Who are you?" Eliza asked coldly, keeping both hands around the sword's blanket-covered hilt.

The woman stood before us, held the light on herself so that we could get a good look at her. Of all the strange sights we'd seen that night, this woman seemed the strangest, the most incongruous.

She was wearing military-style fatigues and a green flight jacket. Her hair was cut very short, almost a crew cut. Her eyes were overlarge, her cheekbones strong, her jaw and chin jutting, her mouth wide. She was tall—over six feet—and muscular and her age was difficult to guess. Older than I was, by perhaps ten years. Nine tiny earrings, in the shape of suns, moons, stars, glittered up and down her left ear. Her nose was pierced and so was her right eyebrow. She could have stepped out of some bar in Soho.

The woman fumbled in a zippered pocket, pulled out something. She flicked the light on it, snapped open a well-worn leather case, and exhibited an ID card. The light was so bright that I couldn't read the card very well and she moved the light off the card again almost immediately. She was an agent of something, or at least that's what I think the card read, but I wasn't clear on what.

"It doesn't matter. You've never heard of the people I work for," she said. "We're a very low-profile organization."

"I have to go back," Eliza said, her gaze going up the mountainside, straining to see her home through the darkness. "My father and mother and Father Saryon are there alone. And without the sword, they're in danger."

"They'd be in worse danger *with* the sword. There's nothing you can do, Eliza," said the woman quietly.

"How do you know my name?" Eliza regarded the woman with suspicion. "And Reuven's. You knew his name, too."

"Our agency has files on both of you. Don't be upset. We have files on everyone. My name's Scylla," the woman continued.

CIA, I thought, or maybe Interpol. FBI or Her Majesty's Secret Service. Some sort of government agency. It's strange, for I had always been extremely cynical about the government, but as we stood in the darkness the thought that some immense and powerful organization was looking after us was rather comforting.

"Look, do we really have time for all this?" Scylla was saying. "You should take the sword to a place of safety."

"Yes," said Eliza. "A place of safety. That's with my father. I'm going home." She lifted the sword, or at least tried to lift it. It appeared heavier than ever.

Scylla gazed at Eliza, measuring her, perhaps; trying to determine if she was serious. A glance at Eliza's pale, rigid, and resolute face could leave no doubt, as Scylla herself must have seen.

"Look, if you're set on this, my air car's not far back," she said. "I'll drive you there. It will be faster."

Eliza was tempted. I don't think she could have carried that sword another three feet, though she would have made the attempt until she dropped down on top of it. And she was desperate to reach her father and mother. I was desperate to reach Father Saryon. I nodded my head.

"Very well," Eliza answered grudgingly.

Scylla gave me an approving clap on my shoulder that knocked me two or three paces back down the hillside. I had the feeling she had done that deliberately, to prove her strength, to intimidate us. She turned and left, running at an easy lope toward the highway, her flashlight guiding her steps.

Eliza and I stood alone in the darkness that was beginning to lighten. It was near dawn, I realized in amazement.

"We could leave, before she comes back," Eliza said.

It was a statement of fact, nothing more. Yes, we could leave. But we wouldn't. We were both too tired, the sword was too heavy, our fear and anxiety too great. We didn't have long to wait. The air car appeared, a blot against the night.

The car soared over the wall, over the trees alongside the highway. It slid quiet as a whisper through the air toward us. When it was near us, Scylla lowered the car to the ground.

"Climb in," she said, twisting around to open the back door.

We did so, bringing the Darksword with us. Settled in the backseat, Eliza placed the sword across both our knees and held on to it, to keep it from sliding off. I was uncomfortable, holding the sword. The touch of it was disquieting, unnerving, as if there were a leech on my skin, sucking out my blood. I had the feeling it was drawing something out of me, something that, before now, I wasn't even aware I possessed. I wanted to be rid of the sword, yet I could not cast it off, not without losing Eliza's trust and respect. If she could bear its incubus touch, then so could I, for her sake.

Scylla sent the air car into a steep climb and we sped up the hill, traveling smooth and fleet as the wind. Eliza stared fixedly out the front window, straining to see her home.

We approached the garden, then the building came in sight. Scylla cut the air car's engines. It hovered noiselessly above the garden wall near the spot where I'd fallen while trying to climb over.

I don't know what I'd expected—anything from the building surrounded by Technomancers to flames leaping from the roof. What I had not expected was to find the building dark and quiet and seemingly as peaceful as when I'd left.

The air car crept forward, drifting over the white flowers with their heavy, drooping heads. The car came to rest not far from the back door.

"There's no one here!" Eliza exclaimed, clasping my hand in her excitement. "They didn't come! Or maybe we're ahead of them! Open the door, Reuven!"

My hand was on the button.

"They've been here," said Scylla. "They've been and gone. It's over."

"You're wrong!" Eliza cried. "How do you know? You can't know. . . . Reuven, open this door!"

She was frantic. I hit the button. The door swung open. Eliza slid out. She turned to retrieve the Darksword, which I was still holding.

"You should leave the sword hidden in the car," Scylla advised, climbing out. "It will be safe here. You'll need it later—for bargaining."

"Bargaining . . ." Eliza repeated the word, licked dry lips.

I slid across the seat, out from under the sword. Even in my worry and fear, I was relieved to be free of its loathsome touch. Eliza stared suspiciously at Scylla, then made a grab for the sword's hilt.

"If I leave it, you'll take it!" she said, struggling to lift the Darksword.

Scylla shrugged. "I can take the sword anytime I want." Hands on her hips, she smiled at us and her smile seemed menacing. "I don't think you two could do much to stop me."

Eliza and I looked at each other and reluctantly we acknowledged the truth. Neither of us was in any shape to battle this woman, although, I recalled, I had not seen her carrying a weapon, either on her person or in the air car.

"But I don't want it," Scylla continued. She slammed shut the car door on her side. To my astonishment, she tossed me the keys.

"What *do* you want?" Eliza demanded.

"Ah, now that's a bit more difficult to explain," Scylla replied.

Turning on her heel, she walked across the garden, leaving us with keys to the air car. We could do what we pleased with the Darksword.

I drew out my electronic notepad, typed swiftly.

The Technomancers could be waiting for us inside! Leave the sword here.

"Do you trust her?" Eliza asked me, agonized.

Maybe, I hedged. *What she said makes sense. She could have taken the sword from us back there on the highway. It would have been like taking candy from two babies.*

"I hope you're right," Eliza said fervently. She shut the door and I locked it. The Darksword, wrapped in its cloth, lay on the backseat of the air car.

I, for one, was glad to be rid of it. I felt stronger, my weariness eased. I was more hopeful. Eliza also seemed relieved to be rid of the burden. We hastened after Scylla and reached her just as she was entering the door through which I'd come out.

The hallway was dark and silent. Perhaps it was my overwrought imagination, but the silence had a chill feel to it. It was not the blessed silence of a house asleep. It was the silence of a house that is empty. A tinge of smoke hung in the air. We came to my room. The door was partially open and I distinctly remembered having shut it when I left.

I stepped to the door, looked inside, and stood, transfixed.

The bed had been ripped open by what appeared to be giant claws. Long slashes cut through the mattress. Gouts of feathers lay in heaps on the floor. My knapsack had been torn apart, my clothes strewn about the room. My other possessions—shaving kit, comb, brush—were scattered everywhere.

"You see," said Scylla. "They were searching for the Darksword."

Despair robbed me of breath. I ran to Saryon's room. Eliza stood dazed in the hall, staring with disbelief at the destruction.

The door to my master's room was wide open. His bed had been torn apart as well, his possessions trampled and flung about. He was *not* there, though whether that was good or bad, I didn't know.

With a wild and incoherent cry, Eliza ran down the hallway, heading for the main living quarters. I followed after her, adrenaline pumping, sparking my tired legs to exertion.

Scylla, shaking her head in sorrow, followed more slowly behind.

We reached the door leading to the warming room. Eliza gave a moan, as if she'd been struck, and her body sagged. I was there to catch her, hold her, support her, though it was all I could do to support myself. I was sick with horror.

Dawn's light filtered through the window, filtered through a faint and rapidly dissipating haze of smoke. Recalling the blast, my first thought was that a bomb had exploded. The floor was strewn with the wreckage of shattered, smoldering furniture. The curtains had been torn from the windows; the glass was cracked and broken. Beyond the warming room, in the kitchen, the table had been overturned. Chairs were smashed.

"Father! Mother!" Eliza called.

Coughing in the smoke, she pushed me away and started toward the door opposite, the door which led to her parents' rooms.

A figure, clad in black robes, took shape and form from the smoke. Eliza halted, appalled and frightened.

"You won't find them," he said. "They are gone."

"What have you done with them?" Eliza cried.

The man cast his hood from his face and I recognized Mosiah. He folded his hands together before him. "I did not take them. I tried to stop the Technomancers, but there were too many of them." He turned his face to me. "They took Father Saryon as well, Reuven. I am sorry."

I could make no response. My hands hung limp at my sides. On the floor, near the hem of Mosiah's black robe, was a smear of blood. I dreaded lest Eliza should see it. Moving close to Mosiah, I shoved a broken chair over the stain. But either I was too late or else Eliza read my thoughts.

"Are they all right?" she demanded, confronting Mosiah. "Were they hurt?"

Mosiah hesitated, before reluctantly replying, "Your father was injured."

"Very . . . very badly?" Eliza faltered.

"I am afraid so. But Father Saryon is with him. I don't think your mother was harmed."

"You don't *think*! Don't you know?" Eliza cried. Her voice broke; she coughed again. The smoke stung our throats, brought tears to the eyes. Both of us were coughing—but not Mosiah.

"No. I do not know for certain what happened to your mother," he replied. "It was all very confused. At least, they did not find what they sought. They did not find the Darksword. You were wise to take it away." Mosiah's gaze went from me to Eliza. His eyes narrowed, his voice softened. "Where is it?"

"Safe," answered Scylla, emerging from the shadows of the hallway.

Mosiah's head jerked. "Who the devil are you?"

"Scylla," she replied, as if that were all anyone needed to know. She strode into the room, glanced around. Again she showed her ID card.

Mosiah took a good look at it. His brow wrinkled. "I've never heard of this organization. Are you part of the CIA?"

"If I were, I couldn't tell you now, could I?" Scylla said, putting away the card. "I thought you *Duuk-tsarith* were standing guard on Joram. What happened? Take the night off?"

Mosiah was angry. His lips tightened. "We did not expect them to attack Joram. Why should they, when it was probable they were going to get what they wanted?"

"Ah, but they knew they weren't," Scylla said. "Kevon Smythe once paid a visit here. He sat in that very chair, or what's left of it. Does that give you a hint?"

"A listening device! Of course." Mosiah was grim. "We should have foreseen the possibility. They knew, then, that Joram had refused to relinquish the sword." He regarded Scylla with suspicion. "You know a lot about the *D'karn-darah*."

"I know a lot about you, too," Scylla retorted. "That doesn't make me *Duuk-tsarith*."

"You're from the government?"

"In a manner of speaking. Let's lay our cards on the table. I can't talk about the work I do any more than you can talk about the work you do. You don't trust me. I accept that. I'll work to correct your mistake. I trust you, but then I've read your file." Scylla regarded him with increased interest. "You're much better-looking than your file photo. What happened here?"

Mosiah appeared somewhat taken aback by this direct approach, though I could see he wasn't pleased with that reference to his file.

"General Boris sent you," he said.

"I know the General. A good man." Scylla smiled. "What happened?"

"It was all over in a matter of moments, too fast for me to summon help." Mosiah's voice was cold, perhaps to keep from sounding defensive. "I was alone, standing watch unseen, remaining hidden in the corridors, as was our custom, so as not to disturb Joram and his family."

"And where were the rest of the *Duuk-tsarith*?" Scylla asked. "You might have been left alone on guard duty, but I know you weren't alone here in the Font."

Mosiah's face darkened. He did not reply. I knew the answer to that question well enough, as I'm sure Eliza did, though she was only now gradually coming to understand. The other *Duuk-tsarith* had been searching for the Darksword. They knew as well as the Technomancers that Joram had refused to give it up. I thought of all these dread forces, with their dread powers, mundane and arcane, searching for the sword, and of Eliza and me, in our innocence, walking off with it, snatching it out from under their very noses. A shiver crept over me. I had guessed we might be in some danger. I had never realized how great. They needed Joram and the Darksword. The rest of us were expendable.

"And so the other *Duuk-tsarith* were off on a little treasure hunt of their own, leaving you alone to stand guard. What made them think—wait! I know." Scylla glanced toward Eliza. "The Darksword had been moved. You sensed its absence, though you could not detect its presence. Very well. You were alone. And then the Technomancers came."

"Yes, they came," said Mosiah curtly. "There is not

much to tell after that." He spoke to Eliza, ignored Scylla pointedly, which seemed to afford her mild amusement. "I never thought I'd say this, but we have that fool Simkin to thank for giving us as much warning as we had."

Eliza and I exchanged glances. "I knew it," she said softly, so that only I heard her.

"Joram could not sleep," Mosiah continued. "He had been out walking, down by the sheep, and had just returned. Your mother was waiting up for him. They spoke together. I left them alone," he said in answer to Eliza's accusing look. "I did not intrude on their privacy. Perhaps, if I had been there . . ." He shrugged.

"It would have made no difference," Scylla said quietly.

"I suppose not. I was here in the warming room when I heard Joram cry out the word *Simkin!* I returned, still inside the magical Corridors, to find what looked like a watered-down version of Simkin waving that ridiculous orange scarf of his and going on about Joram coming under attack from a horde of silver saltshakers or something equally nonsensical, although I must admit that pretty well describes the *D'karn-darah*.

"I guessed what was happening and sent out a warning to my brethren. Joram blazed like fire and left the room. I started to follow, when the *D'karn-darah* stormed the house. It was then I made a mistake."

Mosiah gazed at us steadily. "I thought . . . Well, you'll see. Joram had left the room. Where else would he go, but after the Darksword? The one weapon which would protect him and Gwendolyn—"

"Oh!" Eliza gave a smothered cry, covered her mouth with her hand. "Oh, no!"

"Don't blame yourself, Eliza," Scylla said quickly.

"There was nothing your father could have done. They would have captured him and the Darksword and all would have been at an end. At least now there is hope."

But Eliza was not comforted.

Mosiah was talking, reliving the event, as if trying to figure out what had gone wrong. "I *knew* he had gone after the Darksword! When he came back almost immediately without it, what was I to think?"

"You thought he was deliberately keeping it hidden, refusing to use it even in his own defense," Scylla said.

"Yes!" Mosiah was frustrated, angry. "I revealed myself to him. He recognized me and he didn't seem all that surprised to see me. We didn't have much time. I could hear the *D'karn-darah* coming. I asked him to give me the Darksword. 'I'll take it away!' I promised him. 'I'll keep it safe!' "

"How could you?" Scylla asked. "Its null-magic would have destroyed the Corridors."

"We had designed a special sheath for it," Mosiah said. "Once the Darksword was inside this sheath, we could have transported it easily. Joram refused, of course. He wouldn't give me the sword. I thought . . . I thought he was being stubborn, as usual. I didn't know that he *couldn't* give me the sword. I didn't know then that he knew or guessed who had taken it."

Mosiah raised his head, looked at Eliza. "If he had trusted me. If he had told me the truth—I know. Why should he? It was obvious at that point that I'd been spying on him.

"After that, there's not much to tell. Within moments three *D'karn-darah* entered the bedroom. We could hear more inside the other parts of the house. Then another came to us, dragging Father Saryon. He was all right," Mosiah reassured me, and he smiled slightly. "He is a tough one, Reuven. The first thing the good father said when he saw us was, 'Don't give it to them, Joram!'

"The *D'karn-darah* demanded the Darksword. Joram refused. They told him to give them the sword or he would see those he loved suffer. They had seized hold of Gwendolyn. What was Joram to do? He couldn't give them the sword even if he had wanted to, because he didn't have it.

" 'Take me.' He tried to bargain with them. 'Let my wife and Father Saryon go. Take me and I'll tell you where the sword is hidden.'

"I doubt if they would have ever agreed to such a bargain, not when they held all the cards, but we'll never know. At that moment a teddy bear, which had been lying on the bed, flew up and struck the *D'karn-darah* who was holding Gwen captive."

"Good old Simkin," Scylla said, smiling.

"Yes, good old Simkin," Mosiah echoed dryly. "The *D'karn-darah* was taken by surprise, as you can well imagine. The bear struck the Technomancer on the forehead. The blow was not a hard one, but it rocked her back on her feet. In her astonishment, she let go of Gwen. The bear continued to pummel the *D'karn-darah*, smacking her on the face, buffeting her head, and eventually ended by clamping himself over her nose and mouth. He appeared to be trying to smother her. At that moment Gwendolyn disappeared."

"Disappeared?" Eliza repeated, bewildered. "What do you mean—disappeared? Did my mother run away? What happened to her?"

"I don't know," Mosiah said, angry at himself, at his own impotence. "If I did, I would tell you. She vanished. One moment Gwen was there. The next she was gone. I thought at first that perhaps some of my people had taken her into the Corridors, but later investigation revealed that they knew nothing of what happened to her.

"But Joram thought the worst. He assumed the *D'karn-darah* had taken Gwen. He went wild with rage, flung himself bare-handed at the *D'karn-darah*. He caught them off guard. They had not been expecting an attack by a stuffed toy, nor one of their hostages to disappear. Joram's lunge carried two of them to the floor. I took out the fourth."

Mosiah smiled grimly. "You'll find a charred spot on the bedroom floor. By that time, however, more *D'karn-darah* arrived. They subdued Joram . . . and took him away."

"Subdued him," Eliza said, noting that Mosiah had averted his gaze once more. "How? Tell me. What did they do to my father?"

"Tell her," Scylla said. "She needs to understand the nature of the enemy against which we fight."

Mosiah shrugged. "Very well. They struck Joram over the head, dazing him. Then they inserted the needles. You may have read of a practice known as acupuncture. Needles are inserted into specific areas of the body to produce regional anesthesia. The *D'karn-darah* have developed the reverse. Each needle is charged with electromagic. The stimulus it produces in the body is extraordinarily painful and debilitating. The pain is only temporary, however, and goes away when the needles are removed. But until then, a person is reduced to a state of helpless agony. When Joram was sufficiently subdued, they took him away. Father Saryon demanded to be allowed to accompany him, and of course, they were grateful to have an extra hostage."

"You escaped," said Scylla.

"There was nothing I could do," Mosiah returned coldly. "I risked being captured myself and they have no reason to keep me alive. I deemed that I could be more useful surviving to fight them than throwing away my life needlessly."

Eliza had gone very pale during the description of her father's torment, but she stood strong and quiet. "What happened to my mother?" she asked, her voice quavering only slightly. She was fighting hard to remain under control.

"I don't know," Mosiah confessed. "If I had to guess, I would say that the *D'karn-darah* took her. But, if so . . ." He appeared thoughtful, then shrugged helplessly. "I don't know."

"Do *you* know?" Eliza turned to Scylla.

"Me? How could I know?" Scylla demanded, astonished that she was even asked. "I wasn't there. I wish I had been, though." She looked quite grim.

"Well, what do we do now?" Eliza was calm, very calm, much too calm. Her hands were clenched together, the fingers twined tightly, the knuckles white.

"We wait," said Mosiah.

"Wait! Wait for what?"

"We must wait for them to contact us," said Mosiah.

"To tell us where to bring the Darksword," Scylla added. "To make the exchange. The Darksword for your father's life."

"And I will give it to them," Eliza said.

"No," said Mosiah. "You will not."

CHAPTER SIXTEEN

"Now the game begins in earnest."

—SIMKIN; *FORGING THE DARKSWORD*

"I *will* give it to them," Eliza countered. "You won't stop me. I should never have taken the Darksword in the first place. What they do with it doesn't matter—"

"It does," said Mosiah. "They will use it to enslave a world."

"My father's life is all that matters," Eliza maintained stubbornly.

She swayed where she stood. She was exhausted, her strength almost gone. There was nowhere to sit down; every piece of furniture in the room had been smashed.

Scylla put her arm around the young woman, gave her a bracing hug.

"I know it all looks very bleak now, Eliza, but things are not as bad as they seem. We'll feel better for a cup of tea. Reuven, find something for us to sit on."

She did not speak the instruction aloud. She signed the words to me! Smiling, she quirked her pierced eyebrow as much as to say, *See, I do know you!*

Of course. All that would be in my "file." Once I was over my astonishment, I left the room in search of chairs. And I felt better, having a task to perform. I had to go to distant and long-unused parts of the building to find any furniture that was still intact. Surely the *D'karn-darah* could not imagine that they would find the Darksword hidden in a straight-backed wooden chair, but that's how it appeared. The destruction was wanton and cruel and seemed, to my mind, to have been the result of fury and frustration over not finding what they sought rather than of any true hope of discovery.

If this is what they do to objects, what will they do to people? I asked myself, and the thought was chilling.

I found no chairs, but I did come across several short wooden stools from one of the lower level rooms which must have, I think, been used as a classroom for children. I do not know how the Technomancers missed this room, except that it stood at an odd angle off a corridor and would have been in pitch-darkness during the night.

As I picked up one of the stools I noticed, even in my weariness, how it had been crafted out of a single piece of wood. Crafted by magic, held together by magic, which prohibited the use of nails or glue. The wood had not been cut, but lovingly shaped and coaxed into taking the form the creator wanted.

I rubbed my hand over the smooth wood and suddenly, inexplicably, tears came to my eyes. I wept for the loss, for all the losses—the loss of my master, the loss of Joram and Gwendolyn, the loss of their daughter's peaceful, serene way of life, the loss of Thimhallan, the loss of such simple beauty as I held in my hands, the loss of that other life of my own, the life of which I'd had such tantalizing glimpses.

I startled myself, for I am not given to tears and sobbing. I don't believe that I had cried since I was a child. I was half-ashamed of myself, when I finally forced myself to quit, but the outburst of emotion had done me good, acting like a release valve. I felt calmer and oddly rested, more capable of handling whatever might come.

Picking up four stools, slinging the rungs over my arms, I returned to the main living quarters.

I found I had not been the only one working. The smoldering furniture had been carried outdoors, either by Mosiah or his magic. The smoke was clearing from the room, blown away on a crisp morning breeze. A fire crackled in the fireplace. Water was heating in a kettle which, though dented, had survived the destruction. Scylla was scooping loose tea leaves into a cracked pot. Eliza was sorting through broken crockery, searching for any cups that might have escaped intact. She looked up at me with a wan smile when I entered. She, too, was better for having something to do.

Lifting one half of a large broken platter, she found Teddy lying beneath it.

The bear was in a sorry state. One arm was completely ripped off, one button eye missing. His right leg hung by a thread, his stuffing dribbled out of torn seams. His orange scarf was bedraggled and singed.

"Poor Teddy!" Eliza said, and taking the maltreated bear in her arms, she began to sob.

She had borne up bravely until that moment. That was her release valve.

Mosiah, with a wry smile, seemed about to say something, but Scylla forestalled him with a look and a shake of her head. Mosiah certainly wasn't taking orders from Scylla and would have gone on to have his say, except that even he could see this wasn't the time.

I longed to comfort Eliza, but I felt myself in an awkward position. I had only known her a day and a night—a traumatic day and night, to be sure, but that wasn't really relevant. Her grief was hers alone, and there was really nothing I could say or do to ease it.

I set down the stools near the fire. Mosiah walked over to gaze out the window, his black robes leaving a sinuous trail in the ash on the floor. Scylla poured water from the kettle into the teapot. By this time Eliza had dried her tears.

"I'll sew him back together," she said, using the sleeve of her shirt to wipe her eyes.

"Don't bother," came a weak voice. "I'm done for. Finished. Kaput. The sands of my hourglass are running low. My goose is cooked. My stuffing left to be nibbled by mice. What happened? Did we win? Is your dear father safe, child? That's all that matters. If so, my life has not been spent in vain. Tell me, before I slip away to meet my Maker—"

"He'd only throw you back," Mosiah said shortly. Leaving the window, he came to stare grimly down at Teddy. "Don't fret over this fool, Eliza. Simkin is immortal. And a very bad actor."

"So this is Simkin," said Scylla, joining them. She stood over him, her hands on her hips. "You were my favorite character in Reuven's books, you know."

Teddy gazed up at her with his one remaining button eye.

"Pardon me, madam," he said stiffly, "but I don't believe we have been introduced."

"I'm Scylla," she answered, and handed me a cup of tea.

Perhaps it was my fatigued imagination, but at the sound of that name, Teddy's black button eye glittered in the firelight and stared very hard at Scylla.

"Put me together again, will you? There's a dear child." Teddy spoke to Eliza, but he continued staring at Scylla.

"Put yourself together, fool!" Mosiah said irritably. "Let Eliza alone."

"No, I don't mind," Eliza said.

She found her mother's workbasket, tossed into a corner, and though her lips tightened a moment when she picked up the basket and its scattered contents, she retained control over herself. Sitting down on the stool, she took the amputee bear into her lap and restuffed him, then began to stitch his arm on.

Teddy smirked insufferably, when Eliza was not looking, and made such suggestive noises—particularly when she was poking the stuffing back into him—that I could have cheerfully torn him apart again. But his foolery ceased whenever his black-button gaze fell on Scylla.

We sat down on the short-legged stools, drew them near the fire. Eliza sipped her tea and sewed up Teddy.

"How long will we have to wait?" she asked, trying to sound calm.

"Not long," Mosiah replied.

"According to General Boris's scouting reports, the Hch'nyv will be within attacking range of Earth and Thimhallan within forty-eight hours," Scylla said.

"The Technomancers must have the Darksword away from here and back on Earth before then," Mosiah added.

Eliza glanced at me and a faint flush stained her cheek. "So these . . . aliens really are a threat? It's not a trick? They would really kill us all?"

"Without hesitation. Without compunction. Without pity or mercy," Scylla replied, grave and somber. "*We* have found no level on which we can communicate with them, although it is rumored that others have."

"The Technomancers have made contact," said Mosiah. "That much we know. We fear that Smythe has made some sort of deal with them."

Forty-eight hours. Not very much time. No one spoke, but each sat silent, absorbed in his or her own thoughts. Mine were very black and despairing. And, as if conjured up from the darkness of the mind, the smoke, and the fire, an image took shape and form upon the hearth.

Kevon Smythe stood before us.

"Don't be afraid," Mosiah said swiftly. "It is a hologram."

It was well he said this, for the image appeared very real, not watery, as do many holograms. I would have sworn that the man himself stood before us. It must be the magic of the Technomancers, which so enhanced the electronically created image.

"I have read of such things!" Eliza gasped. "But I have never seen one. Can he . . . can he hear us?"

She asked this because Scylla had her finger to her lips and she, along with Mosiah, was hunting for the source of the hologram. Finding it—a small boxlike object tucked into a recess in the fireplace—they both examined it, both careful not to touch it. They exchanged glances—the first time, I believe, they had looked at each other directly—and Mosiah, nodding his head, drew his hood over his face and clasped his hands together.

Eliza stood up. Teddy slid, forgotten, from her lap. When he looked as if he was about to protest, I set my foot upon him and kicked him backward, none too gently, underneath my stool.

If I had not admired Eliza before now, I would have done so then. She was exhausted, frightened, grieving, anxious. She was well aware that this was the man who was responsible for the abduction of her parents and Father Saryon. Yet she faced him with the dignified reserve of a Queen who knows that any overt show of anger will only demean herself and never faze her enemy.

When I look back on that moment in memory, I see her clothed in gold, shining more brightly than the paltry light of the hologram of the Technomancer. She did not beg or plead, knowing both those to be fruitless. She asked of him what she might have asked of any base intruder.

"What do you want, sir?"

He was not wearing his suit, but was clad in white robes that I later learned were the ceremonial robes of the Khandic Sages. Around the sleeves and hem and neck were laid out in a grid pattern tiny filaments of metal, which glinted and winked as they caught the light. I thought at the time they were merely fanciful decoration.

Kevon Smythe smiled his ingratiating smile. "Since you come so swiftly to the point, mistress, I will myself be brief. Your father is with us. He is our guest. He has come with us voluntarily, because he knows our need is great. He left home in haste and unfortunately neglected to bring with him an object of which he is quite fond. That object is the Darksword. Its absence distresses him greatly. He fears it could fall into the wrong hands and cause inestimable harm. He would like to have it safely back in his possession. If you tell us where to find the Darksword, Mistress Eliza, we will secure it and deliver it to your father."

Half of me believed him. I knew the truth. I had seen the wreckage, the destruction, I had seen the blood on the floor. He was so persuasive that I saw, in my mind, exactly what he wanted me to see—Joram, concerned, willingly going with them. I was certain Eliza must believe him. Mosiah thought so, too, apparently, for he glided forward, prepared to confront the Technomancer. Scylla did not move, but watched Eliza.

"I want to see my father and mother," Eliza said.

"I am sorry, mistress, that is not possible," said Smythe. "Your father had a long journey and he is fatigued, plus being most anxious over the fate of the Darksword. He fears for your safety, my dear. The blade is sharp, the sword unwieldy. You might cut yourself. Tell us where to find it and perhaps, by that time, your father will have recovered sufficiently to be able to talk to you."

His smooth voice and benign manner slid over his threats like a silken scarf.

"Sir," Eliza stated calmly, "you lie. Your minions took my father and mother and Father Saryon by force. Then they destroyed our home, searching for the object which my father would never give to you, so long as he lived. And the same may be said of his daughter. If that is all you came for, you have my leave to go."

Kevon Smythe's expression softened. He seemed truly grieved. "It is not my place to chastise you, mistress, but your father will not like to hear of your re-

fusal. He will be angry with you and will punish you
for your disobedience. He has warned me that you are
sometimes a willful, stubborn child. We have his au-
thorization to take the sword from you by force, if that
becomes necessary."

Eliza's lashes were wet with tears, but she maintained her control. "You do not know my father if you
think he would say such a thing. You do not know me
if you think I would believe it. Get out."

Kevon Smythe shook his head resignedly, then
shifted his head to gaze at me. "Reuven, it is good to
see you again, though, I regret to say, under sad circumstances. It seems that Father Saryon has been af-
flicted with a terrible disease, which will cause his
death unless he receives prompt treatment back on
Earth. Our physicians give him thirty-six hours to live.
You know the good father, Reuven. He will not leave
without Joram and Joram will not leave without the
Darksword. If I were you, I would do my best to find it,
wherever it may be hidden."

His gaze shifted back to Eliza. "Bring the Darksword to the city of Zith-el. Come to the Eastroad
Gate. Someone will be waiting for you."

The image went out. Mosiah removed the ho-
lographic projector, which had been stashed inside the
fireplace. A stone had been pried loose, the projection
machine placed inside. He tossed it on the floor.

"You knew that was there," Scylla said.

"Yes. They had to have some means to communicate
with us. I found it before you arrived."

Scylla stomped on it with her heavy boot, crushed it.
"Are there any listening devices?"

"I removed them. I decided to leave this. We needed
to hear what they had to say. Zith-el." He mused. "So
they have taken Joram to Zith-el."

"Yes." Scylla slapped her hands on her thighs. "Now we can make plans."

"We!" Mosiah looked at her very balefully. "What do *you* have to do with this? With any of this?"

"I'm here," said Scylla, with a sly smile. "And the Darksword is in my air car. I'd say I have a lot to do with this."

"I was right. General Boris did send you," Mosiah said, his tone harsh. "You're one of his people. Damn it, he promised he would leave this to us!"

"You've done such a wonderful job so far," Scylla commented wryly.

Mosiah flushed, stiffened. "I didn't see you around when the *D'karn-darah* attacked."

"Stop it!" Eliza said sharply. "You both want the Darksword. That's all you care about. Well, you can't have it. I'm going to do what he says. I'm going to take it to Zith-el."

Eliza's defiance might have seemed childish and silly, but her grief and her own self-recrimination loaned her the strength she lacked. She spoke with dignity and resolve, and those two people, older and stronger and more powerful, both regarded her with respect.

"You know that you can't trust Smythe," Mosiah told her. "He will try to take the sword and make us all prisoners. Or worse."

"I know that I don't seem to be able to trust anybody," Eliza said with a quaver in her voice. She glanced at me, gave me a sweet, sad smile, and added softly, "Except Reuven."

The pain in my heart was blessed, but it was also too great to bear and overflowed my eyes. I turned away, ashamed of my lack of self-control, when she was so strong.

"I do not see what other choice I have," Eliza continued, now speaking quite calmly. "I will take the Darksword to Smythe and hope that he will keep his promise to free my father and Father Saryon. I will go alone—"

I made an emphatic gesture, which caught her eye. She amended her statement. "Reuven and I will go together. The two of you will remain here."

"I have told you the truth, Eliza," said Scylla. "I do not want the Darksword. There is only one man who can wield it and that is the one who forged it."

Suddenly, Scylla knelt down on one knee in front of Eliza. Pressing the palms of her hands together, in an attitude of prayer, Scylla raised them. "I promise you, Eliza, I swear by the Almin, that I will do whatever lies in my power to rescue Joram and to restore to him the Darksword."

The sight of Scylla—her army fatigues and cropped hair—kneeling there, seemed ludicrous at first. Then I was reminded forcibly of a drawing I had once seen of Joan of Arc, pledging her duty to her king. There burned the same holy fervor in Scylla, so bright and clear that her military fatigues disappeared and I saw her clad in shining armor, offering her pledge to her queen.

The vision lasted only an instant, but it was detailed perfectly in my mind. I saw the throne room, the crystal throne room of the kingdom of Merilon. Crystal throne, crystal dais, crystal chairs, crystal pillars—everything in the room was transparent, the only reality was the queen in her gown of gold who stood on that translucent platform, uplifted, exalted. Before her, kneeling, gazing upward, shining in silver armor, her knight.

And I was not alone. Mosiah saw the vision, too, or so I believe. Certainly he saw something, for he stared at Scylla in awe, though I heard him mutter, "What trick is this?"

Eliza clasped her hands over Scylla's. "I accept your pledge. You will accompany us."

Scylla bowed her head. "My life is yours, Your Majesty."

The title seemed so right, that none of us caught it, until Eliza blinked.

"What did you call me?"

Scylla stood and the vision vanished. She was once again wearing the combat fatigues and boots, her ear lined with the tiny earrings.

"Just my little joke." Scylla grinned and went to refill the teapot. She glanced back at Mosiah. "You are *much* more handsome in person. Say, why don't you take the same oath? Pledge yourself to rescue Joram and restore the Darksword to its owner. You must, you know. Otherwise we won't take you with us to Zith-el."

Mosiah was angry. "You are fools if you think that Smythe will give up any of the hostages once he has the Darksword! The Technomancers need Joram to teach them how to forge more." He turned to Eliza. "Come with me back to Earth. Give the sword into the safe-keeping of King Garald. We will return with an army to rescue your father and mother."

"The army is mobilizing to make a last stand against the Hch'nyv," countered Scylla. "You will get no help from them. And I doubt if they could do much against the Technomancers anyway. They have long been building up their strength in Zith-el, surrounding it with their defenses. An army could not take it. It's all in our files," she added in answer to Mosiah's flashing look of suspicion. "You're not the only people keeping tabs on Smythe."

Mosiah ignored her, continued speaking to Eliza, his tone growing softer. "I am Joram's friend. If I thought surrendering the Darksword would free him, I would be the first to advocate such a venture. But it won't. It can't possibly. Surely you can see that?"

"What you say makes sense, Mosiah," Eliza agreed. "But the Darksword is not mine and so any decisions concerning it are not mine to make. I am taking the sword back to my father. I will make that clear to this Smythe. My father will make the decision as to what to do with the sword."

"Place the Darksword in the hand of its gloomy and doomy creator, and you might be surprised at what happens," advised a sepulchral voice from underneath my stool. "Personally, I think he should give it to my friend Merlyn. I did mention that I knew Merlyn, didn't I? You'll find him hanging around down by that moldy old tomb of his. Quite a depressing place. I can't think what he sees in it. Merlyn's been looking for a sword for a number of years now. Some dolt tossed his into a lake. This isn't it, but the old boy's a bit dotty now and he probably wouldn't know the difference."

We had forgotten Teddy.

I fished him out, dusty and indignant, but otherwise unharmed.

I signed, "Simkin has a point. Not about Merlyn," I added hastily. "About Joram. Once the Darksword is in Joram's hand, it might be used to defeat the Technomancers."

"Have you forgotten that this Darksword is not magically enhanced? No catalyst has given it Life. The Darksword stands no chance of getting anywhere near Joram's hand," Mosiah stated bitterly. "Kevon Smythe will take hold of it and that will be an end. We go upon a fool's journey."

"Just like old times," Teddy remarked with a nostalgic sigh.

"*You're* not coming!" Mosiah said firmly.

"I wouldn't leave me behind," Teddy warned us. "I can't be trusted. Not in the slightest. Much better to have me where you can keep an eye on me as the Duchess of Winifred said regarding the table where she kept her eyeball collection. She had one for every day of the year, different colors. Used to pop them out after breakfast. I recall the day one got loose and rolled across the marble floor. The house catalyst mistakenly trod upon it. You can't imagine the squi—"

"I'll take him," Eliza said hurriedly. Snatching Teddy from me, she tucked him securely into the pocket of her skirt. "He can stay with me."

Mosiah glared around at all of us. "Are you determined to do this? Reuven?"

I nodded. My duty was to Father Saryon. And even if it had not been, I would go wherever Eliza went, support her in whatever she did.

"I go with Eliza," said Scylla.

"And I am going to Zith-el," said Eliza.

"If you are resolved on this, we should leave. You said you have an air car?" Mosiah looked at Scylla. His expression was not friendly.

"You're coming with us?" she asked, delighted.

"Of course. I will not leave Joram and his wife and Father Saryon in the hands of the Technomancers."

"You will not leave the Darksword in our hands, isn't that what you mean?" Scylla said with a sly grin.

"Take my words however you want," Mosiah returned. "I am tired of arguing with the lot of you. Well, are you coming? Even with the air car, we will be lucky to arrive in Zith-el before dark."

"And will your friends, the rest of the *Duuk-tsarith,*

be joining us there?" Scylla asked, raising the eyebrow that was pierced with the tiny gold ring.

Mosiah stared out the window, into the distance, a far distance, that only he could see. "There is no Life in Zith-el," he said softly. "Only death. Countless of our people died there when the quakes struck and the ground shifted, toppling the buildings. They lie unburied, their spirits troubled, demanding to know the reason why they died. No, the *Duuk-tsarith* will not go to Zith-el. There they would suffocate and their magic would be stifled, smothered."

"But you will go," Scylla said.

"I will go," Mosiah said, and he was grim. "As I told you, my friends are being held captive there. Besides, it doesn't make much difference to me whether or not my magic is stifled. After the battle I have little Life left within me. Unless we bump into a catalyst on the way, I will be good for nothing except throwing rocks. Don't count on me to defend you!"

Or defend himself, I thought, recalling how the Technomancers were hunting him.

"And how do we know we can trust you?" Eliza asked.

"I will take your oath," Mosiah said, "on one condition. I will do all in my power to restore the Darksword to Joram, its creator. But if we fail, then I claim the right to transport the Darksword back to my king."

"If we fail, you will have no king. The Technomancers will see to that," said Scylla.

Suddenly, astonishingly, she flung her arms around Mosiah and gave him a hug. She was taller than he was by a head and far stronger. Her hug squeezed his shoulders together and caved in his chest. "I like you," she said. "And I never thought I'd say that to an Enforcer. If you give me the keys, Reuven, I'll drive the air car around front. We'll need food and blankets. I have water with me."

Releasing him, she clapped him on the back and then strode purposefully from the room. I could hear her heavy, booted footsteps all the way down the hall.

As I went to help Eliza with the food and blankets, I looked back and saw Mosiah standing in the center of the empty, decimated room. A gentle breeze from the window stirred his black robes. His hands were clasped before him, he had drawn his hood over his head. I judged, by the tilt of his hooded head, that he still stared far off into that distance which was his alone to view. But now he was searching for someone or something and not finding it, apparently.

"Who the hell are you?"

The words hung like the taint of smoke in the air.

CHAPTER SEVENTEEN

*"And then the magic filled me! It was like the
Life of everything around me, pouring into me,
surging through me. I felt a hundred times more
alive!"*

~MOSIAH; *DOOM OF THE DARKSWORD*

By the time Eliza and I had gathered up bedding and
food, Scylla had driven the air car around to the front
of the building. We loaded the bedding and the food
into the luggage area in the back. That done, we stood
looking somewhat bemusedly at the air car, which only
seated four—two in the front and two in the back. The
Darksword, wrapped in its blanket, lay across the
backseat.

"That should go in the rear," said Mosiah.

"No," Eliza said swiftly. "I want it where I can see
it."

"Put it on the floor in the backseat," suggested Scylla.

Eliza grasped hold of the sword, tugged the blanket over it more securely, and laid it across the floor of the backseat. Mosiah took his place in the front, next to Scylla—if Eliza wanted to keep an eye on the sword, I think Mosiah was determined to keep an eye on Scylla. That suited me well, however, leaving me to sit in back with Eliza. She started to climb in beside me.

"Blessed Almin!" she cried suddenly, straightening and turning to look down the hillside. "The sheep! I can't leave them penned up. I'll water them and turn them out to pasture. It won't take a moment. I'll be right back."

She was gone, running down the hillside.

"We have to stop her!" Scylla said, starting to climb out of the air car.

"No," Mosiah countered, his voice harsh. "Let her see for herself. Then maybe she will understand."

See what? I didn't like this. Jumping out of the air car, I ran after Eliza and soon caught up with her. My legs were stiff, the muscles starting to tighten after the physical exertion from last night. I gritted my teeth against the soreness as we dashed down the hillside toward the sheep pen.

Even from this distance, I could see something was terribly wrong. I tried to halt Eliza's wild rush, but she angrily flung off my restraining hand and plunged ahead. I slowed my pace, to ease the burning in my legs. There was no need to hurry, nothing we could do. Nothing anyone could do.

When I arrived, I found Eliza leaning heavily against the stone fence. Her eyes were wide, the lids stretched with horror and disbelief.

The sheep were dead. All of them, slaughtered. Each

of them bled from the ears. Pools of blood had formed under each mouth and nose. Eyes stared, clouded over. Each lay where it had fallen, with no sign of a struggle. I recalled the blast we had heard. Even from a distance we'd felt the concussive force. The Technomancers, their power running low, had used the deaths of these animals to replenish their supply.

Eliza's head sank to her hands, but she did not cry. She remained standing, her head bowed, so still and rigid that I was frightened. I did what I could, in my poor silence, to comfort her, letting her feel my touch, to know that human warmth and sympathy surrounded her.

The air car slid soundlessly down the hill, pulled up in front of us. Scylla climbed out. Mosiah remained in the car, regarding the slaughter with equanimity.

"Come, Your Majesty," said Scylla. "There is nothing we can do."

"Why?" Eliza asked, in muffled tones, keeping her head down. "Why did they do this?"

"They feed off death." Mosiah's voice came from the air car. "These are the fiends to whom you are taking the Darksword, Eliza. Think about it."

I hated him at that moment. She could have been spared this. She knew well enough, having seen the destruction in her own home, what she faced. But I was wrong, as it turned out, and he was right. He gauged her strength and quality better than I.

She raised her face and she was composed, almost serene. "I will go alone. I alone will take the sword to them. The rest of you should not come. It is too dangerous."

That could not be, as Scylla pointed out with great practicality, refraining from mentioning anything in regard to Eliza herself, but talking only of our own needs. Who would drive the air car? We needed Scylla. As for Reuven, I would not leave Father Saryon to the Technomancers. And Mosiah would never permit the Darksword to venture far from his sight. Each of us had our reasons for going.

Eliza accepted the logic of all this quietly, did not argue. She returned to the air car and slid inside. She glanced once more at the dead sheep and her lips tightened, her hands clasped. She looked away. I climbed in beside her, as Scylla returned to the driver's seat.

The air car skimmed over the surface of the ground, much smoother than when I had driven a similar vehicle. I fumbled for something which had struck a strange chord in my mind. Not an ill-sounding chord. It was pleasant, in fact. But strange. I tried to remember what it was.

Your Majesty, Scylla had called Eliza twice now. *Your Majesty.*

How odd. Yet how fitting.

The start of our journey was uneventful. Scylla had brought a map of the land of Thimhallan, obtained from some archives somewhere—she was vague as to details. Mosiah was both intrigued by it and suspicious of it, for it was apparently recently drawn, contained changes in the landscape that had been made by the devastating quakes and storms following the release of the magic.

The two spent several minutes arguing over the map. Mosiah claimed it had been drawn by General Boris's people, which meant that they had violated the treaty. Scylla countered by saying that the *Duuk-tsarith* had violated the treaty themselves. Mosiah had better look to his own sins before he accused others.

I'm not sure how much longer the bickering would have continued, but Eliza, who had been sitting in the back, white-faced and silent, asked quietly, "Is the map useful?"

Scylla looked at Mosiah, who muttered something to the effect that he supposed it was.

"Then I suggest we use it," Eliza said. She curled up in the corner of the seat and closed her eyes.

After that, Scylla and Mosiah spoke to each other only when it was necessary to discuss directions. The air car soared off down the mountainside, heading for the interior of Thimhallan.

I made certain Eliza was comfortable, covered her with my jacket, for which consideration I received a wan smile, but she did not open her eyes. She held Teddy in the crook of her arm, pressed close to her breast for comfort, as a child might. I was certain that Teddy had arranged himself in this enviable position, but I dared not move him for fear of disturbing her rest.

I settled back in my corner, feeling somewhat cramped in the backseat, which—so far as I could tell—was not intended for transporting any creature possessed of legs. I knew I should sleep, for I would need to be well rested to face whatever it was we would face at the end of our journey.

I closed my eyes, but sleep would not come. My body was in that state of overfatigue where the nerves twitch and the mind travels restlessly over past events.

I felt guilty for having abandoned Father Saryon, although I don't know what good I could have done had I been there. And at least I had warned Eliza away from the Technomancers, although if they had taken the sword then and there, Joram and Gwendolyn and Father Saryon might not have been abducted.

What's done is done, I told myself. You acted for the best.

I spent a few more fruitless moments worrying about what we were going to do when we arrived at Zith-el, for I was certain that Mosiah would never permit Eliza to relinquish the Darksword. Would he try to stop her? Would he try to take the sword? Was he truly devoid of magical Life or was that a deceit to throw us off guard? Scylla had pledged her loyalty to Eliza. Would she fight Mosiah, if it came to that? And who was Scylla anyway?

Was Father Saryon all right? Would the Technomancers kill him, as they had promised, if we didn't give up the sword? Was it wise to give up the sword to these evil people? Was this all wasted effort, if the Hch'nyv were going to wipe us out?

Eventually, these concerns—over which admittedly I had no control—so wore out my brain that it gave up and surrendered to weariness. I slept.

I awoke to darkness, a driving rainstorm, and an urgent need to relieve my bladder.

There being a distinct lack of bathroom facilities on Thimhallan, I would have to make do with the bushes. The rain pelting down on top of the air car did not fill me with any great enthusiasm for going out into the violent storm, but the urgency of my need gave me little choice.

Eliza slumbered in her corner, undisturbed by the tumult of the storm. By her placid face and even breathing, she slept deeply and dreamlessly. Fearful of waking her, I leaned forward as noiselessly as I could and tapped Scylla on the shoulder.

Scylla glanced around swiftly, keeping a tight grip on the wheel. Driving the air car must have been difficult, due to the storm. We were being buffeted by strong winds, the windshield wipers could not keep the window clear of the rain. If it had not been for the radar, with which the air car was equipped and which provided us with a virtual map of the terrain, we could not have kept going. As it was, we crept along, with Scylla fixing her gaze on the radar screen and Mosiah peering out the blurred window.

I made known my request. A bright burst of lightning nearly blinded us. Thunder cracked overhead, the rumble shaking the air car.

"Can't you hold it?" Scylla asked.

I shook my head. She checked the radar screen, found a clear place, and lowered the air car down onto the ground.

"I'll go with him," Mosiah offered. "There are dangers out there for those who don't know the land."

I indicated that I would be grateful for his company, but it wasn't necessary for him to get drenched on my account. He shrugged, smiled, and opened the car door.

I opened the door on my side and started to climb out.

"What? What's happening?" Eliza said sleepily, blinking her eyes.

"Pit stop," said Scylla.

"What?" asked Eliza.

Embarrassed, I didn't wait to hear more.

The wind nearly ripped the door from my hand, pulling me halfway out of the car. I struggled out the rest of the way. Rain soaked me to the skin in an instant. I wrestled with the door, finally managed to slam it shut. The force of the wind blew me several steps toward the front of the car. Mosiah fought his way around the vehicle, his black robes sodden and clinging to his body. He had thrown off his hood, which was ineffectual against the wind and rain. It was at that moment I knew that he truly was devoid of Life. No wizard with any power left would have subjected himself to such a wetting.

"Watch out!" he shouted, grabbing hold of my arm. "Kij vines!"

He pointed, and by the lights of the air car, I could see the deadly vines. I had written about them in my books, about how the vines wrapped around the limbs of the unwary, dug their thorns into the flesh, and sucked the blood of their victims, blood upon which the plants thrived. I had, of course, never seen one. I could have gone much longer without the pleasure. The heart-shaped leaves shone black in the night, glistening with rain, the thorns small and sharp. The plant appeared quite healthy, with gigantic tendrils curling over each other, layer upon layer.

Making certain to keep clear of the entangling vines, I finished my business as quickly as possible. Mosiah stood near me, keeping watch in all directions, and I was glad for his presence. Zipping up my jeans, I started back for the car. Mosiah walked at my side. The storm actually seemed to be abating; the rain was a windswept shower now instead of a torrent. I was looking forward to climbing into the warm interior of the air car when I felt something like wire wrap around my ankle.

The Kij vine! Frantically, I lurched forward, trying to break its hold. Its grip was strong. The tendril pulled my foot out from under me and began dragging me back into the main body of the plant! I gave a strangled cry and dug my fingers into the mud, trying to brace myself.

Needle-sharp thorns pierced the flesh of my leg, sliding easily through my blue jeans and heavy socks. The pain was excruciating.

At my cry, Mosiah sprang to help me. Scylla had seen me fall and was opening the car door.

"What is it?" she shouted. "What's happening?"

"Stay inside!" Mosiah yelled back. "Turn the air car around! Shine the lights on us! Kij vines! They're all over!"

He stomped on something with his foot. I was being dragged slowly along the rain-soaked ground, my fingers scrabbling to gain purchase, digging deep trenches in the mud. The pain was intense—the jabbing sensation of a thorn probing for a vein, and then came the sickening ache of the blood being sucked out.

Mosiah stood above me, peering into the darkness. He spoke a word and pointed with his finger. There was a flash of light, a sizzle, and a snap.

The vine released me.

I crawled forward, only to feel other tendrils grab hold of me. Snaking out of the darkness from all directions, they wound around my wrists and my feet. One curled around the calf of my leg.

The air car had turned. By the car's headlights, I could see the raindrops glistening off the heart-shaped leaves of the deadly Kij vines, and shining on the terrible, sharp thorns.

"Damn!" Mosiah swore, and glared in frustration at the vine. He turned and ran back to the air car.

I thought—I don't know why—that he had abandoned me. Panic welled up inside me, bringing with it a surge of adrenaline. I *will* free myself! I determined. I tried not to give way to fear, tried to remain calm and think clearly. With all the strength I possessed and a great deal I did not, I jerked my wrist and actually succeeded in freeing myself from one of the vines.

But that was only one, and now four more at least had hold of me.

Eliza was out of the car, ignoring Mosiah's orders.

"The Darksword!" Mosiah was saying. "Hand me the Darksword! That's the only thing that will save him!"

My face was covered with muck and my hair was in my eyes. I continued to fight the vine, but my strength was failing. The pain of the thorns was debilitating. I felt sick and faint.

"To me!" Mosiah yelled. "Give it to me! No! Don't risk—"

I heard footsteps and the swish of long skirts.

I shook the hair from my eyes. Eliza stood over me, the Darksword in her hand.

"Don't move, Reuven! I don't want to hit you!"

I forced myself to lie still, though I could feel the vines tightening, the thorns drinking deep.

The car lights illuminated her from behind, forming a halo around her dark hair, an aura around her body. The light did not touch the Darksword. Either that or it absorbed the light into itself. Eliza raised the sword and slashed down with it. I heard it slice through the vines, but to my pain-dulled mind, she was fighting the lethal plant with the night itself.

Suddenly I was free. The plant gave up its hold; the tendrils went limp and lifeless as a hand that has been cut off at the wrist.

Mosiah and Scylla were there to help me to my feet. I wiped the muck from my face and, with their help, stumbled to the air car. Eliza came after us, holding the Darksword ready in her hand, but the Kij vine had apparently given up the attack. Looking back on it, I saw its leaves withered and curling wherever the Darksword had touched it.

They assisted me to the car. Fortunately, the rain had all but ceased now.

"Will he be all right?" Eliza hovered over me. Her obvious concern eased me like a soothing balm.

"The pain fades quickly," Mosiah said. "And the thorns are not poisonous. I know from experience."

"You were always stumbling into them, as I recall," offered Teddy from the floor. He sounded peevish. "I warned you against them, time and again—"

"You did not. You said they were edible," Mosiah recalled with a half smile.

"Well, I knew one of us was," Teddy muttered, then raised his voice in ire. "Is it absolutely necessary for the lot of you to drip all over me?"

"I'd feed *you* to the Kij vines," said Mosiah, reaching inside to pick up Teddy, "but even they must have *some* taste." He started to return the bear to the seat, but instead held him, stared at him. "I wonder . . ."

"Put me down!" Teddy complained. "You're pinching me!"

Mosiah plunked the stuffed bear on the seat beside me.

"How are you feeling?" Scylla asked.

"Not well," said Teddy, groaning.

"I was talking to Reuven," Scylla said severely. She rolled up my pants leg and began examining my injuries.

I nodded, to indicate I was better. The pain was fading, as Mosiah had predicted. The horror was not. I could still feel those tendrils tightening around my legs. I shivered from cold and reaction to the ordeal.

"You should change out of those wet clothes," Eliza said.

"Not here," Mosiah stated. "Not now."

"For once, I agree with the wizard," Scylla said.

"Get back in the car, all of you. I'll turn the heat on. Reuven, take off what clothes you can. Eliza, cover him with as many blankets as we have. You'll find a first-aid kit back there. Use the ointment on those wounds."

Eliza returned the Darksword to its place on the floor, sliding it under the blanket, out of sight. She said no word about what she'd done to save me, and refused to look at me when I tried to sign my thanks. Instead, she searched for and discovered the first-aid kit, then busied herself with the blankets, pulling them out of the back compartment.

The air car rose up from that ill-fated place and slid smoothly forward, making better time now that the storm had abated. A watery sun peered down at us, blinking, as the clouds scudded over its weak eye.

"Mid-afternoon," Mosiah said, gazing at the sky.

"As dark as it was, I thought it was night," Eliza said.

She began treating my cuts and wounds with the ointment. Embarrassed at this attention, I had endeavored to take the tube from her, but she refused to let me. "Lie back and rest," she ordered, and helped me peel off my sodden woolen sweater.

She dabbed ointment on the thorn wounds, which were red and fiery, with dark blood oozing from them. When Eliza spread the salve over them, the redness vanished, the bleeding stopped, the pain eased and was soon completely gone. Eliza's eyes widened at the change.

"This is wonderful," she said, looking at the small tube. "We have medical supplies sent to us by the Earth Forces, but nothing like this!"

"Standard government issue," said Scylla, with a shrug.

Mosiah twisted around in his seat, studied the almost healed wounds on my arms and legs. He looked at Scylla.

"What government issues miracles these days?" he asked.

She glanced at him and grinned. "And where did *you* find that thunderbolt you launched, Enforcer? Just happen to have one up your sleeve? I thought you said your magic was depleted. No Life." She shook her head in mock sorrow, and continued on. "And you asking for the Darksword. Quick thinking. Yet what would you have done with it, I wonder?"

"Used it to free Reuven," Mosiah replied. "Then I would have changed myself into a bat and flown away with it, of course. Or did you think I'd take it and try to run with it, through this godforsaken wilderness, and you with an air car to catch me!"

He sat hunched and huddled in his robes, which were as wet as my clothes. He held his shoulders rigid, to keep from revealing that he was shivering.

"I thought the sword too heavy for Eliza to wield," he added coldly. "I see now that I was wrong."

Scylla made no reply, but from the faint flush I could see rising up the back of her neck, I believe that she was ashamed of having made the accusation. He had given his word to help us and we had no reason to doubt him. If he had a small reserve of Life left to him, that was only sensible. No wizard depleted himself utterly, if he could help it. He had voluntarily gone out into the drenching rainstorm to guard me, and if he hadn't warned me of the Kij vines, I might well have floundered in among them so deeply that not even the Darksword could have saved me.

Eliza offered him a blanket, which he refused with a curt shake of his head. She said nothing; her face was calm and smooth. She still did not trust him and she made no apology for it. She tucked the blanket around me, made certain I was comfortable. She repacked the first-aid kit, then asked if there was anything else she could do for me. She offered me the electronic notepad, in case I wanted to write anything.

I indicated no, smiling, to show her that I was much better. And, indeed, I was. The horror was starting to recede. The air car was warming up rapidly. My shivering ceased, the pain was gone. The ointment deserved some credit, undoubtedly, but no salve can heal the terrors of the soul. Eliza's touch had been the true cure.

Some emotions need no words. Eliza saw in my eyes what I could not speak. A slight flush mantled her cheeks and she looked away from me, to the notepad in her hand. The pad provided her an excuse to change the subject.

"I don't want to disturb you, Reuven, if you're tired—"

I shook my head. She could never disturb me, nor could I ever be too tired to do anything she might ask of me.

"I would like to learn sign language," she said, almost shyly. "Would you mind teaching me?"

Would I mind! I knew she was doing this only out of kindness, to take my mind off the terrible experience I had suffered. I agreed, of course, hoping it might take her mind off her own horrors. She moved closer to me. I began by teaching her the alphabet, spelling out her name. She understood immediately. She was a quick student, and within a very short time she had the entire alphabet and could run through it, hand and fingers flashing.

The air car soared over rain-soaked grasslands, lifted and climbed up over treetops. We were traveling very fast now, though I wondered if our speed would make up for the time we had lost in the storm. Mosiah maintained his cool, offended silence.

The sun continued to shine, though it was often hidden by racing clouds. Scylla turned down the heat in the air car, which—with the wet clothes—was beginning to resemble a sauna.

"Those Kij vines," she said abruptly. "They behaved rather oddly, don't you think?"

Mosiah looked at her, and though I was busy with Eliza, I saw a glint of interest flicker in his eyes. "Perhaps," was all he said noncommittally. "What do you mean?"

"They came after Reuven," Scylla said. "Did you ever know the vines to be that aggressive? And those vines had grown tall and thick. Isn't that unusual?"

Mosiah shrugged. "The *Finhanish* are no longer around to keep them thinned out. The *Sif-Hanar* are no longer here to control the weather. Of course, left alone, the Kij vines would thrive."

"Plants born of magic," Scylla mused. "Created by magic. One would think that when the magic in this land was depleted, the plants would lose their source of sustenance and they would die off. *Not* grow more abundantly."

"Born of magic?" Eliza interrupted our lesson to ask. "What do you mean? We grow corn and carrots and wheat and there's nothing magic about them."

"But there is about the Kij vine," Mosiah replied. "It was created at the end of the Iron Wars, when some of the *D'karn-duuk*—the warlocks and war masters—saw the battle ending with themselves on the losing side. They had already used their magic to turn humans into giants, or twist humans into a combination of beast and man, which became the centaur. The warlocks perverted plant life, developing the Kij vine and other deadly vegetation, used them to ambush the unwary.

"When the wars ended, the ranks of the *D'karn-duuk* were depleted. They could no longer control their own creations, and so the giants and the centaur and the Kij vines were left on their own, to do what they could to survive."

"I heard stories about the centaur," Eliza said. "They captured my father once and nearly killed him. He said they were cruel and loved to inflict pain, but that this came out of their own great anger and suffering."

"I have to work very hard to feel sympathy for the centaur," Mosiah said dryly, "but I suppose this is true. Or should I say it *was* true, for they must have died when the magic died."

"Like the Kij vines," said Scylla, her pierced eyebrow arching. "And certain bears of my acquaintance." She glanced back at Teddy, who smirked at her and winked.

"Here's a thought," she said. "What if the first Darksword did *not* destroy the Well of Life, as everyone has always supposed. What if, instead, the Darksword capped it?"

"Impossible. The magic was released into the universe," Mosiah stated.

"The magic of Thimhallan was released, and perhaps a gush of magic from the Well. Then the Well was sealed. And ever since, the magic has been building beneath the surface. . . ."

"Well, really!" Simkin cried suddenly. "I *won't* stay to be insulted."

With that and a flash of orange scarf, Teddy vanished.

"What was all that about?" Eliza asked, bewildered. "Where did he go?"

"I wonder." Mosiah glanced sidelong at Scylla. "I wonder about a lot of things."

So did I. If Scylla's theory was right and the magic had been building beneath Thimhallan all these years . . . what would happen? One effect was most obvious. Magic—strong and powerful—was available to whoever might be able to use it.

But surely, I argued with myself, if that were true, then certainly the *Duuk-tsarith* would have discovered it long ago.

Perhaps they had. Perhaps that is why they are so desperate to attain the Darksword. Not only could it destroy the Life that might be building beneath the Well, but if the new Darksword were to be given this powerful Life, its own power might be increased.

I turned the question upside down and inside out in my mind and never came to a satisfactory answer. It didn't seem to me that there could ever be an answer. Within forty-eight hours, we would flee this place, most likely never to return.

Mosiah said nothing more. Scylla appeared lost in thought. The two lapsed into an uncomfortable silence. I continued my lesson with Eliza.

I was relieved that Teddy was gone, until I remembered my master's warning—that it was always better to know where Simkin was than where he wasn't.

CHAPTER EIGHTEEN

"It takes nerves of stone to enter Zith-el in this manner."

～*DARKSWORD ADVENTURES*

We reached Zith-el not long after sunset. The afterglow—bright beneath gray storm clouds—tinged the sky with a lurid red that tipped the snow-covered mountains of the Ekard range with blood. It was an ominous sign and one that was not lost on my companions.

"Of all the cities on Thimhallan, Zith-el was the one that suffered the most damage when the Well of Life was destroyed," Mosiah told us. "The buildings of Zith-el soared countless stories into the air. The people also tunneled deep into the ground in search of living space. When the magic was withdrawn and the fearsome quakes shook the land, the buildings fell, the tunnels collapsed. Thousands died, crushed to death, trapped in the rubble, or buried alive beneath the ground."

The air car slowed. Zith-el's Outer Wall, which had protected the city from invasion, had been a wall of magic, completely invisible, much like what we on Earth know as a force field. The wall should have been destroyed.

Perhaps it was, perhaps it wasn't.

We had no way of knowing, and after the Kij vines we could no longer assume that magic on Thimhallan was as depleted as we had once thought. I remembered what the Technomancers had said about "residual pockets."

All that could be seen inside the city was the thick forest, which had been part of the marvelous Zoo, for which Zith-el was known. Oddly, if the wall was gone, the forest had not encroached onto the grasslands.

"Were there any survivors in Zith-el?" Eliza asked. Her voice was strained. Mosiah said no word of blame, but the daughter of the man who had caused the downfall of Thimhallan must feel defensive.

"Yes," Mosiah answered, "and they were the most unfortunate of all. When the magic was weakened, the creatures of the Zoo were set free and took their revenge on those who had kept them prisoner."

Eliza gazed on the city that had once teemed with life, whose walls now encompassed nothing but death. She knew the history of her father and what he had done and why he had done it. Joram was honest, brutally honest, and I do not believe that he would have spared himself in the telling. In all probability he had judged himself more harshly than even his detractors.

But sealed up, safe and secure, inside the Font, Eliza had never been brought face-to-face with the knowledge of what her father had done to this world and to its people. Father Saryon and I had disturbed Eliza's tranquillity by bringing her visions of a different world. The Technomancers had shattered her happy life, her innocent pleasure in her home and her family. Mosiah's words and the crumbled walls of Zith-el shook her faith in her father, the worst and most painful shock of all.

The air car had slowed. Scylla lowered it into the tall stands of grass that surrounded the city. The shadows of the mountains had brought dusk to us on the plains, though the sky was still bright behind them. She kept the lights off.

She and Mosiah discussed how best to proceed, arguing over whether it would be better to remain in the air car or leave it outside the city and enter Zith-el on foot.

"The Technomancers know we are here," Mosiah observed. "With their sensor equipment, they've probably been following us since we left the Font."

"Yes, but they don't know how many we are or if we have the Darksword," Scylla argued.

"We're here, aren't we?" Mosiah returned bluntly. "Why else would we come?"

Scylla admitted that he had a valid point, but she urged stealth as opposed to driving right up to the gate. "At the least, we should not turn over the Darksword until we are assured of the hostages' safety."

Mosiah shook his head.

I left that decision to them. With four of us facing an army of Technomancers, it didn't seem to me to make the slightest bit of difference what we did. Pulling out my electronic notebook, I began looking up some refer-

ence material I had acquired on Zith-el, thinking to let
Eliza read my notes.

When I found them, I started to show them to her,
then checked myself.

Believing herself unobserved, shrouded in the twilight shadows, she had leaned down and, with one
hand, drawn off the blanket from the Darksword. It
was dark against darkness.

Her father had forged the first Darksword. Father
Saryon had given it Life. The blood of thousands had
consecrated it. Now here was a second, another.
Would blood stain its blade as well?

Her face was so open, so honest, emotions passed
across its surface like ripples on still water. I could
guess her thoughts. Her words, spoken softly to herself,
proved my guess right.

"Why did he forge it anew? Why did it have to come
back into the world? And what should I do with it
now?"

Sighing, she leaned against the seat, her expression
sad and troubled.

And yet, what choice did she have?

None that I could see. Unable to offer help, I did not
intrude on Eliza's private pain. I reread the notes written by an unnamed adventurer in the land of Thimhallan, notes that King Garald had taken with him into
exile.

> Zith-el is a compact city whose major distinction
> is that it is surrounded by the most wonderful Zoo in
> all of Thimhallan. Visitors traveling from other cities
> to see the Zoo's wonders provide a large portion of
> Zith-el's income.
>
> History: Zith-el—a Finhanish druid of the
> Vanjnan Clans—was born about 352 YL. He pur-

*chased a wife from a fellow clansman, who had cap-
tured the woman during a raid on Trandar. The
woman, named Tara, was a talented Theldara. Despite a turbulent beginning, the two grew to love each
other. Zith-el gave up his wandering ways and promised to settle in one place with his beloved.*

*He, his wife, and their family traveled up the Hira
River until Tara called a halt. Dismounting from her
horse, she investigated the river, the trees, and the
lands, and if legend is correct, she sat down on the
spot and declared it to be her home.*

The city was built around her.

*Zith-el believed that the ground was sacred and
. . . vowed to the Almin that he would never allow
the city to expand beyond its original borders.*

And that was the reason why, as its population
grew, Zith-el was forced to build up and down. It
could never expand outward.

I glanced up from my reading. The air car glided
forward through the tall grass, which brushed against
its sides with an irritating swishing sound. At first, we
were able to see the trees of the Zoo above the waving
sea of green, but we soon lost sight of them in the
gathering gloom of night. The city itself was dark, that
once must have glittered with light.

Moving out of the foothills toward the gate speci-
fied—the Eastroad Gate—we came upon the Eastroad,
a trail once used by overland traders. So packed and
rutted was the dirt that not even the tough prairie
grasses had yet covered it over. It stretched out before
us, visible in the faint afterglow that purpled the sky.

The stars were coming out. I looked at them and
found myself wondering if any of those sparkling
points of light were the battle cruisers of the Hch'nyv,

bearing down on us. That reminded me forcibly of the time constraint. We had this night, the next day, and the next night before the window of safety slammed shut.

The moon shone, as well, silvering the ragged storm clouds, which had continued to keep clear of us. About three-quarters full, the moon was faint now, but would brighten as the night darkened. That comforted me, though, when I thought of it, I had no idea why it should.

Scylla brought the car to a halt. The Eastroad Gate was built into a small section of the Outer Wall to the west of the city. East Road therefore seemed a misnomer, but the East Road actually took its name as meaning "east road leading away from the Font," all directions in Thimhallan having been determined from the Font, which was considered the center of the world.

I went back to my notes.

> There are two walls around the city, the Outer Wall and the City Wall. The City Wall runs along the lines originally laid down by Zith-el (the city's founder) and marks the place where the city ends and the Zoo begins. The Outer Wall surrounds the Zoo. Completely invisible, it allows a marvelous view of all the creatures, yet keeps them well confined. Its (the Zoo's) nearest point to the city is some four mila from the City Wall.
>
> Four gates in both walls provide the only entrances and exits for overland travelers. These gates are one-way only. You step through the open portal, only to find the back sealed shut. Gates leading into the city are located on the east and west sides of the walls, while gates leading out of the city are located on the north and south sides. It is said that all the

*gates through the City Wall can be deactivated by a
word from the Lord of Zith-el in order to keep the
city protected from attack.*

*The gates have a second and highly startling func-
tion. Upon entering the gate in the Outer Wall, the
traveler must pass through the Zoo that surrounds
the city in order to enter the city proper. Since it
would disturb the sensibilities of those touring the
Zoo to see other humans like themselves wandering
about, the gates temporarily transform the unsus-
pecting entrant into the illusion of some animal.*

We might all turn into Teddies, I thought.

Scylla shut off the engine to the air car. It settled
down upon the road and we sat in darkness and in
silence, watching the gate.

Nothing, no one appeared.

"They are waiting for us to show ourselves," Mosiah said, his voice harsh and overloud in the stillness.
"Let's get this over with."

He drew his hood up over his head and put his hand
on the door. Scylla reached out, clasped hold of his
arm, halting him.

"You should not go. The Technomancers have no
reason to harm any of the three of us. But you . . ."
She leaned near him, said softly, "We are close to the
Borderland. Stay hidden in the car. When the Technomancers are gone, return to the base. Go back to
Earth and prepare King Garald and General Boris.
They have to face the fact that the Technomancers will
soon be in possession of the Darksword. They need to
be forewarned, to make what plans they can."

He regarded her in silence for long moments, such
profound silence that I could hear his breath come and

go. I could hear Scylla's breathing, hear Eliza's, hear my own. I could hear my own heart beating.

"I wish I knew," Mosiah said at last, "whether you were just trying to get rid of me or whether you truly cared about"—pausing, he then said, somewhat lamely—"about King Garald and the Darksword."

Scylla grinned. I could see her face in the lambent light of stars and moon and the setting sun. Her eyes flashed with laughter and that cheered me, too, as had the moonglow.

"I care," she said, and her grasp on his arm tightened.

"About the people of Earth, I meant," he said gruffly.

"Them, too," Scylla responded, her grin widening.

He regarded her in frowning perplexity, for he thought she was teasing him and this was certainly no time for kidding around.

"All right, Mosiah, so I was wrong about you at the beginning," Scylla said, shrugging. "You're not your typical Enforcer, probably because you weren't born to it. And, as I said, you're much better-looking than your file photos. Return to Earth. There's nothing you can do here and you'll only put yourself in danger and maybe us along with you."

"Very well," he agreed, after another moment's thought. "I will remain inside the car. But leave the Darksword here with me, at least until you have proof that the hostages are alive. If the Technomancers try to seize it, they will find me guarding it; something they might not expect."

"A fine guard," Scylla scoffed. "You with no Life and no other weapon."

Mosiah smiled, for the first time since I'd met him. "The Technomancers don't know that."

Scylla looked startled, then she chuckled. "You have a point, Mosiah. If your plan is okay with Eliza, it's okay with me."

Eliza did not answer. I wasn't certain she had even heard, but then she nodded, once, slowly.

"The Almin go with you," Mosiah said.

"And with you," said Scylla, and she clapped him in boisterous good humor on the shoulder. "Ready?" We might have been going to a carnival, for her ebullient spirits.

Eliza's face glimmered pale in the darkness. It seemed as if I were sitting beside a ghost. She stretched out her hand, to touch either Scylla or Mosiah, but she hesitated, then rested her hand on the back of the front seat.

"Did my father do the right thing?" she asked, and my heart ached for the agony in her voice. "All those people dying . . . I never realized . . . I need to know."

Mosiah turned his face away. He stared out the front of the car window, toward the city that had become a tomb.

Scylla's grin vanished. Her expression somber, she rested her hand on Eliza's, and the touch that had been so brash was now gentle.

"How can we ever know, Eliza? Toss a pebble in the lake. The ripples spread out far beyond the entry point, continue long after the pebble sinks to the bottom. Each and every action we take, from the smallest to the largest, has ramifications that we will never see. We can only do what we believe is best and right at the time. Your father did that, Eliza. Given the circumstances, he made the best decision—perhaps the only decision—he could."

Eliza was not speaking only of her father. She was

speaking for herself. In returning the sword to the Technomancers, was *she* making the right decision? Would the ripples from her action fade into the placid smoothness of time's lake or build into a crushing tidal wave?

Eliza drew in a deep breath. She had made her decision.

"I am ready," she said. She drew the blanket over the Darksword.

We opened the doors of the air car and climbed out, all except Mosiah, who hunkered down in the front seat. We left the Darksword on the floor in the back.

Scylla had brought with her a pair of infrared binoculars. With these, she scanned the strange forest, a forest which had remained inside boundaries that were supposedly no longer there. Ahead of us was the East-road Gate—at least that's what I assumed it was. An invisible gate in an invisible wall is not easy to find.

"No one," Scylla said, lowering the binoculars.

"I feel as if someone was watching me," said Eliza, shivering, though the night wind was warm.

"Yes," Scylla agreed. "So do I." She kept her gaze forward, shifting, seeking, searching.

"What do we do?" Eliza demanded. Her voice cracked. The strain was starting to wear her down. "Why is no one here?"

"Patience," counseled Scylla. "This is their game. We have to play by their rules. Remember—we must see for ourselves that the hostages are alive and well. Look inside the gate. Do you see anything?"

I recalled what I had read. In the past, anyone who entered the gate was immediately transformed into the likeness of one of the inmates of the Zoo—a daunting possibility. For if the *Kan-Hanar,* the gatekeepers, discovered that you had been erroneously admitted, you might become a permanent resident of the Zoo.

This edict maintained the integrity of the Zoo. The sight of fat tradesmen tramping through the hunting grounds of the fierce centaurs would spoil the effect. To say nothing of the fact that the centaurs—who were not illusion, but very real—might decide to feast on a fat tradesman. And so the tradesmen were transformed into images of centaurs and thus—if they kept to the path—passed through the Zoo swiftly and safely.

Of course, the elite magi who either lived in Zith-el or had business there entered that city by way of the Corridors, and so did not have to go through the demeaning process of entering the gate. This experience was reserved for peasants, students, peddlers, field magi, and the lower ranks of the catalysts.

"I see nothing inside the gate," Eliza said. "Nothing at all. That's very strange. It's as if there were a huge hole cut out of the forest."

I nodded, to indicate that my view was the same.

"And yet the magic is supposed to be gone," Scylla murmured.

"Not according to *your* theory," I signed.

I have no idea whether she understood me or not, it being difficult to read sign language in near darkness.

"Are we . . . are we supposed to meet them inside there?" Eliza asked, daunted at the prospect of entering the dark maw which gaped before us.

"No," said Scylla reassuringly. "They said to meet *outside* the Eastroad Gate. If the Technomancers are in Zith-el, my guess is that they found some means of entering that did not involve passing through the Zoo."

I could well believe that the Technomancers would be reluctant to enter. Standing before the gate was like standing in the mouth of a cave, feeling the chill air that comes from deep underground touch your skin with clammy fingers. A strange smell emanated from the Zoo, drifting only occasionally to the nostrils, then vanishing. It was the smell of living things, of excrement and rotten food, mingled with the odor of verdure and loam, and, underneath it, decay.

We stood waiting for perhaps fifteen minutes, our uneasiness growing. If the Technomancers meant to unnerve us, they succeeded, at least with Eliza and myself. I'm not sure what it would have taken to unnerve Scylla, who stood beside us, arms folded across her chest, a slight smile on her lips.

Eliza shivered again. I offered to go back to the car for her wrap, but Scylla stopped me.

"Look!" she said softly, and pointed.

A figure was moving toward us, on our side of the invisible wall. It did not walk, but glided over the ground. It was alone and was, by its dress, a woman. Eliza gasped and clasped her hands.

"Mother!" she whispered.

The figure was Gwendolyn, coming toward us, drifting over the ground. I recalled then that she was one of the magi, that she could float where the mundane were forced to walk. But I also recalled that I had not once seen her use her magic when we were at her home. Perhaps that was out of respect for Joram.

Gwen floated toward us, her gaze focused lovingly on her daughter.

"Mother?" Eliza repeated, perplexed, hopeful, afraid.

Gwendolyn dropped gracefully to the ground and held out her arms. "My child," she said in choked tones. "How frightened you must have been!"

Eliza held back. "Mother, why are *you* here? Did you escape them? Where is Papa?"

Gwendolyn took a step toward her daughter. "Are you all right, love?" Reaching out, she took one of Eliza's hands.

Eliza flinched, but then, seeing her mother's worried, loving face so near, she seemed to melt.

"I'm fine, Mother. Only so worried about you and Papa! I heard he was hurt. How is he?"

"Eliza, have you brought the Darksword?" Gwendolyn asked, smoothing her daughter's black curls.

"Yes," said Eliza. "But Papa! Is he well? And Father Saryon? Is he all right?"

"Of course, child. I would not have come to you otherwise," Gwendolyn replied, with a reassuring smile. "Your father is angry with you for taking the Darksword, but if you return it, he will forgive you."

"Mother, I'm frightened for Papa. I saw the blood! And they killed the sheep. All the sheep are dead, Mother!"

"You know how hot-tempered your father is." Gwen sighed. "He was caught off guard when the Technomancers entered our house. Their leader admits that they acted rashly and he has apologized. Your father suffered a slight injury. Nothing serious. His greatest hurt lies with you, Eliza. He believes you have betrayed him!"

"I didn't mean to betray him," Eliza said, her voice quavering. "I thought if I gave them the sword, they would go away and leave us alone and we could be happy again! That's all I meant to do."

"I understand, daughter, and so will your father. Come and tell him this yourself. My pet!" Gwendolyn extended her hand. "We have so little time! Give me the Darksword and our family will be reunited."

I looked at Scylla, wondering if she would remind Eliza of the admonition to see for herself that the hostages were alive and well. Not that I didn't trust Gwendolyn, but the thought came to me that perhaps she was acting under duress.

Eliza gave a deep sigh, as if she were throwing off a heavy burden. "Yes, Mother. I will give you the Darksword."

Turning, she walked back to the car. Gwendolyn remained standing near the wall. Her fond gaze never left her daughter.

I thought Scylla would make some protest, but she kept silent. It was Eliza's decision to make, after all.

Returning to the car, she opened the back door and bent down to pick up the sword. I think Mosiah tried arguing with her, but—if so—their conversation was brief. Eliza slammed the door irritably and started to walk back to us. She carried with her the Darksword, both hands clasped around the hilt, the sword's blade pointed down.

Mosiah climbed out of the car, following after her, moving swiftly, silently.

Eliza had her back turned to him. She was facing her mother. She did not see him or hear him and Gwendolyn had eyes only for her daughter. Mosiah, in his black robes, was difficult to distinguish in the half-light. I saw him because I had been expecting him to do something like this. I had no doubt at all in my mind that he had deceived us, that he was going to try to take the Darksword by force. Scylla saw him, but she only stood, watching, that same slight smile on her lips.

Well, she had as good as admitted that she was attracted to him. But what about her pledge to Eliza? I could trust neither of these two apparently. Perhaps they were in league with each other.

It was up to me.

If I could have, I would have shouted a warning to Eliza. I could not, however, and so, with an inarticulate cry, I pointed toward Mosiah.

At the strange sound of my cry, Eliza looked at me, alarmed and startled.

I pointed again, frantically.

She was just starting to turn when Mosiah reached her. He grabbed hold of the Darksword.

Taken by surprise, she tried valiantly to keep hold of the weapon, but Mosiah was strong and wrested it from her with ease. Then, to my intense astonishment, he turned and, with all his strength, flung the Darksword as far from him as he could manage. He flung it directly into the gate.

The sword disappeared as if it had become one with the darkness.

Gwendolyn reached out to seize hold of Eliza.

Mosiah barreled into the woman, knocking her heavily to the ground.

Eliza screamed, a scream that ended in a strangled gasp.

Gwendolyn vanished. Mosiah wrestled with a being clad in short white robes, white boots, white gloves, and a smiling skull mask beneath a white hood.

"An Interrogator!" Scylla sucked in her breath.

"Run!" Mosiah cried, pinning the white-robed person to the ground. "More will be coming!"

Indeed, we could see the silver shimmer of the *D'karn-darah* surround us as they sprang up from the tall grass and surged toward us.

"Run where?" Scylla demanded.

The *D'karn-darah* stood between us and the air car.

They were bearing down on us. Mosiah slammed the head of the Interrogator into the ground. The skull mask lolled to one side, lay quiet. Mosiah leapt to his feet and made a scrambling dash toward us.

"The gate!" he gasped. "Run for it!"

The *D'karn-darah* had formed a semicircle and were closing in on us, though not very fast. It almost looked as if they were herding us toward the gate, which was now the only retreat open to us.

Eliza stood numb with shock, staring at the hideous being that had taken the form of her mother. I caught hold of her hand, pulled her away, nearly dragged her off her feet. Scylla took hold of her from the other side.

"Your Majesty, we must get you safely away from these evil men," Scylla said firmly. "This way! Through the gate!"

Eliza nodded and started to run, but she stumbled over her long skirts. Scylla and I helped her up and propelled her toward the gate. By now, Mosiah had joined us. We were within a foot or two of the gate, about to enter, when he gave a loud cry and held out his arms, blocking our way. He pointed to what looked like a silver coin, shining on the ground.

"Look out! It's a stasis mine! Go around! Don't step on it!"

Glancing back, I saw the *D'karn-darah* increase their speed. They had been expecting the stasis mine to stop us. Seeing it had failed, they started to close in. But we had already reached the gate.

What made me think that, once inside the gate, we would be safe from our pursuers? For all I knew, they would come in after us. The most we could hope for was to lose them in the forest's darkness, but they were so close behind that this hope seemed a forlorn one.

Of course, I now know what drew me forward. A

good thing I did not know then, I would never have believed it. As it was, I had no chance to believe or disbelieve. I entered the Eastroad Gate, entered the city of Zith-el, and I knew immediately that Scylla's theory was right.

Magic was very much alive on Thimhallan.

CHAPTER NINETEEN

*Magic is the substance and essence of Life—that is
the philosophy of this land and all who dwell here.
Life and magic are one and the same. They are
inseparable and indistinguishable.*

         ∼*DARKSWORD ADVENTURES*

I did not recall losing consciousness, yet it seemed to
me that I awoke from sleep. Then came a frightening
sensation of being compressed, the air squeezed from
my lungs, as if some force were trying to flatten me.
That sensation ended almost before I was fully aware
of it. All I could see around me was a dreamlike shimmer of color. I could hear only indistinct sounds.

I experienced a sickening feeling of falling, as when
one dreams of falling. The fall was gentle, however,
and I hit the ground running, fearful of pursuit. I almost immediately tripped over the hem of a long robe.

I tumbled forward and landed painfully on my hands and knees, scraping my knees against the cloth of the robes and cutting my right hand on an exposed tree root.

The fall left me shaken. My entrance through the gate left me more shaken still. I sat back on my heels, drew a shivering breath, and looked around. My first thought was of Eliza: was she safe? My second thought was in question marks and exclamation points: what in the Almin's name had happened to me?!

My blue jeans and sweater were gone. In their place, I was wearing a long robe, made of cloth that was white in color. The cloth was velvet, and very fine, soft and smooth. Though well made, the robe was plain, devoid of any decoration save for a red band of trim around the hem of the sleeves, and the skirt, which reached to my ankles.

Feeling an unusual coolness on my head, I lifted my hand to discover that my long hair was gone, cut short, and tonsured! Gingerly, and with a certain amount of horror, I felt the smooth round bald spot on the top of my head, where my hair had been shaved, and now grew in a ring that framed my face and just barely covered my ears.

The magic of the gate must have done this, I realized confusedly, yet the information I had just read on Zith-el indicated that the gate would change us into creatures of the Zoo. I had never read that the people of Zith-el kept catalysts in their Zoo, yet that is most certainly what I was dressed as—a catalyst in Thimhallan.

A catalyst in a Thimhallan which no longer existed!

I pondered this amazing and perplexing occurrence and wondered what I should do next. I was alone, so far as I could tell, in a thick and shadowed forest. Had I not fallen over my robes, I would have run headlong into a large oak tree. I was encircled by trees—oaks, mostly, though here and there some pines and ferns grew, vying for the meager sunlight which filtered through the oaks' green foliage. I was just noting in relief that I did not see the heart-shaped leaves of the Kij vine, when it occurred to me that what I was seeing, I was seeing by the light of the sun.

It had been near nightfall when we ran into the gate.

Slowly I rose to my feet, the white robe falling in soft folds around me. I could not call out to my companions to let them know where I was, which was—on second thought—probably just as well. I might have been discovered by our pursuers. I looked around, trying to see some sign of my companions. Almost the moment I moved, I heard a soft voice.

"Reuven? Is that you? Over here."

I heard at almost the same instant another voice say worriedly, "Your Majesty! Are you all right?"

I stumbled through the undergrowth toward the first voice, which I had recognized as Mosiah's, and emerged into a small clearing. He had his back to me, for he had turned at the sound of the other voice. It resembled Scylla's, though its accent was strange.

We heard the clink of metal and the rattle of chain and a crashing in the brush and Scylla's voice again calling to Her Majesty.

I touched Mosiah on the arm to attract his attention.

He turned and looked at me and his eyebrows shot up, his mouth gaped, and his eyes widened. By that I knew that the white robes and tonsured hair were not an illusion of my own making, as I had been most desperately hoping.

"Reuven?" He gasped out my name, and it was more question than recognition.

"I think so," I signed. "I'm not sure. Do you know what is going on?"

"I have no idea!" he replied. His words were heartfelt and uttered with such sincerity that I believed him. My first thought was that he or the other *Duuk-tsarith* had been responsible for this transformation. I knew now that was not the case.

A flash of sunlight glinting off metal some distance away caught my eye.

A knight clad in silver-plate armor worn over chain mail burst through the forest cover, sword drawn. The knight bent over something on the ground and quickly sheathed the sword.

"Your Majesty!" cried the knight. "Are you hurt?"

"I am all right, Sir Knight. Only a bruise here and there and those more to my dignity than my person."

"Allow me to assist you, Your Majesty."

The knight reached out a gloved hand.

A slender, delicate hand that flashed with jewels reached up from the forest floor and grasped the knight's hand. A figure clad in the long, straight skirts of an old-fashioned riding habit rose to her feet. It was Eliza, or rather it had been Eliza, I was not sure who she was now, any more than I was sure who *I* was. The knight in plate and chain mail was undoubtedly Scylla.

"Blessed Almin," whispered Mosiah, and I would have echoed his prayer if I'd had the voice to do so.

"What is going on?" I signed to Mosiah.

He made no answer, but he stared hard at Scylla.

I tried again. "The Technomancers? Did they follow us?"

He glanced around, shrugged, and then shook his head. "If they have followed us, they're nowhere in sight and that's not like them. The *D'karn-darah* don't deal in subtleties."

By which I gathered that if they had followed us we would be their captives by now. I breathed a little easier. Some good had come out of this, it seemed, though the old saying about frying pans and fires came into my mind.

The knight was respectfully brushing dirt from Eliza's gown, which was made of blue velvet, trimmed in black. A golden crown gleamed in her black hair, jewels sparkled on her hands. I realized in baffled amazement and with a sense of growing wonder that I recognized her. This was the Eliza I had seen in that brief glimpse inside another life. Her dress was different, but everything else about her was the same: her hair, now intricately braided and coiffed, her stance, her bearing, the jewels on her fingers. Eliza was ruefully plucking twigs from her hair and wiping the mud and grass stains from her hands, her every movement graceful and regal.

"Where are our Enforcer and our priest?" she asked worriedly, glancing around. "I hope they escaped the mob safely."

"I trust they did so, Your Majesty. The catalyst was to my left when we entered the gate, the *Duuk-tsarith* was behind us. The mob was not that close. Most were at the West Gate, trying to attack the carriage. Our ruse worked perfectly. Everyone thought you were in the carriage, Your Majesty. It never occurred to them that you would dare to enter the Eastroad Gate on foot."

"My brave knights," Eliza said with a sigh. "We fear many have suffered grievous harm for our sake."

"Their lives are pledged to Your Majesty, as is my own."

Mosiah started forward, slipping silently through the undergrowth. I followed after him, trying to emulate his stealth, but at my very first step my foot snapped a tree branch with a sound like a gunshot.

Scylla raised her sword and moved to stand protectively in front of her charge. Eliza looked curiously and without fear in our direction as Mosiah and I walked into the light filtering down from the oak leaves. I was expecting the same astonishment in their faces which I had seen in Mosiah's, even laughter at my expense, at the sight of my odd haircut.

But the only expression on the faces of both was relief and gladness, which emotions were echoed in Scylla's voice.

"Thank the Almin! You are safe!" Scylla's tone altered, becoming commanding. "Were any of the mob bold enough to follow us through the gate, Enforcer?"

Mosiah glanced around. "Why ask me? You can see as well as I."

"Pardon, Enforcer," Scylla returned coolly, "but you *Duuk-tsarith* have magical means at your disposal, means which I lack."

"Pardon me, Sir Knight"—Mosiah's tone was sarcastic—"but have you forgotten that I am devoid of Life and cannot work my magic?"

Scylla indicated me with a nod of her head. "But you have a catalyst with you. He may be a house catalyst and not trained to the specific needs of you warlocks, but he would do in an emergency, I suppose."

They were all looking at me now.

"Father Reuven, you are hurt!" Eliza pointed at my hand and I noticed, for the first time, that it was bleeding. Before I could sign that it was nothing more than a scratch, she had taken hold of my hand and was stanching the flow of blood with a handkerchief that she drew from out of the cuff of her long sleeve. The

handkerchief was lacy and appeared to be made of the
finest cloth. I drew my hand back.

"Don't be ridiculous, Father," she said in an imperious tone which indicated she was accustomed to being
obeyed. She clasped my hand and dabbed at the wound
with the handkerchief, wiping off the blood and dirt.

"We will send for the *Theldara* when our meeting is
concluded and we are safe within the walls of the city,"
she continued.

Her touch was gentle, so as not to give me pain. But
her touch *did* give me pain, a pain that was not of the
flesh but shivered through my body as if I had been
pierced with a sword.

She continued, "The cut is not deep, but it is fouled
with dirt and likely to putrefy if it is not treated."

I bowed my head in humble acknowledgment of her
command and gratitude for the kindness she showed to
me. I noticed that she kept her eyes lowered so as not to
look into mine, and that her hand holding my hand
trembled ever so slightly.

"*Father* Reuven," said Mosiah sharply. "Why do
you call him that?"

Eliza gazed at Mosiah in astonishment. "Do you
speak, Enforcer, even though no one spoke to you? We
must have been in danger, to have so loosened your
tongue! But, you are right." Her cheeks flushed prettily
and she glanced up at me from beneath her long eyelashes. "We should say 'Lord Father' now that Reuven
has been raised in rank. You must pardon us, Lord
Father," she added gravely, "for this promotion was so
newly done that we are not yet accustomed to the new
title."

My hand signed the words, "I owe it all to Your
Gracious Majesty's intercession on my behalf with
Bishop Radisovik."

She gave me a cool, slight smile with her lips and a sparkling, pleased smile with her eyes. She understood me! She understood the sign language, as if we had been speaking it for years, not for only a few hours to pass the time in the air car. And I had known before I signed that she would understand me.

I only wished I understood myself! Who was this Bishop Radisovik I had mentioned? The only Radisovik I knew of was with King Garald back on Earth. Some part of me was cognizant of what I was saying, some part of me had guided my hand to sign the words. If I looked deep into myself, I was certain I would see and understand.

Coward that I was, I turned my face away. I wasn't ready to know the truth. Not yet.

Half turning his body, his motions concealed by his black robes, Mosiah mouthed the words, "Do *you* know what is going on?"

Slowly, I shook my head.

Scylla looked to the blue sky, that was barely visible beneath the oak trees. "It is midmorning, the time set for the rendezvous. We should make our way to the meeting place without further delay. Centaurs still roam this forest, or so I have heard. First, though"— her gaze went to Mosiah—"we should make certain that we are not being followed."

Mosiah turned to me and held out his black-robed arm.

"Open the Conduit. Give me Life, Catalyst," he commanded, his tone mocking, as if he would have added, *Now we'll see this charade come to an end!*

I wanted to run. Nothing I had yet encountered, not even the Technomancers, had frightened me as much as this command. It was not the fear that I couldn't grant

Life that daunted me. It was the knowledge that I *could* do it which made me want to flee in panic.

I would have run, I think, if Eliza's eyes had not been on me. She was watching me with pride and affection. I stretched out a trembling hand and grasped Mosiah's arm. I stepped back and allowed the other Reuven to move forward.

"Almin," he prayed with my thoughts, "grant me Life."

The Conduit opened. The magic of Thimhallan flowed through me.

I felt the Life thrumming beneath my feet, swelling up from the living organisms underground. I was aware of the roots of the oak trees digging in the soil, drawing in nourishment and water. Like the oak, I was drawing in nourishment. I was drawing in the magic.

I breathed it. I heard it singing. I smelled it and tasted it as it flowed through my being. I concentrated it within me and then gave it, a wondrous gift, to Mosiah.

His eyes widened with astonishment as he felt the Life flow into his body. His arm jerked in my grasp. He wanted at first to break the connection. He didn't want to believe this any more than I did. But common sense prevailed. We were in danger. He needed Life and I was supplying it. He held his arm still in my grasp.

And then it was over. The Life was drained from me. As a catalyst, I could neither use magic nor retain it. I could act only as the intermediary. I was exhausted. It would take many hours of rest for me to recover, still more before I would be able to open the Conduit again. Yet I knew that I had been blessed, for I felt within me the touch of this world and all its beings, a touch which would never leave me.

Suffused with Life, looking considerably confused

by it all, Mosiah stared from one to the other of us—
from me, drained and tired, but left with a feeling of
serenity; to Scylla, who was frowning with impatience
and tapping the hilt of her sword with her fingers; to
Eliza, calm and aloof, standing somewhat apart from
the rest of us, in a shaft of sunlight that glittered on the
golden circlet she wore in her black hair.

"I wish I knew what the hell was going on," he
muttered to himself, and then, shrugging, he placed his
hand on the nearest of the oak trees, bent his head near
it as if he were conversing with it.

Branches above my head began to creak and rattle
together as if in a high wind, rubbing against the inter-
mingled branches of the tree's neighbor, who stirred
and began conversation with its neighbor. Soon all the
trees around us were shifting branches and dropping
twigs and reaching out their long arms to touch other
trees.

The leaves rustled and shadows shifted. Mosiah
stood beside the oak, his cheek pressed against its
rough trunk. At length the rustling and creaking
seemed to die down somewhat.

"This part of the Zoo is safe to walk in," he reported, "for the time being. A band of centaurs live
near here, but they are out hunting and will not be
back before nightfall. Because of them, no one else
dares enter. That includes the mob, Your Majesty," he
said, with a slight touch of cynical disbelief remaining
in his voice. "Your knights entered the West Gate
safely, though I fear your carriage is destroyed."

Eliza received this news with equanimity, bowing
her head in gracious appreciation and smiling to hear
those who risked their lives to protect her had not met
with any harm.

"Also," he added, watching the reaction of the other

two, "the Darksword is nowhere to be seen. The trees have no knowledge of such a weapon."

"Well, I should hope not," said Scylla. "You don't suppose it would be lying right out in the open!"

"I might suppose that, since I threw it in here," Mosiah said, but his voice was low. I was the only one who heard him.

"There is one other person inside this part of the Zoo," Mosiah continued. "A catalyst, by his garb. He is in a clearing about twenty paces to the east of our current position."

"Excellent!" Scylla grinned and nodded. "That will be Father Saryon."

I gasped and would have signed something, but Mosiah halted me.

His eyes narrowed with suspicion and displeasure. "What do you mean? You mentioned a rendezvous. Is that with Saryon? How did he escape? Is Joram with him?"

Now it was Scylla who looked astonished. Eliza drew herself up straight and regarded Mosiah with a cold gaze.

"What sort of cruel joke do you make, Enforcer?" Scylla demanded angrily. "To ask of Joram!"

"I make no joke, believe me," Mosiah returned. "Tell me—what of Joram?"

"You know the answer very well, Enforcer," Scylla retorted. "The Emperor of Merilon is dead. He died twenty years ago, in the Temple of the Necromancers."

"How did he die?" Mosiah asked, and his voice was calm.

"At the hands of the Executioner."

"Ah," said Mosiah, and he sighed in relief. "*Now* I know what is going on!"

CHAPTER TWENTY

"For returning to this realm and bringing upon it untold danger, the sentence of death is placed upon this man Joram."

~ BISHOP VANYA; *TRIUMPH OF THE DARKSWORD*

Scylla frowned, her brow creased. "I fear you have taken serious hurt, Enforcer. A blow on the head, perhaps?"

Mosiah put his hand to his forehead. "Yes, for a moment I was quite disoriented. I was loath to tell you. I did not want to worry Her Majesty." Hands folded, he bowed. His tone was respectful, all trace of sarcasm gone.

Eliza had been cold and withdrawn. At this statement, she warmed and drew near him, looking concerned. "Are you all right now, Enforcer?"

"Thank you, Your Majesty. I am recovering. I fear, however, that there may be gaps in my memory. If anything that I say or do sounds odd, you must put it down to that account. I beg you to be patient with any questions I may ask."

How very clever! I thought. Now he frees himself to ask whatever questions he will and they will think it's nothing more than the bump on his head.

"Certainly, Enforcer." The Queen was gracious. "And now we should be going to meet with Father Saryon. We are already late and he will be worried. Sir Knight, will you lead the way?"

"Yes, Your Majesty."

Scylla, sword drawn, took a moment to get her bearings, which she did by looking again at the sun, then searched the ground for signs of a trail. She found one, not far distant, which—by the cloven hoofprints—had been made by some sort of beast.

"This is a centaur trail," Mosiah warned. "Isn't that dangerous?"

"You said yourself they were off hunting," Scylla countered. "We have need of speed and this is faster and easier than slogging through the undergrowth. Besides, centaur prefer ambushing lone, helpless travelers—such as Father Saryon."

"True," Mosiah conceded. "If you will take the lead, Sir Knight. I will guard the rear."

As she walked near him, to take her place at the head of our small group, Scylla paused and looked Mosiah squarely in the eyes. "Are you certain you're all right, Enforcer?" she asked, and there was true caring and concern in her voice, softness in her bright eyes.

"Yes, lady," he said, astonished. "Thank you."

She grinned at him and clapped him on the upper arm with an enthusiasm that made him wince, then she turned and continued moving cautiously and watchfully along the path. Eliza gathered her long skirts and followed.

Mosiah stood a moment staring after Scylla in confusion, a confusion which did not all arise from the strange and inexplicable situation in which we found ourselves, but which was the confusion experienced by any man in any place in any time when confronted with the strange and inexplicable motives of a woman.

Shaking his head, he shrugged and gestured to me to join him.

The trail was wide enough for two people to walk side by side, though, by the prints, the centaurs walked along it in single file.

I signed to Mosiah, "You seem to have some idea what is happening to us."

"So do you, I believe," he said, glancing at me sidelong.

I felt called upon to explain. "I've caught glimpses of myself in . . . another life," was the best way I could describe it. "And I've seen Eliza and Scylla there, too. I didn't say anything before because I wasn't sure."

"Tell me what you saw."

I did so, adding that it wasn't much and wasn't likely to help us. "It didn't seem to make any sense."

"It doesn't make sense now," he said, and his face was grim. "We have been sent to another time, an alternate time. But why? How did we get here? And why do *you* recall another time and *I* recall another time, yet neither Scylla nor Eliza seems to. And how do we get back?"

"The Technomancers?" I suggested. "Perhaps they are responsible. What was that . . . thing . . . you attacked out beyond the Wall. The thing in the white mask that looked like Gwendolyn."

"She was one of the Kylanistic order of the Technomancers," Mosiah replied. "They are known as the Interrogators. They have the ability to take on the face and form and voice of another person in order to induce the victim to do precisely what Eliza was about to do—hand over our valuables, our secrets. They can infiltrate any organization by using such disguises."

"How did you know it *wasn't* Gwendolyn? Could you see through the disguise?"

"Their disguises are not easy to penetrate. They overplayed their hand by having the woman use magic. In all the time we have kept watch on Joram, I've never seen Gwen rely on Life. Not even when she's alone. Eliza noticed and thought it was odd, but she was too willing to believe it was her mother to question it. Then, I saw Joram's injuries. I *know* it was more serious than they let on."

"Why did she abandon the disguise?"

"It takes a great deal of magical energy to maintain the illusion. She could not expend the energy necessary and fight me at the same time, which is why I attacked her."

"If you had been wrong?" I hinted.

"But I wasn't. If I had been, however, and it really was Gwen, then I would have had a chance of rescuing her."

"Do you believe that the Technomancers have her prisoner?"

"I would say yes, since they were able to create such a realistic illusion. On the other hand, I would say no, since Smythe didn't mention her as one of the hostages."

"But what else could have happened to her?"

Mosiah shook his head. Either he didn't know or he wasn't saying.

I tried another question. "That thing you called a stasis mine. What was that?"

"If one of us had stepped on it, it would have trapped us all in a stasis field. We could not have moved until the Technomancers released us."

I hesitated to ask my next question, because I feared his answer. Finally, I ventured, "What if this experience is not real—a hallucination. Maybe they're controlling our minds."

"If that is true," he said with a wry smile, "and they *are* controlling our minds, then I doubt if they would permit your mind to consider the possibility. The Technomancers may be responsible for this, though I can't fathom why they would want to send us to another time when they so clearly had us where they wanted us in the last one."

He was silent a moment, then said quietly, "There were those who once practiced the Mystery of Time upon Thimhallan. The Diviners."

"Yes, but they perished during the Iron Wars," I pointed out. "Their kind was never seen or heard of after that."

"True. Well, we must keep our eyes and ears open and see if we can solve this mystery. Joram is dead." Mosiah pondered. "What would Thimhallan have been like if Joram had died at the hands of the Executioner? If Joram had died before he destroyed the Well of Life and released the magic? I wonder. . . ."

He retreated into his own thoughts, fell back a pace or two behind me to indicate that he wanted to be alone. I was intent on my thoughts for a moment or two and then I noticed that Eliza was glancing at me

out of the corner of her eye and that, by her smile, she
seemed to invite me to come walk beside her.

My heartbeat quickened. I drew near her. With a
small gesture toward Scylla's armored back, to enjoin
silence, Eliza began to sign to me. It amused me to find
that my language of the hands—a poor second to a
voice—was becoming a language of intrigue and secrecy.

"I am sorry for my part in our quarrel last night,"
Eliza signed to me. "Will you forgive me, Reuven?"

I knew well the quarrel she meant, though I could
not have said that a second ago. As words or images
will trigger memories of a dream, so her reference
brought the entire scene to me, only much more real
than any dream. It was not a dream. It had happened—
at least in this here and now, it had happened.

Perhaps it was the influence of the magical Life
flowing through my veins, but my other self—the self
of Earth—was rapidly fading into the background.

"There is nothing to forgive, my dear one," I signed
in return.

I looked at her, the sun glistening on her black curls,
the golden shimmer of her crown, the dappled sunlight
now sparkling on her jewels, the shadows of the trees
now gliding over her, dimming all light but her own.

I loved her. My love for her flowed out of me to her
as the Life had flowed out of me to Mosiah.

I had loved her since we were children together and
I would go on loving her, no matter what happened,
until the day came when I would present that love as a
gift to the Almin and reside forever in His blessedness.

The images of our past, our youth, and our present
were still confused—I remembered her as a newborn
child, I remembered an undercurrent of fear throughout my childhood. I remembered years spent in study at

the Font, holiday time spent in my home with the one who was my foster sister, and so much more. I remembered leaving a sassy, willful child and returning to find a beautiful, spirited woman. But who had raised us? Where had we lived? That was hidden from me.

"Your safety was my only concern," I signed.

"You understand that there could be no other way," she returned. "That this was something I had to do, being my father's heir." She regarded me intently, awaiting my answer.

"I understand," I signed. "I understood then. I only said those things to provoke you. It worked. I thought you'd take a swing at me again, like in the old days."

I was hoping to make her laugh. My mischievous delight as a child, I am sorry to say, had been to tease her until she lost her temper and struck at me with her small fists. Though I always protested that I was the innocent victim, I was not believed and we were both sent to bed without our suppers on those occasions.

She did not laugh, though she smiled at the memory. Impulsively, she reached out, took hold of my hand, and whispered, "Like in the old days, Reuven, I can count on you and you alone to brush away the glittering faerie dust the rest would scatter over my duties. You alone show me the ugly reality beneath. You force me to look at the ugliness and then to see beyond it, to hope. Admit it"—her eyes gleamed with a hint of triumph—"if I had refused to come, you would have been disappointed in me."

"I would have thought that for once in your life you had made a sensible and rational decision," I signed, attempting to look stern. "As it is, my only disappointment would have been if you had not permitted me to come with you."

"And how could I leave you behind?" she asked,

smiling and mocking me. Forgetting herself, she spoke out loud. "I'd have to hear you whine about it for days. 'Eliza got to go and I didn't!' " she concluded in a childish voice, talking through her nose.

"Hush!" said Scylla, turning. "I beg your pardon, Your Majesty. It's just that—"

"We're not on a picnic, Your Majesty," Mosiah said dourly, gliding up to stand beside us.

"You are right, both of you," Eliza murmured, her cheeks flushed. "It won't happen again."

"We are very near the meeting place," Scylla said. "Enforcer?"

The oak trees had creaked and rattled their limbs as we walked along and I guessed that they must be continuing to provide Mosiah with information.

"Father Saryon is in the clearing and he is alone. He has, however, heard our approach and is more than a little unnerved. I suggest we ease his fears."

"I will go forth into the glade," said Scylla. "You remain here with Her Majesty."

"Oh, nonsense!" said Eliza, losing patience. "We'll all go together. If it is a trap, we've already walked into it. Come, Reuven."

Emerging into a glade, we came upon an elderly priest, who had been looking nervously to his right and left previous to our appearance.

At the sight of us, he breathed a gentle sigh. He smiled and extended his hands, one to either of us.

"My children," Saryon said in heartfelt tones.

My eyes blurred with tears. I knew then the man who had been father to Eliza and to me, the man who had taken two orphans into his home and into his heart.

No wonder I had felt the love of a son for a father in

that other life. Such love knows no bounds, would stretch across the gulf of time.

He gave me his hand and looked with pleasure and pride upon my white robes with their red trim. The white marked me a house catalyst, one who is in the employ of some noble family. The red indicated that I was a Lord Father, a high rank for one of my years.

He would have bowed and kissed Eliza's hand, but she forestalled him by flinging her arms around his neck and kissing him heartily on the cheek. He hugged her and held her close, all the while keeping firm hold of my hand, and we had a most joyous family reunion there in the glade in the Zoo of Zith-el.

"It has been so long since I've seen both of you," he said, releasing us to look at us fondly.

"We do think the Emperor might let you come to visit us in Merilon," said Eliza, a tiny furrow creasing her forehead.

"No, no, Emperor Garald is right," Saryon said, sighing. "The ways are dangerous, very dangerous."

"The Conduits are safe."

"The *Thon-li* refuse to guarantee it these days. Menju the Sorcerer has many allies on Thimhallan. Not that I care for any danger for myself, mind you," he added with a touch of spirit. "I am more than ready to go to my rest, to be reunited with your father and your mother." He patted Eliza's hand. "But I cannot put down the great burden I bear. Not yet. Not yet."

I blinked my eyes free of the glad tears, and now that I could see Father Saryon more clearly, I was shocked at his appearance. He had aged far beyond his years, was gray and stooped, as if the burden of which he spoke was a physical one. He was not frail or fragile in spirit, only in body.

Scylla and Mosiah had held back at the edge of the

glade, to give us a moment's privacy for our reunion and also to make certain no one and nothing was lying in wait. Now they walked forward, both making respectful bows to Father Saryon. He greeted Mosiah with pleasure, mentioning that he had heard Mosiah was now in Queen Eliza's service. Mosiah stood with hands folded before him, silent and observant.

Scylla was not known to Saryon, apparently, for Eliza introduced her as her knight and captain of her guard. Scylla was polite, but her manner was brisk. She was obviously ill at ease.

"We should stay here no longer than is necessary, Your Majesty. With your gracious permission, I would suggest that we leave immediately."

"Is that well with you, Father Saryon?" Eliza asked him, regarding him anxiously. She, too, was concerned and dismayed at his wan appearance. "You look tired. Did you walk all this way? The journey must have been a strenuous one for you. Do you need to rest?"

"There can be no rest for me until I have completed my task. Yet," he added, looking earnestly and searchingly at Eliza, "yet I would go to my grave bearing this secret if you are the least bit unsure, Daughter. Will you take on this heavy responsibility? Have you considered well the perils you will face?"

Eliza gripped him by both hands. "Yes, Father, dear Father, the only father I have ever known. Yes, I have considered the perils. They've been shown to me in vivid detail," she added with a glance and a smile for me, before she turned back to Saryon. "I am prepared to take the responsibility; to finish, if need be, what my father began."

"He would have been proud of you, Eliza," Saryon said gently. "So proud."

"Your Majesty—"

"Yes, Scylla, we are leaving. Father, you must guide us, for you are the only one who knows the way."

Saryon shook his head and I guessed that the way of which he was thinking was not the sun-dappled path through the forest, but the path forever cloaked with darkness which leads into the future.

Eliza walked at his side, holding on to his arm in a close and confiding manner which pleased him immensely. The trail not being wide enough for three of us to walk side by side, I fell a pace or two behind, which put me between Saryon and Eliza in front and Scylla and Mosiah in back.

"Perhaps I am still suffering from the effects of my injury," Mosiah said, "but what is there to fear, besides the usual fears which always attend anyone insane enough to walk through the Zoo of Zith-el? You said yourself that the centaurs would not attack us."

Scylla made a disparaging sound in her throat. "Short work to them if they did. No, it is not the centaurs I fear, nor darkrovers, nor giants, nor faeries." She paused a moment, then said quietly, "I wonder that you cannot guess."

"You fear the *Duuk-tsarith*. Of which I am one."

"True, but you have always been of an independent nature, Mosiah, and were not afraid to go your own way, if you thought the other way wrong. That was why Her Majesty chose you to accompany us. You are the only one of her Enforcers she felt she could trust."

"What is it you fear the *Duuk-tsarith* will do?"

"Why, try to seize the Darksword, of course," Scylla responded.

"So that is why we're here," Mosiah said thoughtfully. " 'I am prepared to take the responsibility,' the Queen said. Eliza means to use the Darksword. And Father Saryon knows where it is."

"Certainly. Didn't Her Majesty explain this to you before we left?"

"Perhaps Her Majesty does not put as much faith in me as you do," Mosiah said wryly.

Scylla sighed. "One can hardly blame her—after all that's happened. Emperor Garald believes that the *Duuk-tsarith* are under his control and will obey his commands. Certainly, they've given him no reason to think otherwise, but still . . ."

"You don't trust them."

"The Darksword is a great prize. It could give them enormous power, especially if they discovered the secret to making more swords."

"I don't see how. No one with Life can use it. The Darksword would drain them of their magic and leave them helpless."

"That bump you took *must* be severe," Scylla said. "Or maybe it's a recurrence of those injuries you suffered in the collapse of Lord Samuel's house during the battle. Whatever it is, you're obviously not thinking straight. The Dead among the *Duuk-tsarith* would wield the Darksword. *You* were the one who told me that is why the Dead were recruited in the first place. And then it's widely known that the *Duuk-tsarith* don't believe in the Bishop's prophecy. Like many others, they think it's a political device cooked up by the Emperor and Radisovik to frighten the rebels."

"My head throbs," Mosiah said, and he sounded very plaintive. "Remind me of this prophecy."

Scylla lowered her voice, spoke solemnly. "That the Devil himself was raising an army against us. Demons armed with Hell's Light would come down on us from the skies and destroy every living thing in Thimhallan."

So startled and alarmed was I by this prophecy that I turned in consternation and stared at Mosiah.

"The Hch'nyv!" I signed.

"What?" Scylla demanded. "I don't understand. What is he talking about?"

"A previous conversation we had. It is not important." Mosiah made a swift motion with his hand, counseling me to keep quiet. "This prophecy . . . when is it to be fulfilled?"

"This time tomorrow, the demons will launch their attack. Thus Bishop Radisovik was told: 'Only the Darksword in the hands of Joram's heir can save us.' "

"And who gave the Bishop this infor—this prophecy?"

"A being of light," said Scylla, sounding awed. "An angel sent from the Almin."

"I can understand how my brethren in the *Duuktsarith* could be skeptical," Mosiah said. "I must admit I find it hard to believe."

Scylla drew in a deep breath, seeming about to argue or reprimand. Slowly, however, she released it. "This is not the time for another of our theological debates. Though I do worry about your soul and pray for you nightly."

Mosiah appeared considerably taken aback by this statement and didn't seem to know what to say. Scylla was also silent, preoccupied.

I was watching them and listening as best I could while keeping one eye on the path ahead. He started to speak, but she interrupted him.

"I wish Her Majesty had discussed this with you!" she said, then added decisively, "Still, it is only right that you know. But this must be kept secret. The Emperor sent a message to Earth, to General Boris."

Scylla paused, expecting Mosiah to look shocked. He accepted this news very calmly.

"What is wrong with that? General Boris and King—I mean Emperor Garald are friends, after all."

"Hush! Never say such a thing aloud! Don't even think it! It would be worth the price of the Emperor's life if it were known that he had ties with the enemy."

"The enemy. I see. What did our enemy General Boris have to say about this heavenly missive?"

"That the Devil is indeed coming, though not perhaps in the form we might expect. Boris went on to add details about an invasion force that had destroyed Earth's outposts and was now rapidly closing in on Earth. He said that Earth Forces would do what they could to protect Thimhallan, although he added in a closing note that he feared they fought a losing battle and warned us to ready our defenses."

Mosiah and I again exchanged looks. I turned away with a sigh. The Hch'nyv. It had to be. I had hoped that we had left them behind in that other time, but that apparently was not the case. They were coming and they were right on schedule. We had less than forty-eight hours to stop them.

The Darksword in the hands of Joram's heir. The Darksword in Joram's hands. How could a sword in anybody's hands halt the advance of an alien horde, when neutron bombs, photon missiles, laser cannons— the most sophisticated, powerful killing machines humans had ever devised—had not put even a dent in their armor?

I felt suddenly very tired, my footsteps dragged. This was all so futile! Hopeless! Our feeble struggles were doing nothing more than alerting the spider to the fact that we were tangled in its web. I was thinking it would be far better to sit down beneath these lovely oaks with a couple of bottles of good wine and drink a

final toast to humanity, when a hand smote me between the shoulder blades.

"Cheer up, Lord Father!" Scylla said, and after
nearly knocking me flat, she very kindly assisted me to
keep my balance. "Joram's heir will soon have the
Darksword and then all will be well."

She strode past me, going to the front of the line in
response to a gesture from Eliza, a gesture that I had
not even seen, so dark were the thoughts surrounding
me.

All during this conversation, our path had been
veering downward at a gentle slope. The oaks gave way
to poplar and aspen, these gave way to willows. I had
long heard the sounds of rushing water, and rounding
a bend, we came in sight of a narrow, swift-flowing
river. The Hira River, or so I recalled from my research; it cuts right through the heart of Zith-el. Like
the inhabitants of Zith-el, the Hira was tame and
placid when it was inside the city, but became rough
and dangerous and wild when it entered the Zoo.

The sun shone bright on the water, its light warm
on my face. Looking into the heavens, I saw the white
wisps of clouds drawn like flimsy veils over the blue
sky. Cotton from the cottonwoods drifted down
around us, a summer snowstorm.

The water was green where it ran smooth, foaming
white where it leapt over rocks, black where it ran
beneath the overhanging limbs of the trees lining the
bank. Some distance from us was one enormous willow, which leaned far out over the river, its arms gracefully outstretched, its leaves trailing through the water.
Its exposed roots were gnarled and huge, like knuckles
on a boxer, from the effort of keeping fast hold on the
soil.

"There." Father Saryon pointed. "That is our destination."

We walked along the bank, approaching the willow, and none of us said a word. I do not know what the others were thinking, but in my mind I saw the river red with blood, the willow withering in flame, the blue sky gray with smoke. But whereas before I had been despairing, now I was angry.

We would fight to save this: the sun, the sky, the clouds, the willow. Hopeless though it might be, though no one would be left alive to tell of it, we would fight to the very end.

Father Saryon pointed at something else downstream from our position and said something; I couldn't hear what, due to the bubbling of the water. I moved closer, coming level with Scylla and Eliza. Mosiah did not immediately join us. When I looked back for him, I saw him kneeling down on the path, in apparent conversation with an enormous raven with bristling black feathers, which gave it a hunchbacked appearance.

The *Duuk-tsarith* often used ravens as an extension of the Enforcer's ears and eyes.

"—not far," Saryon was saying. "There at the bend. Be careful. The path along the riverbank is muddy and very slippery."

There was a slight drop-off from the path in the woods to the path along the riverbank, caused by the churning of the water in a small pool below us, which had eroded the bank. Saryon was about to make a clumsy descent. I interceded, offering to go first and stand ready to assist those who came after.

Scylla remained on the highest part of the path, her hand on her sword hilt, keeping watch all around us. I gathered up the skirts of my robes and half jumped, half slid down to the river trail. Once I had regained my feet, I turned and reached out my arms to Eliza. She did not hesitate, but made the jump with skill. She did not really need my help, but she ended up in my arms anyway.

For a brief moment we held fast to each other. She looked up into my eyes and I gazed down into hers. She loved me! I knew then that she loved me, as I loved her. My joy was bright as the sunshine on the water, but the next moment the joy flowed into a shallow, stagnant pool, dark and dismal.

Our love could never come to anything. She was Queen of Merilon and I was her house catalyst, a mute catalyst at that. She had duties and responsibilities to her people, duties in which I could assist her, in my humble calling, but only in my humble calling. She was betrothed. I knew her future husband well; he was the son of Emperor Garald and was much younger than Eliza. They were waiting for the boy to come of age. The marriage would strengthen the Empire, forever bonding the kingdoms of Merilon and Sharakan.

Provided, of course, that the Hch'nyv did not kill us all first.

Eliza slipped out of my grasp. "You help Father Saryon now, Reuven," she said softly, and walking a slight distance from me, she turned away from me and stared out across the glistening water. I watched her a moment, saw her hand reach up to her eyes, but the movement was swift and was not repeated.

She had accepted her duty and was resigned to it. Could I do less, with her brave example before me?

I held out my hand to Father Saryon, and helped him safely to the bank below.

"It wasn't this difficult twenty years ago," he said. "At least not that I remember. I managed by myself without any trouble at all. I was much younger then, of course." He came level with me and looked at me intently. "Are you all right, Reuven?"

"Yes, sir, I am," I signed.

He looked from me to Eliza, who remained standing with her back to us all, and his expression grew sad and sorrowful. I saw that he knew, that he must have known for some time.

"I am sorry, my son," he said. "I wish—"

But I was never to know what he wished, for he was unable to express it. Shaking his head, he went to Eliza and rested his hand gently upon her arm.

Scylla jumped and landed beside me, with a rattle of armor and a thud that shook the ground. She brushed off brusquely my attempt at assistance.

"Where is the Enforcer?" she asked impatiently, and turned back to peer up the bank.

Mosiah stood above us, a dark and ominous figure in his black robes, which fluttered in the wind. The raven hopped on the ground at his side.

"Father Saryon," he called. "Where are you bound?"

Saryon gazed up at him. "There is a cave in the bend of the river—"

"No, Father," said Mosiah, and his voice was deep and stern. "You must find some other path. We dare not go near that cave. The raven has warned me. That cave is the dwelling of a Dragon of the Night."

Scylla looked alarmed. Eliza paled and her eyes widened. Father Saryon was not the least bit disconcerted by this news. He nodded and smiled. "Yes, I know."

"You know!" Mosiah leapt from the bank. His black robes billowed around him. He drifted like a sooty wisp of cottonwood to the bank and landed in front of Saryon. The raven, taking wing, flapped and fluttered at his shoulder. "You know and you will go anyway?"

"Do you realize, Father," Scylla added, "the risk we run? An army of warlocks could not win a battle against a Dragon of the Night, should it awake and attack us."

"I know the risk well," Saryon said, with a flash of his old spirit. "I ran that risk myself, all alone, twenty years ago. Not out of choice, mind you, but out of desperation. I don't need you three to remind me."

He gazed at us, his eyes narrowed. "If you want to recover the Darksword, that is where we must go. The Dragon of the Night is the Darksword's guardian."

CHAPTER TWENTY-ONE

*Saryon caught Joram in his arms. Touching the
fabric of the crimson-stained robes, the catalyst felt
the warm wetness of life's blood draining from
Joram's body, falling through Saryon's fingers like
the petals of a shattered tulip.*

⟿ TRIUMPH OF THE DARKSWORD

Eliza listened gravely to Mosiah's arguments against
going. She asked Father Saryon if there was any way to
retrieve the Darksword without facing the dragon. On
his replying that there was not, she said it was her
intention to go with Father Saryon, but that she would
not ask any of the rest of us to go with her. In fact, it
was her express command that we remain behind.

Needless to say, that was one command in her reign
she could not convince any of us to obey. After some
further discussion we headed for the cave—all five of
us.

"Now at least," said Mosiah as he trudged along behind me, "we won't have to worry about dying at the hands of the Hch'nyv."

"According to Father Saryon," I signed, "the dragon is charmed. As I recall, a person is able to control one of these dragons if he touches the charm the warlocks embedded in the dragon's head."

"Thank you, Mister Encyclopedia," Mosiah retorted sarcastically. We had left the sunshine and returned to the shadows, walking beneath the willows and cottonwoods that bordered the river. "It takes a very strong and powerful personality to cast a charm on a dragon. My respect for Father Saryon is vast, but 'strong' and 'powerful' are not words I would use to describe him."

"I think you underestimate him," I signed back defensively. "He was strong enough to sacrifice himself when they would have turned Joram to stone. He was strong enough and powerful enough to assist Joram in fighting Blachloch."

Mosiah remained unconvinced. "Twenty years have passed since he left the Darksword with the dragon! Even if Father Saryon *did* actually charm the beast, the charm could not possibly hold it that long!"

I felt regretfully that Mosiah was right. The Dragons of Night had been designed by their creators as killing machines, made to slaughter on command. During the Iron Wars some of these dragons had escaped their creators and wreaked havoc among their own forces. After the war the *D'karn-duuk*, who had made the dragons and controlled them, were mostly dead. Those who survived were too battle-shocked and exhausted to deal with the Warchanged. The Dragons of Night escaped and fled below ground, seeking to hide from the light of day, which they loathed and feared, in the endless night of tunnel and cave.

They have no love for man, remembering always who had doomed them to this dark life and hating them for it.

We had now arrived at the cavern entrance. Halting on the riverbank, we stared at it bleakly. The opening—dark against the gray rock face—was an enormous archway of gray stone, easy for all of us to enter, or it would have been had not most of it been sunk underwater! A part of the river had branched off, flowed, swift and deep, into the cavern.

"You're out of luck, Father," Mosiah said. "The river has changed course. Unless you would have us swim these treacherous currents, we can't go inside." The raven, perched on a tree limb, gave a raucous caw.

I am ashamed to say that my first reaction was one of relief, until I saw Eliza.

Up to this time she had borne calmly and courageously all dangers and setbacks. This disappointment was too much for her to bear. She clenched her fists.

"We must get inside!" she cried, her face white to the lips, adding wildly, "I *will* swim if I have to."

The water flowing into the cave was fast-moving, with small, swirling whirlpools and dangerous eddies that splashed and foamed among sharp rocks. Swimming was not an option.

"We could build a raft," said Scylla. "Lash together some logs. Perhaps the Enforcer with his magic—"

"I am not a conjurer, nor am I *Pron-alban,* a craftsman," said Mosiah coldly. "I am not learned in boatbuilding, and I don't think you want to wait while I study up on the subject."

"I wasn't asking you to build a full-blown sailing vessel," Scylla returned, her eyes flashing in anger. "But

I *do* think you might be able to use one of your fire spells to burn out the inside of a log so that we could make a canoe."

"Canoe!" Mosiah snorted. "Perhaps we'll use your head, Sir Knight. It must be hollow enough! Has it ever occurred to you that I will need to conserve all the Life I have left to extricate us from the clutches of this dragon, which—I have the feeling—isn't going to be exactly *charmed* to see us."

All this time Father Saryon had been attempting to say something. At last, he had his chance. "Do you have so little faith in me, to think I would bring you to a drowned cave?"

He smiled as he said the words, but we felt the rebuke, especially myself and Eliza.

"Forgive me, Father," Eliza said, looking remorseful. "You are right. I should have had faith in you."

"If not me, then at least in the Almin," Saryon said, and he cast a glance at Mosiah which indicated that the elderly priest had also heard at least part of our former conversation.

Mosiah said nothing, made no apology. He stood stoic and silent, his arms crossed, his hands concealed in the black sleeves of his robes.

Saryon continued, adding briskly, "There is a path, over here. A rock ledge runs above the water level. This path leads to a corridor which takes us away from the river, down into the bowels of the cavern."

The path along the riverbank made a meandering turn to the left, circling around a large willow, whose limbs and trunk sheltered part of the cave entrance from view. Saryon parted the swaying, leafy branches and there was the rock ledge, leading into the cavern.

Mosiah offered to go first and I thought perhaps

this was his way of making amends for having been so short-tempered.

"Don't follow me until you receive my signal," he cautioned.

He entered the cave, taking the raven with him, and soon passed beyond our sight. I wondered why the bird had been invited to come, then realized—when it came flapping back out of the cave entrance, like an over-large bat—that the raven was to be the messenger.

"Come ahead," the bird croaked in a raspy voice. "One of you at a time."

Eliza went next, entering the cavern stalwartly and without fear. My fear *for* her was enough for both of us, however. I watched her as long as I could, as if my will alone would hold her on that ledge and she must fall when she was out of my sight.

The raven had flown in with her and I waited in agony until the bird returned. "She is safe. Send the next."

"You go, Reuven," said Saryon, a smile in his eyes.

I could not believe I was actually eager to enter that cave, but now nothing could have kept me from it.

Chill damp air washed over me and I had to wait until my eyes adjusted to the darkness. The light shining outside the cavern gleamed off the rushing water and lit my way for a short distance. The path was wide here and I was able to make fairly good time.

But then the path narrowed, until I could barely place my two feet side by side. The ledge rounded a bend in the wall, which cut off the light. I expected this part to be dark and was astonished to find the way bathed in a warm reddish glow. One of the stalactites overhead radiated light and warmth, as if the rock had been heated. I could see the path, a shimmering ribbon of gray above the black and shimmering water. The raven winged past me, returning to Mosiah.

I understood now why the Enforcer had offered to go first. He had walked the darkness in order to light the way for the rest of us.

The path began to rise and here it narrowed farther, until I was forced to place my back against the wall and shuffle sideways. I crept along, out of sight of my friends behind me, not yet within sight of Mosiah and Eliza ahead of me. One false step and I would plunge into the murky, foaming water below. Sweat beaded on my brow and trickled down my breast; the cold air set me shivering. I had never in my life felt so alone.

I took another step and I could see the end, and there, waiting for me, were Mosiah and Eliza. I was so eager to reach them that I was tempted to fling caution to the winds and make a dash for safety.

"Easy now," Mosiah warned. "This is the hardest part."

I controlled the urge to bolt. I pressed so hard against the rock that I scraped the flesh off my back and edged carefully along the path. It grew wider as I went and I was able to quicken my pace. I stumbled into Eliza's arms and we clung to each other for comfort, our shared warmth driving away the thought of falling into the swirling water. I blessed Saryon for having sent me ahead to have this time with her.

Mosiah watched us with a faintly sardonic smile on his lips, though he said nothing, merely sending the raven back with the message, "Next!"

Father Saryon arrived, his movements so awkward and ungainly upon the ledge that we thought more than once he must topple over. He would always manage to save himself, however, his hands snagging an outcropping of rock when his foot slipped or his feet maintaining a toehold when his hands could not find purchase.

He reached us at last and wiped dirt from his palms. "That was much easier than the first time I made that trip," he said, keeping his voice low. Though the dragon was far down in the very bottom of the cavern, we dared not take a chance on its hearing us. "I did not have a wizard with me to provide light." He nodded his thanks to Mosiah. "And I was carrying the Darksword at the time."

"What drove you to make the trip at all, Father?" Mosiah asked, his eyes visible in the shadows of his hood only by their reflection of the red-glowing stalactite. He had sent the raven back for Scylla. "Were you pursued?"

Saryon was silent a moment, his face pale and haggard at the memory. "I think, on reflection, that I probably was not, but I had no way of knowing that at the time. Besides, to be safe, I had to believe that they *were* in pursuit. What led me into this cave? Instinct, maybe, the instinct of the hunted to seek a dark place in which to hide. Or maybe the hand of the Almin."

Mosiah lifted an eyebrow, turned away, and watched the path. We heard the clash of steel against rock and Mosiah muttered, "So much for stealth."

The sound was immediately muffled. A short wait, and then Scylla appeared, rounding that same treacherous bend, the red of the stalactite burning like flame in her silver armor.

She was having a difficult time of it. The breastplate prevented her from flattening her back against the wall, as the rest of us had done. She was inching her way along, clinging to the wall with her hands. And then she came to a halt, leaned her head back against the wall, and closed her eyes.

"Tell her," Mosiah said to the raven, "that this is no time for a nap!"

The raven floated over, hovered near Scylla. We could not hear what she said, but the words seemed forced out in a gasp that was audible from where we stood.

"She says she can't move," the raven reported. Landing on the path beside Mosiah, it began to clean its beak with a clawed foot. "She knows she's going to fall."

Frozen in terror, Scylla clung to the wall. My heart ached for her. I had known the same fear and the Al-min only knew what had kept me going. The sight of Eliza, I think.

"She needs help," said Father Saryon, gathering up the skirt of his robe.

"I'll go," said Mosiah. "I don't want to have to drag both of you out of the river!"

He returned along the treacherous path. Facing the wall, he edged his way forward, until he was within an arm's length of Scylla.

"What's the matter?" he asked.

Scylla could not move her head to look at him. She could barely move her lips. "I . . . I can't swim!"

"Bless the girl!" Mosiah said in exasperation. "If you fall into the water, you won't have to worry about swimming. You'll sink like a boulder in that armor."

At this, Scylla gave a brief, mirthless laugh. "You're such a comfort!" she said through clenched teeth.

"I have my magic," Mosiah told her. "I don't want to use it, unless I have to. But I will not let you fall. Look at me. Look at me, Scylla."

Scylla managed to twist her head, looked at Mosiah.

He extended his hand. "Here, take hold."

She raised her arm, the armor scraping against the rock, and slowly reached toward Mosiah, her hand outstretched. He clasped his hand over hers, and held on to her tightly. Her face smoothed in relief. She ventured forward. He drew her along the path, holding her steady.

At the end, when they reached safe ground, Scylla gave a great shuddering sob and covered her face with her hands. I think Mosiah would have put his arms around her, but for her armor. Hugging her would have been tantamount to embracing an iron stove.

"I have shamed myself," Scylla whispered fiercely. "Before my queen!"

"By what? Proving you're human like the rest of us. I, for one, was happy to see it. I was beginning to wonder."

Scylla uncovered her eyes and looked at Mosiah, as if she suspected there might be more to this statement than appeared. He was half-amused, half-sympathetic, nothing deeper.

"Thank you," Scylla said, her voice husky. "You saved my life, Enforcer. I am in your debt." Subdued, she walked over to Eliza and knelt before her on one knee. "Forgive me, Your Majesty, for my cowardice in the face of danger. If you wish to remove me from the position of trust in which you have placed me, I will readily understand."

"Oh, Scylla!" cried Eliza warmly. "We are of Mosiah's opinion. We are glad to see that you are flawed, like the rest of us. It's very difficult to love a paragon."

Scylla was overcome and, for a moment, could not speak. At length, wiping her hand across her nose and eyes, she stood up and threw back her head, faced us proudly, if somewhat defiantly.

"Which way do we go now, Father?" Eliza asked.

We had been concentrating so hard on the path behind us that we had given no consideration to the path before us. The river veered off to the right. Our ledge ended, but we could see the shadowy opening of what appeared to be a tunnel.

"We go down," said Saryon.

CHAPTER TWENTY-TWO

"Perhaps the killer's gone. . . ."
"I doubt it. He didn't get what he came for."

~SARYON AND JORAM;
TRIUMPH OF THE DARKSWORD

We went down. And down. And down.

A flaming brand lit our way. Mosiah had been going to expend more of his magical Life to provide light, but that proved unnecessary.

"You will find a brand, tinderbox, and flint in a small chamber near the entrance to the tunnel," Saryon advised us. "I left them there myself, on the chance that someday I would return."

"Tools of the Dark Arts," Mosiah said, with a slight smile, harkening back to a time on Thimhallan when the use of such "tools" as a tinderbox and flint was prohibited. Such objects gave Life to that which was Dead.

Scylla carried the brand, walked in front with Saryon. I remained at Eliza's side, our hands twined together. From this point on, our lives would be changed for good or ill. Perhaps, in a short time, we would be dead. It didn't matter anymore that she was a queen and I was her house catalyst. Our love, a love that had sent down its roots in early childhood, had grown strong like the oak, and though the tree might be cut down, it could never be uprooted.

Mosiah followed behind alone, the raven having refused to accompany us anywhere near the dragon.

The path ran smooth, cutting down through the rock in a steep spiral that was almost a corkscrew. It was easy to walk, almost too easy. It seemed to be hurrying us downward—a circumstance which we found ominous.

"This was never formed by nature," Mosiah observed.

"No," Saryon agreed. "So I thought when I first discovered it."

Mosiah came to a halt. "And you descended this all unknowing, Father? When anything from griffins to darkrovers could have been at the bottom? Forgive me, Father, but you were never the adventurous sort. I think you should tell us how you first found this cave. Before we go on."

"We will not have this!" Eliza was angry. "You have insulted Father Saryon for the last time, Enforcer—"

"No, child," Saryon said. Looking about, he found an outcropping of rock and sank down upon it. "Mosiah is right. Don't tell me, Daughter," he added with a smile for her, "that you yourself are not curious about what we will find when we reach the dragon's lair. I could use the rest. We must not be long, though. We must reach the dragon's lair before night falls, while it is still sleepy and lethargic."

"Amen to that," Mosiah said.

What I write now is Father Saryon's story, in his own words.

I have sometimes wondered what would have happened if Simkin had not tricked Menju the Sorcerer into sending him to Earth. I think matters might have turned out much differently. Had Simkin been here, I am certain that he might have saved Joram's life. Emperor Garald does not agree with me and I must admit that I see his view. There is no doubt that Simkin set Joram up for the ambush, for it was Simkin who suggested that Joram find help for your poor mother in the Temple of the Necromancers. And it was there the Executioner waited for him and killed him.

I will never forget that terrible day.

I had gone to the Temple with Gwen and Joram, at his request, though I feared traveling to such a dreadful place. Joram was desperate. Gwendolyn was drifting further from us every day, it seemed. She spoke only to those who were dead and gone. She had no care for the living, not even for her own husband, whom she had once dearly loved. Her parents were sick with grief. When Simkin told us his fool story about having a little brother who was cured by the dead, Joram grasped it as a drowning man grasps at a bit of wood.

I tried to dissuade him, but he refused to listen. Simkin told us to be at the Temple at noon, when the power of the Temple would be greatest. The Emperor believes that Simkin knew in advance that the Executioner would be there waiting for Joram, but I don't think so. I think Simkin merely wanted Joram out of the way, so that he—Simkin—could pretend to be Joram and so travel to Earth, which is exactly what he did.

I don't suppose it matters now, one way or the other. Your father and I went to the Temple. I remained with Gwen, who was exceedingly troubled by the voices of the dead. Joram stood by the altar. I heard four sharp, distinct cracks, one after the other.

I was paralyzed with fear, not knowing what dread fate these awful sounds portended.

The cracking sounds stopped. I looked about and saw nothing amiss, at first. I was about to take Gwendolyn into the Temple, where she would be safe, when I saw Joram slump against the altar.

His hand was pressed over his chest and blood welled from between his fingers.

I ran to him and caught him in my arms. I lowered him to the ground. I did not know then what had happened to him. Later I learned that he had been killed by a heinous tool of the Dark Arts, a weapon known as a "gun."

All I knew then was that he was dying and there was nothing I could do except hold him.

"The Darksword . . ." he said, his voice coming in painful gasps. "Take it, Father. . . . Hide it . . . from them. My child!" He clasped my hand with his dying strength, and I believe that he willed himself to live the few moments longer it took him to impart this message. "If my child is in need . . . you must give the sword. . . ."

I had not known then that Gwen was pregnant. Joram knew, and that was another reason he had wanted so desperately to find a way to help her.

"Yes, Joram!" I promised, through my tears.

He looked past me, to Gwen, who stood above him.

"I am coming," he said to her, and closed his eyes and slipped away to join the dead.

She reached out her hand, not to the body, but to his soul. "My beloved. I have waited for you a long, long time."

You know what happened after that. The forces of Menju the Sorcerer attacked Thimhallan. Our armies were crushed, utterly defeated. If Menju had had his way, we would have been exterminated into the bargain, but the man we know now as General Boris protected us.

Menju did not insist on our destruction. He had what he wanted. He sealed up the Well of Life so that magic no longer flowed into the world of Thimhallan. Bereft of their magic, most of the people in Thimhallan said bitterly that they might as well be dead. Many did kill themselves. It was a terrible time.

Fortunately, Garald, who was then King of Sharakan, following the death of his father, was able to act quickly and take control. He brought in the Sorcerers, the practitioners of the Dark Arts, and they taught our people how to use tools to do what magic had always done for them in the past. Gradually, as the years went by, we rebuilt the cities, though the buildings were crude and ugly, compared with what they had once been.

But all that would come later. Joram was dead. I had two responsibilities now, or rather three. The Darksword, Gwen, and the child she bore. Whoever had killed Joram must still be in the Temple and, indeed, I saw the Executioner rise and start to move toward us.

He was a powerful *Duuk-tsarith*. I could not hope

to escape him. Suddenly, however, he was pushed backward, almost to the edge of the cliff. I saw him struggling, but he fought an invisible foe!

And then I knew—the dead were giving us a chance to escape.

Picking up the Darksword, I grabbed Gwen's hand. She came with me docilely. We fled that sorrowful place. Later, when the Emperor sent to recover Joram's body, it was found laid out in state inside the Temple of the Necromancers. The hands of the dead tended him, who had been Dead in his lifetime.

All of Thimhallan was in confusion, as you can imagine. Bad as that was for some, it was good for me, for no one cared about a middle-aged catalyst and a young woman they took for my daughter. My first thought was to go to the Font. I am not sure why, except that it had been my home for so long. Arriving there, I realized my mistake, for though the place was in an uproar, there were people who knew me and connected me with Joram. In order to be truly safe, I would have to take Gwen and travel to a part of the country where neither of us were known.

It was while I was at the Font, however, that I came across a child, a little boy of about five years of age. He was an orphan, they said. His parents were catalysts, and had been killed in the first assault. The boy was mute. He could not speak, and whether that was due to the shock of seeing his parents slain before his eyes or if he had been born mute, none could say.

I looked at that silent boy and I saw in his eyes the same emptiness, the same grief, the same loss I felt in my own heart. I took him with me. I named him Reuven.

We started our journey. I chose to relocate to Zith-el. Although I had heard that the city was heavily dam-

aged in the war, it was one place where I was certain
that no one would know me.

The magical wall that guarded the city was gone.
The Zoo creatures had mostly escaped and returned to
the wild. The inhabitants were dazed and disbelieving.
All of the tall buildings had been destroyed, but Zith-el
is also a city of tunnels, and the survivors moved underground.

We found a small place for ourselves, little more
than a niche in one of the tunnels. Here Gwen and little
Reuven and I dwelt, living on the sustenance that was
brought to us by our conquerors.

Gwen never did return to the world of the living.
She was happy with the dead, for Joram was with her.
She remained with me only long enough to bring her
child into this world, and then she died. Reuven and I
were left alone with the baby. I named her Eliza.

But I am getting ahead of myself.

I had carried with me, all this time, the Darksword.
And not a day dawned but that I feared someone
would find me and then they would find it. Menju the
Sorcerer was searching for the Darksword, so I heard.
Fearing the use he might make of it, I determined to
hide the sword in a place where it would never be
discovered.

I prayed to the Almin for guidance and that night I
dreamed I was walking in the Zoo. The next morning I
wrapped the Darksword in a blanket and carried it to
the Zoo. This was dangerous, even foolhardy, you
might say, for though many of the Zoo's creatures had
run off, others had stayed behind. I might run into a
centaur or worse.

But it seemed to me that the Almin guided me and
though my faith had wavered in the days before
Joram's death, when I saw the rest and peace he found

in death—a peace he had never known in life—I could only believe that all had happened for the best.

I wandered through the forest, searching for something, though I didn't know what. And then, coming down the same path we walked, I saw this cave.

I saw something else, too. A black dragon.

The dragon was lying outside the cave and my first thought was that it was sunning itself, for it lay stretched out full-length, with its head upon a rock, basking in the sunlight.

As Mosiah has said—I am not much of an adventurer. My impulse was to flee, but I turned in such haste that I lost my footing. I dropped the Darksword. It fell among the rocks on the riverbank, landing with a clang that must have been heard by the dead back in my small house.

I froze, terrified, and waited for the dragon to rear up its head and attack me.

But the dragon never moved.

Of course, you are all laughing at me, because you know that a black dragon—a Dragon of the Night—would never be out taking a sunbath. The creatures loathe the sunlight, which burns into the eyes, causing such intense pain that the dragons lose consciousness.

At last, I remembered what I should have known all along. This Dragon of the Night was either unconscious or dead.

Cautiously, I approached the dragon, and as I drew near I saw its body rise and fall with its breathing. It was not dead.

I knew then why the Almin had sent me this way. A comatose Dragon of the Night can be easily controlled by means of the charm on its forehead. Here was the perfect guardian for the Darksword, the dragon's cave the perfect hiding place.

I did not have much time. As I told you, I was
fearful of pursuit. That fear gave me courage, for otherwise I do not believe I would ever have found the nerve
to do what I did.

I had never seen a dragon this close before. The
beast was monstrous, beautiful, awful. It was so black
that it seemed to be a hole cut through daytime, revealing night beneath. I saw the charm upon its head,
an oval diamond, shaped smooth, without any facets.
It alone sparkled in the sunlight, which did not touch
any part of the dragon, did not gleam on the scales or
shine on the leathery wings.

I stretched out my hand, which was trembling so
that I first missed the diamond completely and touched
the dragon's hide. It was dry and rough and hot from
the sun and I jumped as if I had touched flame. Then,
finally, I put my hand upon the diamond.

A feeling of power and authority suffused me. I
knew that I could prevail over anything. You will laugh
again, but I tell you that I never experienced the like
before. I had such confidence in myself and my own
abilities that I felt as if I alone could rebuild Zith-el,
brick by brick. (Yes, we were using bricks, those creations of the Dark Arts.)

To charm this dragon and bend the creature to my
will seemed a paltry thing. A child could do it. Words
of potent magic flared in my brain. I spoke them aloud.

The dragon did not move, did not respond at all.

My power and my confidence began to ebb.

I pulled back my hand and noted that it was wet.
Wet with blood.

Of course! That was why the dragon had been
caught in the sunlight! The creature had been
wounded. It had emerged from its cave at night, proba-

bly to drink from the river, when it collapsed and was now caught out in the sun.

Had the charm worked? Would it work on an unconscious dragon? Surely it would, I argued. The charm was meant to work on the beast when it was comatose.

Yet, argued that cursed part of me which never fails to play devil's advocate, the charm was meant to work when the dragon was comatose from lying in the sun, not from being struck by one of the mundane's killing lights. Plus, for all I knew, the dragon might be dying.

A sensible man—or a less desperate one—would have walked away. But here was the perfect guardian and the ideal hiding place for the Darksword. I could not rid myself of the notion that the Almin had guided me here for this reason. I settled down to wait, at least until nightfall. If the charm had not worked, the wounded dragon would be sluggish and I had some chance of escaping. I settled down upon the rocks a short distance from the dragon and waited for night.

The hours I passed provided me an excellent opportunity for studying the dragon. I found myself awed by the beauty and magnificence of the creature and saddened by the fact that it had been bred to nothing but dealing death. The Dragon of Night has an inborn hatred for all other living beings, even those of its own kind. It cannot bear young and when the last of these great beasts dies, that will be the end of them.

A good thing, you say. Perhaps. The Almin knows best.

I watched its even breathing, which seemed strong, so that I eventually concluded the dragon was not dying.

Night came early to the forest. When the deepening shadows blocked the sunlight from its eyes, the beast began to stir. The dragon's huge body lay on the rocks, but one wing dipped into the river water. I heard the water lap against the rocks and saw the shoulder bone twitch. The dragon snuffled and blew and its lower jawbone scraped along the rock as it shifted its head, endeavoring to move into even deeper shadows.

My heart was in my throat. I would have run then, but for one hopeful sign. The diamond on the head of the dragon had begun to glow dimly. Which meant that the charm had worked.

I hoped. And prayed.

I had spent the daylight hours waiting impatiently for night. Now it seemed to me that night came all too fast. Darkness closed in with a vengeance. The dragon was one with the darkness. I could no longer see it at all.

The diamond's light was very bright now, shining with a prickly brilliance. It did not radiate light. I could not see the dragon by the gem's glow. I could see only the diamond itself. When it suddenly lurched into the air, I knew that the dragon was fully awake and had lifted its head.

I rose hastily to my feet, leaving the Darksword lying on the ground nearby. I could have used it to defend myself, but I feared that the sword's powerful null-magic might undo the charm. Time enough to pick it up if I needed it.

The dragon rotated its head. I could see the diamond moving and I could hear the dragon—its claws pushing its body up from the rocks, its wings lifting with a mighty splash from the water.

The dragon was searching for me. Certain that all vestige of sunlight was gone, the dragon opened its eyes.

They shone pale and cold as moonlight.

I averted my gaze, for even though the beast was charmed, if you look into the eyes of a Dragon of Night, you will end up a raving lunatic.

The dragon reared up on its hind legs and lifted its wings, spreading them out like the wings of a bat.

I was struck with such awe that if I had died then and there, I believe I would have deemed it worth death to have seen that terrible, magnificent sight.

A thousand thousand tiny pinpoints of white light glittered in the blackness of the wings, as if the dragon's wings were made of the starlit sky. Thus, in battle, do the dragons mimic the night sky in order to swoop down unseen upon their enemies. Those tiny pinpoints of light not only resemble stars, they are also deadly weapons. A flip of the wing causes them to fall like meteors. The small shooting stars burn easily through flesh.

The lights glittered before my eyes, but none fell on me. The charm had worked. I gave fervent thanks to the Almin.

The lunar-white eyes stared at me, bathing me in moonlight. I kept my eyes lowered.

"You are the master," the dragon said, and hatred shook its voice.

"Yes," I replied, as boldly as I could. "I am the master."

"I am constrained to do your bidding," the dragon said with cold fury. "What do you want of me?"

"I have an object here," I said, and very carefully I lifted the Darksword. I had to control the fear in my heart, or else the sword would sense that I was threatened and start to disrupt the magic of the charm. "I command you to take it with you into your cave and guard it well. You must give it up to no one except to me or to Joram's heir."

I held up the Darksword and it was now the dragon's turn to shield its eyes. The lids dropped, the white light was hooded. The dragon's wings shivered, the false stars winked out. I could not see the sword for the darkness, yet its null-magic must have been piercing and deadly as daylight in the eyes of this creature of magic.

"Wrap it! Cover it!" the dragon cried in anger and in pain.

Hurriedly, I did so, shrouding the Darksword with the blanket.

Once the sword was concealed, the dragon again opened its eyes. Its loathing for me had increased tenfold, a thought that was not comforting.

"I will guard the Darksword," the dragon said. "I have no choice. You are the master. But you must take it down to my cavern and there bury it under a cairn of rock so that no part of it is visible. I am hungry. I will go to hunt food now. But do not fear. I will return and I will do what you ask of me. You are the master."

Spreading its wings, the dragon leapt from the rock and soared into the air. I lost sight of it immediately, for I could not tell what was night sky and what was the dragon.

But now my heart was lightened with hope. Carrying the Darksword, I entered the cave and made my way down to the very bottom, where I found the floor littered with shining black scales and bones. The dragon's lair.

I placed the Darksword on the floor of the cavern, in a part far distant from what I took to be the dragon's nest. I covered the sword with rocks, forming a large mound.

I had just finished when the dragon returned, entering through a back way, for it emerged suddenly into the cave. The body of a male centaur hung from its cruel teeth.

The dragon eyed the cairn, which was now illuminated with a pale, chill light.

"Leave," it commanded, adding the single word, "Master," in grudging tones.

I was glad to obey, for the smell of the blood of the freshly slaughtered centaur sickened me. I made my way back up to the world of true starlight. By the time I reached the cave opening, I was exhausted and could go no farther. I rested there until morning. Leaving behind the tinderbox and flint and the brand which I had carried in the tunnel, I returned home.

The Darksword was as safe as I could possibly make it. Many times I have wondered if it was still there, if the dragon was still guarding it, if the charm was still holding. Many times I was tempted to go to see for myself, but then a peaceful feeling would steal over me. Now was not the time.

It was the Almin, reassuring me.

And so I have not been back here since that day twenty years ago when I left the Darksword beneath the rock cairn with the Dragon of Night.

I would not have come back now, but the peaceful feeling is no longer in my heart. In its place is an urgency, a fear, which leads me to believe that it is the Almin's will that the Darksword be recovered.

That it be given to Joram's heir, to Joram's daughter.

CHAPTER
TWENTY-THREE

"*Have they truly found peace in death? Are they
happy?*"
"*They will be, when you free them.*"

~JORAM AND GWENDOLYN;
TRIUMPH OF THE DARKSWORD

I could not help but cast Mosiah a glance of triumph,
hoping to impress upon him how thoroughly he had
misjudged Saryon.

Mosiah appeared preoccupied, and did not notice.
"You made one statement which I find curious, Father.
You said that magic had vanished from Thimhallan.
Yet Father Reuven gave me Life. The magic lives
around us. I can feel it."

Father Saryon regarded Mosiah with an expression
of astonishment. "Well, certainly, my son. You were

partly responsible for magic's return. The raid upon the Well of Life . . ."

"Forgive him, Father," Scylla interrupted. "He received a blow to the head during our fight with the thugs outside the Eastroad Gate. He has great gaps in his memory."

"I would be obliged if you would refresh that memory, Father," Mosiah said. "Just so that I know what to expect."

"Well . . ." Father Saryon was nonplussed. "There isn't much to tell, I suppose. Or rather, there is a lot to tell but we don't have time for most of it. How those calling themselves the Dark Cultists arrived from Earth. A man named Kevon Smythe drove King Garald from power, almost succeeded in having him assassinated, but Garald was warned in time and escaped.

"How you and King Garald lived the lives of outlaws in the wilderness. You don't remember that?" Saryon gazed anxiously at Mosiah, who merely smiled and remained silent.

"And then Simkin returned from Earth—"

"Ah," said Mosiah, and then he again fell silent.

"Simkin returned. He told Garald how the Well of Life had not been destroyed. It had been merely capped—"

At this, which was exactly the theory we had postulated, I made a sign to Mosiah, who made me a sign to keep silent.

"The Dark Cultists had a secret source, however. They were bleeding off the magical Life, using it for themselves. In a daring raid, you, Mosiah, Garald, and his friend James Boris broke open the Well and released the magic back into the world. We were then able to fight Smythe and the Dark Cultists. Smythe fled back to Earth.

"Garald returned to the rulership of Sharakan and also that of Merilon. I traveled to Sharakan to congratulate him and to present to him my wards." Saryon looked fondly at Eliza and me. "King Garald was struck by Eliza's beauty and was deeply touched to hear that she was Joram's daughter. He granted her the right to claim the throne of Merilon, as Joram's heir.

"Garald made Eliza Queen of Merilon. Reuven traveled to the Font, to enter into his training as a catalyst. Merilon and Sharakan became allies. Cardinal Radisovik was made Bishop, following the death of Vanya. The Bishop was kind enough to appoint me as Eliza's adviser until she came of age." Saryon smiled, shook his head. "I considered myself most unsuited to the task, but Radisovik turned all my noes into yes before I truly knew what was happening. Besides, Eliza needed very little advice."

Eliza reached out, pressed Saryon's hand gratefully.

"Times are difficult," Saryon said, sighing. "Magic has been restored, but it is weak. Though the barrier around Thimhallan has been rebuilt, we know that magic is seeping out of it and there doesn't appear to be anything we can do to stop it. Undoubtedly, Smythe and his Dark Cultists are responsible.

"We are forced to live on a combination of sorcery and steel. The *Duuk-tsarith* have grown ever more powerful, since they are capable of absorbing more Life than anyone else in the world. Emperor Garald trusts them, but I—" Saryon halted, somewhat confused.

"I understand, Father," Mosiah said quietly. "Now that you talk, much of my own memory returns. You have good reason not to trust many among the *Duuk-tsarith*."

"I trust you, Mosiah," Saryon said. "And that is what is important. Knights"—he smiled at Scylla—

"now guard the realm. Though at first Garald was viewed as a savior, he has come to be reviled. Smythe, in exile on Earth, has his followers upon Thimhallan. They are managing to foment unrest among the lower classes, foretelling the coming of the end of the world unless Smythe is permitted to return to save it.

"You heard about the warning which came to Bishop Radisovik?"

We nodded in silence.

"The Darksword must be returned to the maker of the world. That was the message, though we are not certain what it means. The maker of the world was Merlyn, but he's been dead and gone these many years . . ."

Not according to Simkin! I thought suddenly and, pondering this, I lost, for a moment, the thread of what Saryon was saying.

". . . recovered by Joram's descendant. Emperor Garald came to me in person"—Saryon flushed, embarrassed—"to ask for the Darksword. I agreed, but only if I were permitted to seek it in secret and, in secret, give it directly into the hands of Eliza, Joram's daughter. The Emperor gave me his word of honor that we would not be followed, that no one would attempt to take the sword from us."

"The Emperor's word is not the word of the *Duuk-tsarith*," said Mosiah.

"But, surely, they would be constrained to obey," Saryon said, and it seemed to me that he was pleading for reassurance.

"Since when, Father? There is a saying on Earth. 'They have their own agenda.' I do not see them being impressed by a visitation from an angel."

"Do you think we were followed?" Eliza asked him.

"I think we should be very careful," Mosiah answered her gravely. "And that we have taken enough time."

We resumed our journey, moving with greater caution but more speed. It was already late afternoon. We had less than twenty-four hours before the arrival of the Hch'nyv. The part of me that remembered Earth wondered, with a pang, if our planet was now under attack.

No use fretting about events over which I had no control. I would do my part here. We continued following the corkscrew tunnel, which delved straight down and which had perhaps been shaped by the warlocks who had brought the Dragons of Night into being.

We walked at a good pace, for the way was easy, and we made good time. Still, our walk lasted over an hour from our starting point, which leads me to believe that we must have descended at least three or four miles below the surface of Thimhallan.

Though we could neither see nor hear the dragon, which would be slumbering during the daylight hours, we could smell it and its refuse. The air grew fetid and various odors of a most unpleasant nature—stale urine and dung and decay—soon caused us to gag and cover our noses with handkerchiefs or whatever cloth came to hand.

The one consolation we had, if you could call it such, was Mosiah's pronouncement. "The dung smells fresh," he observed. "This must mean that your dragon is still alive, Father, and still making this cave its residence."

"I don't remember the smell being this bad," Saryon said, his voice muffled by the sleeve of his robe.

"The dragon's had twenty years to add to it," Scylla observed. "I don't like to think of what else we'll find in that lair. Mounds of rotting corpses, among other things."

"Fortunately, dragons will not eat humans," Eliza said, shivering, "or so we've heard. We taste bad."

"Don't believe all you hear, Your Majesty," Mosiah said, and that effectively ended that conversation.

Our enthusiasm had begun to wane, though not our hope and hope is what carried us on. We were tired, our legs ached, and we were all of us half-sick with the stench, which tainted everything, even the water we had brought with us. We rounded yet another corner, our feet dragging, when Scylla, who was in the lead, came to a sudden halt, her hand raised.

The torchlight that had before gleamed off curve after curve in the rock wall now illuminated nothing. A vast yawning darkness gaped before us.

"This is the dragon's lair," Saryon whispered, and so quiet were we that his whisper carried clearly.

We hardly dared breathe, for we could hear the sound of other breathing, stentorian breathing, as if someone were pumping a giant bellows.

We hesitated, at that tense point when the gambler at the craps table breathes on the dice, then clutches them in his hand for a single, heart-stopping instant, asking for the win. And then throws.

"I will go first," Saryon said. "Do not come until I call that all is safe. If the dragon attacks me, Scylla, Mosiah"—he gazed at them intently—"I expect you two to do everything possible to protect my children."

"I promise, Father," Scylla said reverently, and raised her sword, hilt first.

"I promise, as well, Father," Mosiah said, his hands folded. "Good luck. I'm sorry . . ." He paused, and did not finish his sentence.

"Sorry?" Saryon repeated mildly. "Sorry for what, my son?"

"I'm sorry about Joram," Mosiah said.

Saryon lifted his eyebrows. Joram had, after all, been dead twenty years.

He had been dead to them, but not to Mosiah.

Eliza hugged Saryon close. Blinking back her tears, she managed a smile. "The Almin go with you, Father," she whispered. "My father, the only father I have ever known."

I, too, embraced him in the name of father. It was right, eminently right.

He asked the Almin's blessing on us all and he alone entered the chamber.

We waited in the tunnel, ears strained to hear the slightest sound. I was so tense, I no longer noticed the stench.

"Dragon of the Night," came Saryon's voice from the darkness. "You know me. You know who I am."

Scraping sounds, as of a massive head sliding along the rock floor, a gigantic body shifting position. And then a pale, cold white light lit the chamber.

We could see Saryon, a stark black silhouette against that white light. We could not see the dragon, for its head was far, far above Saryon, out of our view. I remembered that I was not to look directly into the dragon's eyes.

We held our breath for the answer, which might be instant death. Eliza and I clasped each other by the hand.

"I know you," said the Dragon of Night, hating him. "Why have you come to disturb my rest?"

We breathed again. The charm had held! Impulsively, Eliza hugged me. I put my arm around her.

Mosiah flashed us a stern, reproving glance. Neither

he nor Scylla had lowered their guard. She stood with the torch held high in one hand, her sword in the other. He had his hands clenched, magic spells in his mind and on his lips. He reminded us silently that there was still great danger.

Accepting the rebuke, Eliza and I drew apart, yet our hands again found each other's in the darkness.

"I come to relieve you of your burden," Saryon said. "And to free you of the charm. This young woman is Joram's heir."

"I am here," Eliza called.

Releasing my hand, she walked into the chamber. Scylla and I both would have followed, but Mosiah held out his arms, blocking the way.

"Neither of you were mentioned in the charming!" he said swiftly. "You could break it!"

His caution was sensible. He certainly knew more about charms and spells than I did. I was forced to stay behind, though it took every ounce of self-control I possessed to remain there in the tunnel and watch Eliza walk away from me, walk into deadly peril.

Scylla was pale, her eyes dark and huge. She, too, understood the wisdom of Mosiah's words, yet she was in agony at the thought of her charge going where her knight could not follow. Sweat beaded on the knight's brow. She bit her nether lip.

We could do nothing but wait.

Eliza and Saryon stood in silhouette before the dragon, bathed in that pale, white light, which did not illuminate, but turned all it touched a ghostly gray.

"She is Dead," said the dragon. And then, in a terrible voice, the dragon repeated the Prophecy. " 'There will be born to the Royal House one who is dead yet will live, who will die again and live again. And when he returns, he will hold in his hand the destruction of the world.' "

"That was spoken of my father," said Eliza, proudly, calmly.

"You are indeed what you claim. Take that which is yours. Remove it from my lair. It has troubled my sleep these past twenty years."

The two walked to a large mound of rocks, which stood just to the left of our line of sight. With Eliza's help, Saryon began to shift the rocks, working swiftly. Neither wanted to stay in there any longer than they had to. The three of us, waiting for them, dared not stir. Though we could not see the dragon, we knew that it was aware of our presence. Its hatred and loathing were almost palpable. It longed to slaughter us, not for food, but for revenge. The charm held it back, but just barely.

And then the work was finished. Saryon and Eliza stood above the cairn. She saw for the first time her father's creation. Repulsed, her courage failed her. Then, jaw tightening, she reached down and picked up the Darksword.

Without warning, black-robed figures materialized out of the darkness. Five surrounded us. More appeared in the dragon's lair, their black robes and hoods standing out in stark contrast to the white light.

"Keep still!" Mosiah warned softly, urgently. "Go quickly before it is too late! You will destroy us all!"

"Silence, traitor."

One of the *Duuk-tsarith* raised his hand and Mosiah doubled over in wrenching pain and fell to his knees. Still he was defiant.

"Fools!" he managed to gasp.

Scylla advanced a step, her sword raised.

The same *Duuk-tsarith* again moved his hand.

Scylla's steel blade changed to water, ran down her upraised arm, and dripped upon the stone at her feet. She stared, in openmouthed astonishment, at her empty hand.

"What is the meaning of this?" Father Saryon demanded angrily.

"Relinquish the Darksword," another of the *Duuktsarith* commanded. He approached Eliza. "Relinquish it and you will come to no harm."

"We have no need of you. Leave us. We will take the Darksword to the Emperor!" Eliza said imperiously.

"Emperor no more," countered the *Duuk-tsarith*. "Garald and his false, lying bishop have been deposed. We rule Thimhallan now. Give us the Darksword."

Eliza fell back before them. "You have no right—"

Red flame sprang from the fingertips of the *Duuktsarith*, formed into fiery tentacles that reached out to encircle Eliza and make her captive.

Instinctively, she lifted the Darksword to shield herself from the magic.

Tentacles of flame struck the Darksword. The darkstone drank them in greedily and began to glow with a white-blue flame of its own.

"The child of the traitor Joram is hereby sentenced to death," the *Duuk-tsarith* pronounced.

Magic surged and heaved and sparked.

"Stop! Cast no spells!" Saryon cried in terror. He stumbled forward, to put himself between Eliza and the *Duuk-tsarith*. "The dragon—"

The Darksword sucked in the magic. The metal seemed superheated, the white-blue glow of the flame was dazzling, blinding. . . .

The Dragon of the Night roared in pain and fury. It lifted its wings, the deadly stars glittered. The dragon opened its eyes wide. Its mind-shattering light flared

within the cavern. Saryon clutched his head and reeled
in pain, then he collapsed upon the stone floor. White
stars of death showered down around us. The *Duuk-
tsarith*'s black robes burst into flame. They and their
spells withered in the horrific blaze.

"Fools!" Mosiah repeated, with the grim quiet of
despair. "You have doomed us all!"

I looked for Scylla, but could not find her.
Weaponless and alone, she must have gone forth to do
battle with the dragon.

"Eliza!" I cried, and ran into the cave, not to save
her, for nothing could do that, but to die with her.

I ran and it was as if I had leapt off an immense cliff.
I spread my arms and discovered I could fly.

CHAPTER
TWENTY-FOUR

*"Simkin's a monumental liar. I don't see how you
can put up with him!"*

*"Because he's an amusing liar. And that makes
him different."*

"Different?"

"From the rest of you."

~MOSIAH AND JORAM; *FORGING THE DARKSWORD*

Again, the frightening sensation of being squeezed,
the air forced from my lungs, my body compressed and
flattened like that of a mouse squeezing itself into a tiny
crack. My flight ended abruptly and painfully in a tum-
ble. I rolled down a rocky incline, came up hard against
a stone wall.

For a moment I lay there, dazed and bruised and
cut, gasping for air like a landed fish. Fearing the
dragon, I opened my eyes, prepared to do what little I
could to defend myself and Eliza.

I looked around, blinked.

The dragon was gone. The *Duuk-tsarith* were gone. Father Saryon was gone. Scylla was there, and Mosiah, and Eliza. We were in a cavern, the same cavern. It smelled the same. The floor was covered with refuse, bones lay scattered about. Eliza stood in the center of the cavern, holding the Darksword.

Dropping the sword, she hurried to me, bent over me.

"Reuven! That was a nasty fall! Are you all right?"

Was I? No, I wasn't.

Eliza no longer wore the blue velvet riding outfit, no glittering golden circlet adorned her head. She was dressed in the plain woolen skirt and simple blouse she had been wearing when we first set out upon this strange journey.

I started to push myself up, mindful of entangling myself in my robes, except that I wasn't wearing robes. I was wearing jeans and a blue sweater.

"Scylla! Quick! He's hurt!" Eliza cried.

Scylla, clad in combat fatigues, her earrings winking and sparkling in the light of a flashlight, squatted down and peered at me intently. Reaching out her hand, she brushed aside the hair on my forehead.

"The cut's not deep. The bleeding's already stopped. He may have a headache for a while, but no permanent damage."

Eliza drew out a handkerchief—a plain, white handkerchief—and began to dab at the cut on my forehead.

Angrily, I thrust away her hand. Scrambling to my feet, I backed up against the wall and glared at the two women, who were regarding me in astonishment. Had it been a dream? A hallucination? If so, it was the most incredibly real dream I had ever experienced.

"What's going on here?" Mosiah demanded, coming over to us.

"Reuven's foot turned on a stone and he fell and hit his head," Eliza said. "Scylla says it's not serious, but look at him. He's staring at me as if I were a dragon about to tear him apart!"

"And you," said Scylla, confronting Mosiah. "Where have you been?"

"I don't know," he said harshly. "Where *have* I been?"

"How the hell should I know?" Scylla demanded, looking amazed. "What's wrong? Did you hit your head, too?"

Mosiah was suddenly grave, thoughtful. "Yes," he said quietly. "Come to think of it, I did."

He knew! He had been there, wherever it was! Limp with relief, I leaned back against the cave wall and tried to collect my thoughts. Most of them were too far scattered to get hold of, but at least I knew I wasn't going insane. I started to ask Mosiah one of the thousand questions that was in my mind, but he made me a discreet sign with his hand.

"Say nothing. Not yet," he counseled.

"There," Scylla said, dusting off my clothes with an enthusiasm which nearly had me back on the stone floor again. "You look a little better."

Eliza bent down, picked up the Darksword. I had a sudden, horrifying vision of a black dragon, claws stained red with blood, knocking the Darksword from her hands. She fell. The claws ripped and tore her flesh. Her screams . . .

The vision faded, though not the horror. My body was wet with sweat and I shivered in the cavern's dank air.

"You do realize that we are standing in a dragon's lair," Mosiah said sharply.

"That's what Scylla told me." Eliza shrugged. She was too preoccupied with worry over her father to evince much interest.

"It's an old one," Scylla said. "No need to be afraid. All the dragons died when the Well of Life was destroyed."

"It certainly *smells* occupied," Mosiah maintained, frowning. "And how did the Darksword end up *here*? I threw it through the gate—"

"And damn near made me into a shish kebab," came a plaintive voice from a dark corner. "Bear-on-a-Spit. Teriyaki Teddy. Lucky for you I was around. Those silver-plated goons would have snapped it up if it hadn't been for me. As for the cave, it's hermetically sealed. Like Tupperware. Keeps the rot fresh for centuries."

Flashing her light around the cavern, Scylla located the source of the voice.

"Teddy!" Eliza cried in delight.

The stuffed bear sat propped up against a stalagmite. "I thought you'd never get here," he said peevishly. "What *have* you been doing? Going on picnics, I suppose. Taking bus trips to Brighton. I've been waiting and waiting. It's been frightfully dull, I don't mind telling you."

Still carrying the Darksword, Eliza walked over to Teddy, bent down to pick him up.

The bear's beady black eyes glittered in alarm. The stuffed body squirmed out of her reach. "Don't bring that ugly thing near me!"

"The Darksword?" Eliza said, wondering, then added, "Oh, of course. I understand."

"I don't," Mosiah said sharply. "The Darksword

disrupts his magic. He can't stand to have it near him. And yet he maintains that he brought it here!"

"You'd be amazed what I can do when I put my mind to it," Simkin said, sniffing. "And I never said I brought it here. I do have friends left in this world, you know. People who appreciate me. My dear friend Merlyn, for one."

"Merlyn. Of course." Mosiah's lip curled. "Kevon Smythe for another?"

"Sticks and stones may break my bones but Darkswords will never hurt me," Teddy said, and the bear grinned.

"What does it matter how the sword came to be here?" Eliza asked impatiently. "Now that we have it, we must find my father and mother and Father Saryon."

Startled, I looked at Mosiah.

"Your father. Joram," Mosiah asked. "He's alive?"

"Of course he is!" she answered, and repeated emphatically, "Of course he is."

"Oh, yes, Joram's alive, all right," the bear said in languid tones. "In a foul temper, though. Can't blame him. Locked up in a prison cell with only the elderly bald party for company."

Eliza grasped the Darksword tightly, her knuckles whitening on the hilt. "You've found him? He's safe?"

"He's seen better days, as the Duchess of Orleans said when she discovered her husband impaled on the door knocker. He's conscious, and taking solid food. Your father. Not the Duke. There was nothing much we could do for him, beyond polish his head every Sunday."

"What about my mother?"

"*Nada*. Nothing. Zip. Sorry and all that, but I sighted neither hide nor hair of her. She is not being held captive in the same location as your father and the catalyst, that much I can tell you."

"You've been there." Mosiah was skeptical.

"Certainly," replied the bear.

"To the Technomancers' prison. Where they're holding Saryon and Joram."

"If you would remove that black hood from over your head, Mosiah," the bear said in nasty tones, "you might be able to hear better. Isn't that what I said? I was just returning from there, in fact, when you hurled that great bloody sword at me."

"And where is this prison?"

"Right there," the bear replied, and gave a bored glance upward.

"Above us!" Eliza exclaimed. She had looked pale and downcast at hearing no news of her mother, but now the color came flooding back to her cheeks.

"In the upper chambers of the cave. Not far. A good, brisk walk on a summer's day, straight uphill, of course, but think what wonders the climb will do for your calves."

While this may have been good news in one respect, it was certainly chilling in another. We flashed alarmed glances at each other.

"I'll watch the door," Scylla offered. "And keep your voices down!"

That warning came a bit late. We hadn't been shouting, but we hadn't been talking in whispers, either. And noise echoes in caverns.

"If the Technomancers are in the chambers above us, why did you bring the Darksword here?" Mosiah demanded of Simkin. "Unless you meant to give it to them."

"If I did, I wouldn't be down here in this smelly, dank hole with the lot of you, now, would I?" Simkin said, his nose button twitching. "I'd be up there where it's dry and comfy and stinks of nothing worse than Kevon Smythe's cheap cologne. He may be a man of the people, but I don't see why he has to smell like one."

"Why bring the Darksword here?" Mosiah pursued with extraordinary patience.

"Because, my dear thickheaded clodhopper friend, this is obviously the *last* place they would think to look! Having lost you, they are this moment turning Zith-el upside down searching for you and the sword. You don't see them searching down here, do you?"

"He's got a point," Scylla admitted.

"He always does," Mosiah grumbled. "Why didn't we see the Technomancers or they see us when we entered the cave?"

"You would have, if you'd come in the front."

"You're saying we came in the back?"

"I didn't see any flashing signs, exit or egress, don't you know, but if you want to think of it that way, yes, you came in the back."

"Is my father in a cell?" Eliza asked. "Is he being guarded? How many guards?"

"Two. As I said, everyone is certain you're in Zith-el—"

Scylla moved away from the cavern door, back toward us. "We should go now," she said. "Quickly."

"I don't trust him." Mosiah was grim. "He betrayed Joram once and caused his death—*almost* caused his death," he amended. "Whatever Simkin does, he does for his own amusement. Don't fool yourself, Eliza. He cares nothing for you, nothing for Joram, nothing for any of us. I have no doubt that if he thinks the Hch'nyv would provide him a moment's entertainment, he'd wave that orange scarf of his and direct them to the landing site."

Eliza turned to the bear, only to find its eyes closed. It was gently snoring. "Simkin!" she said, imploring.

The eyes snapped open. "What? Oh, pardon. Must have dozed off during that long harangue. As for me, what our cow-turd-kicking friend says is absolutely true. I'm not to be trusted. Not in the slightest."

The black button eyes glinted. The black-stitched mouth quirked. "Listen to Mosiah, the wise *Duuk-tsarith*. Now, *there's* a trustworthy bunch. We are all ears, my friend. I could be, if I wanted, you know—all ears, that is. What is *your* suggested plan of action?"

Mosiah's lips tightened. He said nothing, however. I am sure he was remembering that in that other life of ours, it was the *Duuk-tsarith* who had betrayed us. Simkin knew this, too. I could tell from the squint in the bear's eye. He knew and he was laughing at us.

Eliza made her decision. "If the Technomancers are searching somewhere else for us, we should not pass up this opportunity to rescue my father and Saryon. We may never have another chance."

"It could be a trap," Mosiah warned. "Just as the Interrogator impersonating your mother was a trap."

"It could be," Eliza said calmly. "But if so, it really doesn't matter, does it? We're running out of time."

"But which time? That's the question," Mosiah muttered.

Eliza hadn't heard him. I did, and it gave me cause for thought.

"What about the Darksword?" she was saying. "Should we take it with us?"

"Too dangerous," Scylla advised. "If they capture us, at least they won't have the Darksword. We may still be able to use it to bargain our way out. Why not leave it here where it will be safe?"

"Out in the open?"

Scylla flashed the light around the cavern, halted the beam. "There's all these rocks stacked up over here. We'll hide the sword underneath them. Build a cairn over it."

Eliza placed the Darksword on the cavern floor. She and Scylla gathered stones, began to build a cairn around it. It was like watching a video rewind. I saw them build the cairn up, whereas only moments before, I had seen Eliza and Father Saryon tear the cairn down. At this, my mind rebelled.

I hurried over to join Mosiah, who was standing silent, hands folded, watching.

"Tell me what is happening!" I signed frantically.

"Do you mean our little game of time hopscotch? I'm not sure," he mused, sotto voce. "It appears that there is a time line running parallel to the one in which we now find ourselves. An alternate time line, for in that one Joram died twenty years ago and in this one it was Simkin, disguised as Joram, who 'died' at the hands of the assassin. But why is this happening? And if Scylla and Eliza are present in both worlds, why is it that you and I appear to be the only ones conscious of both worlds?"

"Do you know the answer?"

He shrugged. "Your guess is as good as mine, Reuven. I am sure of one thing, though. The Hch'nyv were coming in that other world. They're coming in this one. As Her Majesty says, time is running out."

I asked the question I had most feared asking. "Time ran out for us in that last world, didn't it? We were all killed. I know, because when I try to catch a glimpse of that other life, I see nothing anymore. I only feel a great and terrible anger at those who betrayed us, and bitter sorrow over what will be lost."

"You are right," Mosiah said. "The dragon slaughtered us. I saw you die. I saw Eliza die. I saw my own death approaching. The one person I didn't see, though, was Scylla," he added. "Now, isn't that interesting?"

I waited for him to continue, but he said nothing more.

I signed, "Do you think we've been given another chance?"

"Either that," Mosiah replied, "or someone is being highly entertained by our struggles against the inevitable."

We both looked at the bear, who was again slumbering contentedly against the stalagmite. And it may have been my imagination, but I thought I saw Teddy smile.

CHAPTER
TWENTY-FIVE

"Strike me dead. I'm rotten."

∼SIMKIN, UPON CHANGING HIMSELF INTO A TREE;
FORGING THE DARKSWORD

The Darksword was buried under the cairn, a cairn that was exactly like the one I had seen before, down to the placement of the last rock. I could not look at it without feeling a shiver creep up from my tailbone and I was glad when we left the chamber.

We moved cautiously through the spiraling tunnel, this time going up instead of down. It did not appear as if the Technomancers had searched the lower levels— there was no reason why they should. To judge by the thick layer of undisturbed dust on the smooth floor, no one had been here for perhaps as many years as the magically shaped tunnel had been in existence. We took no chances, however, and crept along as silently as possible, guided by the ghostly image of Simkin and the faint eerie glow of his orange silk scarf.

Simkin's transformation had come about under duress. Before leaving the chamber, Mosiah had insisted on carrying Teddy, in order to keep an eye on him.

"Absolutely not!" Teddy was appalled at the indignity and pleaded and bleated. Finding Mosiah proof against both the bear's threats and Eliza's intercessions on his behalf, Simkin had abandoned his stuffed self and condescended to appear before us "naked," as he put it.

"It takes a great deal out of me, maintaining this form, as you can see. Or can't see," Simkin said in gloomy undertones as we walked through the tunnel. The orange glow from his scarf lit the way for Mosiah and me. Scylla and Eliza came behind us, using Scylla's flashlight.

"Odd," said Mosiah. "The Kij vine finds enough magical Life to thrive. I am surprised you don't."

"The Kij vine," Simkin observed, "is a weed."

"Precisely," Mosiah said dryly.

"Oh, very funny. Ha-ha and all that. According to you, I have Life coming out my ears and I'm just frittering it away, scattering it to the four winds in a blithe and merry dance of revelry. I'll have you know," Simkin added in aggrieved tones, "that I haven't changed clothes in twenty years! Twenty years!"

He dabbed at his eyes with the scarf, which was the only solid piece of him.

"Perhaps you're using your magic for other purposes," Mosiah suggested. "Such as sending us hopscotching through time."

"What do you take me for?" Simkin demanded,

sniffing. "A bloody amusement park? There are lots of places I would be glad to send you, Mosiah, but bounding gleefully among the nanoseconds is not one of them.

"I say!" Simkin came to a halt, glared at us indignantly. "*Have* you been leaping the years? *Annus touristi*? And you didn't take *me*!"

"What now?" Scylla demanded, coming up from her position as rear guard. "What's the matter?"

"Nothing," Mosiah said.

"Then keep moving! This is no time to stop and have a chat!" Scylla stalked on ahead of us.

"Got you in trouble!" Simkin said in smothered tones, and laughing, he flitted back to walk beside Eliza and flirt with her, most shamefully.

"An interesting point, don't you think?" Mosiah said to me softly. "Simkin *wasn't* with us in that other time. And Simkin would never throw a party that he himself didn't attend!"

I conceded that this might be true. Still, as I glanced behind me, watching uneasily the orange glow bob along close to Eliza, I recalled that in each of the alternate lines of time, Simkin had betrayed Joram. Why were we to suppose that this one would be any different?

Except that now he would not be betraying Joram. The treacherous kiss would be given to Joram's daughter.

The tunnel seemed much longer going up than coming down. By the time we neared the top, my legs ached, I was gulping for breath, and the difficult part was only beginning.

I had pictured the top portion of the cavern as being

the same as in the alternate time, if that's truly where (or should I say *when*!) we had been. I soon realized I was wrong. Rounding a bend, Scylla, in the lead, suddenly switched off her light and jumped backward.

"Light!" she whispered. "It's coming from ahead!"

Now that her flashlight was turned off, I could see the glow of another light reflected on the cavern walls. There had been no light in the other cavern, I recalled, remembering that Saryon had left a tinderbox and flint and a brand behind.

"What's up there?" Mosiah asked Simkin.

"Rock, air, water." Simkin waved the orange scarf. "Oh! You want specifics! Well, let's see." He frowned in deep thought. "This tunnel ends at the river. At the opening to the tunnel, there is a small chamber, just off to the right as you're facing the tunnel. Or is it the left, as you're facing the river? Of course, if you're *in* the river, it's rather behind you and—"

"Simkin, please!" Eliza said, and her voice quavered.

"What? Sorry, dear girl. Truly." Simkin looked very contrite. "Forgot that you're taking this personally. Let's see. Where was I? In the river . . . Right. We don't want to go in the river. Not if it can be avoided. No need to, really. Joram and the Father Skinhead are being held prisoner in the small chamber which is to the right—no, make that left. . . . Anyway, the small chamber. You can't miss it."

"No, and they won't be able to miss us," Mosiah said grimly. "They'll spot us the moment we walk into the light. If only I had Life enough—"

"I don't see what's stopping you, Enforcer. You have a catalyst right here," Eliza said. "Father Reuven. He may be a house catalyst and not trained to the specific needs of you warlocks, but he would do in an emergency, I suppose."

"Father Reuven!" Scylla chuckled. "How funny."

Mosiah and I did not laugh. We stared at Eliza. She had spoken of me as if we were in that other time, using the very same words Scylla had used in a similar situation.

"Why are you looking at me like that? What did I say—oh." Eliza blinked in confusion. "What *did* I say? And why did I say it? Father Reuven. House catalyst. But it sounds so natural. . . ."

Mosiah was looking at me now, his expression thoughtful. Suddenly he thrust his black-robed arm out. "Catalyst," he said softly, "give me Life."

I would have laughed. My hand lifted to sign that I did not know how. . . . And yet, I did know how. I remembered. I remembered the wonderful feeling as the Life flowed into me. I remembered how to reach out for the magic with one hand while the other held Mosiah's arm. I was the vessel, the magic ran into me, and for that brief moment I was blessed.

I closed my eyes and willed the Life of Thimhallan to come to me.

At first I felt nothing, and fear that I would fail, fail Eliza, twisted inside me. I concentrated all my effort, praying to the Almin, pleading. . . . The Life came suddenly, in a great surge, as if it had been pent up and was waiting only for release. The energy gave me a severe jolt. My body tingled and burned, as if each drop of blood was a tiny spark. The sensation was excruciatingly painful, not pleasant, as it had been in the alternate time.

Frightened and hurting, I tried to end it, tried to snatch my hand from Mosiah's arm, but he refused to let me go. The magic leapt between us in a blue arc that twined around his arm and mine.

The flame of the arc crackled out. I was empty, the fire replaced by a sensation of cold that left me numb and shaking. I sank to my knees, my strength sapped.

Eliza knelt and put her arm around me.

"Reuven, are you all right?"

I nodded, though I felt sick and dizzy.

"Blessed Almin," said Scylla, awed. "I've never seen anything like that!"

"I doubt you ever will again," said Mosiah, massaging his arm. "That was the Life transference of a catalyst to a warlock. We thought such transferences had died with the magic, for it has not been successfully performed since the war ended. Strange," he murmured to himself. "Very strange."

"Not so strange if the magic hasn't died," Scylla observed.

Simkin yawned. "While you all are playing at being magi, I'm off to reconnoiter. Wait for me here. Do you know, I'm quite enjoying this!"

"Wait—damn!"

Mosiah clutched empty air. Simkin had vanished.

"Now what do we do?" I signed.

"Hand ourselves over to the Technomancers," Mosiah said bitterly. "We might as well."

"Nonsense," Eliza said crisply. "We'll wait here for him to return. He *will* return. I have faith in Ted—Simkin."

"So did your father," Mosiah said grimly. He glanced around, stiffened. "We're missing someone else."

We could see a short distance down the tunnel by the light reflecting off the rocks. Scylla was nowhere in sight.

"Back!" Mosiah urged, and he started herding Eliza and me down the tunnel. "Back the way we came! We can hold out—"

"Psst! Over here!" came a piercing whisper.

A hand waved at us from the darkness.

An arm attached to the hand appeared and Scylla emerged from the shadows. "I've found another chamber. We can hide in here and keep watch!"

Eliza gave Mosiah a reproachful glance and went to join Scylla. I started after her. Mosiah clamped hold of my arm.

"Do you remember another chamber in the cave the last time we were inside it?"

I shook my head. "But it was dark and confused."

"Wasn't it," Mosiah said coolly.

The chamber Scylla had found was located directly across the tunnel from where we had been standing. It provided a clear view of a small cavern. Two Technomancers, in their silver masks and robes, stood guard outside the entrance.

Long minutes passed. Nothing happened, and the thought occurred to me that Simkin had been right about one thing, at least. The Technomancers must have felt their prisoners were secure and that we were far away. Either that or the prisoners were not in there at all. I was wondering if Simkin had led us on a wild-goose chase when one of the Technomancers spoke.

"Time to check on them," he said.

The other nodded and turned on his heel, took a step, and fell headlong, sprawling on the cavern floor.

"Son-of-a-bitch!" the man swore as he picked himself up.

"What the hell happened to you?" his companion asked, turning to stare.

"I fell over a rock! That rock!" The Technomancer glared and pointed.

"Well, watch where you're going next time."

The Technomancer stared balefully at the rock. "I'll swear that wasn't there before."

"You're just clumsy," said the other Technomancer, shrugging.

"No, I'm serious. I've been in and out of this blasted prison cell thirty times today and I'll swear that rock wasn't there!" The Technomancer picked it up. "I'll be damned!" he said, amazed. "This rock has . . . eyes!"

Those of us hunkered down in the chamber exchanged glances. None of us said the word, but we were all thinking it.

Simkin.

"What the devil are you two doing? Standing there discussing a rock," came another voice. I recognized it and so did Mosiah.

"Smythe!" he whispered.

"If you've taken up geology," Smythe continued, "do it on your time. Not mine."

The two Technomancers snapped to attention. Smythe appeared, coming from the direction of the cavern entrance. He was not wearing the business suit in which I'd last seen him, but was dressed in the robes, trimmed in gold, that he'd worn in the hologram. His face was in the light and it was a good thing I had recognized him from his voice. I might not have done so otherwise. The face that had been so handsome and charming was grim and contorted with suppressed rage. Four bodyguards in silver trooped after him.

"But, sir, look at this rock—"

"Is it darkstone?" Smythe demanded impatiently.

"No, sir, it doesn't appear to be. Ordinary limestone, maybe. But it—"

"Darkstone is the only rock in which I'm interested. Toss it in the river."

The Technomancer looked again at the rock and seemed to want to argue. A glance at Smythe's scowling face, and the Technomancer gave a heave, flung the rock into the dark, swiftly flowing water.

I could swear that I heard a faint indignant shriek as the rock sailed through the air. It hit the water with a splash and sank . . . like a rock.

"How are the prisoners?" Smythe asked. "Any change?"

"That Joram's growing worse, sir. He won't be with us long if he doesn't get help."

Eliza, beside me, made a choked sound.

"Hush!" Scylla breathed.

Mosiah cast them both a warning glance. I found Eliza's hand. Her flesh was chill to the touch. Her fingers tightened convulsively around mine.

"I'm going to talk to Joram," Smythe was saying. "If he's that bad off, he may be willing to cooperate. Two of you come with me. The rest of you wait outside."

Smythe entered the chamber where the prisoners were being held. Two of his guards followed after him. The others took up positions out in the corridor.

There was nothing we could do but wait. Not only would we endanger ourselves if we tried to fight such overwhelming numbers, we would place the prisoners' lives in jeopardy. There was every possibility the Technomancers would kill their prisoners rather than let them be rescued.

We hid in the darkness, straining to hear.

The first voice we heard was Father Saryon's. His tone was strong and indignant, which meant that he was well. I closed my eyes and breathed a prayer to the Almin in thankfulness.

"Joram is very ill, as you can see, Mr. Smythe. My friend needs medical attention immediately. I insist that you take him to the outpost. They have a medical facility there—"

"Certainly," said Smythe, and his voice was smooth and eager to please. "We will provide him with the antidote to the poison—as soon as he tells me where to find the Darksword."

"Poison?" Saryon was horrified. "You poisoned him?"

"A slow-acting variety. We use the same to cause the deaths of the organisms in our perpetual generators. Death comes very slowly and very painfully, I am told. Now, my friend. Where is the Darksword? Tell us that, and you will feel much better."

"He does not know!" Saryon said angrily.

"Ah, but I think he does," said Smythe. "He gave it to his daughter to hide. We saw her in possession of the sword, so you needn't trouble to lie about it. We are on her trail—"

"If you hurt her . . ." The voice was weak, but it was definitely Joram's.

We heard scuffling sounds and a stifled cry.

Eliza turned her head into my shoulder. I held her tightly and the rage I felt toward Smythe at that moment appalled me. I had always thought of myself as a pacifist. Now I knew I had it in me to kill.

"Don't! Leave him alone!" Saryon cried, and we heard a rustling sound, as if he threw himself protectively in front of Joram. "He is weak and ill."

"He will be far more ill if he does not cooperate."

"He can be of no use to you dead!"

"He isn't going to die. At least not yet. As you say, I

have need of him. Give him the stimulant. There. That will keep him alive a little longer. He won't feel very good, but he'll live, which is more than I can say for you, Father Saryon. You are of no use to me whatsoever. I have catalysts of my own, prepared to give the Darksword Life, once it is recovered.

"Listen to me, Joram. You have five minutes to reconsider your stubborn refusal to tell me where your daughter is hiding. If you do not, Father Saryon will be flayed alive, a particularly nasty way to die. Bind his feet and his hands."

We four stared, horrified, at each other. We had five minutes to act, five minutes to rescue the hostages, or Father Saryon would most certainly be tortured and murdered. There were six guards, plus Kevon Smythe, and only four of us.

"Scylla, you have your gun," Mosiah began, speaking in a tense whisper. "You—"

"Gun," she said. "I don't have a gun."

Mosiah glared at her. "You don't carry a gun! What kind of agent are you?"

"A smart one," Scylla returned. "From what I've seen, carrying a gun is an open invitation for someone to shoot you."

Mosiah was grim. "We have no choice, I guess. We have to take on all six of the *D'karn-darah*—"

"Make that seven," Scylla said.

Another silver-robed Technomancer had apparently entered the cavern. I say "apparently" because I had been watching the cavern entrance and I had not seen anyone come inside. The new arrival glided up behind the two guards waiting at the entrance. Reaching out a silver-gloved hand, the *D'karn-darah* tapped one of them on the shoulder.

It was the Technomancer who had thrown the rock

in the river. He jumped, turned. His robes flowed around him like liquid mercury.

"What the devil—who are you?" he demanded. "What do you want? And don't come sneaking up on someone like that. It's bad enough being on this blasted planet, with rocks that have eyes and God knows what else! What do you want?" he repeated nervously.

"A message from HQ for the master."

"He's inside the prison cell."

"It's urgent," said the *D'karn-darah*.

"I'll go tell him," volunteered the other Technomancer.

"Wait," said the first. His tone was suspicious. "Why didn't they just send the message the usual way—using the seerstones?"

"None of your seerstones are working. Try them."

The first Technomancer put his wrist to his ear. The second did the same. The second looked at the first, who shrugged and jerked his head toward the prison cell. The Technomancer left to report.

Smythe emerged. His choleric face was a fierce red, his brows drawn tight in a vicious scowl.

"What do you mean the seerstones aren't working?" he demanded.

"We don't know, sir," returned the newly arrived Technomancer. "Perhaps it's this cave, blocking the signal. I have an urgent message for you, sir."

"Deliver it!" Smythe snapped.

The silver-hooded head revolved, glanced in the direction of the other *D'karn-darah*. "It is for you alone, Master. We should speak in private. It is most urgent, sir."

Smythe looked back in frustration toward the prison. His unhealthy choler increased. "Of all the damn luck. I just about had him broken! This better be good!" He turned to one of the guards. "Remind the good father that he has three minutes left. Three minutes."

"Come over here, Master," said the messenger, and he gestured—alarmingly—in the direction of our small hidden cavern.

The two walked toward us. The silver robes of the *D'karn-darah* swished about his ankles, revealing his silver-slippered feet, and I suddenly noticed that this Technomancer was wearing orange socks.

"Simkin!" Mosiah breathed into my ear.

Beyond all reason, it was, it had to be Simkin, disguised as a Technomancer and leading Kevon Smythe straight toward our hiding place.

"That bastard!" Mosiah whispered. "If it's the last thing I do, I'll—"

"Shhh!" Scylla hushed him.

Eliza gripped my hand tightly. We didn't dare move, for fear he'd hear us. We went completely immobile in the darkness, every breath seeming to whistle loud as a cyclone, our heartbeats booming like thunder. Mosiah's body tensed. He was readying his magic for one gigantic, lethal burst.

Desperate, frantic plans rushed through my mind, none of them making any sense, or offering any hope.

Four more paces and Kevon Smythe would bump right into us. At the second pace, the *D'karn-darah* that was Simkin came to a halt.

Smythe stopped, turned to face him.

"What's all this about?" he asked irritably.

"Sir," said Simkin, "the representatives of the Hch'nyv have arrived in Zith-el."

I heard a soft gasp, as if Mosiah had been punched in the solar plexus. Scylla exhaled softly.

Smythe's color went from red to sallow yellow, as if

someone had opened a major artery and drained all his blood in an instant. Such stark terror was on his face that I could almost have felt sorry for him. He quickly recovered his equanimity, but the vestiges of that fear remained.

"What do they want?" he asked, his voice under tight control.

"The Darksword," said Simkin laconically.

Smythe cast a furious glance back toward the prison. "We haven't recovered it yet. We will. They must give us more time."

"Earth Forces are in retreat. Earth takeover is beginning. You haven't much time. Such were their words to us. It is their religious leaders that are pushing the issue, sir. Their gods or whatever it is they worship have warned them that the Darksword is a distinct threat."

"I know all about their blasted gods!" Smythe said, his voice shaking with fury and fear. Once again, he clamped down hard on himself. "We made a deal. Remind them of it. They have Earth in exchange for the Darksword. We have Thimhallan. They provide us with Death. We provide them with Life. We will recover the Darksword and we will give it to them, but in our own good time. Tell them that."

Simkin shook his silver-hooded head. "They will not listen to those they consider underlings."

Smythe fumed, glanced again at the prison, in an agony of indecision. "Very well. I'll go deal with the matter."

He turned on his heel, stalked away, shouting orders.

"My guards! Come with me. I'm needed back at HQ. You two. Kill the priest. I don't care how. Do it slowly and make certain Joram has a ringside seat."

"What if he decides to talk, Master?"

"Get his information, then transport him immediately to me at HQ. Use the teleporter."

"Yes, sir. Do we still kill the priest?"

"What do you think?" Smythe demanded impatiently. "He's of no use to me."

"Yes, sir. Could you leave someone to help us, sir? The teleporter is not functioning efficiently on this planet."

"I'll stay here and give them a hand," said Simkin from beneath his silver hood.

"Very well." Smythe was obviously anxious to be gone. He left the cavern, his four bodyguards trooping after him.

I looked at the others, to see my own feelings of revulsion, horror, and fury reflected on their faces. I could not comprehend how any human could be so consumed with power that he would make a deal with a heinous enemy, a deal sacrificing millions of his fellow humans on the altar of his own ambition.

The two Technomancers went into the prison to retrieve the captives. Simkin remained outside, rocking back and forth on his heels and humming to himself. The humming was off-key and extremely jarring to the nerves. He did not once look in our direction or give us the slightest sign.

I was beginning to think that we had been mistaken. Perhaps the Technomancer wasn't Simkin, after all. Perhaps it was merely a Technomancer with an odd taste in footwear.

Mosiah shared my doubts. "That fool! What's he doing? If it *is* him . . ."

"Whether it is or it isn't, he got rid of Smythe," Scylla pointed out. "And four of the guards. We should attack now."

"Let them bring the hostages out of the cell first," said Mosiah. "They're probably using a stasis field to hold them and we'd never be able to remove it ourselves."

"Good point, Enforcer," said Scylla admiringly. "What's the plan?"

"Plan!" Mosiah snorted. "*I'm* the only one with a weapon and that's my magic."

"Not even a laser pistol would have any effect on that protective armor of theirs," Scylla returned in a hoarse whisper. "Besides, I have my own weapons."

"Which are?"

"You'll see. I guarantee you that I'll put one out of commission, if you can handle the other."

Mosiah didn't like it, but this was no time to argue. We could hear scuffling sounds from inside the prison. Simkin's humming grew louder and more nerve-racking, if that was possible.

"At my signal, Scylla, you attack," Mosiah ordered. "Reuven, you and Eliza rescue Joram and Father Saryon."

"Where do we take them?" Eliza asked.

"Down the tunnel. Back to the cavern where you hid the Darksword."

"What then?"

"Let's get that far first," Mosiah said.

Simkin's humming was setting my teeth on edge. I've never heard such a strange and ear-piercing sound come from any living human throat. But then, this was Simkin. The two Technomancer guards emerged. One had hold of Father Saryon. He looked upset and anxious, but I knew that his anxiety was for Joram, not for himself, though he was the one who was about to be put to death. Saryon kept twisting his head, trying to see over his shoulder, trying to see Joram, who was being dragged out behind him.

At the sight of her father, Eliza gave a small moan and immediately covered her mouth with her hand to prevent any further cries from escaping her.

Joram's skin was a grayish white, beaded with sweat. Blood matted his hair and was caked on one side of his face, where a deep, ugly wound crossed over his cheek, almost laying the bone bare. His right hand was clasped over his left arm, which hung limp. His shirt was torn, blood covered the shirtfront, and the sleeve of the left arm was saturated. The stimulant, his fever, and his anger gave his eyes an unnatural luster. He was weak, but grimly alert and defiant.

"Release Father Saryon. Then and only then will I tell you where to find the Darksword."

"You'll tell us," said one of the Technomancers. "When you see the priest lying there with half his flesh flayed from his body, screaming for us to end his torment in death, you'll tell us."

The Technomancer flung Father Saryon to the ground. His hands were bound, he was unable to break his fall, and he landed heavily, crying out in pain. I would have rushed forward then and there, but common sense and Mosiah's whispered warning prevailed.

Simkin approached Father Saryon, looked down at him.

There was a sharp snapping sound.

The Technomancer standing nearest Simkin stared wildly, gasped, and backed away.

"What are you doing?" he cried shrilly.

"Following orders," said Simkin. "Giving you a hand."

He held out his own hand, which he had broken off at the wrist.

CHAPTER TWENTY-SIX

*The magic that Joram longed for and sought every
morning to feel burning in his soul never came to
him.*

*When he was fifteen, he stopped asking Anja
when he would gain the magic.*

*Deep inside of him, he already knew the
answer.*

~*FORGING THE DARKSWORD*

"In addition, I'll help you get ahead," Simkin added.
He lifted his head from his shoulders—unscrewed his
head would be more precisely the term—and flung it
straight at one of the Technomancers.

The man may have had some small magical powers,
although from what I had seen, the Technomancers
were so beholden to Technology as to make the magic
almost irrelevant. Certainly he had never seen magic in
such maniacal form. He gaped when Simkin broke off
his own hand. But when Simkin's head, covered with a
silver hood, the ends flapping, flew through the air at

him, the Technomancer gave a strangled cry and flung his arms over his face. Simkin's head exploded with a force that stopped my heart, shook the cave . . . and resulted in a shower of daisies.

"*Now!*" Mosiah yelled.

The Life flowed through him and transformed him as he ran. His black robes writhed around him, flattened to cover his body in spiky black fur. His head elongated, changed to a muzzle with yellow fangs protruding from beneath black, curled lips. His legs transformed into the legs of a beast, his forearms were covered with black fur, claws sprouted from the fingernails. The hem of his robes twisted into a tail with a barb sharp as a razor. Mosiah had become a darkrover, the type known as a hunterkill, one of the most feared of all the creations of the ancient war masters.

The Technomancer uncovered his eyes, gazed in bafflement at the daisies drifting down around his head. They might have been scattered over his grave. The next sight he saw was a terrible one—a hunterkill bounding across the cavern floor, running upright on its powerful hind legs, jaws snapping, its claws reaching for the Technomancer's throat.

His silver robes acted as armor, capable—as Scylla had said—of deflecting all attacks by conventional weapons. The darkrover was certainly not a conventional weapon, however. Mosiah hurled himself on the Technomancer. The silver robes crackled and the darkrover shrieked in pain, but Mosiah's claws scratched and tore. His weight carried the Technomancer to the ground.

The other Technomancer guard was not quite as befuddled by the magic surging around him as his fellow. A weapon appeared in his hand, a scythe, that gleamed with a fell energy. He stood over Father

Saryon, swinging the scythe in a vicious arc. The blade sang as it whipped through the air, reminding me of Simkin's off-key humming.

Eliza and I held back, agonized, afraid for the captives. But there was nothing we could do. Saryon lay flattened on the ground. Every sweep of the scythe came a little closer to him. Joram was behind the scythe-wielding Technomancer, leaning up against the cavern wall, his eyes bright and burning with the effects of the poison. He lurched forward, with the idea of knocking down the Technomancer from behind.

The guard heard him, however. Whipping the scythe around, he struck Joram on the side of the head with its handle. Joram fell, landed near Father Saryon. Even then, defiantly, Joram raised his head. Blood, fresh blood, covered his face. His head sank between his arms. He lay still.

Eliza cried out and would have run to her father, regardless of her own danger. I caught hold of her, held her.

"Allow me, Your Majesty," said Scylla, and advanced, bare-handed, on the Technomancer wielding the scythe.

"Be careful, Scylla!" the darkrover shouted, using Mosiah's voice.

The jaws of the hunterkill dribbled blood and saliva, its claws were red, blood smeared its black fur. I glanced over at its prey and was sorry I did. Hastily, I averted my gaze from what was left of the Technomancer's body. It was covered with blood and daisies.

"That scythe can drain a person of Life," Mosiah cautioned.

"I don't know why you think that would affect me," Scylla said, flashing Mosiah a grin and a wink.

She advanced on the Technomancer, watching his movements, and suddenly kicked out her leg in the path of the swinging scythe. Eliza covered her eyes. I watched in horror, expecting to see Scylla's leg hacked off by the vicious blade.

The blade struck her combat boot and shattered, flying apart in thousands of tiny sparkling shards as if it had been brittle and fragile as ice. I could not see the expression on the silver-hooded head, but I could guess that he was staring at his weapon in astonishment. He quickly recovered, however, shifted his hands to use the scythe's handle as a club, and tried to jab Scylla.

She struck out with the heel of her boot, catching the Technomancer full in the nose of his silver-hooded head. I heard a sickening, crackling sound and thought at first it was the silver armor's defensive shield activating. A smear of blood blossomed on the silver hood. The sound had been the man's nose breaking. He toppled over backward. A kick to the head while he was on the ground finished him.

"What's going on in there?" a voice shouted from outside the cavern. "Is everything all right?"

"More Technos," said Mosiah. He had retained his darkrover shape, his eyes glowed red and hideous. "They must be the ones guarding the teleporter. They'll be here quickly. They've got a hover barge! Go!" he urged, waving bloody claws at us. "Take Father Saryon and Joram and go! I will deal with these."

Saryon was on his knees, bending over the unconscious Joram. Eliza was at her father's side, holding his hand. I wondered how we would manage to carry him with us, for he was a tall man and muscular.

"I won't leave Joram," said Saryon firmly.

"Nor will I," Eliza said. Tears streamed down her face but I don't believe that she was aware of them.

"Smythe has the antidote to the poison." Saryon's gaze went to Eliza. "Do you know where the Dark-sword is?"

"Yes, Father."

"Then we must find it and give it to him. It is the only way to save your father's life."

"He may not keep his end of the bargain," Scylla cautioned.

"Perhaps he will," Saryon said bleakly. "He must."

"We must carry him away from this place," Scylla urged. "We should not leave him here for them to find. They might take out their wrath at your escape on him."

She touched Joram on the forehead. Her deft hands glided smoothly over the broken skin, wiping away the blood.

Joram opened his eyes, blinked, as if he were look-ing into a dazzling light.

"The guards aren't answering. Something's wrong," came the voice from outside the cavern. "I'm going to go check."

"Go!" Mosiah snarled. He bounded over to hide in the shadows near the cavern entrance.

"I can make it," Joram said, fending off all offers of assistance. "I don't need any help."

As it was, he stumbled when he tried to rise, but Scylla was there, her strong arm and shoulder support-ing him.

"Reuven," she called, "take hold of him from the other side."

I did as she commanded. Hastening to Joram's side, I caught hold of him around the waist. He glowered at both Scylla and me and for a moment I thought he was going to defy us.

"If you don't allow us to help you, sir," Scylla said

quietly, "you will not move ten paces from this spot. When you fall, your daughter will remain with you, as will Father Saryon. The Technomancers will catch them and that will be an end to all which you have struggled to protect. Is that what you want?"

Joram's forbidding expression dissolved. He shook his head. "No. I will accept your help." He glanced over at me. "And Reuven's."

"Eliza, you lead the way," Scylla said. "Hurry now."

"Wait!" Eliza turned to Father Saryon. "Where is Mother? Was she in that prison with you?"

"No, child," Saryon said, looking concerned. "She was not. I thought perhaps you might know—"

Eliza shook her head.

"She is not here," Saryon said. "And that is a hopeful sign. If the Technomancers had made her captive, they would have made use of her by now. I think that somehow she managed to escape them."

"Then where is she?" Eliza demanded.

"Perhaps I have an idea," Saryon said. "Do not worry. I believe that wherever she is, she is safe. Safer than we are."

Eliza gave her father a gentle kiss on his blood-stained cheek, then grabbing hold of Saryon's hand, she led the way back down the spiraling tunnel. Scylla and I, half carrying Joram, hastened after. He groaned with pain only once, when we first started to move, then gritted his teeth and tightened his lips over his agony.

Behind us, we heard a savage howl and a scream.

It occurred to me to wonder, just as we left the area, what had become of Simkin.

I glanced back. There, lying on an empty pile of silver robes, was a teddy bear. Its head was missing and so were both of its arms. The orange ribbon that had been tied in a jaunty bow around Teddy's neck lay limply across the body.

I hurried on, thankful that Eliza had been too preoccupied with her father to see.

"It's very strange," said Saryon, after we had traveled about a mile down the corkscrew tunnel, "but this place seems familiar to me. And I know I've never been here in my life."

"Not in this life, perhaps, Father," said Scylla, "but who knows where you've been gallivanting around in other lives?"

Saryon glanced back at her with a weak smile, thinking she was joking and politely pretending to be amused, although he must have been thinking that this was not the time for levity. Eliza was endeavoring to find our way, using Scylla's flashlight as a guide, and paying no attention to what was being said. Joram was too intent on combating his pain to search for hidden meanings.

I alone realized that there might be more to Scylla's statement than appeared. I glanced at her sidelong, with Joram between us, and caught her looking at me, a smile on her lips. I could not question her; my hands were occupied in supporting Joram.

I had no thought, then, of the truth. I'm not certain I would ever have figured it out, but I began to see how a few small pieces of the puzzle might fit together. I wished that Mosiah were here, to see what he would have made of her peculiar statement.

But for all I knew, Mosiah might very well be dead. We had heard nothing of him since we left. Our only sign that he had lived long enough to perform his task was that we had not been overtaken by the guards.

We continued on. Joram grew heavier as his strength flagged and he relied more on us to support him. Scylla bore most of the weight, but I had my share and my shoulders burned and ached with the strain. I thought of the pain he must be enduring in silence, with no complaint, and I felt ashamed. Resolutely, I put the thought of my own discomfort out of my mind and trudged on.

Saryon came to a sudden halt. "I don't like this," he said. "Something lives down here. Can't you smell it? A dragon," he added, his brow furrowed. "A Dragon of the Night."

"Something *used* to live down here, Father," Eliza answered, flashing the light around the smooth-sided, smooth-floored tunnel. "I'm not sure what it was, but it's gone now. It must have died when the magic died. Why do you think it's a dragon?"

"I don't know." Saryon was perplexed. "The thought came to me, that's all." He was shrewd and he had lived most of his life in magical Thimhallan. He looked at Scylla, his expression puzzled and uneasy. He was beginning to take her joke more seriously. "Perhaps we should wait here for Mosiah. Not travel any farther until we find out what has happened to him. Are you certain we have to go deeper into this awful place?"

"Yes, Father," said Eliza. "I'm sorry, but we must go on. The Darksword is down here."

At this, Joram raised his head. His pallor was frightening, the blood formed dark streaks over his face. He had once again lapsed into unconsciousness, his feet dragged, his eyes closed. Except that I could feel the beat of his heart beneath my arm, I might have thought he had died. The word *Darksword* on his daughter's lips was perhaps the only thing that could have roused him.

"Where is it?" he gasped, and his voice was little more than a breath. "Is it safe?"

"Yes, Father," Eliza answered, and her suffering for his suffering choked her. "It is safe. Oh, Father, I am so sorry! I had no right—"

He was shaking his head. "I was the one who had no right," he said, and then his head lolled. His eyes closed and he sagged in our arms.

"Whatever happens, I have to rest!" I signed urgently, afraid I would drop him.

Scylla nodded and we lowered him to the cavern floor.

Painful warmth flooded through my cramped shoulders. I bit my lips to keep from crying out.

"Is he going to be all right?" Eliza asked fearfully, crouching down beside him. She smoothed the black curly hair from his face, the hair that, but for the streaks of gray at his temples, was the exact match of her own. "He looks so ill."

"We don't have much time," Scylla admitted. "Either for Joram or for ourselves and the rest of those who are counting on us."

"I am confused," I signed. "I have lost track of time—any time! How long do we have?"

"Until midnight this night," Scylla said, consulting a green-glowing watch she wore on her wrist.

"That's when the last ship leaves the outpost?" Saryon asked.

Scylla gave him a strange look. "The last ship has left," she replied coolly. "Midnight is when the Hch'nyv will arrive."

"What?" My frantic gestures revealed my fear and

alarm. "How will we return the Darksword to Earth? What good would it do? Why do we persist in this folly? We're all going to die anyway!"

She was about to answer when the sound of footfalls, moving rapidly, echoed down the tunnel. The noise silenced us all. Scylla was on her feet, placing herself between us and whoever was coming down the tunnel.

"Douse the light!" she hissed.

Eliza shut off the flashlight. We huddled together in the dark, our fear a living thing that seemed to take shape and form around us. Then I heard a voice, a soft voice, Saryon's voice, speaking to the Almin in prayer. His hand, strong and warm, closed over mine. He was offering me comfort and a gentle reminder that our lives were being guided, watched over, protected by one greater than ourselves. Though this should all come to some terrible end, we would not be alone. I said a prayer myself, asking for forgiveness for my lack of faith and strength to go on.

A figure lurched out of the darkness, nearly ran headlong into Scylla. "What the—" came a voice.

"Mosiah!" Scylla breathed a sigh in relief.

Eliza switched on the light.

Mosiah glared around at us. "What the devil are you all doing?" he demanded angrily. "Having a picnic? Why—"

He caught sight of Joram, lying unconscious on the tunnel floor. "Oh," Mosiah said, and he shook his head. His gaze shifted back to Scylla. "Is he dead?"

"No, but he's not doing well," she answered guardedly, with a glance at Eliza.

"We can't wait. I took care of the Technomancers, but more will be coming through the teleporter at any moment. I could not prevent them from sounding the alarm. We must recover the Darksword and get out of here quickly! You and I will carry him."

"You don't look able to carry yourself," Scylla said as they bent together to lift up Joram. "Do you have any Life left?"

"Not much." Mosiah grunted from the exertion. He had changed back to his usual form, but the alteration must have been a draining one. He looked exhausted to the point of dropping.

"Perhaps I could give you Life again," I said, feeling guilty that I had failed them.

Saryon regarded me with amazement. "You gave Mosiah Life, Reuven? How? When?"

"It will take too long to explain, Father," said Mosiah. He and Scylla, supporting Joram between them, started moving down the tunnel. He refused my offer, stating that I should conserve my strength, for we were not out of this yet.

The Hch'nyv would be attacking Thimhallan at midnight. Smythe and his Technomancers would be desperate to find the Darksword. Where could we go that they would not discover us? And how would we fight the massive armies of the Hch'nyv with one sword, however powerful? On a more mundane level, the word *picnic* reminded me that we had not eaten. Our water supply was running low. All of us were thirsty and hungry and who knew how long it would be before we could find food and water? Joram was near death. Perhaps he was the lucky one among us, I caught myself thinking.

Of course, I should have faith, as Saryon had silently counseled. But it was very hard for me to trust in the Almin when reason and logic were so overwhelmingly against us.

I was trying to nurture hope's flickering flame when I heard a sound that doused it utterly.

It was a sound I had heard before in this tunnel, a sound I'd heard in that other life, a life that had come to such a horrible end.

Stentorian breathing rumbled from the cavern that was not all that far below us.

CHAPTER
TWENTY-SEVEN

*"Here's to folly," Simkin announced, and together
they tottered forward into the fiery illusions, the
champagne glasses clinking along behind.*

~*DOOM OF THE DARKSWORD*

"The dragon," Mosiah said. "A Dragon of the
Night."

"But that's impossible!" Saryon gasped. "The dragons were creations of the magic. They must have all
died when Life disappeared from Thimhallan."

"The Life didn't disappear, Father. The Well was
shattered, but the magic didn't escape, as we had
thought."

"We believe that the Well may have been capped,
Father," Scylla added.

"I don't believe there's a dragon. There can't be," Eliza argued. "We were just down there."

"If you remember, I *said* that cave smelled occupied," Mosiah returned.

"But . . . I still don't understand. . . ." Saryon appeared bewildered. "How do you know that a Dragon of the Night lives in that cavern? It could be anything! A bear, maybe."

"A bear? Yes, of course. Dear Teddy! Well, that explains it. Or doesn't, as the case may be. As to the cavern, we've been there before. In fact, we've died there before." Mosiah was looking directly at Scylla. "Haven't we, Sir Knight?"

Scylla shrugged. "If you say so." She rolled her eyes and, leaning over to me, whispered, "Humor him."

"The Darksword is there, too," Eliza reminded us. "We must return to the cavern to recover the sword."

"We cannot challenge a Dragon of the Night," Saryon protested vigorously. "They are terrible creatures. Terrible!"

"The dragon is before us, but the Technomancers are behind us," Mosiah pointed out. "We can't very well go back."

At last, as I said, I was beginning to have a glimmer of understanding. I touched Saryon's arm, to draw attention to myself.

"You can charm the dragon, Father," I signed.

"No," he returned hurriedly. "Absolutely not."

"Yes," I repeated. "You did it before, in the other life."

"What other life?" Saryon stared at me in perplexity. "I charmed a dragon? I am certain I would recall doing such a thing," he added more testily, "and I assure you that I do not."

"If he's going to do it, he must act swiftly," Mosiah

warned. "While the sun is still shining. When night falls, the dragon will awaken and go out in search of food. It is twilight now."

Eliza kept watch beside her father, her attention divided between ourselves and him. She did not understand completely what we were saying, but she understood the urgency and did not interrupt us with demands for us to explain. She trusted us. I smiled at her reassuringly.

"I tell you I know nothing about charming dragons!" Saryon was shaking his head.

"You do," said Mosiah. "You are the only one of us who does. I cannot."

"You are *Duuk-tsarith*!" Saryon argued.

"But I was trained on Earth. The only dragons I ever saw were created by special effects. I can't take time to explain, but in an alternate time, Father, a time in which Joram died twenty years ago, you came upon a Dragon of the Night—this very dragon, or so I believe—and you were able to charm it. Think, Father! Lessons you learned at the Font. All catalysts were taught the spells of the war wizards."

"I . . . It's been so long. . . ." Saryon put his hand to his temples, as if they ached. "If I fail, we would all die. Die most horribly."

"We know," Mosiah said.

I noticed in all this that Scylla kept silent. She did not venture to persuade or argue. I could not yet understand, but I was beginning to understand, if that makes any sense.

"Father Saryon." It was Joram who spoke.

So intent had we been on our discussion I had not noticed that he had regained consciousness. His head was pillowed in his daughter's lap. She wiped the sweat from his brow, smoothed back the damp hair, and watched over him anxiously, lovingly.

Joram smiled. He lifted his hand. Saryon knelt and clasped Joram's hand to his breast. It was obvious to him, to all of us, that Joram had very little time left to live.

"Father Saryon," he said, and it took an effort for him to speak. "You were able to charm me. What is a dragon, compared to that?"

"I will," Saryon said brokenly. "I will . . . try. The rest of you . . . wait here."

He stood up and would have rushed down the tunnel, then and there, if we hadn't stopped him.

"You cannot charm the dragon and retrieve the Darksword at the same time," Mosiah pointed out. "The Darksword would disrupt the charm."

"That's true," Saryon admitted.

"I will recover the Darksword—" Mosiah began.

"*I* will recover the Darksword," said Eliza firmly. "It is my legacy."

A spasm of agony contorted Joram's face. He shook his head, but he was too weak to argue or try to stop her. A single tear tracked through the blood on his cheek. A tear that was not wrung from him by his own physical pain, but by the pain of regret, remorse.

Eliza saw the tear and gathered her father close, hugging him to her. "Don't, Father!" She wept with him. "I am proud to bear this! Proud to be your daughter. You shattered the world. Perhaps it is left to me to save it!"

Kissing him, she rose quickly to her feet. "I am ready."

I was afraid Mosiah would argue or try to dissuade her. He regarded her intently for a moment, then he bowed. "Very well, Your Majesty," he said. "I will go, and of course Reuven will go as well. I may need my catalyst," he added.

I was filled with pride, so much that it almost pushed out my fear. Almost. I could not forget the terror of the last time we had faced the Dragon of the Night. The terror and pain of my own death. Worse— the horror of seeing Eliza die. Resolutely, I trampled down the memory. I would never have found the courage to stir a step otherwise.

"Someone must stay with my father," Eliza said, looking at me. "I had hoped that Reuven—"

"I will stay with Joram," Scylla volunteered. She grinned at us. The ring in her eyebrow glinted. "You're on your own now."

"I do not understand any of this," Saryon said plaintively.

"You must have faith," I signed to him.

"And you are impertinent to your teacher," he said with a wan smile. He gave a bleak sigh. "Come, then. We will go charm this dragon."

The Dragons of the Night loathe sunlight to such an extent that even though they burrow down into the deepest, darkest parts of Thimhallan they can find, they sleep during the daytime. This dragon was asleep, to judge by its rhythmic breathing, but its sleep appeared restless and shallow. We could hear the gigantic body move, scales scraping against the rock floor. I recalled in that other life what the dragon had said about the presence of the Darksword in its lair, how it had disturbed its rest. Either that, or its waking time was very near.

I remembered the stench from my last visit to this place. The smell seemed worse, this time. We all of us covered our noses and mouths, to keep from retching. We brought no light with us, for fear that even the beam of the flashlight might wake the dragon and arouse its ire. Moving slowly and silently, feeling our way with our hands, we crept along the last few yards of the tunnel. We rounded a corner, and came upon the dragon's lair.

The diamond embedded in its forehead shone with a cold, sharp brilliance. It did not illuminate. We could not see the dragon. We could see nothing, not even each other, though we stood bunched together, side by side.

The dragon's breathing reverberated through the tunnel. It shifted its body again as we stood outside its lair, and the floor shook as it flopped over on its side, its tail thrashing against the wall. The diamond lowered, the dragon had settled its head on its side, apparently. We stood in the darkness, immersed in fear and awe.

I could not have ventured inside that cavern. I don't know where Saryon found the courage to do so. But then, where had he found the courage to suffer himself to be turned into living stone?

"Wait here," he said to us, his words no more than a breath. "I must do this alone."

He left us and walked into the cavern. I could not see him, but I could hear his robes rustle and the soft padding of his feet. His figure passed in front of me, blotting from my sight the light of the diamond.

Eliza clasped my hand. I held on to her tightly. Mosiah stood beside us, tense. Sometimes I could hear whispered words and I guessed that he was rehearsing his magic in his mind. Not that it would do us much good. We'd been through that before.

The *Duuk-tsarith*! Were they here now as they had

been here in that other time? Would they try to seize the sword?

Taking hold of Mosiah's hand, I signed my question with my fingers pressed against his palm. If he could not see my words, at least he could feel them.

"I thought of that myself," he said back to me, his mouth against my ear. "I have sought my brethren. They are not here."

At least that was one worry off my mind.

I had not forgotten Saryon. I walked with him in spirit every step of the way. The dragon snuffled and shifted once again. A gleam of pale light beamed from a slit in its eyelids. My heart stopped. Eliza gripped my hand so tightly that she left bruise marks on it, yet I don't recall feeling any pain at the time.

Saryon halted, held still. The dragon breathed a great sigh, and the eyelids closed. The light vanished. Those of us in the cavern added our sighs to the dragon's.

Saryon moved forward once more. He must be very close to the dragon's head now, I thought. I could see the diamond again, since the dragon had changed position. The massive head was lying completely on its side, resting on the jawbone. And then I saw a hand, Saryon's hand, looking frail and fragile, silhouetted against the diamond's bright chill light.

The hand hesitated a moment. He must be asking the Almin for strength, as I was praying to the Almin to protect him, protect us all.

Saryon's hand touched the diamond.

The diamond flashed. The dragon twitched, muscles contracting, a tremor passed through it. In the alternate time the Dragon of the Night had been injured, caught out in full sunlight. This dragon was probably very healthy and it was inside its dark lair. The dragon made a rumbling sound, deep in its chest. Its claws scrabbled against the floor.

"Now!" Mosiah whispered urgently, though Saryon could not hear him. "What is he waiting for? Cast the spell now!"

I cannot imagine what it would have been like to have had my hand on the dragon's head, to feel that great beast move beneath my fingers. I could not blame my master for faltering at this juncture. His hand jerked back, the fingers clenched.

Mosiah took a step forward. Eliza pressed her cheek against my arm.

The diamond moved. The dragon was raising its head.

Saryon gave a great gasp, that I could hear distinctly, and then his hand pressed down hard against the diamond.

He spoke words that I didn't understand. Words of power and authority. The dragon ceased to move. It might have melded with the stone around us.

Saryon finished speaking the charm and stepped back, removing his hand from the diamond.

This was the moment when we would know whether we lived or died.

The dragon reared its head up off the cavern floor. The eyes opened and the pale light that was like the light of a gibbous moon bathed us.

"Do not look into the eyes!" Mosiah cautioned loudly, loud enough for Saryon to hear.

The dragon spread its wings. I could hear the rustle and the creaking of its tendons, and thousands of tiny, sparkling deadly lights appeared in the cavern's darkness.

The dragon spoke, the voice vibrated with fury, and I breathed easier.

"You are the master," it said.

"I am," Saryon replied, his own voice firm. "You will do as I command."

"I do so because I am constrained to do so," the dragon answered. "Take care that you do not lose your hold over me. What is it you want?"

"In your lair is an object which we greatly value. We want to retrieve it safely and take it away with us. After that, we will trouble you no more."

"I know of that object," said the dragon. "It is a sword of light. It hurts my eyes, destroys my rest. Take it and be gone."

"A sword of light?" Eliza whispered wonderingly.

"Eliza," Saryon called to her, without turning his gaze away from the dragon. "Come and take the Darksword."

"Go with her, Reuven," said Mosiah.

I could not have stayed behind. We walked forward, Eliza and I, into the dragon's lair. The light of the eyes focused on us, flared around us.

Though spellbound and constrained not to harm us, the dragon was tempting us to lift our gaze and meet its eyes, hoping we would fall victim to the madness. The feeling was in my heart that it would almost be worth the madness in exchange for a single glimpse of a creature of such wondrous, cruel beauty.

To banish the temptation, I kept my gaze on Eliza. She looked to the rock cairn that covered the Darksword.

"Make haste, my children," urged Saryon quietly.

Was he at last recalling that other time? The time in which we were his children? I hoped he was. Though it had ended in tragedy, I wanted him to know the love I bore him flowed from that time, as well as my own. He was my father.

Reaching the rock cairn, Eliza and I began to take it apart. We worked as swiftly as we could, lifting the rocks and tossing them aside. At last, the Darksword came into view. It did not shine, as I had almost expected from the dragon's words. It did not reflect the moonlight of the dragon's eyes. It seemed, instead, to reflect the dragon's darkness. Eliza took hold of the Darksword by the handle and raised it up.

"Cover it!" the dragon shrieked, and the light from its eyes was hooded, plunging us into darkness.

Hastily, Eliza wrapped the Darksword in its blanket, which had been lying near it.

"Take it and get out!" The dragon writhed and thrashed, as if it was in the most terrible pain.

"This way!" Saryon called, his voice alone guiding us, for we could not see.

Clasping hands, finding comfort in each other's touch, Eliza and I advanced cautiously toward his voice. We tried to hurry, but we were afraid of falling over the rocks, bones, and other debris scattered around. The journey across the dragon's lair, with the great beast roaring and lashing out so near us, was terrifying. Saryon's voice, calm and steady, guided us through the nightmare.

"Here, I am here!" Saryon cried, and his hands found us in the darkness, his arms gathered us to him. "My children!" His embrace on us tightened and I knew then that he had seen into that alternate time. "My children!" he repeated.

My heart swelled with love for him, love that enhanced the love I felt for Eliza, expanded that love until it filled me completely, admitted no room for fear. I was no longer afraid of the darkness or the dragon, the Technomancers, or even the Hch'nyv. The future might be filled with horror. I might never see the sunrise, I might be dead by morning. But this moment, with this blessed feeling warm inside me, would be enough.

Saryon's grip tightened still further. I felt his body tense.

"Be careful," he warned softly. "Someone is in here."

"Father," came Mosiah's voice at almost the same moment. "Get out of there! Now!"

The dragon had ceased its pain-filled roar. It lay still on the cavern floor, its eyes hooded, so that only a slit of pale light shone from them. I could still sense its hatred of us, but that hatred was now tempered with fear.

"Father!" Mosiah's call was urgent.

"Wait," said Saryon quietly.

A figure stood before us in the middle of the dragon's lair. Calm and relaxed, she might have been standing in our living room back home. She took no notice of the dragon, who had pressed its body back up against the wall, as far from her as it could manage.

"Mother!" Eliza breathed.

Mosiah was beside us. "It could be another trick!"

My first thought was that the Technomancers must be very brave or very desperate to enact a charade before such a dreadful audience as the Dragon of the Night. Then I realized that desperate was an apt description of Kevon Smythe as we had last seen him.

Gwendolyn looked exactly as I had seen her when we first met, except that the lines of care and worry had been smoothed from her face. Her expression was serene. She had eyes for only her daughter, and no Interrogator could have mimicked the love and pride with which she gazed upon Eliza.

"It is my mother," Eliza said, her voice aching with longing. "I am sure of it."

"Wait," Mosiah counseled. "Don't go near. Not yet."

Remembering the horror of the last meeting with the Interrogator, Eliza remained standing beside Saryon. She wanted this to be real. Yet how could it? From where had Gwendolyn come? And why had she come to us now, in the middle of the dragon's lair?

"I want you to meet someone, Daughter," Gwen said.

She reached out her hand, reached into the darkness, and another figure appeared, shimmering into view at Gwendolyn's side. I was reminded of Simkin, for this second figure had the same watercolor, transparent look to it that Simkin had exhibited when he wasn't playing at being stuffed. Gwen led the figure by the hand, drew the figure close to us.

And then I recognized the person. I gasped and looked wildly at Eliza. I even reached out and touched her, to make certain she was real. Eliza stood beside me and Eliza stood before me, both at the same time or, rather, one in one time and one in another. The one before me I recognized as Queen Eliza. She wore the same blue riding habit, the same circlet of gold glinted in her dark hair.

Mosiah sucked in his breath. Saryon smiled wistfully, sadly. He kept his arm around Eliza, supporting her.

"What . . . what is this?" Eliza, my true Eliza, cried brokenly. She stared at her reflection in time's mirror. "*Who* is this?"

"You, my daughter," said Gwendolyn. "You as you might have been in another time. She cannot speak to you, for in her time she is dead. I alone can understand her words. She wanted to prove to you, to all of you"—her gaze swept over every one of us, lingered longest on Mosiah—"that everything you have experienced has been real. That *I* am real."

"I don't understand!" Eliza faltered.

"Look at yourself, Eliza. Look at yourself and open your mind to the impossible."

Eliza stared long at the shimmering figure and then she suddenly looked around at Saryon, who smiled and nodded yes to her unspoken question. She next looked wildly at me and I signed, "I am as you remember, in this time and the other."

Her lips parted, her eyes glistened. Her gaze next went to Mosiah, who grudgingly and reluctantly inclined his hooded head.

"I am your Enforcer, Your Majesty," he said, a hint of irony in his voice.

"Your Majesty. So Scylla called me. I never even noticed that until now. So some part of me did know, even then," Eliza said softly, wonderingly, to herself.

"And now, my daughter," Gwendolyn said, "you must heed my instructions and obey them. You must take the Darksword to Merlyn's tomb. Now. This moment. It must be lying on Merlyn's tomb at midnight."

"Merlyn!" Eliza was amazed. "Teddy kept talking about Merlyn. He said something about giving the sword to Merlyn—"

"Oh, Blessed Almin!" Mosiah snorted in disgust.

"But . . . Father. You don't know, Mother!" Eliza went back to her point of main concern. "They've poisoned him! I must give them the sword or Father will die."

"Take the sword to Merlyn's tomb," Gwen repeated.

"Why?" Mosiah asked harshly. "Why take it there?"

"Trust me, Daughter," said Gwendolyn, ignoring Mosiah. "Trust yourself. Follow your heart."

A cry shattered the darkness. From back in the tunnel, where she was guarding Joram, Scylla shouted, "Mosiah! They're coming! Look out! I can't stop—" Her voice was cut short.

We heard scuffling sounds and then the tramping of many pairs of booted feet. The dragon lifted its head, anger rumbled in its chest. The eyes opened wider, the light that drove men to madness gleamed more brightly.

Gwendolyn was gone and so was the image of Eliza.

"Father!" Eliza cried.

"No time!" Mosiah said urgently, catching hold of her. "We have to find a way out. Simkin said there was another exit. Father Saryon! The dragon! It must know another way. You must command it to show us."

"What? Oh, dear, no!" Saryon was alarmed and appalled. He cast the dragon a sidelong glance and shuddered. "Not again. The spell is slipping. I can feel it."

"Father Saryon," Eliza pleaded. She held the Darksword, wrapped in the blanket. "Mosiah is right. This is our only chance. How else can we take the sword to the tomb in time?"

Leaning down, he kissed her on the forehead. "I could never deny you anything. Reuven used to complain that I spoiled you. But then, you two were all I had."

Saryon left us. He walked over to stand, once more, in front of the dragon. He kept his eyes lowered.

"Make certain the sword is hidden," Mosiah said to Eliza. "You remember what happened the last time."

Then it had been the *Duuk-tsarith* who had attacked us. Then Eliza had wielded the Darksword and its power had broken the spell. Outside, in this time, I could hear the footsteps coming nearer. I wondered what had happened to Scylla and hoped with all my heart that she was safe. I trusted that they would not hurt Joram any more than he'd been hurt already. They needed him alive still, so long as his daughter was in possession of the Darksword.

"Dragon," said Saryon. "I command you. We are in danger. Help us to escape those who pursue us."

"You are in danger, old man," said the dragon, its lip curling to reveal hideous, yellowed, and blood-stained fangs. "Your danger lies ahead of you, not behind."

The diamond's light was rapidly dimming. As Saryon had warned, the spell was slipping. The dragon started to crawl toward us. It began to lift the night-dark wings. I could see the sparkle of the deadly stars.

Saryon drew himself up tall. I saw in him now what I had seen in him before, in our living room, facing a king, a general, and the dread leader of the Dark Cultists. His inner strength, his love for us, his faith in his Creator shone brighter than the dragon's hideous light.

"Dragon, you will obey me," said Saryon.

The diamond on the dragon's head flared, glittered with brilliance. The dragon glared at him balefully, but it was constrained by the charm's unseen force to lower its head. The Dragon of the Night bowed before Saryon. The pale eyes were slits of enmity, but the dragon kept them hooded.

"If you dare, old man, climb upon my back."

"Quickly, children!" Saryon urged. "Mosiah?"

"I will stay behind to cover your escape," Mosiah said.

"But they'll kill you!" Saryon cried.

"Come with them, *Duuk-tsarith*," the dragon said,

its voice grating. "I will deal with those who pursue you. I feel the need to kill *something*!"

Mosiah did not wait to be asked twice. I now trusted him. He was loyal to his word and would have defended us to the death, but he still had hopes of obtaining the Darksword and was loath to let it out of his sight.

By this time I was climbing up onto the dragon. I followed Saryon, who appeared to have been riding dragons all his life, though I know for certain he had never done such a thing. We crawled up the bony structure of the enormous black wing, being careful—as he warned us—not to step on the membrane or we might tear it. The dragon's body quivered beneath us, as the ground in the vicinity of a volcano quakes from the pent-up fire within. Saryon and I both helped Eliza, who would not relinquish the sword to anyone, not even for a moment. We were settling on the dragon's bony back, which proved extremely uncomfortable, Mosiah had just climbed off the wing and onto the back, when the Technomancers in their silver robes entered the cavern.

"Hide your eyes!" Mosiah shouted to us, and pulled his hood over his head.

I did as he ordered, covered my eyes with my hands, but I could still see the white glare, so intense was the pale light beaming from the dragon's eyes. The beast roared and reared its head and lifted its wings, but even as it attacked it took care not to dislodge us, who were seated on its back.

I heard dreadful, agonized screams. Star bursts flashed on the backs of my closed eyelids. The screams ended very suddenly.

The body beneath me began to move, to ripple into motion. The wings creaked, the glow of the white light faded. A rush of fresh air, cool and sweet smelling after the rank stench of the cavern, struck me in the face. I opened my eyes. Before me was a gigantic opening, like a huge chimney, large enough for the dragon to ascend.

We soared out and upward, the dragon's wings beating slowly, carrying our weight without effort. We were nothing more than annoying insects, clinging to its hide.

I looked up into the night sky and I gasped.

It was filled with stars, more stars than I remembered having seen when we first arrived. And then the truth hit me a terrible blow, even as Mosiah put it into words.

"Those aren't stars. Those are spaceships. Refugees. The last survivors from Earth. They have come here, the final hope. The Hch'nyv are behind them."

CHAPTER
TWENTY-EIGHT

*Merlyn looked upon it with eyes that had seen
centuries pass, chose this place for his tomb, and
now lies bound by the Last Enchantment in the
glade he loved.*

⁓FORGING THE DARKSWORD

We flew over the darkened land of Thimhallan,
while above us the sky was bright with the lights of
thousands of starships, carrying millions of people.
Hope sparkled above us. Hope and desperation. They
must have sighted us on their sophisticated instru-
ments. I wondered what they made of us—a gigantic
black winged shape flying just above tree level. Probably nothing. Dismissed as animal life indigenous to the
region.

A few knew the truth, perhaps; knew that the image
showing up on their radar screens was a dragon. King

Garald, Bishop Radisovik, and General Boris would have recognized the creature. But they could not know that we rode the Dragon of the Night. They had come here out of faith and because this was the last place to run to. They could not know where we were bound or upon what errand. For that matter, now that I thought of it, we knew little more. Did the Technomancers know it all? Was this a trap? Had Gwen and Queen Eliza been an illusion?

Mosiah thought so, apparently, but then he was one who would always term the glass half-empty. I did not know what to think. Gwendolyn had seemed so real, the love and affection for her daughter had been genuine, of that I am certain. And how could the Technomancers have conjured up an illusion of Eliza from an alternate time? When I thought of all this, my spirit soared with the dragon.

But they could have knowledge about that time, I realized, and my spirit plummeted to the ground. Kevon Smythe and the Dark Cultists had been present in that time as well. Perhaps everything we had experienced had been their doing.

I looked up into the sky again, the sky that was pocked with life. I thought of the millions up there, afraid, despairing, bewildered. All that remained of mankind, who had fled the only home he'd ever known and embarked into space, a cold and lonely place to die. The assault ships of the Hch'nyv would come soon, once their conquest of Earth was assured. I imagined the sky bright with fire. . . .

Shivering, I turned my gaze away. When I looked back, the sky was covered over with storm clouds and all was darkness. I felt a certain amount of relief, hidden away from the pleading, trusting, frantic gazes of those who were—all unknowing—depending on us.

The ride was not a pleasant one. We flew through a rain squall and were thoroughly soaked. The chill air rushing over the dragon's wings set our teeth to chattering. We huddled together for warmth, clung together to keep from falling off. The dragon's back was broad and we sat between the wings, but the bones of the spine were sharp and dug painfully into my backside, while my thighs soon ached from the uncomfortable position. And though the dragon was under a geis to fly us to Merilon and the tomb of Merlyn, the beast's enmity toward us was strong.

The dragon loathed our touch, our smell, and, if the charm had failed, would have immediately rolled over and dumped us to our deaths. As it was, the dragon would occasionally veer to one side, forcing us to cling to its mane and scales to avoid sliding off before it would reluctantly and slowly level off. I suppose it considered that if one of us was clumsy enough to fall, that was our own concern and it could not be held responsible.

Eliza grasped the Darksword. Mosiah kept hold of her, as did Father Saryon. I hung on to a bony protuberance right above the main tendon for the wings. I could see nothing below us, except when the frequent flashes of lightning illuminated the ground and then it was only for an instant. All I saw at first were thick stands of forest or the smooth grass of the plains. Then I located a winding river.

"The Famirish," shouted Saryon over the rush of air swirling past us. "We are getting close!"

We flew along the course of the Famirish, the dragon sinking lower until it seemed to me that we must crash among the treetops. The dragon knew its business, however, and though it came perilously close, so close that I should think the treetops must have tickled its belly, it never collided with any of them.

A flash of lightning more brilliant than the rest spread across the sky in a blanket of flame. By its light, I obtained my first glimpse of the city of Merilon.

According to lore, when the ancient wizard Merlyn had removed his followers from the persecutions of Earth and led them to Thimhallan, the first place they came to was a grove of oak trees on a plain between two ranges of mountains. Merlyn was so taken with the beauty that he founded his city here and proclaimed that this grove would be his final resting place.

He and the other conjurers and shapers created a floating platform of delicately carved, translucent marble and quartz, which they had called the Pedestal. Upon this Pedestal, which drifted among the clouds, they built the city of Merilon. But what had once been considered a wonder in a world of magic where wonders abounded now lay in ruin, its broken body slowly being covered over by a shroud of encroaching wilderness.

It was a sad sight, an oppressive sight, reminding us all too clearly that man's works, no matter how glorious, are but temporary, that there must come a time when the workman's hand falls, forever stilled, and then Nature will do her best to erase all trace of him.

"Did Merlyn's tomb even survive, Father?" Mosiah asked.

"Why, yes, don't you remember? No, of course, you wouldn't." Saryon answered his own question. "I forgot how grievously you were injured in the attack on the city. The grove burned to the ground, but the tomb remained untouched. The firestorms swept right over it. Some have later claimed that the grass around the tomb was not even scorched, but that is not true."

Saryon shook his head and sighed, his memories sad ones.

Another flash revealed Eliza's face. She was very pale, her expression one of awe, mingled with profound sorrow. She was seeing, as I myself saw it, Merilon rebuilt, in that other lifetime, and contrasting that image with the bleak, bitter reality.

I closed my eyes and I saw, in that other time, Merilon. The floating platform was gone; no one was able to summon up the powerful magicks needed to perform such a feat. The buildings—made of ordinary stone, not crystal—stood on the ground. The palace was a fortress, solid and thick-walled, made to withstand attacks, not play host to glittering parties. The Grove of Merlyn had been replanted. A stand of young oak trees, small but sturdy, kept guard over Merlyn's tomb.

I looked into that time and saw the end. I saw the young oaks wither and die in the laser fire of the Hch'nyv. I turned my gaze away and looked into that time no more.

The dragon began to spiral downward. We could see nothing of where we were headed, because another of those fierce, sudden storms closed in on us. Rain slashed my face, forced me to shut my eyes. Lightning flared much too close, thunder cracked and boomed. I saw the ground only when we were almost upon it, a flash of lightning illuminating wet grass and the burned-out stumps of dead trees. The dragon was descending much too fast, it seemed to me, and I wondered if the beast might be going to kill itself, and us along with it, thereby relieving itself of the geis and a foe at the same time.

At the last possible moment, when I was certain that we were going to crash headlong, the dragon lifted its

wings, gracefully swooped upward, and reached out
for the ground with its powerful hind legs. The landing
was rough for us, though not for the dragon. We were
thrown forward by the force of the impact. I hit my
head on the bony mane and scraped my hands on the
scales.

"I have brought you to the tomb," said the dragon.
"Now leave and trouble me no more."

We were only too happy to obey. I slid down
the dragon's rain-wet back and landed heavily on the
ground. I helped Eliza, who was still clutching the
sword. She was shivering with the cold, her skirt hung
in sodden folds around her, her blouse clung to her
breasts. Her hair was a mass of wet, tangled ringlets,
straggling over her face. She was grim, composed, resolute, prepared to do whatever might be asked of her.

Saryon and Mosiah joined us. The dragon reared
up, its wings spread, the starlike deadly darts shining
through the lashing rain. The pale eyes flared.

"I have obeyed your command," the dragon declared. "Release me of the spell."

"I do not release you," Saryon said, seeing the trick
the dragon was attempting to play upon him. "Once
you return to your lair, the spell will be lifted."

The Dragon of the Night gave us a parting snarl and
a frustrated snap in the air with its jaws, then it leapt
into the storm, wings beating, and soared upward to
disappear into the clouds.

Saryon slumped when the dragon was gone, relieved of a terrible burden.

"Perhaps we should have ordered the dragon to remain," Mosiah said, "or at least return if we called. We
might need to make a swift retreat."

Saryon shook his head. "My strength was giving
out. The dragon fought me every second. I could not

LEGACY OF THE DARKSWORD   371

have held the spell much longer. Besides"—he looked
around at where we stood in the wind and the rain—
"for good or for ill, our journey ends here."

"Where is the tomb?" Eliza asked, the first words
she had spoken since we left the dragon's lair.

"I'm not sure," said Saryon. "It's all so different. . . ."

The storm was beginning to subside. Thunder still
rumbled, but now from a distance. The clouds remained overhead, however, blotting out the starlight
and the lights of the starships. Without the flaring lightning, we were all but blind.

"We could stumble around for hours searching for
the tomb," Saryon said, frustrated. "And we don't
have hours. It's nearly midnight."

Mosiah spoke a word, lifted his hand. A globe of
soft yellow light appeared in his palm. I don't know
when the sight of something has been more comforting.
It was as if he had reached back to Earth and snatched
a bit of sunshine from a summer day, brought it here to
cheer us and light our path. The light seemed even to
ease the chill. I stopped shivering. Eliza managed a sad
smile.

"There is the tomb," said Saryon, pointing.

The light shone on the ruins of the oak trees that
had once been the tomb's guardians. It was a dismal
sight until, moving forward, I saw where several thin,
supple saplings, growing from the seeds of their parents, were preparing to take over the guardianship duties.

The tomb, made of pure white marble, stood in the
center of the circle of trees. The rest of the grove was
overgrown with plant life run amok, but no plants had
come near the tomb. Vines creeping that direction
twined away, went around it. The grass had grown tall,

but the blades bent away, as if they would not, from respect, touch it.

Mosiah held the light high, for us to see. "I remember when I first came here," he said quietly. "I felt very peaceful. This was the only part of Merilon where I was truly at home. I am glad to know that, though much has changed around it, the feel of the place remains the same."

"It is a blessed place," said Saryon. "Merlyn's spirit remains."

"Now that we are here, what should I do?" Eliza asked. "Should I lay the Darksword on the tomb or—"

She caught her breath. I did the same, both of us having seen the same thing at the same time.

Something already lay on the tomb, a dark form against the tomb's whiteness.

"I knew it!" Mosiah muttered, with a bitter oath. "This was a trap. We—don't! Eliza! Stop!"

He reached out to grasp hold of her but he was too late. Her loving eyes had seen clearly what was only a vague shadow to the rest of us. With a wild, stricken, hollow cry, Eliza ran toward the tomb. Reaching the marble sarcophagus, she flung the Darksword down onto the wet grass. Hands outstretched, sobbing, she threw herself on the body that lay on the tomb's cold white surface.

The body was Joram's.

Mosiah paid no attention to the body on the tomb. His responsibility was the Darksword and he hastened to retrieve it, where it lay in the grass, a thing of ugly darkness, not illuminated by his magical light. He had his hand almost on it when he halted.

"Scylla!" Mosiah shone his light upon her.

It was not surprising we had not noticed her earlier. She was a huddled mass, leaning against the tomb.

Blood covered one side of her face. She opened her eyes and looked up at Mosiah.

"Flee!" she warned, with a gasping breath. "Take the Darksword and—"

"Too late for that, I'm afraid."

A man clad in white robes emerged from the shadows of the charred oaks. Mosiah made a dive for the Darksword. A beam of light flared out from the darkness, struck Mosiah in the chest, slammed him back against the tomb. He slid down it, collapsed onto the wet grass.

Bending down, Kevon Smythe picked up the Darksword.

"A pity you came too late, my dear," he said, speaking to Eliza. He did not even glance at the two wounded people at his feet. "We had the antidote all prepared, but as you can see, it will do your poor father little good now. His last words were to you. He said he forgave you."

I lunged at the smug, triumphant man. I had no weapon, but I think—I know—I could have strangled him.

I did not go far. Strong hands caught hold of me, hands covered in silver gloves. They affixed a silver disk on my breast. Pain tingled through my body and I found myself unable to move. Just to breathe was a struggle. My limbs were paralyzed.

They attached silver disks to Saryon, who stood near me, and to Mosiah. I was glad to see that they feared him, for it meant that he was not dead. Scylla's hands remained free. Her feet were bound by some type of metal restraints that clamped over her combat boots. Weakly, she pushed herself into a sitting position, and I realized that she could not move the lower portion of her body. She looked up at Eliza.

"Forgive me . . . Your Majesty," Scylla said softly. "I . . . failed you. I failed him."

Eliza said nothing. I don't believe she even heard. She was lost in her grief. Her head lay on her father's still breast, her arms cradled him. She urged him to come back to her by every term of endearment, but he could not respond, not even to her loved voice.

"Bring the mother," Smythe called. "We might as well have the entire family."

A Technomancer emerged from the shadows of the burned trees, dragging Gwendolyn by the arm. She was disheveled, her clothes stained and torn, but she did not appear to have been harmed.

The image we had seen in the dragon's lair must have been a trick, I thought. Yet even now, with proof at hand, I doubted. I had seen the love in her eyes. No disguise, however clever, could have feigned that. Her first concern was for her grieving daughter.

Gwendolyn put her arms around Eliza, who sobbed against her mother's breast.

"Oh, Mother, it is all my fault!"

"Hush, child!" Gwen smoothed Eliza's black curls, the curls that were so like her father's. "It would not have mattered. If you had not taken the Darksword, your father would have used it and they would have killed him. Your father loved you, Eliza, and he was very proud of you."

Eliza shook her head, unable to talk. Gwen continued to soothe her.

"Your father is well, now, child. At long last, he is well and he is happy."

Silence fell, a silence broken only by Eliza's lessening sobs. I glanced worriedly at Saryon. His body trembled with the enormity of his own emotion. Tears slid unchecked down his cheeks. He could not lift his hand to wipe them away.

Kevon Smythe stood before us, holding the Darksword. His lip curled slightly. "An ugly thing, isn't it?"

"You're no beauty yourself."

I knew that voice. Simkin!

I looked about expectantly, hopefully, my eyes searching the darkness.

Nothing appeared, not a teapot, not a stuffed bear, not a washed-out, watercolor transparency of the foppish young man.

I began to doubt myself. Had I really heard the voice? Had anyone else heard it? Smythe was still gazing triumphantly at the sword. The Technomancers, who outnumbered us at least three to one, were at ease, relaxed. Why not? Their captives were completely immobilized. Scylla was concerned with Mosiah, who was starting to regain consciousness. Gwen and Eliza comforted each other. Saryon wept for the man that had been dearer than a son.

I must have imagined it, I thought, despair closing in on me.

"It is almost midnight, sir," said one of the Technomancers, speaking to Smythe.

"Yes, thank you for reminding me. I will take the sword to the meeting place. Once I hand it over to the Hch'nyv—"

"You'll be a fool if you do," Scylla told him. "They will never keep their bargain with you. They will allow no humans to remain alive."

"On the contrary, they appear quite well disposed toward us," Smythe countered smoothly. "Perhaps because we have shown them how we can be of use to them."

"What are your orders while you're away, sir?" the

Technomancer asked. "What do we do with these?" The silver-gloved hand gestured, included all of us. "Kill them?"

"Not all of them," Smythe replied after a moment's thought. "Hand the Enforcer over to the Interrogators. He'll soon be glad to die. Turn the girl and her mother over to the Interrogators as well. Joram must have told them something about how he forged the Darksword, where he discovered the darkstone, and so forth. They may yet be of use to us."

I bent every ounce of my strength, my will, into attempting to break free. I focused all my energy upon lifting my hand, to tear the paralyzing disk from my chest. I could not move so much as my little finger.

"As for the priest and the mute and the CIA agent or whatever she is," Smythe continued, "we will give them to the Hch'nyv, as a symbol of our good faith. The rest of you, make the arrangements for the first of those refugee ships to land. Go aboard and start the culling process. You know those we want: those who are young, fit, and strong. Pull out the elderly, children below an age where they might be of use, and any who are sick or handicapped. They will be given to the Hch'nyv, as we agreed. Also remove any magi who possess Life and who refuse to join our ranks. Execute them immediately. Once they are back on their homeland, they might be a danger to us."

Smythe held up the Darksword, his two hands clasped just beneath the hilt. "Now that the Darksword is mine—"

"*Am* I yours?" cried the sword in a mocking voice. "Oh, this is the happiest day of my life! Give us a hug, snookums!"

The Darksword began to wriggle and writhe. The bulbous head atop the hilt nodded back and forth, the crosspiece—that was like two arms—waved up and down. The blade twitched this way and that. Smythe stared wildly at the undulating sword, clutching it as he might have clutched a snake which he fears will bite him if he lets it fall.

The crosspiece arms elongated. The bulbous head expanded, the hilt became a neck, the blade transformed into the body of a man not old, not young, with a face like a fox wearing a silky beard. He was dressed all in orange, from his feathered hat to his velvet doublet to his shapely legs and glittering shoes.

The astonished Smythe still held on to Simkin—a solid, flesh-and-blood Simkin—who laughed and, flinging his arms around Smythe, gave him a smacking kiss on the lips.

"Did you mean it? Did you truly mean it? Am I yours?" Simkin asked, holding Smythe at arm's length and regarding him with grave solemnity.

"Seize him!" Smythe shouted in rage, and struck at Simkin with his hands.

"Wrong answer," said Simkin softly.

A Technomancer ran forward, fixed one of the silver paralyzing disks onto the orange velvet doublet.

"Why, how kind!" Simkin regarded the disk with an appraising frown, then looked up at the Technomancer. "But I don't think it goes with my outfit." Casually, he plucked off the silver disk and placed it neatly on the breast of the startled Technomancer.

The man's body jerked, went rigid.

"Tell me what you have done with the Darksword," Smythe demanded, almost choked with rage, "or I'll order them to shoot! You'll be dead before you can draw your next breath."

"Fire away," said Simkin with a yawn. He leaned against the tomb and stared very hard at his fingernails.

"What was that, Smythe? The Darksword? I'll tell you exactly where it is. It is being guarded by a dragon, a Dragon of the Night. You might be able to recover it, but not before midnight. Poor Cinderella. I'm afraid you're going to turn into a pumpkin."

Smythe gnashed his teeth in fury. "Shoot him!"

Silver robes shimmered and coalesced. Each Technomancer held a sleek, shining silver handgun.

A beam of blinding light slashed through the darkness. It did not hit Simkin, but struck the tomb right next to him. The marble exploded, fragments of rock flew through the air. A second beam of laser flared. Simkin caught the light in his hands. Molding the laser light as if it were clay, he made it into a shining ball, and flung it up in the air. The ball transformed into a raven, which took wing, flew once around Simkin's head, then fluttered down to perch on the tomb. The raven began to clean its beak with a claw.

Kevon Smythe's face was mottled red and white. Saliva flecked his lips. "Shoot him!" he tried to command again, but he was so hoarse with fury and fear that his lips formed the words but no sound came out.

"Oh, I say. I find this quite fatiguing," said Simkin languidly.

He waved an orange silk handkerchief and the Technomancers' handguns changed into bouquets of tulips. The silver disk fell from my breast onto the ground, where it turned into a mouse and scampered off into the grass. I could move again, breathe again.

Scylla reached down, plucked off the ankle manacles, as she might have plucked off a pair of shoes. She assisted Mosiah to stand. He was very pale, but fully conscious and alert. He regarded Simkin with narrowed eyes, not trusting him. Saryon was freed as well. His expression was troubled. Simkin was having a good time, playing with us all, not just the Technomancers. Certainly, it appeared that he was on our side, but we had no way of knowing how long that might last, especially if he grew bored.

Right now, though, he was simply having fun.

The Technomancers produced other weapons: stasis grenades, morph guns, reaper scythes, only to have them transformed into objects strange, useless, and grotesque—anything from saltshakers to bananas, clock radios, and pink gin fizzes adorned with tiny umbrellas. The magic burst around us in a dazzling array like a fireworks show gone berserk.

I began to fear I was losing my mind and I was not surprised to see some of the Technomancers bolt and run.

In the midst of all his foolery, Simkin caught sight of Eliza. She stood near her mother, staring at him in bewildered astonishment.

He ceased his magic show. Doffing his feathered hat, he extended his leg, and made a graceful bow. "Your Majesty." Rising, he replaced the hat at a jaunty angle on his head and asked, "Do you like my outfit? I call it Apocalypse Apricot."

Eliza looked dazed. The sight of Simkin emerging from the Darksword had shocked her from her grief. But she didn't know what to make of this. Like the rest of us, she wondered if he brought victory or if he was fixing the lock and seal on our doom.

"Who *are* you?" Kevon Smythe demanded.

"A pocket of residual magic," said Simkin with a sly smile. "That's the problem, isn't it? You don't know me. You and your kind never did. Oh, you tried to manipulate me. You tried to use me. But it never truly worked, because you never really believed in me."

Simkin turned on his fancy orange heel. He gave the

raven a pat on the head and smoothed its feathers, to
which affectionate gesture the bird answered with a
rude croak. Grinning, Simkin walked around the marble tomb to stand at Joram's head.

We watched him in silence. None of us moved, not
Eliza nor Saryon, not Mosiah, Smythe, nor the Tech-
nomancers who still had nerve enough to remain.
Simkin held us all in thrall.

He gazed down at Joram's ashen face that was still
and cold as the marble on which he lay. Simkin ran his
fingers through Joram's black curls, carefully arranged
them on the dead man's shoulders.

"He believed," Simkin said. "He could make no use
of me whatsoever. I betrayed him, I mocked him, I used
him. He shattered a world to free me, he gave his life to
protect me. What I do now, I do for him."

Again, Simkin transformed, shriveling and shrink-
ing, withering in upon himself. He was, once again, the
black and unlovely Darksword. Except that this time I
noted the sword had a flashing orange jewel embedded
in the hilt.

The Darksword placed itself across Joram's chest.

A wind rose from the west, strong and biting cold.
Above us, in the night sky, the storm clouds blew
away, torn to shreds by the wind. The light of star and
starship glittered white against the darkness. And then
the wind died. The air was still.

All waited, stars and wind and ourselves.

Scylla stretched out her hand. "You can wake up
now, Joram. Hurry. It's nearly midnight."

Joram slowly opened his eyes. He looked first at
Scylla.

She nodded. "All is well."

I knew then that my vague understandings had been
right. *She* was the one who had sent us hopscotching

through time. She was the one who had brought all this about. She was an agent, as she had claimed, but she did not work for the CIA or the FBI. She was an agent of God.

Joram turned his head, looked over at Gwen and Eliza.

Gwen smiled, as if she had been a party to the charade. I saw then, gathered around her, shadowy figures, hundreds of them. The dead. She had once spoken for them and they had not forsaken her. She had escaped capture by the Technomancers. The dead had rescued her. The vision we had seen in the dragon's lair was true.

Eliza gasped, wanting to believe, yet not daring to believe.

"No!" Kevon Smythe cried, half-strangled. "It can't be! You were dead!"

" 'There will be born to the royal house one who is dead but will live, who will die again and live again,' " Joram quoted. He sat up, hearty and vigorous, and jumped down from the tomb.

"Quidquid deliqusti. Amen," said the Darksword.

Joram laid the Darksword on Merlyn's tomb.

A man appeared beside the tomb. He was tall, with short-cut white hair and a gray, grizzled beard. He wore armor of an ancient design over chain mail. He bore no weapon, other than a staff of oak twined with holly.

Reaching down, he clasped his hand around the Darksword and picked it up.

"You're no Excalibur," he said, "but you'll do."

"Thank you," the sword said coldly.

The old man held the sword high in the air and spoke words long forgotten. Light began to shine from the sword, a light that was blinding to some, for

Smythe cried out in pain and flung his arms over his head. His followers clapped their hands over their eyes, lowered their heads, unable to look.

I could not take my eyes away.

The light expanded, spreading outward, banishing the darkness. A globe of light surrounded the tomb, and then a globe of light surrounded those of us standing near the tomb. The light flowed outward, to the grove, the broken city of Merilon, the shattered world of Thimhallan.

The light lit the heavens, encompassed the starships.

The light lifted us up.

I stood in a radiant globe that was bearing me upward. Looking down, I saw the dark rain-wet grass below my feet. I saw Smythe gazing up in wonder and horror; seeing his own doom swarming out of the skies to claim him. Thimhallan, a world founded by exiles, fell away from me.

We would be exiles ourselves, refugees fleeing to some new world, lit by some far distant star.

But we bore the magic with us.

EPILOGUE

Having read and reviewed my manuscript, Saryon suggests that I include a detailed explanation of our time "hopscotching," for fear that many of my readers may be confused. Certainly, as he said, it was confusing enough just living through it. When Scylla explained it to me later, after we had settled ourselves in our new world, it made much more sense. I have therefore included her descriptions of the alternate time lines in an appendix, which follows.

I have written before about the various Mysteries of Life that existed on Thimhallan. There were nine of them, seven of them which existed in the world during Joram's lifetime. Two of the Mysteries—that of Time and that of Spirit—were lost during the Iron Wars. It was believed that all the practitioners of these Mysteries died. That was not the case. Scylla herself was of the Seventh Mystery, that of Time. She was a Diviner.

Possessing the ability to look into the future, as well as into the past, the Diviners were said to be closest to seeing the Mind of God.

"We do not view the future as one long path," Scylla told me. "Rather, we see it as several paths branching off a main road. Mortals can walk but one path at a time, the paths of their choice. The rest are alternate futures, what might have been."

The Diviners looked into the future and saw the Hch'nyv. They saw the ultimate defeat of Earth Forces, the eradication of human life from the universe.

"That existed in all paths," said Scylla. "All except one and that in only one of his many paths. If Joram could come to the tomb of Merlyn on the very last night at the very last second of the very last minute of the very last hour and in that second present the Darksword to Merlyn, the greatest of all magi would be able to cast a spell that would save humankind from destruction, transport them to a new world.

"Unfortunately, every path we took to reach that second ended in disaster.

"We generally do not meddle in time, but this was critical. There was a chance, a slim one, but that chance could be obtained only by a manipulation of times—of jumping between times. It would be tricky, for the participants must be rescued from one time before they died and transported to another. The four of you had to be dropped down in the middle of alternate lives you never knew you had been leading.

"It was imperative that two of you—you, Reuven, and Mosiah—recalled the alternate time, even though it would confuse you, for you had to be able to take what you learned in one and transfer it to another.

"As for Eliza and Father Saryon, the tasks each had to perform were so dangerous that I deemed it best, for their own peace of mind, if neither knew of the alternate time. Such knowledge might cause them to hesitate at a critical moment. Also, the fact that they were so comfortable in their own times helped you and Mosiah to adapt more quickly."

Scylla grinned at me. "Better to have two of you confused than all of you."

That depends on how you look at it, I suppose.

And this, I believe, wraps up my story. I must put my manuscript aside now, for it is my wedding day. It has been a year to the day that we have spent on this wonderful new world and Eliza and I are marking the anniversary with our wedding.

Her father, Joram, has accepted our union, though

of course he does not consider me at all good enough for his daughter. He will never love me, but I think he is at least beginning to like me a little. He says that he sees much of Father Saryon in me and he smiles his dark smile when he says this, so that I believe it to be a compliment. Most of it, anyway.

In Gwendolyn, I have found the mother I never knew. She has learned sign language for my sake and we spend a part of each day in study, for she is teaching me much I need to know about how she uses Life. Magic is abundant on this new world of ours. Even we catalysts can use it.

All but Father Saryon. And Joram.

He will not even try, though both Gwen and Eliza tease him to do so. He is content with himself as he is, which must be the greatest blessing to come to him in this lifetime.

As for Scylla and Mosiah, they were married almost as soon as we arrived in our new part of the universe. Theirs is an interesting and exciting life, if dangerous. For, just as there are dark and shadowed parts to the human heart, so there are dark and shadowed parts to the world of our creation.

Father Saryon is, at last, truly happy and content. He is spending his time formulating a new theory of relativity, having figured out where Einstein went wrong on the last one.

As for Simkin, we have not seen him since we left Thimhallan.

But I always look twice at anything orange. . . .

APPENDIX

This was taken from Scylla's description of our "time hopscotching," as Mosiah so inelegantly put it. I have written out each of the three time lines involved. You can see where they have been cut and spliced in my story.

THE FIRST TIME LINE

The Darksword is forged. Joram goes Beyond and is gone for ten years. He comes back to Thimhallan to warn of Menju the Sorcerer, a Dark Cultist (one of the blood-doom knights) who has plans to attack Thimhallan. Earth Forces attack. Joram goes to the Temple of the Necromancers, seeking help for his wife, Gwendolyn, who does not communicate with the living but talks only to the dead. Here, due to Simkin's betrayal, Joram is killed by an assassin's bullet.

The Darksword is recovered by the grieving Father Saryon, who rescues Gwen and flees with her to the Font. Earth soldiers attack the Font, and some of the catalysts are killed. Many more are able to hide in the numerous catacombs and tunnels. Here Saryon finds a five-year-old boy whom he names Reuven, crouched near the bodies of his dead parents. Saryon rescues the child and takes him along with Gwen to safety.

Gwen continues in her madness, only now she is happy for she can talk to Joram, who has become one of the dead. She longs to join him and remains among the living only to give birth to their daughter, Eliza. Gwen dies soon after. Saryon is left to raise Eliza and

Reuven. Keeping Eliza's identity a secret, Saryon flees with the children to Zith-el.

The armies of Earth win. Menju the Sorcerer plans to take over Thimhallan. Fearful of attack from the magi, he orders that the Well of Life be sealed. The source of magic is shut off, except from a chosen few—Menju and the other Dark Cultists. Magic dies in Thimhallan. The people are forced to learn to live without it. They must rebuild their cities and they turn to the Sorcerers to help them.

A schism arises among the Dark Cults. Menju is put on trial before the *Sol-t'kan*. He is found guilty of innumerable crimes, the main one being that he intended to rule Thimhallan alone, without offering to share any of its resources with his brethren. Menju is put to death. Kevon Smythe takes over rulership of the Dark Cultists.

Smythe travels to Thimhallan.

Saryon discovers that the Dark Cultists are searching for the Darksword. Guided by the Almin, he ventures into the Zoo, which has been damaged in the assault on Zith-el. The magical boundaries that surrounded the Zoo have been destroyed, its creatures roam free. Saryon comes across the lair of a Dragon of Night. The creature was stunned during the attack on Zith-el. Having been caught outside in the light, it is comatose.

Saryon charms the dragon, who swears its loyalty to him. Saryon leaves the Darksword with the Dragon of Night, telling it that it should give the sword only to himself or the heir of Joram, Eliza. Bound by the charm, the dragon agrees. Saryon returns to Zith-el, continues to live there with his adopted children, Eliza and Reuven.

Smythe was going to put Prince Garald to death,

but foreseeing his doom, the Prince fled Sharakan before the soldiers could capture him. He and his followers hid out in the Outlands, always on the run from the Technomancers. Garald dreams of driving Smythe from Thimhallan, but without magic, there is little he can do against the powerful Technomancers.

At this juncture Simkin returns from his travels to Earth. Garald accuses Simkin of betraying Joram and orders him put to death.

Simkin bargains for his life. He knows of a source of magic, if Garald is interested.

The Well of Life is sealed, but Simkin reveals that there is a tap, used by Smythe and his people to renew their own magic. In a daring raid, Prince Garald, his friend James Boris, Mosiah, and their knights steal into the Well and, following a swift, bitter battle, unseal the Well.

Magic is once again released into Thimhallan. Garald forces Smythe and his Technomancers to retreat to Earth.

Garald's one worry is the Darksword. He knows that Smythe is searching for it and fears that if the Technomancers find it, they will use it to once more rule the world. Garald believes that Saryon knows where the Darksword is hidden. He finds Saryon and his wards—Reuven and Eliza. Garald is struck by Eliza's beauty and guesses her parentage. Saryon reveals her true identity. Garald asks about the Darksword. Saryon is evasive.

Garald puts Joram's daughter, Eliza, on the throne of Merilon. Merilon and Sharakan are allies. Bishop Vanya has died. Cardinal Radisovik has been made Bishop and he decrees that Father Saryon should be Eliza's adviser until she comes of age. Father Saryon accepts this task reluctantly, thinking himself unsuited.

He leaves Reuven behind at the Font, in training as a catalyst.

Magic is restored, but it is weak. Though the barrier surrounding Thimhallan is rebuilt, magic is found to be seeping out of it and there doesn't appear to be anything anyone can do to stop it.

The people live on a combination of sorcery and steel. The *Duuk-tsarith* are the wizards, they being the ones with the most power left in magic. Prince Garald trains more knights to guard the realm.

Times are difficult. Though at first Garald was viewed as a savior, he has come to be reviled. Smythe, in exile on Earth, has his followers upon Thimhallan and they foment unrest among the lower classes, foretelling the coming of the end of the world unless Smythe is permitted to return to save it.

The Hch'nyv have attacked outposts and are closing in on Earth. Smythe is secretly plotting with the Hch'nyv, agreeing to give them Earth if he is given Thimhallan. The Hch'nyv have no intention of honoring the agreement, planning to kill Smythe as soon as he hands over the Darksword, which their own Diviners have warned them means ultimate defeat.

Taking the form of an angel, Scylla appears to Bishop Radisovik and warns him of a great doom coming to all peoples on Earth and Thimhallan. The Darksword must be taken to the tomb of Merlyn and this must be done by Joram's descendant, Queen Eliza. Radisovik informs King Garald. At the same time a messenger arrives from General Boris, telling of the Hch'nyv's approach. Garald is convinced of its truth.

Garald sends the *Duuk-tsarith* for Father Saryon. Garald explains their desperate situation and begs Saryon to reveal the location of the Darksword. Saryon at length agrees, but he will give it into the hands only of the heir. Garald gives his word of honor that this will happen.

More and more people are being drawn under Smythe's sway. Mobs roam the countryside. Eliza, guarded by her knights, travels to Zith-el. On the way, the carriage is attacked. Alerted ahead of time, the Queen; her house catalyst, Reuven; her Enforcer, Mosiah; and one of her knights, Scylla, sneak in the side gate.

They are met in the forest by Father Saryon, who guides them to the cave of the Dragon of Night.

The dragon recognizes Saryon, who introduces Eliza. She goes forward to recover the sword. As she picks it up *Duuk-tsarith* appear in the cavern. They do not believe Radisovik's vision of the angel, they think that the Hch'nyv are part of a plot designed by the Technomancers. The *Duuk-tsarith* have deposed King Garald and taken up rulership of the world. They demand the Darksword.

Eliza raises the sword to defend herself. The Darksword begins to draw Life from the *Duuk-tsarith*. The sword's null-magic breaks the charmed hold Saryon has on the dragon.

The Dragon of Night kills Eliza and everyone in the cave. The dragon hurls the Darksword into the deepest part of the River Famirish.

The Hch'nyv destroy Earth and Thimhallan. The human race is extinct.

THE SECOND TIME LINE

Saryon and Reuven travel to Thimhallan from Earth to meet Joram. They warn him of the coming of the Hch'nyv. Saryon tries to persuade Joram to return to Earth with his family.

Fearing that this is a trick to steal the Darksword, Joram refuses.

His daughter, Eliza, steals the Darksword during the night. She leaves the house, intending to take the sword to the military outpost, hand it over to the people of Earth. Reuven sees her leave and, realizing her danger, goes after her.

The Technomancers arrive, confront Joram, and demand that he hand over the Darksword. Joram seeks the weapon in its hiding place, discovers that it is gone. Eliza is gone as well. Joram realizes what has happened. He battles the Technomancers and is joined in his fight by Mosiah, who has been keeping Joram and his family under guard.

The Technomancers capture Joram and Father Saryon. They are about to capture Gwen, but she is rescued by the dead, who take her away to their realm.

Scylla finds Reuven and Eliza. They return to the house, discover Mosiah, and hear that Joram has been captured by the Technomancers. Smythe appears and tells Eliza that he will exchange her father's life for the sword. She is to meet him in Zith-el, where the Technomancers have their headquarters.

Scylla, Eliza, and Mosiah travel to Zith-el, accompanied by Simkin, in the form of a teddy bear.

Eliza and her escort reach the gate. An Interrogator, disguised as Gwen, tricks Eliza into giving up the Darksword.

Mosiah recognizes the Interrogator, seizes the Darksword, and hurls it into the gate. He, Reuven, and Eliza enter the gate and run straight into the arms of the waiting Technomancers.

In the ensuing battle, Eliza is killed. The Technomancers seize the Darksword. They transport it and their prisoners to Earth.

Despondent over the death of his beloved daughter, blaming himself, Joram dies of his wounds on the trip back.

The Hch'nyv attack Earth. Kevon Smythe hands over the Darksword, expects his life to be spared.

It isn't.

The Hch'nyv destroy Earth and Thimhallan. The human race is wiped out.

THE THIRD TIME LINE

As you know, having read the book, Scylla managed, by jumping between time lines, to create a third time line, one in which we had a chance to survive. Simkin was the key and Scylla admitted that she herself didn't know until the very end whether he would help us or blithely cast us all aside.

"We were fortunate that the Technomancers lost no opportunity to insult him. As he told Smythe, they didn't believe in him," Scylla said. "In the end, that's why he decided to help."

Not even she knew, or so she claims, that Simkin had taken the form of the Darksword. But thinking back, I realize now that was why the dragon complained so bitterly of the sword's bright light, hurting its eyes. The dragon could see more than we could, apparently.

As for the Darksword itself, does it still lie in some cave back on flame-ravaged Thimhallan?

We will not discover the answer in our lifetime, but who knows? Perhaps, when thousands of years have passed and the Hch'nyv have been vanquished by some more powerful race, one of our descendants might read this book of mine and return to Thimhallan, to Zith-el, to the cave of the dragon. . . .

MARGARET WEIS and TRACY HICKMAN are the *New York Times* bestselling authors of the *Dragonlance*® series, the *Darksword* trilogy, the *Rose of the Prophet* trilogy, and the seven-volume *Death Gate Cycle*.